The Queen's Priest

The Story of Blessed Thomas Abell

Theresa Abell Haynes

Tall Tree Press

This is a work of historical fiction. While inspired by real events and figures, some names, characters, and events have been fictionalized for narrative purposes.

ISBN: 979-8-9928398-1-4 (printed softback)

ISBN: 979-8-9928398-0-7 (printed hardback)

ISBN: 979-8-9928398-2-1 (ebook)

Cover design by Hannah Linder

Editing by Julie Frederick and David Aretha

Proofreading by Allison Ramirez

Typesetting by Theresa Haynes

Find out more at www.Theresaahaynes.com

for my father
a man of truth
Robert David Abell

Yet for all of it, my conscience would not suffer me
to hold my peace, but compelled me to offer, with ye
poor widow, a farthing of my learning to the honor
of almighty God. -- Thomas Abell

Invicta Veritas The Unconquerable Truth   1532

To Serve the King

Tall Tree Press

1

A Cardinal and a Priest

September 1527   Hampton Court

Thomas Abell squeezed the rough wooden cross in his sweaty palm. His stomach burned. *Why am I here?* Church bells rang in the distance, a distant call to prayer. But Thomas could not pray. He could not speak. He stared at the polished oak floor and scolded himself for not looking up. Look up, Thomas. Look up!

"Father Martin sent me," Thomas finally stammered, glancing at Cardinal Thomas Wolsey. "Said you requested me."

Thomas eyed the cardinal's red velvet biretta. The square, flat-topped hat rested on Wolsey's broad forehead while the lord chancellor's gold chain draped heavily across his crimson cassock. The combination made Cardinal Wolsey one of the most powerful men in England, second only to King Henry VIII. *What does he want with me?*

Thomas drew in a sharp breath and began again.

"Ah, well, perhaps you know it is the first week of class. My students... "

Cardinal Wolsey laughed.

"Father Abell, don't worry about your students," he said with the flick of his fat, ringed hand. He stepped toward Thomas, and his red velvet robe pooled around his feet.

"Father Martin didn't tell you?" Wolsey's small mouth pursed in amusement. "Ah, well, perhaps I neglected to tell him." He laughed again.

Was it possible for the great Cardinal Wolsey to neglect anything? If he had forgotten to tell Father Martin, it must have been intentional. Father Martin would never have sent him into the lion's den without preparing him—not Father Martin.

"Follow me," Wolsey said briskly, and though Thomas's strides were long, he nearly stumbled to keep up as they left Wolsey's private chamber and clipped down a long corridor. In the polished wooden panels, Thomas glimpsed a blurry reflection of his thin, pale face with high cheekbones and wide blue eyes. He turned away from the distorted image and pressed on.

Music and voices, the muffled sounds of a raucous party, echoed up the hallway. Hadn't the bells just chimed eleven in the morning? *Wasn't it Wednesday?* Didn't the royal court observe the autumn Ember fast days? Wolsey stopped before a giant double door that seemed to throb with laughter on the other side.

"Have you had the honor of meeting His Majesty, our king?" Wolsey asked with a coy smile, his large green eyes crinkling like he had said something funny. "No, of course, you haven't."

Thomas's knees suddenly felt weak. When Father Martin had told him to make haste to Hampton Court, Cardinal Wolsey's new sprawling estate west of London, he had not realized the king and his court were in residence there. He would have considered it if he had not been so focused on that new Greek grammar Father Martin had given him. Of course, the king was with Wolsey. The king was always with Wolsey.

Thomas's heart raced. Sweat broke out on his forehead. He closed his eyes and took a deep breath. Pressing the wooden cross through the opening in his black vestments into a hidden leather pocket, he ran his trembling hands through his thick brown hair and drew in a deep breath. *Jesus Christ, Son of God, have mercy.* He touched the heavy pewter crucifix that hung around his neck and clasped his shaking hands. A thousand images ran through his mind, but he forced his focus forward, beyond the doors that stood like an enormous barrier between the present and the future.

"Don't be nervous, Thomas," Wolsey whispered. "The king rarely hangs the clergy."

King Henry VIII roared with laughter, his eyes twinkling as he focused on one person, a slight woman with dark hair and an amused smirk on her face. The king handed the Italian lute he had been playing to a servant and opened his hands to embrace hers.

The king was every bit as imposing as Thomas had heard. He was taller and broader than anyone else in the room, a monarch known as much for his wrestling abilities as his jousting. And from the way his flushed face twitched when he smiled, Thomas had no trouble imagining that he could turn from laughter to shouting in an instant. At least, that was the king's reputation.

The dark-haired woman stepped toward the king, placing her gloved hand in his, never taking her eyes off his face as if she dared him to look away.

A crowd of colorful courtiers gathered around the couple like the king's menagerie of exotic animals: velvet padded doublets and silk stockings, capes and furs, feathered felt hats, flowing brocade gowns, and jewels—ropes and ropes of jewels.

The king thrust a silver chalice into the air.

"To Anne!"

The courtiers cheered and raised their own sloshing goblets. Their ruddy faces, already warmed by wine, turned toward the king.

Thomas searched the room for a familiar face. None of the young men and women looked familiar, though he knew he might know their names by reputation. Plenty of royal gossip traveled up the Thames, seeping into the holiest halls of Oxford chapels. For the most part, Thomas preferred to ignore the idle chatter. But there was one name that always caught his attention, one person he prayed for when her name came to his consciousness. And looking around the Great Hall, he did not see her. Katherine of Aragon's throne sat empty. *Where was the queen?*

A courtier leaned onto the king's arm and said something low, causing the king to look up sharply at Thomas and Wolsey. He seemed surprised and then curious.

"My Lord Cardinal, my dear Wolsey!"

The king set down his goblet, parted his flock of courtiers, and strode heavily toward Thomas and Wolsey.

Wolsey bowed solemnly, and Thomas quickly did the same.

"What are we celebrating today?" Wolsey asked, looking past the king to a servant who dashed around the room, refilling the courtiers' raised glasses.

King Henry scowled like a scolded child. "Just a toast to celebrate our little Nan's birthday."

The dark-haired young woman on the king's arm smiled coyly, though her brown eyes, fixed on Wolsey, seemed less than festive.

"Well, a happy birthday to you, my dear," Wolsey said. "It is good to see the king celebrate his loyal friends." The young woman gave Wolsey a slightly sour look, and Thomas wondered what had been said between the two. The king winked at Anne.

"You heard us singing?"

"Yes, of course, Your Majesty."

Thomas looked from the cardinal to the king.

Wolsey pressed his hands together.

"I have come to introduce you to Thomas Abell, the priest I have chosen for our dear Katherine."

"Oh!" King Henry exclaimed, his bright blue eyes abruptly turning to Thomas.

Suddenly, the room began spinning. Thomas pinched the inside of his palm to keep from giving in to the downward swirl. *Breathe, Thomas, breathe!* He focused on the king's commanding face—his wide forehead and eyes bright as a summer sky. *Katherine? Queen Katherine?*

Thomas tried to say something, but his dry tongue stuck in his mouth.

Wolsey chuckled.

The cardinal's laughter shot through Thomas like the cry of a hawk over an empty meadow, and he was suddenly fully alert. And angry. How dare Wolsey surprise him like that? Giving him no opportunity to consider such an offer? Had he ever appealed for such a position? Who had nominated him? And why? What of his life in Oxford? His students? His studies? What game was the cardinal playing with him?

His face flushed.

Wolsey shook his head with a soft laugh.

"Your Majesty, you will have to forgive our young priest. I have quite sprung this on him." He slapped Thomas on the back. "I should say, this is the man I believe would best serve Katherine at this time. He is an Oxford tutor, an accomplished scholar, and a talented musician. Ah, and he knows several modern languages, including Spanish."

The king smiled slowly and tapped Anne's gloved hand. Anne turned her chin up slightly as she moved away from him and joined a group of whispering women.

"Does Katherine need a new priest?" Henry asked distractedly, his eyes bouncing from Wolsey to the courtiers and their little circles of conversation. It was apparent who ran the country. *Alta Rex*—Latin for "high king"—was the nickname whispered behind Wolsey's back.

"Yes, Your Majesty," Wolsey continued, undaunted by the king's divided attention. "Perhaps you will remember we removed her Spanish priests last month and agreed to replace them with ones loyal to Your Majesty."

Wolsey nodded as he spoke, as if studying the king's face for a moment of recognition. Thomas's stomach turned. Loyal to Your Majesty?

The king slowly nodded.

"Well, yes, Wolsey, I do remember that conversation." He drummed his fingers on his fur-trimmed doublet and glanced over at Anne before turning back to Thomas. "I trust you have vetted this ..."

The king's piercing blue eyes scanned Thomas from the top of his dark head to the leather boots protruding from beneath the floor-length priestly robes.

"His name is Thomas Abell," Wolsey said.

"Abell," the king said slowly. "An unusual name. Like Cain's brother?"

"No, Your Majesty," Thomas said, finding his voice. "Like a bell that one rings, Your Majesty." He swallowed hard. "Our family is from Essex."

"Yes," the king said thoughtfully. "I know the family—some gentry."

King Henry turned to Wolsey and pursed his lips, eyeing the cardinal's sallow face. The king was silent as if he wanted to make an offhanded remark, perhaps about Wolsey's lack of family connections, but after an awkward moment, he merely nodded, leaving his unspoken opinion lingering loudly between them.

Wolsey squared his shoulders. "Your Majesty, Thomas comes to us with the best recommendations from Oxford. I believe you will find him more than suitable for overseeing the queen's spiritual needs and, of course, our current needs."

The king glanced at Anne Boleyn, now huddled in a circle of ladies plumed in yellow damask. An older woman in blue silk pressed her hands around Anne's ear and whispered something that made Anne look sharply in Thomas's direction.

"Yes—well—don't let me keep you from your work," the king said, stepping away from Wolsey. The king walked over to Anne, pulling her away from her ladies and possessively slipping his arm around her child-sized waist. When she did not immediately look up at him, he raised her chin toward him, forcing her to meet his eyes. He mouthed something that Thomas could not hear, but

Wolsey seemed to understand. The cardinal's lips twitched, and he smiled nervously.

Back in Wolsey's private chamber, the cardinal was quiet. Thomas let out a sigh and drew up his courage. His heart had stopped racing. The panic was gone, for now. He was ready to talk.

"Cardinal Wolsey," he said, straightening his shoulders, "you wish me to serve the queen?"

Wolsey nodded. "I see I have your attention. And you are not pleased? Most men in your position would be honored. Perhaps you would prefer a formal request."

Wolsey tilted his head, his large green eyes mocking, despite his formal tone.

"Father Thomas Abell." He dipped his chin, staring directly into Thomas's eyes. "King Henry VIII, your sovereign king and lord over England, would be greatly obliged if you would serve his queen in the royal household as her official confessor and chaplain," he said.

Thomas watched the cardinal's face. *Why?*

"It is his personal request," Wolsey added with a sniff.

Thomas's cheeks flushed.

"The king requested?" *The king who was surprised to meet me five minutes earlier? The king who had forgotten his wife needed a new priest?*

The cardinal smiled, assuringly. "You should know that the king and I are of the same mind. Our will is one."

Thomas was silent as he considered the cardinal's words. Wolsey could demand the king's counsel at any time. His word was the same as the king's. He and the king were one.

"We keep a keen eye on the universities," Wolsey continued. "We are aware of upcoming scholars. We recruit them for His Majesty's service," he said, and then added, "but I would think that you already know this."

Thomas nodded. "Yes, certainly, of course. But Cardinal Wolsey, I have been teaching in Oxford for years. I am not a new graduate."

The cardinal smiled. He was prepared. "Yes, Thomas, we know that you are a tutor. You have also served at Frideswide's Shrine. *And* you were the royal secretary of wine and beer regulation at Oxford."

"I am not fond of administration."

Wolsey laughed out loud at this, and Thomas felt his cheeks flush again. He did not enjoy Wolsey laughing at him.

"We know. We have not called you here to manage the king's wineries or any of his financial concerns."

Cardinal Wolsey looked Thomas in the eyes.

"We want you to be Queen Katherine's personal chaplain, her confessor... Father Thomas, it is a role of extreme honor," he said with more gravity than anything else he had said. Then he lowered his voice. "It is a place of great influence, Thomas. You would have the ear of the queen."

Thomas thought about Father Martin and his friends in Oxford. A heavy weight settled on his chest. He had never wanted to be anyone's personal confessor, not even Queen Katherine's.

"Perhaps there is someone else that our King Henry would consider, perhaps one with experience already in the queen's household?"

Wolsey sighed impatiently and looked at his ringed fingers.

"The king and queen are making some changes to the queen's royal household," he said. "We would like to provide her with English priests. As you may have heard, some of her Spanish priests have returned to Spain. Others have passed on." He narrowed his eyes. "We believe it is in our best interest to replace them with English priests, English priests loyal to their English king."

Loyal to the king?

"You have many admirable qualifications, Thomas. You are fluent in Spanish and other languages. We have been told that you know French, Italian, and some German. Of course, your Latin proficiency is well known at Oxford."

Thomas felt his cheeks redden again. He was wary of the cardinal's flattery. Why flatter him? Surely, there were a dozen Oxford doctors who would happily serve in the royal household.

"Personally," Wolsey dropped his voice, causing Thomas to lean closer, "I know that you are a compassionate man. I believe that you would handle the queen's, ah, temperament well. I remember the day you caught our falling lady."

Frideswide?

Thomas sighed, the weight on his chest increasing. Did he have a choice?

The cardinal cleared his throat.

"There is more," he said. "As you must know, I spend a great deal of my time tending to the king's personal affairs."

Thomas nodded.

"It would be a comfort for me," he said, covering his heart, "to know that the queen is content, that she is cared for, that she is well in both heart and soul."

Thomas nodded, listening.

"And ... I would like you to make a habit of updating me on the queen's state of mind, what she is thinking and saying." Wolsey's eyes narrowed. "Do you understand what I am asking?"

Thomas hesitated, and Wolsey continued.

"This is important to the king. He wants to know what his wife is thinking, what she is saying privately to her priests and ladies. If you met with me regularly ... you could inform me. ... Then I could advise you on the best way to counsel her, to direct Queen Katherine."

Thomas was silent, suddenly aware that his mouth was open but unwilling to close it. He had heard the gossip that King Henry was unsatisfied with his wife Katherine. She had failed to produce a prince. Everyone in Oxford was aware of it—everyone in England. And more recently, there were rumors that the king was considering a divorce. The Pope would have to approve it, of course, and the king would need Katherine's consent. She would have to be convinced that the dissolution of their marriage served England best. An English priest bent to Wolsey's will could be a powerful tool in convincing the queen.

Thomas looked beyond Wolsey to his tapestry-covered walls. It felt like they were closing in around him, smothering him. Did he have a choice? Did anyone have a choice when the king's cardinal made such a request? No. The noose was set. He suddenly wished he had not hurried to Hampton Court. But Father Martin had asked him to go, and he had always listened to him.

"Serve God, honor the king, eat the meal prepared," Father Martin always said. Christ himself drank the cup the Father gave.

Thomas unclenched his sweaty palms. He opened them quietly in a posture he had learned long ago, a private sign of surrender. *Not my will, God*, his open hands said. *Yours*. He would seek to serve both God and king.

But no.

Surely, this could not be God's will. Thomas closed his trembling hands and shook his head. How could he use his holy calling to be a spy for Wolsey? He could not. Surely, Christ would not want him to serve Him in that way. No. He would not.

Thomas cleared his throat. "I am honored that you would consider me, but your Grace ..." He paused, and the cardinal raised an eyebrow. "Cardinal Wolsey, I would prefer to retain my position in Oxford. It is my home, you see."

The cardinal's cat-like eyes narrowed.

"The queen's accommodations and the salary accompanying such a position would give you a comfortable life. You would have access to the latest books and meet the world's best scholars visiting court."

Thomas nodded. He had already considered this.

"I enjoy teaching. I like the university."

Wolsey nodded. Perhaps he could understand this.

"You and I have much in common," Wolsey said thoughtfully. "I miss Oxford, myself." And for the first time, Thomas thought the cardinal had said something genuine.

"But perhaps, Thomas, you might consider God's call to care for his people. The queen needs a priest who cares for her body and soul, especially in this difficult time. Your service would be useful to both the king and the queen."

Thomas said nothing. He did not trust himself to say anything more.

The cardinal waited for a minute and then extended his hand. "Give my regards to Father Martin," he said. "He is a good man."

2

FRIDESWIDE

1518   Frideswide's Chapel Oxford

Thomas closed his eyes and smiled, his frosty breath lingering like incense as it drifted through the cavernous church. He gently plucked the Spanish lute, feeling each warm note as it flowed through his fingers, reverberating off the ancient stones. How he cherished these rare predawn moments! Alone in the abbey, he could feel his soul expand, relax, rejoice. This was peace.

As Thomas played, the dawn slowly illuminated the panes of Frideswide's stained glass windows, bathing the room in colorful light. Soon, the narthex would be full of English pilgrims, candles, and tearful women falling prostrate on the pedestal that promised miracles. Soon, he would unlock the heavy wooden doors and usher in the faithful, the hopeful. Soon, he would be priest and pastor, both a guardian of Oxford's ancient shrine and a minister to the people. But for now, for one more self-indulgent moment, he would play.

A loud knock on the door made Thomas jump, nearly dropping the instrument onto the stone floor.

"Thomas!" he heard a familiar voice demand. "Unlock the door!"

Thomas rushed to unbar the door, and the balding Father Martin scrambled inside.

"Light the candles!" Martin cried, breathless from running across the priory. "Arrange the chairs!"

Martin raced around the room, gathering candles, lighting them, muttering incoherently. Thomas knew better than to ask what was going on. He gently settled the Spanish lute in the corner, out of sight, and began arranging wooden chairs in rows before the shrine.

Thomas began his own prayer, whispered just loud enough for Martin to hear.

"*Pater Noster, qui es in caelis, sanctificetur nomen tuum.*" Our Father in Heaven, hallowed be thy name.

Thomas finished the prayer, and Martin smiled, grasping Thomas's young hands in his wrinkled ones. "Thank you, my son," he said, his clear blue eyes holding Thomas's gaze. "Thank you!"

Martin returned to arranging candles, but this time more slowly, at a pace more typical for his creaking knees and shaky hands.

"The queen is coming... here," he said between breaths as they finished illuminating the chapel that needed no candles in the bright morning light. By now, the sunrise was pouring through the eastern windows, overpowering the flickering candles.

Thomas raised an eyebrow. "The queen?"

"Her messenger... just arrived... said... open the chapel... keep away pilgrims... Queen needs to be alone."

The old priest was out of breath, relating the information. Thomas's eyes widened, and his heart pounded like he had also sprinted across the abbey. *The queen?* Suddenly, the humble chapel lacked luster.

It was too late to polish the brass fixtures or clean the stained-glass windows, but Thomas rushed over to Frideswide's altar, a stone pedestal in the center of the side chapel, and reverently wiped the polished surface with his loose vestment sleeve bunched in his palms.

There was no dust, of course. The pedestal was swept clean daily by the women who thrust themselves onto it, rubbing their scarves and handkerchiefs over its surface, hoping to absorb just a bit of the saint's healing presence into their threadbare clothing.

The door opened, and a detachment of armed soldiers, swords clanking against metal armor, filed into the church, their bodies flanked to conceal a trio of people. As the soldiers dispersed to the sides of the room, Thomas could see the portly Cardinal Thomas Wolsey piously escorting an anxious woman, partially hidden behind a black laced veil. Wolsey's face was severe, like a man advancing before the judge, his hopes pinned on a verdict yet to be revealed. He strode half a step ahead of the woman whom Thomas recognized instantly.

She was Katherine of Aragon, daughter of the mighty Ferdinand and Isabella of Spain, the Queen of England, queen consort to King Henry VIII. Thomas had only seen her once before, and then she had been a young bride dressed in white. On that midsummer day in 1509, Thomas had been a young boy, holding his mother's hand, and she had been Henry's beloved Spanish princess. Her cascading auburn hair blazed in the afternoon sun as she floated through the streets of London to her coronation.

And now she made her way to Frideswide's Shrine, his Frideswide's Shrine.

The third person in the queen's trio was an olive-skinned Spanish priest, somberly dressed in floor-length black vestments with a giant silver crucifix weighing on his chest. He was undoubtedly the queen's confessor, her most privileged spiritual confidant. And now, as he walked beside Katherine, his hand supported her delicate jeweled one, guiding her along like a ship captain ferrying his vessel into port.

As the queen neared the shrine, the Spanish priest and Wolsey fell back, giving her space to make her petitions.

Thomas heard the heavy church door slam shut and looked back to realize the entire chapel was already crowded with the queen's entourage—her soldiers, priests, ladies, and gentlemen in waiting. It was an enormous crowd to be assembled at the chapel just after dawn, and Thomas had no doubt that they had begun their procession in secret, walking through Oxford under cover of the predawn darkness. It seemed that everyone important to the queen was there—everyone, with the notable exception of her husband, the king.

Katherine pulled back her veil. She lifted her weary, red-rimmed eyes and gazed upward at the silk canopy that hovered over the shrine like a veil separating Heaven and Earth.

Like countless women before her, she knelt before the altar, extending her empty arms. She pressed her body onto the altar—her palms, forehead, and lips. Her shoulders quaked as she silently sobbed under the sarcophagus that held Frideswide's bones.

Thomas shifted uncomfortably back toward the stone wall. He was accustomed to the endless lines of women unburdening their souls to the saint. Above all else, they begged for the miraculous power to conceive and give birth to healthy children.

Thomas watched the queen, prostrate on Frideswide's pedestal. The saint had never been a mother, never been a wife. She had been a princess, but she rejected the throne. She spent her life serving the poor, anointing the sick, touching their bodies with the power of Heaven. People walked for miles across England to spend a moment in her presence. And now, eight hundred years later, they still did, hoping that her remains still served as a bridge between Heaven and Earth.

Thomas was accustomed to desperate pilgrims, but this was different. This was the queen, her body smothered in a mountain of crushed velvet robes, surrendered on the shrine. It felt as if she brought the weight of England with her, collapsed at the feet of Frideswide.

Thomas swallowed the lump that rose in his throat. His eyes stung. His own mother had wept like that when she bore his brother cold. Thomas had been young, but old enough to remember being shuffled aside and told in hushed tones to go back to bed. But he would never forget that night. Thomas wiped away a stubborn tear that spilled down his cheek. He still missed her.

Katherine had lost four children, two of them sons, one a few months old and the other a nearly developed infant, a son dead before he breathed his first breath. Two years ago, the queen had finally given birth to a daughter, Mary. Oh, how joy and royal wine flowed through the streets that day! But it was not enough. The king and his country would only be satisfied by the birth of a male heir.

And now, Katherine sought the help of Oxford's patron saint. Thomas had heard priests whispering that the queen was pregnant again. This might be her last chance. Nothing could be more critical. The child she carried had to be Henry's crown prince. Without an heir, England could fall into another dynastic power struggle.

Thomas pressed his hands together. *Jesus Christ, Son of God, have mercy.*

The queen quaked and quivered silently on the shrine's altar for nearly an hour until her Spanish priest, looking embarrassed and impatient, stepped forward and tugged her elbow. The queen lifted her head, searching the chapel rafters as if looking for a sign from Heaven. Taking a deep breath, she rose on unsteady feet, still searching through disoriented, tear-filled eyes.

But as she stood, Katherine stumbled, her velvet-slippered feet sliding off the marble pedestal, her body twisting in a clumsy effort to find her balance. Her soft forehead caught the rough edge of the shrine as she collapsed. Courtiers gasped.

Thomas lunged forward to catch the queen. His long arms encircled her body as she fell. Her bloodied face pressed into his vestments.

Cradling the queen like an infant, Thomas hoisted her down the remaining pedestal steps, pushing aside a burning candelabra as he laid her, now pale and unconscious, on the chapel floor.

Instantly, one of the queen's ladies produced a pillow for the queen's head and a lace shawl to cover her ankles. The royal physician, a thin, gray-haired man standing in the back of the queen's entourage, pushed through the crowd of murmuring courtiers and knelt beside her, gently taking her hand in his.

Thomas stepped back, conscious of his own place and that of the queen's servants.

He wanted to retreat and return to the safety of the shadows, but before he turned his head, Katherine took a sharp breath and opened her eyes.

She looked straight at him.

Like a pilgrim returning from Heaven, she seemed both here and there, an ethereal spirit still hovering between the body and the world to come. She held her gaze on Thomas, and he had the overwhelming feeling she was seeing through him into Heaven and the world beyond. It was as if she saw his future and his past, his greatest hopes, his deepest fears, his pain, his losses, and especially the loneliness that weighed on his heart in the darkest of nights. He felt so naked he wanted to turn and run—run out of the church and down the lane into the grassy meadow. Instead, he turned away, bolting the door to his soul. There were some places not even a queen was allowed to go.

Katherine closed her eyes and exhaled, the color returning to her pallid cheeks. Thomas retreated into the shadows, relieved that the crowd was focused on the queen and could not see him shaking. When he dared look up again, he saw Cardinal Thomas Wolsey watching him, fingers laced over his ample middle.

3

THE DEBATE

September 1527   Hampton Court

Thomas tossed and turned. The bed the cardinal had given him was a generous one, usually reserved for men of higher rank. But it might as well have been a servant's reed mat on the cold floor. *Serve God, honor the king, eat the meal prepared for you.* Life in the king's court was not what he wanted, not in the least. He had always imagined a life among the college halls, days and nights discussing theology, Aristotle, and Church law. He would see young men grow to become leading priests and lawyers. It had been a simple life, a simple routine, but it had been his life. He turned over again. The feather bed felt as hard as a rock.

When Thomas finally fell asleep, he was at Frideswide. The queen was falling, and he was not close enough to catch her. Though he tried to move, his feet were attached to the stone floor, attached like Christ's feet to the crucifix in his parish church, the pitiful Christ that he had learned to kneel before as a child when the priests gave him the Body and Blood. And now, nails held his feet to the floor.

The queen fell in slow motion, her blood covering the floor.

Thomas tried to scream, but the words stuck.

He awoke, choking, gasping as if some invisible hand were wrenching his throat.

Water!

Thomas stumbled out of the high poster bed, still gasping, and fell heavily on his hands and knees. Enough moonlight trickled through the high window for him to make out the pitcher of water at the other end of the room. He crawled on his knees to the pitcher and drank deeply.

Will you serve me?

The question was unfair. Wasn't he already serving Christ? He was teaching young priests Latin and Greek. Many of them would serve in parishes around England. Why did Christ need him in the queen's household? Surely there were men more capable, more willing.

Thomas rested his forehead on the cold stone floor. *More willing?*

"My God," he whispered.

Thomas was unaccustomed to such casual prayers. He searched his heart for a piece of liturgy that would suffice. He found none.

"Jesus," he whispered, "I do not want..."

I know.

The voice in his heart came so clearly that Thomas knew it was more than just his thoughts. He swallowed hard.

"But, Lord, I have never wanted to live in the royal court."

Silence.

"I like Oxford," Thomas whispered, heat rising to his cheeks at the simplicity of his protest. A moment passed, and then another.

Thomas shook his head and clenched his fists. "No, Lord."

Silence.

Thomas let out a deep sigh. "Do you want me to serve the queen?"

I want you to serve Me.

Thomas opened his hands and nodded his head. "Then I will," he whispered into the darkness. And for a brief moment, a wave of peace washed over him. He rose to his feet. His life in Oxford was over.

4

KATHERINE OF ARAGON

The next morning, Cardinal Wolsey and Thomas stood at the threshold of the queen's chambers at Hampton Court. Thomas clasped his clammy hands together and took a deep breath. To step forward was to begin a new life. He hesitated. The cardinal did not. He strode straight into the royal quarters like he owned the castle—which, Thomas remembered, he did.

"Your Majesty, Queen Katherine!" Wolsey bellowed. "I trust you are well this morning."

The queen did not respond.

From the open doorway, Thomas could see the great Katherine of Aragon slumped in her window seat, her face hidden under the shadow of an English gable hood. She absently traced the lines of the first autumn rain trickling across the other side of the diamond-cut window.

"Your Highness?"

A young lady in a simple blue damask dress whispered to the queen. She gently pulled the Latin book from Katherine's slack hand, rescuing the worn devotional from tumbling unceremoniously to the black and white checkered floor.

"¡Se está cayendo el cielo!" Katherine whispered. The sky is falling.

"Your Highness," the girl repeated louder, touching the queen's hand this time. Katherine groggily glanced at her young lady-in-waiting. She blinked, drawn from her thoughts like a prisoner slowly facing the light of an open cell door.

"Please, Your Highness, Cardinal Wolsey and your new chaplain have arrived. They wish to see you now."

The young lady's bright brown eyes motioned to the doorway, and the queen woke with a start. She turned to see Thomas and Wolsey.

"You should have sent notice," Katherine said with a frown. She rose to her feet and folded her arms in front of her thick waist.

Wolsey smiled, unaffected, and gestured back to Thomas.

"My Lady. This is Thomas Abell, your new chaplain. I trust you will find him a suitable replacement for your late confessor."

Katherine's face flushed.

"Confessor! I have not requested a new priest!"

Wolsey walked toward the queen while Thomas stood in the doorway.

"Your Highness, this is the confessor your husband, the king, has requested."

The queen looked at Thomas suspiciously.

"Cardinal Wolsey, you know that I have always selected my own confessor. And my dear husband knows I have always had a Spanish friar." Her eyes narrowed. "I doubt he would send my priests away and order me an English boy!"

Wolsey continued across the checkered floor and opened his hands.

"You, Your Highness, are English," he mewed in a quiet, measured tone.

"Yes," Katherine quickly agreed, taking a tiny step back toward the open window seat. "I am indeed English, the Queen of England! And, I am capable of interviewing and selecting the members of my own household."

"Indeed," Wolsey said slowly. "I would agree, most capable, Your Majesty."

He paused dramatically.

"But, Queen Katherine," Wolsey continued as he stepped forward again. "Your gracious husband, the King of England, who *knows* your needs better than anyone, has observed that you *do* need a confessor. You wrote to your husband of Friar Pedro Velasquez's unfortunate passing, God bless his soul." Wolsey stopped to sign the cross. "And the king has asked me to locate a suitable replacement. You will find this priest, Thomas Abell, to be well-educated and likable, a man of the highest morals. He comes with the best recommendations from his service in Oxford. And he is, by the way, most definitely not a boy."

As Wolsey spoke, he took two more small steps and stood within a handbreadth of the queen.

Thomas, however, remained at the door, watching the queen's face and her thinly veiled emotions. She looked angry, and he wondered why she didn't simply order him out.

"I have always chosen my household," she repeated quietly. "I have not requested any new priests. In fact, you know that I have two remaining priests in my household at this moment."

Wolsey nodded as if he had anticipated this objection. He looked at his manicured fingernails stained black with ink of the king's business.

"Very well," he said with a dramatic sigh. "I will leave this priest with you. You may interview him at your leisure and return him to me if he does not suit your needs."

Katherine eyed Wolsey suspiciously.

"In the meantime, your remaining Spanish priests will accompany me when I leave tomorrow. The king needs them, at least temporarily, you see."

The look on the queen's face clearly showed that she, in fact, did not see.

She charged to a table with paper, a flask of ink, and a quill.

"I will write to King Henry at once," she declared, picking up the quill and poking it into the inkpot. "My Henry would not remove my two last priests and replace them with this ... this ... There must be some mistake."

"Of course, Your Majesty, you must do what seems right to you," Wolsey said with a yawn.

Wolsey sat heavily on the window seat, leaving no room for the queen's young lady, who quickly jumped up and darted to her mistress's side.

"I have always chosen my household. I *will* select the members of my household," the queen restated as she wrote.

"Queen Katherine ... I think you will find Thomas to be most sympathetic," Wolsey said, as the queen wrote feverishly. "He speaks Spanish fluently. He will hear confessions in your mother tongue. And he is adept at playing several musical instruments. Perhaps he could help you continue your studies as well."

"I am not in need of a tutor!" she exploded. "Nor do I need any more court musicians. Especially priests who play."

Thomas stretched his hand out.

"Mi Reina Catalina ..."

The queen stopped writing.

"Lamento que no se le haya dado la oportunidad de elegir." I am sorry that you have not been given the opportunity to choose. Thomas spoke the words carefully, evenly, and did not translate for Wolsey.

The queen's face softened, though she kept her eyes on the parchment.

Wolsey stood up. "Oh, and dear Queen Katherine, I believe that you have, in fact, been acquainted with Father Thomas Abell."

The queen eyed Thomas critically.

"Father Abell served Mass the day we visited Oxford," Wolsey said casually, *too* casually. "St. Frideswide."

Katherine's face darkened.

"That was a sad day," she said bitterly. "God did not hear my prayers."

Wolsey shrugged. "Well, yes, Your Highness, our prayers were not answered as we had wished. But you know, my Queen, that we must trust God in these things."

He took her finished note and started walking toward the door, his errand completed.

Thomas watched Wolsey's red robe slither away and glanced back at Katherine. She stood scowling, arms crossed, lips pursed. Perhaps she did not remember him. Why would she? Their eyes met, and she turned away. Thomas remained in the doorway and waited.

5

THE QUEEN'S PROTEST

The next morning, Thomas peered into the queen's darkened room. He blinked, waiting for his eyes to adjust to the unexpected bleakness. The queen's servants had drawn the heavy shades and tucked extra tapestries into the corners of the window, smothering any light that might have leaked into the room. The candelabra stood bare, bereft of even half-burned candles. Only the faint light of the dying embers glowed in the giant stone hearth.

Thomas drew his cloak around his thin shoulders to shield himself from not only the damp cold but also the despair that hung in the queen's bedchamber.

The queen's maidservant Margaret, the young woman he had seen take the queen's prayer book yesterday morning, padded over to him.

"Father," Margaret whispered as she reached for him with cold fingers. "The queen wishes to be alone today."

Thomas looked over at Katherine, a heap of blankets and pillows huddled in a high-post bed. Her faithful dog, Crimson, lifted his head and looked at Thomas forlornly, then resettled next to his master, tucking his paws under his chin.

Bed dogs were common enough among the English peasantry, but Thomas had not expected to find a canine companion in the queen's bedchamber. Most nobles would not suffer the animals sleeping among their expensive feather beds and silk cushions.

"Please understand," Margaret mouthed, holding her small forefinger in front of her lips.

"Is the queen ill?" Thomas inquired, relieved at the thought of being released from his morning obligations to the queen. But then, feeling a stab of guilt for shirking his new responsibilities, he added, "Does she need confession—Mass perhaps?"

"The queen is fasting," Margaret answered. She turned her face up to Thomas.

Something about her tiny chin, proudly perched atop her little neck, reminded him of his niece, his sister Agnes's daughter. She must be at least fourteen now. It had been five years since he had spent Christmas with them in Essex. She would be grown and starting her own family before too long.

Thomas smiled sadly.

"Shall I return later?"

"No," Margaret said with quiet resolution. "The queen has sent word to the king. She has requested that her Spanish priests, and only her Spanish priests, attend her. We will wait until the king relents and returns Father Juan Pedro and Father Enrique Francisco."

Thomas nodded. Of course. He was not the priest that the queen wanted. Well, at least they could agree on something. Perhaps he would return to Oxford after all.

Thomas stood in the hallway in front of the queen's chamber. Silence. No light shone from below the door. It had been almost a week, and she had not received him or the Holy Eucharist. Each time he came to her door, Margaret ushered him away, saying that the queen was fasting. She wanted only her Spanish priests. Thomas wondered how long it would continue and at what cost. If the queen fell ill on account of him, could he ever forgive himself? He touched the pewter cross around his neck. *Would Wolsey? Would the king?*

"Is the queen ready to take Holy Communion?" he asked, pushing open the door. The dark room was beginning to smell sour, like the chamber of a sick man. He had attended too many of those with Father Martin, offering prayers and assurance, absolution, only moments before death claimed weary eyes and silenced rattling coughs.

"No," Margaret whispered, although this time her chin trembled a bit. Perhaps she was worried too. "She will not receive you. Nothing has changed since yesterday."

Thomas bowed his head and turned to go.

"But please, Father," Margaret added, blinking back tears, "pray for our queen. She does not seem well to me." She reached out for his hands. "I am concerned."

Thomas looked over Margaret's shoulder to Katherine's motionless body, bundled in the bed.

"I should call for the doctor."

"No." Margaret shook her head, the tiny brown ringlets on the sides of her face shaking. "It would make no difference. Queen Katherine is determined to refuse food until Cardinal Wolsey returns her priests."

Thomas nodded. The situation had not changed. He would return to his own quarters and pray.

Thomas continued the routine for another week, rising at dawn, preparing the morning elements, and traipsing to the queen's chamber with the Holy Sacrament on the queen's own silver platter.

"No," he was told every time. No, the queen would not see him. Not today. Not ever. But as he turned to go, he could not help but notice Margaret's large brown eyes watching him, waiting, pleading. "Please, Father, please, don't give up."

"Father!"

Thomas opened his eyes to see a candle pressed close to his face and Margaret's wide eyes and freckled nose hovering.

"Please! Come with me!"

Thomas got up, taking only a moment to splash his face with water and gather his cross and rosary.

He followed Margaret's tiny bobbing orb of light down the long, dark corridor to the queen's privy chamber.

The room was awash in light, and King Henry himself was seated on a padded stool next to the queen's bed. He held her hand and brushed her fingertips with his lips, concern deepening the furrows of his brow.

The servants had lit every candle on the three candelabras, and there was a roaring fire in the hearth, radiating both heat and light. Even the chamber pot had been emptied, and someone, probably Margaret, had scattered crushed rose petals along the floor.

Thomas bowed, his heart suddenly racing.

"Forgive me, Your Majesty, I did not expect you."

The king frowned.

"I live here too," he said. "My chambers are just down the corridor." Thomas shook his head—of course! He had nearly forgotten the king's presence. The queen's quarters felt leagues away from the rest of the household.

"My queen is starving," King Henry said, his eyes both accusing and worried. "Would you have let the Queen of England wither away and not send word? Surely you could have sent a message."

Thomas had wondered if he should write to the king. He had tried to contact Wolsey, but was informed that the cardinal was at business, important business. He should have tried again.

Thomas stood silently, heart racing. Was this it? Had he already angered the king? He hoped Wolsey was right, hoped the king rarely hanged the clergy. He had been given one job, and he had managed to fail. *Oh, sweet Jesus!*

"Bring her the Eucharist," the king demanded. "If she will not eat meat and bread, she will eat the Lord's Supper."

Thomas nodded and hurried away, retracing his steps down the darkened corridor and out to the kitchen, and prayed he could find bread and wine, though he had never navigated the kitchen himself, let alone in the middle of the night.

The king's kitchen staff were asleep, bundled together on straw mats in the narrow room adjacent to the kitchen. If the king's kitchen servants were anything like those who served in the great houses in Essex, Thomas knew they worked hard all day, ate and drank what they could at night, and huddled together for sleep, waking only to stir the kitchen fire that cooked the food by day and warmed the servants at night.

Margaret had warned Thomas that no one was admitted entrance to the kitchen at night, but perhaps she was wrong. Priests were given privileges others were not. Priests moved in the service of both God and king.

When the kitchen's maidservant, Olivia, heard Thomas, she quickly rose and showed him the cabinet of unleavened wafers made each morning by local monks.

"For the queen?" the old cook asked. "Been days since she took victuals or drink."

Thomas nodded, and Olivia clucked her tongue in her toothless mouth.

"Such a shame, dear one. Will she survive? Does the good doctor know what ails her?"

Thomas looked at the woman's face, weathered from years of service, softened by affection for Katherine. He took her hands in his.

"Pray for the queen," he said simply. And he left with a tray of bread and wine, praying as he hastened back to the queen's privy chamber.

The queen lifted weak eyes without acknowledging Thomas.

"My Queen, *Corpus Christi.*" The Body of Christ.

Thomas would have said the words in Spanish as he placed the wafer in Katherine's mouth, but under King Henry's watchful eyes, he thought better of it. He would speak their common language lest he give King Henry another reason to be vexed.

"Sanguis Christi." The Blood of Christ. He gently raised the golden chalice to the queen's dry lips. The queen drank and sank back to her bed. The king let out a long sigh and got up to leave.

He and Thomas walked to the door.

"The doctor will attend to her in the morning. You should not have let her go a week on water alone," he said.

Thomas nodded. No, of course not, but how was he to know it was his responsibility to make the queen eat? The queen had many other servants and courtiers who could have alerted the king. Where were they?

"The queen's servants informed me that she was fasting and praying," Thomas said quietly, hoping that would not enrage the king. "I did not think that I should interfere in her devotion."

King Henry pursed his lips.

"She does that," he said after a moment, "sometimes for days, always has." He closed his eyes, and then, as if tearing himself away from the past, looked directly at Thomas. "But don't let her."

Thomas nodded. It would not happen again.

"I was told that Queen Katherine was waiting for her Spanish priests to be returned," he said as the king turned to go. "I thought perhaps she did not want me here."

The king whipped around, glaring at Thomas through narrowed eyes.

"Is that what this is about?!"

The king's face flushed.

"I will not be manipulated!" His ears grew red, and he searched the room until his angry gaze fell on Margaret, who was dutifully extinguishing the candles now that the queen had fallen asleep.

"You can tell your mistress when she wakes tomorrow that I will not be manipulated by foreign operatives in my own court!" His voice rose, and Margaret's eyes widened in her pale face. Thomas glanced over to see that the queen had awoken. She watched him.

"Her Spanish priests will be sent back to Spain, and if she carries on like this," the king said, shaking a finger at Margaret, "I WILL send her Spanish conspirators to the gallows."

Thomas's blood went cold, his heart racing. His palms began to sweat. The bright room grew dim—*No, not now!* He dug his fingernails painfully into his palm. *Calm yourself, Thomas!* It was a threat. Just a threat. No English king would execute an ambassador, priest or otherwise, from a foreign house. That would only invite retribution. He may be a capricious king, but he was not so foolish as to tempt war with Spain over the death of a priest. He might expel them from England, but he would never lay a hand against them.

An English priest, on the other hand... Thomas shuddered.

King Henry glanced over at Thomas and chuckled. The king's anger, so quickly ignited, vanished, the violent tempest a mere passing storm. Perhaps Henry had seen him sweating.

"Just make sure she eats."

6

BETTER

The next morning, Thomas found the bedchamber door open, the shades parted, and the queen dressed in a dark blue velvet dress, sitting primly at a wooden table. Her hair was neatly tucked under a black gabled hood. Her face was washed. When she looked up at him, she gave him a polite nod.

A polished silver tray with a loaf of bread and sliced green pears sat on the table. At least half of the bread had been eaten. Good. The fast was over.

Queen Katherine was attended by three women: Margaret; a Spanish woman Thomas did not recognize; and the saucy woman he had noticed on Henry's arm the day he first met the king at court—Anne Boleyn.

"You are well, my Queen?" Thomas asked, bowing slightly.

The queen nodded, pulling a needle with black embroidery thread through a stiff white shirt. She turned the garment over and pulled the needle through again, forming an intricate pattern of black flowers on the white sleeves. In the center of the pattern was a prominent "H.R.," *Henricus Rex*.

It was a good sign. The queen was back to her favorite pastime, sewing the king's shirts and marking them with his initials. Thomas exhaled a breath he had not known he was holding in. The queen was recovering.

Anne did not seem so pleased by the queen's embroidery. Her small mouth curled into a scowl as she watched Katherine's hands work.

"Father Abell, you have met Margaret, of course," the queen said, not looking up from her work. "These are two of my other ladies, Maria de Salinas, from my country, and ..."

Katherine paused and glanced sideways at Anne Boleyn, who dipped her head, her lips twisted in an amused smirk. Katherine squared her shoulders and took in a sharp breath. "This is Lady Anne Boleyn."

Anne raised her head, her steady brown eyes meeting Thomas's. "A pleasure," she said, flashing a confident smile. Thomas returned the smile, feeling Katherine's heavy gaze. Did she know? How could she not? Everyone knew.

"My *dear husband*, the king, and I were up at dawn," Katherine said stiffly, addressing Thomas directly. "We took Mass with Father John in the royal chapel."

At the mention of the king, Anne raised her chin and looked away. But Margaret smiled at her mistress, nodding with appreciation as the queen continued. "You will join us tomorrow."

"Yes, Your Majesty," Thomas said with a polite bow. Perhaps he would be able to serve the queen after all.

7

TROUBLED QUEEN

December 1527   Greenwich Palace

Thomas knelt on the cold chapel tile. Incense mingled with the damp winter evening as he gazed up at the brass crucifix on the gilded altar. The Lord's head, crowned with thorns, bowed over his tortured body. *Jesus Christ, Son of God, have mercy.* The last of the day's light filtered through high stained-glass windows, illuminating the cross in splashes of red.

The queen and her host of ladies, both the gentry and the servants, knelt behind Thomas. He could hear the rustle of velvet and satin, the murmuring of whispered prayers. One lady's rings clicked as she moved a string of rosary beads through her fingers.

Thomas focused on the cross in front of him and did not turn to see which one of the women made the noise. The queen preferred that he face the altar during the evening vespers.

The light faded, and Thomas opened his mouth to sing, his deep voice echoing through the royal chapel. As he sang, the queen's voice joined his, along with a chorus of women, the liturgy of their shared experience resonating through sacred space.

Lucis Creator optime,
Lucem dierum proferens,
Primordiis lucis novae,
Mundi parans originem.

Thomas closed his eyes and let the sound wash over him. "Creator of light, by whom each day is kindled out of night." The simple words comforted his soul, and he marveled at how the common experience of day and night pointed to the greater truth of life and death and the God who reigns over all.

Thomas opened his eyes and ran his thumb over a worn prayer book in his hand. He opened it to the evening's reading, though he knew it by heart, and stood. The dresses swished behind him. Psalm 113. He read it in Latin, but his heart translated it: "Praise the Lord. Oh, you servants, praise the name of the Lord. Blessed be the name of the Lord from this time forth and forever."

The tall white candles on the altar seemed brighter as the light from the window faded. The queen liked silence, so Thomas waited several minutes, watching the candles flicker, until whispering reminded him that the queen's young ladies were not so patient.

Thomas inhaled deeply and began the final song, the "Canticle of Mary." The song always drew a response from Katherine, and now her voice lifted and filled the chapel, soaring over the other women, her spirit uniting with Mary in their submission to God's will. Yes, and amen. She would obey her Lord.

Magnificat anima mea Dominum,
Et exsultavit spiritus meus in Deo salutari meo.

When the nightly service concluded, Thomas continued to kneel, facing away from the women. He led by example, but he was not one of them. They came and left without acknowledging him. It was a cold arrangement, but it was as it had been for the two months since Thomas entered the royal household. The queen tolerated his presence, but only so much.

But this evening, long after the sound of slippers on the floor had left, the shadow of a single kneeling figure remained.

"My Queen," Thomas whispered, not turning around.

"Please," Katherine said in a low voice. "Stay." She was silent for a moment, and then her voice cracked. "I want to confess my sins."

The shadow slumped, shoulders quaking with sobs, and Thomas longed to turn around to touch Katherine's shoulder. But he could not. Decorum demanded otherwise. They had roles to play. He focused his gaze on Jesus's bowed head and made the sign of the cross. "Your Majesty, I am listening."

"How is our dear Katherine?" Wolsey asked the next morning as Thomas entered the cardinal's private room. Sitting behind a heavy wooden desk littered with open ledgers, parchments, and an ink pot, Wolsey extended his bejeweled hand to Thomas with an impatient smile and glanced down at the open ledger.

Thomas had grown used to these weekly meetings and had long since stopped trembling in Wolsey's presence. The cardinal was too busy attending to the king's business to worry much about him. But it bothered Thomas how Wolsey called the queen "our dear Katherine," as if he were talking about his own elderly mother or dependent daughter.

Though it was never discussed, Thomas and all the other courtiers knew that the cardinal had fathered a daughter in his youth. The unfortunate, illegitimate daughter was serving God in a nunnery, miles from court, conveniently located in the northern county of Yorkshire. Wolsey provided financially for her, as was fitting of the wealthiest cleric in England, but he was no more of a father to her than he was a father to the whole country. It seemed to Thomas that this was often the sad case of children born to "celibate" churchmen. How was it that some children came unwanted, and other children, so desperately wanted, never came?

"Queen Katherine is growing more comfortable with me," Thomas answered truthfully, hoping the progress would please Wolsey. "Although she is still distant. She grieves her lost children, I think."

Wolsey pursed his lips thoughtfully, leaned back, and laced his ringed fingers over his giant chest.

"Does she make confession?"

Thomas searched Wolsey's face. Did the cardinal expect him to break the Seal of Confession? He squirmed. "Cardinal, it is not appropriate for me to say ..."

Wolsey waved his hand. "I was not asking you what she said, only that she made confession." He shook his head and then narrowed his eyes. "But Thomas, if she is making confession, and I assume from your demeanor that she is, that is good for us."

Thomas wrinkled his forehead. "Us?"

Wolsey leaned forward. "Yes, Thomas, us."

Thomas's stomach began to churn. He should have asked Wolsey to explain, but maybe he did not want to know.

"Perhaps a visit from the king would help," Thomas suggested.

"Help?" Wolsey asked.

"Help her state of mind, help her grief," Thomas said with a hint of impatience. Wasn't that why he met with Wolsey, to help the queen? "The king came to Queen Katherine when she was ill. I believe it revived her."

Wolsey nodded thoughtfully and pursed his lips. "Yes, I remember," he said absently, then looked down at his open ledger. "Perhaps, if it comes up, I will mention it to King Henry."

"Thank you, Lord Cardinal."

Wolsey stood up, signaling the end of the meeting. Would he speak to the king? Somehow, Thomas doubted he would. Their meetings were beginning to feel like a staged masque in which he, Thomas, was cast as the fool.

8

OXFORD CONVERSATIONS

January 1528   Greenwich Palace

The day was dawning, but Thomas had been awake for hours, lying on the cold straw mattress in the furthest quarter of the queen's household suite. Thomas could already hear servants bustling through the halls, more activity than usual. The royal company was moving today, and even though the queen rarely left the sanctity of her private quarters, Katherine intended to join the procession to Richmond Palace, one of the king's favorite winter homes. And, as always, the queen's entire household—all of her courtiers, servants, clerks, and clergy—would go with her.

Thomas rose and stretched.

He looked around the meager room and gathered his few possessions: an extra tunic, his summer vestments, and his woolen winter one, the lute, and a prayer book he had brought from Oxford. When he was finished, he knelt on the floor.

"*Pater Noster, qui es in caelis ...*" he began his Latin prayer. Our Father, Who is in Heaven.

"Heaven." He looked out the window at the frosted fields below and the cold, gray river that would ferry the royal company back toward London later that day.

"You are in Heaven," he whispered. "Are you not here as well?"

Thomas closed his eyes. He was weary, so weary of being in the royal household, weary of Wolsey and his constant questions, weary of serving a queen whose moods seemed as changeable as the seasons. Weary of the court gossip. Weary of the king's problem. He missed his students and his books. He missed academies alive with conversations and ideas, both exciting and dangerous. He smiled, remembering heated discussions about Erasmus of Rotterdam and his friend, the king's counselor Thomas More. About Martin Luther, the renegade German theologian who had enraged the establishment. All of it was interesting to Thomas, and he relished nothing more than an easy walk down Oxford's cobblestone streets with his mentor, Father Martin.

Spring 1520   Oxford

"He's a heretic," Father Martin scowled, quickening his pace.

Thomas was quiet, watching the road as they walked. Tiny spring wildflowers pushed through the cracks between the paving stones.

"The German's thoughts on indulgences are nothing new. I know that you yourself have been troubled by this practice. I believe I have heard you say so, many times," Thomas said carefully, mindful of Father Martin's wisdom and years. "Even Erasmus agrees with him on these points."

Father Martin nodded as he walked. "Yes, yes, that is true."

Thomas waited for the "Perhaps, however ..." but it did not come. The two walked silently for several minutes, quietly contemplating until Thomas spoke again.

"Perhaps Luther was right in starting the conversation. We are not unaware of corruption ... in certain areas of our Church," Thomas finally said carefully, still watching the uneven ground.

"Perhaps," Martin said. Then, almost wistfully, he added, "I wish it had come from Rome, though."

Thomas nodded. Martin was right, of course. "But perhaps it could not," Thomas said thoughtfully. "Perhaps, criticism and changes have to come from outside Rome."

Thomas respected the old priest who had served so long at the Lord's altar. If he saw things that were corrupt, he passed them by for the sake of all that was good, and Thomas knew that. In a way, he felt the same. He loved the Church. When he knelt at Mass with the entire community, he felt peace. He believed in the saints and how their example served as signposts to those still on the earthly pilgrimage to Heaven. He loved to pray the Latin prayers. It felt right. But he also loved the conversation.

Last night, Thomas had stayed up late with friends at the Old Bear tavern, discussing Luther and his pamphlets. William Tyndale was there, arguing again for Scripture in the common language, a regular point of discussion between the scholars.

"But what about Latin words that have no real English equivalent? Should the English translator just make up new words?" Thomas challenged.

William Tyndale shrugged. "Maybe English needs new words to communicate the gospel."

"But William, with Latin, we know that we are all reading and teaching the same words the Church has taught for centuries. There is a continuity, a quality, I think that is worth protecting and preserving ..."

William interrupted, shaking his head. "But what good does it do the common Englishman who knows no Latin? It's easy for us to say here, in Oxford, that Scripture should be in Latin because we know Latin. Thomas, you love the Vulgate, but to the common plowman, it means nothing."

Thomas shook his head. "If more people were educated in Latin, they could read and understand the Bible properly. Plenty of London merchants are teaching their boys Latin; we just need to make sure that it is accessible to all the boys of England."

"But why, Thomas? Why should everyone learn Latin? Why should there be any barrier at all between common people and the Word of God?"

"Because faithful transmission of the Scripture, of the traditions of the Church, matters!"

Their conversation was taking on the typical cycle, but Thomas continued anyway.

"If heretics can read and interpret the Scripture in any way they want... William, consider how irresponsible that could be. Wrong ideas do real damage!" Thomas ran his hand through his thick hair. He could feel himself getting upset, though he relished the argument.

"Yes, yes, they do!" William agreed.

It was nearly half past eleven, and the old tavern was mostly empty. The few remaining tables of patrons began eyeing the Oxford scholars. Suddenly, Thomas felt like they were two actors in a play, delivering the leading lines of a debate being waged in academic halls and taverns across the cities of Christendom. Tonight, he and William took the stage. Tomorrow night it might well be someone else in England, France, Germany, or Brussels.

A skinny lad, several years younger than William and Thomas, edged his way over. He wore the traditional shirt of an underclassman. The young fingers wrapped around his half-finished half pint were ink-stained from the long days of reading and writing.

"If I might add," he boldly started in, "what if there was an official commission that oversaw translation from Latin into English? Then even people who cannot read and write could hear the Bible in the language they understand when they come to Mass."

William smiled broadly at the young student's remarks.

"See, that is exactly what I would like," William said.

Thomas swirled the remaining ale in his cup slowly. He could not agree too quickly with William.

"It would need to be authorized by the Pope, by leadership in England, by Wolsey himself," Thomas added. "Yes, it would need to have the legitimacy of being an official translation authorized by the Church."

William stood up from the table, jostling what was left of the ale in their mugs. "And Wolsey would never authorize it. He is too busy handling the Church's money, managing the Church's lands, and sticking his hands in the king's pocket too. I doubt he cares about ..."

"That seems rather harsh," Thomas interrupted, standing up too. William's list of offenses against Wolsey and his cronies was long, and Thomas had heard most of it before.

"Well, Thomas, do you think he would authorize translating the Bible into English?"

But before Thomas could answer, William turned to the young scholar. "And by the way ... ah?" William raised an eyebrow.

The young man bowed slightly. "Robert Barnes, *sir*."

William smiled. "Master Barnes, the Bible needs to be translated from its original Greek and Hebrew, not Latin. Our New Testament was written in Greek, the Old in Hebrew."

The young man nodded thoughtfully, and Thomas smiled, happy for the diversion that landed them somewhere off the logic circle they were traversing. He turned to the boy and placed his hand on his thin shoulder. "Perhaps you can learn Greek and Hebrew for us. It might be needed in the future."

Thomas looked over at William. "And pray we get an authorization for an English version of the Bible. The heart of the king is in the Lord's hand."

William raised his glass. "Yes, indeed, my friend! Pray!"

January 1528   Greenwich Palace

Thomas looked out over the frozen field, his heart heavy. He closed his eyes.

"Holy Father, give England an authorized commission to translate the Bible into English," he whispered. "It could be such a beautiful thing."

He thought about it for a moment.

William had left for the continent long ago, and his first English New Testaments arrived in England two years ago. Thomas's friends in Oxford told him that William was working on the Pentateuch, although no one knew for sure. Not even his friends knew where he lived.

But here Thomas was, in London, like it or not, in the queen's household, regularly speaking to Wolsey, the head of the Church of England, the very man who had issued a warrant for Tyndale's arrest two years earlier.

Perhaps the Lord had put Thomas there for a reason. Perhaps. He would wait for an opportunity. And he would pray.

Adveniat regnum tuum. Fiat voluntas tua, sicut in caelo et in terra.

Let your kingdom come.

Let your will be done on Earth as it is in Heaven.

He prayed the line in Latin and English. As he looked out over the frozen land and watched his frosty breath hang in the morning air, he felt something he had not felt in a long time: hope.

9

Daily Bread

May 1528   Hampton Court

Thomas stood in the doorway, watching the queen run trembling fingers through her thick, unkempt hair. The famous auburn tresses, once her youthful glory, were now darkened and streaked with silver.

Katherine stared blankly out the tall glass windows onto the manicured gardens. The spring rosebuds, glistening with morning dew, shimmered in the sunlight, but Katherine seemed unaffected by their beauty. Instead, her face reflected the inner turmoil Thomas had often sensed.

In many ways, the queen was still a mystery to Thomas. Outside of confession, she rarely spoke to him, and she continued to regard him as Wolsey's appointment, planted in her house.

Most days, Thomas spent less than an hour with the queen. He knelt faithfully by her side as she carefully pronounced every word of her routine prayers. Be it winter darkness or summer sunlight, every morning began with Latin prayers.

Staring at her small, delicate hands, the queen whispered quiet confessions to Thomas. They were minor sins of the heart and mind, weeds in her holy garden, and Thomas hoped that when he whispered absolution, he helped her pluck out each undesirable thought. The daily practice lessened her burden, Thomas hoped, but what did it do for the great ache of her soul?

Their interactions were sterile—carefully choreographed. When she rose to her feet, prayers completed, Katherine of Aragon retreated into the privacy of her quiet shell. Thomas took his cue and left her chambers. There was little he could do to help anyway. After more than six months of daily serving, the queen was still an enigma.

And when Thomas thought about it, he realized he had grown comfortable with their distance. He offered daily Mass, then withdrew to his books and private study. At this rate, he would master Greek by the end of the year. With a little more practice, he might even be able to assist in translating Scripture. While it was still illegal in England, the law might change if it suited the king. In France, the theologian Jacques Lefèvre d'Etaples had already begun translating a French New Testament. If the old Lollardy laws were dropped, translators could begin working on a Church-approved English version.

The thought filled him with a giddy hope. If only the king could see the wisdom in authorizing an English Bible. If Thomas could discuss his thoughts with Wolsey, perhaps the cardinal could be convinced, and then the king would authorize it. If only King Henry were not so preoccupied with other things. Other things ... The thought drew him back to the task at hand.

Thomas looked at the queen standing in the cold morning light. It was Ascension Day. Already, the aroma of roasted lamb and venison filled the house as the kitchen staff prepared the court for an afternoon of feasting. There would be church services to honor the day, and then feasting and music, even dancing. Last year, they had been at Greenwich Palace, and the performing choir had brought tears to the queen's eyes. Thomas had hoped she would stay for the dinner, but she retreated to her quarters... again.

Today did not look more promising. Queen Katherine's ladies had dressed her in an elegant, new gray velvet dress, but Katherine hardly looked prepared for a party. She looked unmoored, lost in thought. Her hair hung loose, tumbling down her back.

Margaret stood by with a heavy brush, a rope of pearls, and the queen's characteristic square-gabled headpiece, but Katherine had taken a step away from the young woman, a quiet protest against the encroaching day.

Thomas turned to leave. Perhaps he should return later when the queen was presentable.

"Father Abell," the queen called after him.

Thomas turned to look at Katherine.

"I need... I need... " She lowered her eyes and twisted a handkerchief. Thomas stepped toward her, kneeling a bit to reach her eye level.

"I am afraid I am losing. I am afraid I have already lost." She looked away. Crimson, who had been sleeping at her feet, raised his head. She stroked his head, feeling each silky ear, and continued.

"My mother was a fighter, a real fighter, a *conquistador*!" Her voice rose, and Thomas raised an eyebrow. "No, Father Abell, it is true. She led troops into battle against the Moors. With my father. They were king and queen together—did you not know?"

"Yes." Thomas nodded, holding her steady gaze. "I have been told."

"It is true," Katherine said bitterly. "I am the daughter of Queen Isabella, the great liberator of Spain. And I have failed in the only task, the only battle that matters!"

Margaret and Marina Salinas froze in silence, and Thomas felt their presence.

"You have not failed," Thomas tried, clearing his throat.

"Oh yes, yes I have," Katherine said, stepping away. "I am failing the only task that matters. And I am nearly forty-three years old."

Margaret hurried to the queen's side to hold her hand. "No, my Queen," she cooed, stroking Katherine's hand. Marina Salinas picked up the queen's night dress and cap and began folding them carefully, preparing them for the wardrobe keeper to take away and store for another day. Anne Boleyn was nowhere to be seen. The queen sat heavily on a padded stool.

"I've been wed to the king for nearly nineteen years and have not given him one living prince. Mary, yes, but no sons. Even the daughter I carried to Frideswide came early and died in my arms. Why does God punish me?"

She covered her face with her hands, shoulders slumped, and wept.

"Sometimes I think God is cruel," she whispered between her fingers.

She took in a deep breath and said in a half-whisper, "King Henry has given up. *Dice que soy demasiado vieja.*" He says I am too old.

The ladies looked away from Katherine, but Thomas held her gaze, patiently waiting for her to finish unburdening her heart.

"I can produce a son for England," she said, straightening her back and wiping her eyes. "I can. I know I can. If I could have just one more chance. *Solo uno más.*" Just one more.

Thomas stood at a distance, uncomfortably conscious of the elements he had brought for the queen. The Body and Blood of Christ, the Holy Incarnation in his hands.

The Lord had told his disciples to ask for Daily Bread, and truly, He was the Bread that came from Heaven, and yet, in the moment, it hardly felt sufficient. Mere bread and wine? By faith, incarnate God? Were they enough to soothe the heartaches of life? Dashed hopes? Unanswered questions lay bitterly at his feet. Unaccustomed to such a heartfelt outpouring from the queen, Thomas was lost for words. He let the hallowed silence hang between them.

"*Mi Reina Catalina,*" he finally said quietly. "It is Ascension Day."

She nodded, and he continued. "And I have brought you the Bread of Christ."

Margaret handed Katherine a fresh tissue embroidered with the black H and K.

"Thank you," she whispered.

"My Queen," Thomas said carefully, looking his queen directly in her troubled gray eyes. "This is the Body of Christ, broken for you. Take it and eat."

As Thomas held her gaze, he could not help but feel a little bit of the depth of her pain. Tears gathered in his eyes too. Pools reflecting pools. Spirits communicating without words. He would never know this heartache, the rejection of a spouse, the loss of children, but somehow, he felt it. And his heart translated it into every pain he had ever known. The grief when his mother died. The sorrow of leaving home. His father... The lump in his throat was so full he wanted to immediately retreat to his own chambers, to look away, to think about something else, to be somewhere else. But he continued. It was his service to God.

He handed her trembling hands the familiar golden chalice, elaborately decorated with pomegranates, worn where his hands, and the hands of priests before him, had held the cup.

"This is the Blood of Christ, shed for you," he said.

She lifted the cup to her lips, closed her eyes, and slowly drank the wine.

The daily practice of remembering the Lord's death through wine and bread had always been the queen's morning routine. Rise. Remember the Lord. Receive his Body and Blood. It was her life. It was Christ's life living in her.

Some days it was the only thing they had in common. It was Thomas's daily bread too.

"*Pater noster, qui es in caelis,*" Thomas began in Latin, their common language of prayer. Our Father, who is in Heaven. "*Sanctificetur nomen tuum.*" Hallowed be Thy name.

The queen joined Thomas in the cadence, inhaling life as she breathed out holy words, the comfort of them soothing her furrowed brow, relaxing the lines on her face.

When they finished, Margaret smiled at Thomas. She picked up the brush and continued her work.

"Thank you," Katherine murmured.

Thomas nodded and turned to leave, his morning duties completed, but he stopped. Instead of leaving, he took the queen's hand in his own. The human touch was both comforting and shocking to him.

"My Queen," he implored with a sudden fierceness, "do not give up hope."

The corner of Katherine's mouth turned up into a slight smile for a second and then faded. "Thank you, Father. Thank you for being here."

Thomas turned to leave and was halfway down the marble hall when he felt a tug on his vestment sleeve. Turning, he saw Margaret's beaming face.

"Thank you, Father Abell," she said. "The queen says she will attend the Ascension Day Feast tonight at court. There will be music and dancing, marzipan and sugar doves. She says you should sit at our table. Will you?"

Thomas nodded. "Nothing would make me happier."

10

CONVERSATIONS WITH A CARDINAL

September 1528   Hampton Court

"How is our dear Katherine?" Wolsey began as Thomas strode into his expansive working apartment. Since Thomas had joined the queen's household, nearly an entire year had passed, and now the trees were changing again. And despite shifting between castles—Hampton Court to Greenwich Palace, Greenwich to Richmond, Richmond to Windsor Castle, then on to Woodstock and back to Hampton—little had changed in the queen's life.

Every day, Thomas continued one heavy step after another, the ache of loneliness, both his and the queen's, growing in his heart. Perhaps the king would release him to return to Oxford. It was not too late to begin tutoring this year's students. Perhaps.

"Be faithful, Thomas." That was what Father Martin had written him. *"Give your service to God and be faithful."* He could do that. One day at a time. But sometimes, more than sometimes, the routine was just too much. It felt meaningless. Despite the queen's regular confessions, there seemed to be very little he could do to advise or comfort her.

Thomas watched Wolsey's tired face. Over the summer, the cardinal had become increasingly busy and harried. This morning, his red cardinal's cap was set aside, and the remnants of his thin white hair stood up at ragged angles as he raked fingers through what was left of it.

These days, Wolsey rarely looked up from his stack of ledgers, inkpot, and correspondence. Wolsey's new assistant, Thomas Cromwell, on the other hand, watched Thomas Abell with narrowed eyes and pursed lips, tapping his thumb over his folded arms.

Thomas had no doubt that Wolsey and Cromwell had been working on the king's business since long before the first light of dawn. The royal court whispered that, in recent months, the cardinal had barely slept. He burned candles on both sides of the night to keep King Henry's country running. And now that Cromwell had joined his inner circle, it seemed that the inseparable two were always busy, very busy.

At least the royal household had returned to Hampton Court, where the cardinal was at home in his own libraries and chambers. And, from what Thomas had seen, the king planned to make Hampton Court a regular habitation. He frequently made pointed comments about the estate's luxuries. On more than one occasion, he had noted loudly that Hampton Court was indeed larger and finer than any of his own castles.

Cardinal Wolsey seemed to take these comments warily, noting always that he was pleased the king liked the humble house he had built. He had designed it, he said, to offer the royal household the hospitality they deserved. Nothing more. All in service for the king. Thomas couldn't make sense of how the king's own chancellor had amassed such wealth.

Thomas looked at the cardinal with his head bowed over the ledgers, Cromwell pointing to a figure, whispering. Thomas wondered if Wolsey had forgotten the question as quickly as he uttered it. Thomas cleared his throat.

"Queen Katherine is well in body but troubled in spirit," he answered, exactly as he had for as many weeks as Wolsey had been asking him.

He sighed and rubbed his hands. How he longed to talk about other things! Surely Wolsey had read Erasmus's *Hyperaspistes*. He wondered whether Wolsey had an opinion on Erasmus and

Luther's debate over free will or on the growing call for an official English translation of the Scriptures. Surely Wolsey was aware that Londoners were reading smuggled copies of Tyndale's New Testament. Maybe he could convince Wolsey to allow the translation to happen in England under the watchful eye of faithful theologians who could oversee the work. Then the English could have an authorized version of Scripture. That conversation would make Thomas's time in the royal household worth the days of monotony.

Thomas watched the cardinal and Cromwell continue with their figures, ignoring Thomas's stock answer to Wolsey's standard question. Thomas watched them, waiting. Perhaps today was not the day to talk about biblical translations or Dutch philosophers, but maybe he could help the queen.

"Does the king intend to visit my lady?" Thomas asked abruptly. "To my knowledge, he has not been alone with the queen for nearly a year."

Wolsey looked up in surprise, set down his quill, and pushed aside the note he had been writing. Cromwell took the quill from him and continued. "You must understand, dear Thomas, that the king is most occupied with matters of state," Wolsey said.

"Yes, of course," Thomas said carefully. "But it seems to me that the queen is distressed that her opportunity to bear a son is waning. She is getting older, as you know."

Thomas tried to say this as delicately as possible, but out of the corner of his eye, he saw Cromwell smirk. Thomas's cheeks felt hot, and he wished that he did not have to discuss the queen's womanly cycle with the cardinal and Cromwell. But, of course, the queen's menstruation and pregnancies had been national gossip for years. Her most private and shameful details were a source of national concern.

The cardinal touched his thumb to his fingertips and pursed his lips, a habit he seemed to have before speaking. "Thomas, you care about the queen. I can see that, and that is good."

Thomas did not smile or nod. Wolsey continued.

"You want what is best for her?"

Thomas nodded. He disliked acquiescing before he knew the cardinal's direction. Wolsey narrowed his eyes. "Then you should know that the king will never be intimate with Katherine again."

Thomas could not mask his surprise, and Wolsey continued.

"And, Thomas, it would be best if you helped her accept this reality."

Thomas could feel his mouth was open, but he did not bother closing it. "Why?"

Cromwell glared at Thomas while Wolsey stood up, laced his fingers behind his back, and began pacing as if he was formulating the thoughts as he spoke. "The queen is not able to bear the king a son. She has demonstrated this over and over, as we all know."

Cromwell, watching Wolsey, nodded slightly. Cromwell would not dare interrupt the cardinal, but it seemed to Thomas that he had a way of encouraging Wolsey with the slightest tilt of his head. And this seemed odd to Thomas, odd that the cardinal needed Cromwell to approve what he said.

"The queen has had six pregnancies and no live children," Wolsey calculated.

"Except Mary," Thomas interrupted.

The cardinal waved his hand like he was slapping a gnat. "Well, yes, of course, but Mary doesn't count. Does she?"

Thomas felt heat rising in his cheeks.

"I am aware of the queen's miseries," Thomas said, willing himself to move past the slight to Katherine's only living child. "But I am surprised that the king would give up on his heir while his wife is still able to carry a child."

"Is she?" Wolsey demanded.

"She has told me so," Thomas said. He furrowed his brow. He had not thought to question the queen's claim.

"Is it possible that she has simply told you what she wants to believe?" Wolsey asked.

Thomas felt his cheeks burning, but did not look away from the cardinal.

"Yes, I suppose that is possible," he conceded.

Wolsey smiled. He had won a small point in their argument.

"Then how will the king have his heir?" Thomas asked.

Cromwell glared at Thomas. "It is not your place to question His Majesty the King or His Lord Chancellor," he said, crossing his arms.

Thomas stared at Cromwell, pushing down a stab of resentment.

"Of course," he said with a slight nod. "I apologize."

Wolsey raised a scolding eyebrow at Cromwell and gave Thomas a conciliatory smile, reminding him that above all, Wolsey was a great diplomat.

"The king has options for his heir," Wolsey began, then listed all the strategies Thomas had heard in court gossip. He could elevate his illegitimate son Henry Fitzroy, a young boy born to one of Katherine's maids. He could appoint a distant cousin, or *more practically*, he could replace Katherine with a new queen.

So, there it was, out in the open. The king was no longer content with his mistresses. He wanted a new queen. Thomas had heard the gossip, but he had hoped, he had prayed...

"The king has come to believe that his marriage to Katherine was a mistake," the cardinal said, as if his ledgers were off and the king had spent too much money on a visiting dignitary.

"Was it not approved by the Pope?" Thomas asked.

"Yes," Wolsey said slowly. "Yes, it was, but perhaps *that* pope did not fully understand the situation."

Cromwell lifted his chin. "It would be helpful, Father Abell, if you understood the king's predicament and helped the queen make peace with it," he said.

Wolsey nodded, crossed his arms, and waited.

Thomas swallowed hard, his mind spinning. Of course, it was increasingly unlikely that the queen would bear another son, especially since the king refused to share her bed. Of course, the king needed a prince, an heir. The whole world expected it. The country demanded it. Yet, what Wolsey suggested, what Cromwell seemed eager to adopt, was unfair, cruel, immoral. *Lord Jesus, give me wisdom and courage.*

"I will serve the queen however I can," he said quietly, his troubled eyes searching Wolsey's face.

Wolsey smiled.

"Thank you, Thomas. I will need your help in the coming weeks," he said. "This will not be easy for Katherine."

Wolsey sat down heavily, and Cromwell handed him a parchment. Wolsey rubbed his eyes. "That is all, Thomas."

They would not be discussing Tyndale or Erasmus today. The conversation was over.

11

THE QUEEN'S PRINCESS MARY

October 1528

"I would like to see my daughter," Queen Katherine announced as Thomas walked into the room. In the weeks that had passed since his meeting with Wolsey, he had intended to talk to Katherine, to let her know that she must be prepared for the king to seek an annulment. But it had never seemed the right time.

With every passing day that the king did not visit her chambers, the queen seemed to grow more desperate, spending hours staring out the window or lying prostrate on the chapel floor. When she shared her thoughts with Thomas in confession, she talked about the king's absence and the sins that might have turned God's favor away from her. Thomas feared the queen's frail heart might break if he suggested she begin preparing for the king to divorce her. Even bringing up the conversation might cause the queen to take to her bed, refuse food, fast in sackcloth. King Henry would not tolerate it.

But this morning the queen looked uncharacteristically awake, alert, like she had spent the last watch of the night in contemplation and had come to an urgent decision.

"Princess Mary? She is in Wales?" Thomas asked, looking to the queen's attendants. Margaret nodded. Thank God for Margaret. She always knew.

"I oversee the princess's education myself," Katherine declared with more energy than she had displayed in a month. "She has the best Latin and French instructors, of course. And perhaps you have heard that she is also learning Greek." The queen straightened her back, tilting her chin. "I thought, Father Abell, that you would be particularly happy to hear that she is learning Greek." She clasped her hands to her heart. *"La princesa leerá la Santa Biblia en griego."* Then, as if Thomas did not know Spanish, she shook her head, her earrings bobbing against her cheeks. "The Holy Bible in Greek!"

"Yes," Thomas said carefully. "Indeed, Your Majesty."

Katherine continued pacing around her private chamber, head tall, back straight. Her hands danced with her words. Thomas did not know what to make of the sudden change in demeanor.

"My Henry and his Wolsey decided that she would be best prepared for her future by sending her to Wales, *as she is the Princess of Wales.* But of course, it is nearly Advent, and she must return home for Christmas."

"It is October, my Queen," Margaret said, looking down at the embroidery work in her hands.

"Yes, I am well aware that it is October," the queen said, stopping short to address her lady. "But Christmas will be coming soon."

"Yes, Your Majesty," Margaret said with a polite curtsy.

"Father Featherstone," the queen suddenly said. "Where is Featherstone?"

"The princess's tutor?" Thomas asked.

"Yes, of course," the queen said with less patience than Thomas expected.

"He is not in our household at the moment. He was sent to Wales with the princess," Margaret said, this time looking up at the queen.

"I am aware of that," the queen said irritably as if she had not just asked his whereabouts. She started pacing again. "We should call him back... with Mary. They could resume their studies here."

She stopped short at her desk. Her wide Spanish farthingale bounced around her as she snatched a piece of parchment and a long feather quill.

"I will write to the king immediately," she said, scratching ferociously onto the parchment, ignoring the drops of ink that splattered across the paper.

"You will deliver this to Wolsey this afternoon," she demanded as she handed Thomas the unfolded paper. "I need my princess here."

"She wants her daughter and the tutor Richard Featherstone to return to London immediately," Thomas stated flatly as he handed Wolsey the note an hour later.

"Christmas?" Wolsey said, eyes scanning the queen's note, handing it to Thomas Cromwell. "Does our dear Katherine understand that it is October? The trees are yellow."

Cromwell smirked.

"Yes, Cardinal," Thomas said sharply. "I mentioned this to her."

Wolsey looked up quickly at Thomas, eyeing him carefully. It never ceased to unnerve Thomas, this public undressing. Wolsey's eyes narrowed. "Are you weary of Katherine's company?"

Thomas did not answer. This was not about him.

Wolsey waved his hand dismissively.

"Ah, the company of unhappy women. I understand."

Thomas said nothing. It was none of Wolsey's business how he felt about Katherine, and even if it were, he would not complain about the queen in Thomas Cromwell's presence. The way the cardinal's assistant watched Thomas put him on edge. Besides, Cromwell did not personally know the queen. Unlike Wolsey, Cromwell had never had an intimate conversation with her. To Cromwell, the queen must have seemed like another problem to solve.

Wolsey waited through Thomas's silence and then said, "You are a wise man. You keep your thoughts to yourself."

Thomas said nothing, and Wolsey tilted his chin.

"Perhaps it would be good for Katherine to have her daughter here. Tell our dear Katherine the king will send for her. Mary will return for Advent and stay with us through Twelfth Night," he announced.

Thomas's heart lightened. Would Wolsey grant the queen's desires unconditionally?

"In the meantime," Wolsey said, beginning to pace the room, "Katherine must be thinking about her own future as well as her daughter's."

The cardinal stopped pacing and looked at Thomas, narrowing his eyes. "Has Katherine discussed our conversation?"

Thomas looked at Wolsey quizzically. He could feel Cromwell's gaze following him. Katherine had not mentioned a meeting with the cardinal. "No."

Wolsey crossed the room and stood squarely in front of Thomas. "How our king wishes she leave court and retire to a nunnery?"

Thomas raised a brow.

"I see not," Wolsey continued. "Well, Thomas, you should know that King Henry has requested that his sister-in-law retire to a nunnery. I discussed this with her last week. I am surprised Katherine did not tell her chaplain. Perhaps she is better at keeping secrets than you thought."

Thomas cleared his throat, mind spinning. *The king's sister-in-law?*

"The king believes that his *sister-in-law* has failed him, quite miserably so," Wolsey stated like an attorney winding up on an indictment.

Thomas willed his face to remain passive, listening to Wolsey, but his heart raced beneath his vestments. No wonder the queen seemed so desperate in recent days. Wolsey was accusing her of somehow failing the king, and now he denied she had ever been rightly married to the king.

"She had one task for king and for country, and she has not produced a male heir because their union was, is, and always will be, a sin before God." Wolsey's cadence fell like a judge's gavel: *was, is, and always will be.*

Wolsey had marched in the London procession with Katherine and Henry on their wedding day. He stood over their infant son, the little Duke of Cornwall, when they baptized him in the chilly winter chapel. And he had been in Richmond Palace when the little prince died. He had told Thomas that he would always remember the queen's heart-wrenching wail echoing through the cold corridors. He knew how desperately Katherine had wanted a son. Cardinal Thomas Wolsey knew.

Thomas bit his tongue, tasting a bit of blood. But he kept silent and felt Cromwell's icy stare as Wolsey continued.

"Over the past several years, it has begun to trouble the king... this marriage to Arthur's widow." Wolsey's portly face took on an unexpected posture of sympathy for Henry. "He has consulted Scripture, and he has been greatly troubled by what he has found, particularly Leviticus 20."

Thomas nodded slightly. He had heard rumors of this.

"The scriptures say that if a man takes his brother's wife, then their union shall be unclean and thus unfruitful."

Wolsey lingered on the pronouncement of "unfruitful."

"As I have told you before, the king intends to ask the Pope to annul his marriage to Katherine, as it was a grievous sin of incest for him to marry his brother's wife. We are in the process of making that request now, and I think it is likely that Pope Clement will make an allowance for this, as it has been done in the past."

Wolsey clasped his hands together as if the problem were solved.

Thomas neither nodded nor spoke. He had heard some of this whispered, spoken about among the queen's household, but he had hoped it was all speculation. Unclean? Unfruitful? Incest?! Could there be any more damning words?

"This news surprises you?" Wolsey asked curiously.

Perhaps it had been naïve to hope the king would tire of Anne Boleyn, but even after his last conversation with the cardinal, Thomas had hoped it was possible. The alternative was just too complicated, too painful for Katherine.

"I did not know that the king was *determined* to request an annulment," Thomas answered.

"Oh yes," Wolsey said, raising his brow and looking Thomas square in the eye. "Yes, indeed." He sighed and began pacing again. "I am sure, Thomas, that you will see how this is in the best interest of everyone."

Everyone but the queen.

"It is a difficult situation," Thomas finally managed, the slight taste of blood still lingering in his mouth.

Wolsey stopped pacing and looked over his shoulder at Thomas. "Indeed! I have already notified the queen of the king's desires," he continued. "I am surprised she has not conveyed them to you."

"She has conveyed her distress at falling out of favor with the king," Thomas said carefully, watching Cromwell's eyes follow the cardinal.

Wolsey interrupted. "No, no. It is not *she* who has fallen out of favor, Thomas. *She* has failed to bring favor to her husband by producing an heir. It is, perhaps, a kindness to her to recognize that it is not strictly her fault, you see."

Thomas shook his head, not understanding.

"If the Pope recognizes that the marriage should never have been made, that it was always in sin, then the death of her children is not only her fault but also that of Henry as well. The king wishes, therefore, to do what is right by Katherine and *repudiate* their marriage. He would thus repent of this sin and provide her with an opportunity to do so as well. It is for the well-being of Katherine's soul. Surely you can appreciate that."

The logic of the cardinal's proposition spun around Thomas like the king's acrobats flipping somersaults at court. The annulment was to protect Katherine's soul?

"You see, Thomas, it is the *right thing* for our good King Henry to seek an annulment," Wolsey said.

"And where would that leave Queen Katherine?" Thomas asked.

Wolsey nodded and continued to pace, hands behind his back.

"Our dear Katherine would return to being the Princess Dowager, as she was after the death of her lawful husband, Arthur, the king's brother."

Thomas nodded.

"She would retain that title," Wolsey said brightly. "And perhaps, if she agreed to repent as well, she would live out the remainder of her life in the solace of the Church. She would be highly esteemed in such a position, and I would recommend her to our best nunnery."

Like your illegitimate daughter?

"And the king would remarry a younger woman who could give him a son," Thomas said, pulling all the pieces of the cardinal's puzzle together.

"Yes!" Wolsey said. "It would be a great gift to the country for Katherine to comply in this way."

Thomas pursed his lips, and Wolsey continued.

"Thomas, if the king dies without an heir, England could face a civil war! Think how many lives Katherine could spare by simply acknowledging that her marriage to King Henry was never meant to be."

Thomas shook his head. A mistake? After twenty years? Was there no other way to preserve the state of England and the queen's dignity? Could they not do right by them both?

"You must convince her to accept this reality," Wolsey pressed. "It is the best solution for everyone." He paused like he was waiting for Thomas to say something, but there was nothing he could say, nothing that Wolsey wanted to hear.

Wolsey leaned in and continued his case.

"She is *old*, Thomas. She will never bear a son. And even if she could, the king will not give her another chance. Surely you understand this by now. He will not allow himself to live with the sin of their union any longer. And I doubt the queen is capable of safely bearing another child anyhow," Wolsey added, raising one eyebrow.

Thomas was quiet. How could something so holy as the sacrament of their marriage be conveyed as such filth?

"I see that you do not agree," Wolsey said as if suddenly impatient with the conversation.

"It is not that I disagree with our king," Thomas said quickly, considering the veracity of his words as he spoke. "I am considering the situation. It is not an easy one for the queen."

Wolsey nodded. "No."

"I will speak to her," Thomas promised. "I will see if she can be convinced."

Wolsey smiled broadly. "My dear Thomas, that is what I hoped to hear."

Wolsey added casually, "And tell her that we shall have her Mary home early for Christmas this year."

12

TELLING KATHERINE

The queen looked radiant as she knelt in the morning light that cascaded through the diamond-cut panels in the royal chapel. On cold, dark days, the room was lit by an abundance of white candles, enough to light a rural parish all winter. But there was no need for candlelight this morning. It reminded Thomas of the morning, a decade earlier, at Frideswide.

The morning sun shone brilliantly on the queen, illuminating her worn face, teasing Thomas with a vision of Heaven, a moment when all would be made new, an eternal spring, all things right and beautiful again. Eden. Someday, Katherine's sorrow would be forgotten. He smiled.

"Did you speak with Wolsey?" Katherine asked hopefully, still kneeling with her Latin prayer book in hand.

"Yes," Thomas said carefully. "He has agreed that Mary should come home early."

Katherine clapped her hands together and closed her eyes. *"Gloria a Dios!"* She kissed her rosary. "You are always faithful to hear your servant."

Thomas sat down on a wooden bench placed several feet back from the altar and held his hands in his lap.

"Mi Reina Catalina?"

"Sí?"

"Hay más," he began, as a cloud of concern crossed the queen's face. "The cardinal has told me about your conversation."

The queen froze.

"He has told me that the king is determined to seek an annulment, and it is his conviction that the Pope will allow it. They will use a passage in Leviticus to argue that your marriage should never have been made."

The queen's face paled.

"But... as I told Wolsey, we had a dispensation from the Pope," she said.

Katherine's chin trembled, and her eyes filled with tears.

"We asked permission from Pope Julius, and he granted it!"

Thomas was quiet, grasping for words. He hunched his shoulders and looked down at his hands.

"It was a holy marriage!" Katherine continued, her voice rising with every word. "Sanctioned by the highest authority in Rome. We did nothing wrong in the eyes of God."

Thomas nodded. Katherine stood up abruptly and walked to the window.

"Cardinal Wolsey believes that Pope Julius was wrong to admit your dispensation," Thomas said carefully. "And he thinks Pope Clement will grant the annulment."

Katherine spun around to face Thomas. She covered her mouth and shook her head.

"No, no," she whispered. "No! This cannot be so."

Her forehead wrinkled in worry.

"My Mary would be an illegitimate child!" Her eyes widened in alarm. "A common bastard!"

Trying hard to keep his own emotions in check, Thomas watched her, his heart pounding, resounding Katherine's alarm. *Lord, help me to answer carefully.*

"Cardinal Wolsey is a powerful man, my Queen," he said. "He has brokered peace between France and England, arranged state marriages, and the affairs of kings. He has the attention of both King Henry and the Pope. You know this."

"No. It is not right," she said, rocking back and forth on her heels. "Our marriage was granted by the Pope. We were married before God! The priest, he said, '*Quod Deus coniunxit, homo non separet!*' 'No man should separate! Not a cardinal nor a king nor a Pope in Rome!'"

Thomas nodded slowly.

"Yes, I know."

She looked up at him as if surprised.

"You believe I am right?"

"My Queen," he said cautiously. "I have not studied this Leviticus passage, but it seems that the king is determined to have his way. Perhaps it is the best course of action to find a way to appease him."

Katherine opened her mouth and closed it.

"You know Cardinal Wolsey can crush those who oppose him," Thomas continued quietly.

Katherine sat down heavily on the prayer stool that was intended only for kneeling.

"But who is Cardinal Wolsey to me? I am the Queen of England, the daughter of Ferdinand and Isabella of Spain. I will be ruined," she said, and then, in a cracked voice, added, "I am ruined, aren't I?"

"No," Thomas smiled sadly. "If you were to go to a nunnery, you would be treated well for the rest of your life," he said. "You would have time for learning and improving your mind, as I know you love to do. You would be treated with respect for the princess that you are."

"But I am *the queen*," she replied quietly. "I will not be demoted. I have been faithful to the king from the first—though, as you know, he has not been the same to me."

Her cheeks burned with shame at the mention of her husband's well-known infidelities.

"Try to think of it from the perspective of England," Thomas said. "If England has no prince, there could be a civil war. Families will fight families."

The challenge invigorated Katherine. She stood up, hands on her hips.

"Yes, but there are other options," she said, pacing like a general plotting the attack. "Mary is being educated as a regent. I myself have ruled in Henry's absence, as you know, at the Battle of Flodden, at which we soundly defeated the Scots!" She smiled. "And my mother, of course, was always a ruling queen in her own right. She didn't even need my father to be the Queen of Castille!"

Thomas nodded. But that was not England.

"Mary would be a fine ruler," she said, her voice now echoing off the chapel walls. "She is an intelligent and principled child. She would not suffer fools well."

She gave a bitter laugh, and then the corner of her mouth turned up in a sour expression.

"And if that was unacceptable to the people of England ... the king has a bastard son, Bessie's boy, whom he has elevated to the Duke of Richmond." She raised a single eyebrow at the thought. "Surely King Henry could name the boy his heir if he so needed a male heir."

Thomas nodded. The queen was not wrong, though he had also heard gossip that the king's illegitimate son lacked intelligence and a proper princely education.

"I disagree with Wolsey's belief that the dissolution of my marriage is the best course for England, for Christendom," she said. "If my Henry divorces me and marries his whore, it might very well produce a male heir for England, but it would be wrong. It undermines the Pope's authority, the whole order of how things should be. It is not right!"

Katherine's chest heaved.

Thomas stared at the stone-cold chapel floor. The queen was not wrong. But still ... "The king will not make your life easy if you oppose him," he finally said.

"¡Amo a mi esposo! I love my husband. I love my king," she said, standing tall with her hand on her hip. "I will be faithful to him for the rest of my life. But I *will not* allow him to dispose of me in this way! I will not allow him to do this to our daughter!"

"Then you will not consider a life married to the Church?" *It would make matters so much easier.*

She shook her head violently and crossed her arms.

Thomas sighed. "I have not found such a situation too difficult," he said.

Sometimes he wondered what joy he had missed out on by embracing the priest's calling. But he had shut that door long ago. He would not allow cold, lonely nights or the sweet laughter of children who would never be his own to pierce his soul. That part of his heart had been safely closed to both joy and sorrow. He was a priest, a servant of God, and that was enough.

Katherine shook her head and grabbed Thomas's shoulders, forcing him to look at her directly.

"Father Abell, your sacrifice has not been in vain!" she said with the same conviction with which she had just defended her marriage. "No! But your story is not mine. I am not a nun. I am a queen. I was destined to be the Queen of England since I was two years old. Indeed, I am married to the King of England, and I will remain so until I die."

13

LEVITICUS

October 1528   Oxford

Thomas inhaled and smiled. Books. It was good to be home, in the library, breathing in the smells of ink and parchment, books and bindings. The tall wooden bookshelves surrounded him like rows of towering trees in a hallowed forest, secluded in their quiet dignity.

There were libraries he could have used in London. Certainly, Wolsey had a decent collection at his home in Hampton, and there were other libraries in London with owners who would have permitted the king's priest to peruse for a day or two at leisure. But it was the old library in Oxford that Thomas longed for, the familiar vellum pages of the Vulgate he had spent so many hours reading. Like a poor pilgrim pining for the precious relics of saintly bones, he felt that being in the presence of this old book was to be just a bit nearer to God.

Thomas reverently touched the page and noticed the faint lines supporting the handwritten words. The Oxford library had a printed Bible, also in Latin, but it was this old one, chained to the podium for centuries, that connected Thomas to the lives of so many scholars who had lived before him. He turned to Leviticus 20 and read carefully.

"Qui duxerit uxorem fratris sui, rem facit illicitam: turpitudinem fratris sui revelavit: absque liberis erunt." If a man takes his brother's

wife, it is an unclean thing. He has uncovered his brother's naked-
ness. They shall be childless.

The king had married his brother's wife. *Was it an unclean thing?*
But they had children... The marriage to Katherine had produced
six children, even if most had not lived long enough to breathe the
air of this world. *Did Mary not count as a child because she was a girl?*
She may not be a male heir, but she was every bit a child. *Did the
king expect her to die too? Leave them truly childless? Was King Henry,
right? Had his marriage been a sin all along?* Thomas rubbed his eyes
and gently closed the Bible.

He would have to consult Father Martin.

"Yes, yes," Father Martin said. He scratched his chin the way he
always did when Thomas asked him troubling questions. "This is
the problem everyone is talking about."

Martin carefully pulled his candle closer to the giant Vulgate.
The old priest's eyes were growing dimmer. Although candles were
forbidden in the library, the warden overlooked Father Martin's
habit of taking a candle to help him illuminate the page.

"Well, it does say that it is unclean," Father Martin said, gently tapping the page. "But the problem is, there is another text in
Deuteronomy. Are you familiar with that one?"

Thomas shook his head.

Father Martin's eyes twinkled. He never tired of a good theological debate. Using both hands, he carefully turned several pages
of the old Bible until he got to Deuteronomy, the fifth book of the
Law of Moses. Martin silently read the twenty-fifth chapter, his lips
moving as he moved down the page until he came to the fifth verse.
"There it is," he said. *"Quando habitaverint fratres simul et unus ex eis
absque liberis mortuus fuerit uxor defuncti non nubet alteri sed accipiet
eam frater eius et suscitabit semen fratris sui."*

Thomas nodded.

"I see," he said curiously. "If two brothers live together and one dies, the living one must marry his brother's widow and produce an heir for the dead brother." He tapped the page for emphasis. "So, by that rule, the king not only should have married Katherine, but he should have considered their first son Arthur's child."

Father Martin pursed his lips, and Thomas waited. The old priest always had something more to say.

"But we are not obligated to live under the Jewish law," he said, throwing up his weathered hands.

"No." Thomas raised an eyebrow. "These laws contradict each other?"

"It is certainly ambiguous. The king will at least argue that with Rome," Father Martin said. "He hopes Pope Clement will see things his way."

Thomas eyed the old Vulgate.

"Is it possible that these are two different situations? The Leviticus passage does not say anything about the man dying childless, and the Deuteronomy passage explains why the man is to marry his brother's widow... so his family line will continue. Perhaps this has more to do with inheritance and family line."

"Yes, perhaps," Father Martin said, raising a single heavy gray brow. "But doesn't the king's concerns also have to do with inheritance and family line?"

"Perhaps," Thomas conceded.

"But," Father Martin began thoughtfully, "I believe that the principle of the Leviticus passage could be to protect women against abuses... incest, adultery, and the like, particularly while her husband is alive." Father Martin paused. "That seems to be the plainest interpretation of these two together... But we should consult canon law. Surely, this is not the first time this question has been posed."

Thomas smiled.

He knew that Father Martin would eventually get to canon law. That was, after all, his favorite. The Church's 1,500 years of canon law were like a moral compass, interpreting the difficult passages and informing his religious beliefs. Father Martin would never admit it, but Thomas felt that his mentor hardly allowed himself to accept any opinion unless he first found it spelled out by Church fathers and philosophers somewhere within the canon.

"Interestingly, Pope Julius ruled that King Henry and Katherine's marriage was admissible," Father Martin said, rubbing his chin and staring into the distance. "If he ruled that the marriage was permissible under Church law, then it is quite bold for King Henry to ask Pope Clement to reverse this ruling. Pope Clement would effectively be saying that Pope Julius was wrong."

Father Martin shook his head enough to make his jowls tremble.

"This is not the right time for the Pope to admit that another Pope made a mistake, not with half of the German princes becoming Lutheran. To say Pope Julius read Scripture wrong would only encourage heretics."

"But if Pope Julius was wrong," Thomas gently pushed, "then, of course, this annulment is right for England."

Martin narrowed his eyes.

"Well, let's see what we can find. Do you have time for a walk?"

14

A WALK PAST FRIDESWIDE

"Cardinal Wolsey is building his college here. I am sure you already know about that," Father Martin said as they strolled down Oxford's streets, walking under half-timbered houses that hung over the cobblestone road. They carefully sidestepped the overflowing sewage ditch that ran toward the river as they made their way out of town.

"I heard a rumor," Thomas said as he watched two men struggling with a cart of rough paving stones. The men were heading toward a cleared field where several buildings were in various stages of destruction and reconstruction. A massive stone structure resembling a London cathedral already dwarfed the adjacent chapel.

"Frideswide's Abbey," Thomas noted sadly.

Father Martin nodded. "They say it will be beautiful." He shook his head. "But it's sad to see the old monastery closing. I've been coming here my whole life."

Thomas watched the men pushing the wobbly stone cart. He understood why Cardinal Wolsey and his friends at the court wanted to disband some of the old monasteries. Only a few monks were left at the abbey to maintain Frideswide's Shrine. It would be difficult to argue for its existence, although he hated to see it go. People still needed a place to go, a place to pray, a place to remember that God still does miracles.

"They won't tear down the main chapel, though," Father Martin said.

"That's good," Thomas said, feeling surprisingly relieved.

"It is too important, because of the shrine," Father Martin continued. "They say it will be in the back of the new cathedral. Wolsey's cathedral."

Frideswide, with its land holdings, must have been a financial windfall for Wolsey. It was amazing that the old cardinal had waited so long.

As a scholar, Thomas appreciated that the money would be spent on educating England's next generation of bright minds, establishing a modern, humanist college. Still, it was sad for him to see the old saint's shrine marginalized. Before Oxford was Oxford, it was her shrine that drew so many pilgrims to this hallowed spot on the river.

"How is our queen?" Martin asked.

"Not well, as you might imagine," Thomas replied. He walked a few more paces.

"Her grief can be overwhelming to me," Thomas confessed. "I don't know how to help her. And, sometimes, to be honest, Father, I am not sure why I am serving the king instead of teaching here. Father, you know I would rather be here."

"Ahh, Thomas, the things that we love tell us who we are."

"Thomas Aquinas?"

Martin nodded.

Thomas looked at the ground. "I love the university, the conversations, the learning. Is it wrong to love the pursuit of knowledge?"

"No, Thomas," Martin said. "God has given you a mind to learn *and* a heart to understand. He will give you the courage to persevere."

"Aquinas?"

"No, just a prayer from an old Oxford man," Martin said shyly.

Thomas smiled.

Father Martin stopped walking and turned to study Thomas's face. The corners of his eyes clouded with tears.

"Be faithful where you are," he said, nodding. "And pray always, Thomas. Listen for the Holy Spirit. The Spirit is the one who leads us. He is the Spirit of Truth. That is why we pray, *'Veni Sancte Spiritus.'* Come, Holy Spirit."

Father Martin smiled broadly, the wrinkles around his eyes deepening.

"Every disciple has to learn to listen to and obey the Holy Spirit." He looked around the construction site. "You know, Frideswide traveled in the other direction, no? She left her palace and came here to serve God."

Thomas looked back at Wolsey's new cathedral, rising out of the jumbled heap that had been Frideswide's Abbey. Of course, he remembered the Frideswide story, the young Saxon princess who fled home rather than marry a wicked prince. Her heart, her true calling, was to serve God as a nun. She would settle for nothing else.

When the prince discovered her whereabouts, he came with his soldiers to force her hand in marriage, but God came in a flash of light, and like Paul, the foolish prince was struck blind.

Queen Katherine had come to Frideswide to find healing, but her daughter was born dead just the same. Perhaps Katherine did not understand why God had let her children die, but she believed with all her heart that God had chosen her to be a queen, not a nun. The queen would not cower in a nunnery. She would not let any human prince come between her and her God-given duty. Would God strike King Henry blind like the foolish prince in Frideswide's story?

Thomas shuddered. If only he knew.

"Wolsey wants me to convince Queen Katherine to join a nunnery. If the marriage is annulled, she could live out her life serving the Church," Thomas said. "But she says that she won't, Father, and I don't know how to counsel her. I know we should obey the king, but the queen feels this would dishonor God."

"Hmm ..." Martin considered this.

"I want to do what is right, Father," Thomas said, furrowing his brow. "But I am afraid that if Queen Katherine fights the king, she will lose."

Father Martin nodded. "She may."

The two walked silently for a few moments.

"The world is shifting, Thomas," Martin finally said. "I feel it."

The old man glanced back at the construction site around Frideswide.

"Keep your heart anchored," he said.

Thomas nodded and breathed in his mentor's precious words.

"And Thomas, be careful... pick your battles wisely... Perhaps you should not tell Wolsey or Katherine how you feel until the Holy Spirit instructs your heart. Do you understand what I am saying?"

"Yes."

Father Martin sighed. "And you don't have to convince the queen to give up her fight and join a nunnery. Others can take up that cause. Listen to her confessions. Offer Mass. That is the gift you offer. That is why you are in her house."

"Thank you, Father," Thomas said as the weight of Wolsey's request lifted off his chest. His pace quickened.

"Now, where do we read what the Church fathers said about Leviticus? Are you available to consult the library tomorrow?" he asked.

Father Martin smiled.

"Of course, my dear son," he said, affectionately embracing Thomas, holding him close for a long minute. Thomas breathed in Father Martin's scent—sweat, faint lavender, and a little smoke from sitting too close to the hearth. A lump formed in Thomas's throat, and he blinked back tears. Oh, how he had missed him!

"Tomorrow, then," Thomas said.

But by the time the sun rose the next day, Thomas was already in a carriage heading back to London. An urgent message from Thomas Cromwell demanded his immediate audience. Further inquiry into Church doctrine would have to wait.

15

THE KING WILL HAVE HIS WAY

"And how is our dear Katherine?" Wolsey asked dryly, not looking up from the thick leather-bound ledger he was entering figures into. There was no sense of urgency. Thomas suppressed a flash of irritation. He could have used a few more days in Oxford. Wolsey's calling him back had felt pressing. Now, he was not so sure.

Thomas Cromwell glanced over the cardinal's shoulder, pointing to a figure and whispering in his ear. Neither of them looked up to acknowledge Thomas, so he said nothing. He watched and waited.

It worked.

Cromwell looked up at him.

"Priest," he said, resting a hand on his hip. "Our cardinal has asked you a question."

Thomas waited until the cardinal set down his quill and met Thomas's eyes.

"Our queen is the same as the last time we spoke," Thomas said dryly. "Perhaps you did not expect a change."

Wolsey raised an eyebrow.

"I had hoped that you might have spoken some sense into her, convinced her to give up her devilish fight with her sovereign, the king," Wolsey said, rubbing his forehead.

"I have spoken to her, Cardinal Wolsey, and she may be considering our proposition. But she is quite proud. You know this is true."

The cardinal swore.

"But you did give her good reasons why her submission to the king would serve England?"

"Yes, of course," Thomas said truthfully. "I counseled her against fighting the king's wishes. My very words were to tell her that the king will have his way."

"Really?"

"Indeed. He is the king."

"And you disagree with him."

"It is not my business to have an opinion."

"Ha. You sound like Thomas More," Wolsey said ruefully.

Thomas Abell nodded. He could do far worse than being compared to Thomas More. The philosopher was known for his loyalty to the Church and traditional English values, but he seemed to know how to dance around the politics at court. He disturbed and amused the king in equal parts, and that balance seemed to ensure him a perennial place in the king's company.

Cromwell narrowed his eyes.

"Thomas More is a royal irritation," Cromwell said icily. "He should do the king a favor and ship himself off to his *Utopia*."

Thomas flushed, opened his mouth, and then shut it.

Wolsey rose like an old schoolmaster, ready to separate two disgruntled boys before their first blows interrupted Latin studies.

"Well, all of this anxiety need not be," Wolsey said, placing his fat hand on his chest. "This will all be resolved quite soon. The popes have allowed for many annulments on many occasions. It is a thing of necessity, as I am sure you are aware."

Thomas knew of a few royal annulments, but they were few and far between. Wolsey's confidence rang hollow, and Thomas was sure they all knew it.

"Of course, getting an annulment can be difficult," Wolsey conceded. "Some men, like myself, feel it is best never to become entangled in matrimony. But our kings are different, Thomas, as you know. They have no choice in the matter. Their marriages are state affairs. Their children, state interests."

Wolsey began to pace around the room, wringing his hands. "Oh, surely Pope Clement will grant King Henry this one request. He knows that our good king has been quite the defender of the faith, a good man, a good king … you do understand?" Wolsey stopped pacing and took in a deep breath.

"Yes," Thomas said truthfully. "I understand what is at stake."

"Then please continue to work on convincing Katherine." Wolsey's voice quaked, and he sat down heavily at his desk.

Cromwell handed the cardinal a piece of paper, which he took with shaking hands. He stared absently at it for a moment and then spoke without looking up at Thomas.

"There is one more matter," Wolsey said. "It would be best if you informed me the next time you leave the queen's side. I don't like getting unpleasant surprises from my people in Oxford."

Thomas looked up sharply. He had not expected Wolsey's spy network to include Oxford.

"Yes," Wolsey said, seemingly satisfied with Thomas's response. "I have people everywhere, especially in Oxford. You should know this."

Cromwell crossed his arms and glared triumphantly at Thomas.

"I apologize, Cardinal, for not informing you that I would be leaving London for a few days. The queen asked me to offer my opinion on Leviticus," he said truthfully. "I wanted to conduct a bit of study myself to know how to answer her."

"Have you no Bible in London?"

"Yes, there are Bibles here," Thomas said carefully. "But I wanted to speak with an old friend I trust about the matter. He has always given me wise counsel."

Wolsey smiled knowingly.

"Father Martin?" the cardinal asked with a nostalgic smile. "A simple man, but a good scholar. He is wise. He knows Katherine's place." His eyes narrowed. "But I would prefer that you consult with me first."

Thomas nodded, of course.

"And Thomas, you should know that the king requested the Pope send an emissary to England. Even now, he is preparing to send Cardinal Campeggio. When he arrives, we will form a Legatine Court, representing the Pope's desire in this matter. Together, we will hear all the evidence, and, God willing, we will give the king his final answer."

Wolsey clasped his hands, exhaled, and fell heavily into his padded seat.

"Your Grace and Cardinal Campeggio will decide the matter on behalf of the Pope?" Thomas clarified.

"Yes."

Thomas nodded. At least he understood what the queen was up against. The king's own friend would decide on behalf of the Pope? Katherine did not have a chance.

"That should be interesting," Thomas said dryly. "Was this the urgent matter you wished to discuss with me?"

"No," Cromwell interjected. "*I* asked you to return because your king and cardinal want you here. That is enough."

16

THE QUEEN'S SCRUPLES

November 1528

Margaret pushed the chapel door open and motioned Thomas toward the queen, kneeling alone before a statue of Our Lady. Dried rose petals cascaded over the altar and onto the floor, where the queen rocked back and forth, her lips moving in silent petition.

"She has been here all day," Margaret whispered. "No food. No water." She pointed to an empty candelabra. "We lit all of those candles this morning at dawn. This is the second day this week."

Thomas looked at the spent candles, then at Katherine, who was rocking feverishly, repeating the same prayer in Latin. He knelt beside her and placed his hand on her shoulder. "My Queen."

Katherine stopped, eyes still closed.

"My Queen," Thomas continued. "Why are you troubled?"

The queen resumed rocking slowly, ignoring Thomas while she finished the rotation of her rosary. Thomas said the last few words with her and gently took the beads in his hand. "My Queen, please tell me what troubles you."

"Father, forgive me," she mumbled. "I have sinned. Surely, I have sinned, grievously sinned."

Thomas nodded. "I am listening."

"I thought a hateful thought about one of my ladies. I imagined her dead. I know it is a sin, a mortal sin, to commit murder. Our

Lord said a hateful thought was like murder. I am a murderer, and God has not forgiven me."

She began rocking back and forth again. "And I was not kind enough to the king. I spoke harshly to him the last time he visited. It was a sin. I know it now. God is punishing me for my grievances against him."

"My Queen," Thomas began. "I know you are sorrowful, but these are sins you have already confessed to me... twice. The Scripture says that when we confess our sins, the Lord Jesus is faithful to forgive. You are forgiven in the name of the Father, the Son, and the Holy Spirit. You do not need to confess again."

The queen stopped rocking, her lips trembling. "But I feel ... I feel as if *I do* need to confess." She pressed her fingers into her palm until they left red marks. "I must confess again."

Thomas nodded. "Then I am listening."

"Father, I have sinned, most grievously, and I confess that my sins are great before God," Katherine recited. She beat her breast. "I am a sinner, and for that, God has not allowed my children to live."

Thomas pulled back his hand, the change in the queen's scrupulous routine surprising him.

"What new sin have you committed, my Queen?"

The queen crumpled to the floor and sobbed into the pavement. Thomas let her struggle for a minute and then pulled her elbow until she sat up.

"My Queen, I cannot give penitence if you do not tell me what sin you have committed," he said.

She looked at him through puffy eyes, puzzled. "Father, I have already told you all my sins. I cannot think of any other sins, but I know there must be some that I do not remember! It is not enough. I am not enough. My king finds fault with me, and so does God."

Thomas studied Katherine's face. She was troubled, but she was sincere. The weight of it crushed him, and he shook his head. "My Queen, if God has not revealed a sin to confess and you have already confessed every sin you know, rest. God has forgiven you."

Katherine closed her eyes and shook her head.

"My Queen Katherine, be at peace. You were forgiven the first time you made confession."

The queen let out a long sigh and rose on shaky legs. "Thank you," she said. "Thank you."

Thomas gave the queen his arm to lean on. "Let me take you back to your ladies," he said.

As she leaned into him, Katherine's lips began to tremble again. "Father?"

Thomas looked down at her. "Yes?"

"Is it my fault that the king's sons died?"

Thomas walked with the queen in silence out of the chapel and down the hall. He had thought about this question many times. Some priests privately told him that it had to be, that it *must* be the fault of someone, either the king or the queen. But somehow, he knew that was not true, could not be true.

"I do not know why your children have died," he said carefully. "But I do not think it is because of your sin."

The queen's body relaxed. "The king is telling his council that our children are dead because it was a sin for King Henry to marry me," she said with a sniff. "He is seeking an annulment from the Pope."

Thomas listened to the sound of their feet on the stone pavement. One. Two. Three steps. "I know, my Queen. I have heard. I am sorry."

"The king tells Wolsey and his friends that I was not a virgin when we married." Katherine stopped walking and faced Thomas. "It is not true. Henry has been my only true husband ... in that way." Her cheeks burned a little, and she bit her lip and looked away. "The king's brother, the prince, was not well. He was only fifteen." She swallowed hard. "I never wanted to embarrass him. He was not ready. ... I thought we had more time. Do you understand?"

Thomas nodded. Listening.

Katherine continued walking, then stopped again. "Some people don't believe me, don't believe that... you know." She looked up at Thomas. "My mother, Queen Isabella, sent Pope Julius a letter and asked him to put it in writing that Henry and I had permission to marry even if the prince and I... " She swallowed. "Even if I had been married in body as well as name."

Katherine's steps quickened, and her voice rose shrilly. *"Le dije que no era necesario. ¡Era una vergüenza!"* I told her it was not necessary, an embarrassment. *"Le dije que era virgen cuando me casé con el rey."* I told her I was a virgin when I married the king.

Katherine's hands clenched. "Pope Julius wrote to her *with his seal* and said Henry and I had permission to marry *even if* I had been intimate with the prince. I have a copy."

"Even if?"

"*Sí*, Pope Julius said even if I was not a true maid, *a virgin*, the king and I could be married with the blessing of the Church. Our marriage was holy before God from the beginning." She exhaled. "But I was a true maid, so it was unnecessary."

"You have a copy of this brief? It could be an important legal document."

"Yes, I have a certified copy of the papal brief. The original is in Spain."

Katherine's pace quickened as they walked. "The Pope declared our marriage holy *before God*, no matter who I had been married to before. So... was the Pope wrong?"

Thomas was silent, and Katherine caught his sleeve. "The Pope cannot be wrong! Don't you agree?" she asked, a little breathless from her walk.

"I need to pray about it," he said weakly, and she dropped his vestment.

"Then pray," she said and walked away.

17

MARY COMES HOME

"My sweet, my dearest princess," Katherine gushed as Thomas ushered the queen's only child and her tutor, Richard Featherstone, into Katherine's private chamber. "Oh, how I have missed you."

The gangly twelve-year-old with her mother's auburn hair tucked under her petite French headdress blushed and curtseyed shyly as if she were a visiting dignitary. Richard Featherstone bowed. "Your Majesty," he said in a voice that seemed too low.

Katherine stretched out her arms for Mary, addressing her daughter like a toddler. *"¡Infanta! ¡Mi corazón! ¡Mi tesoro!"*

Princess Mary stepped forward awkwardly, approaching in half steps as if the very movement hurt her delicate feet. When she neared Katherine, the queen snatched Mary and pressed her into her bosom. *"¡Mi preciosa!"*

Then she pulled Mary back and looked at her solemn face. She kissed her on her left cheek, and then her right, and then both sides again. "Oh, my dear, my dear! How you have grown!"

"I've improved my Latin," Mary said stiffly.

"Yes, I know," her mother replied, raising her chin and smiling. "I've read all your letters, all of them. *Todos.*"

"I wrote them in my own hand," Mary said, her vacant gray eyes staring at the floor.

"Of course," Katherine said, still smiling but now wiping away tears. She looked up at Thomas and reached out to take his hand. "Thank you."

Thomas read Wolsey's note slowly. "Did you speak with our dear Katherine about our king's Great Matter?"

Thomas groaned and set the note down on the writing table. Was there anything "great" about the king's desire to divorce the queen? Wolsey had begun calling it the king's Great Matter, and every time Thomas heard the phrase it was like biting into an apple and finding the rancid remnants of a worm.

Thomas rubbed his eyes. He had yet to speak again to the queen about the king's proposition since Princess Mary arrived, and he knew Wolsey was impatient. The cardinal had delivered the girl early for the holidays, and now he expected some return on his investment. Politics and prelates! Could Wolsey not let the queen have her joy for a moment? He stood up and began pacing.

"You are very distracting," Richard Featherstone remarked dryly without raising his bald head from a book he was reading. The princess's tutor had taken to lounging in the same study Thomas used, and now he was sprawled comfortably on Thomas's velvet armchair, reading.

"Sorry," Thomas muttered, glancing over at Richard. The priest was about the same age as he, shorter in stature and thicker around the middle. And if what Margaret had whispered was true, the tutor loved a good marzipan treat. Probably a venison roast too.

Thomas squinted to see the title of the book he was reading by candlelight: *The Education of a Christian Prince*. "Erasmus of Rotterdam?" Thomas asked.

Richard looked down at the book in his hand. "Indeed, it is."

Thomas smiled. "'He acquires most who requires nothing, but commands respect.'"

Richard returned the smile. "You agree?"

"I was an Oxford tutor before I came here. Teaching students—my life, my delight." He sighed, looking out the window at the misty gray rain. "I have not always served in the king's household."

Richard closed the book and sat up. "Do you want to talk about it?"

Thomas looked over at Richard and shook his head.

"I am not at liberty to discuss my concerns," Thomas apologized. How could he explain his worries to a man he hardly knew? After his hasty departure from Oxford, Thomas was beginning to think anyone could be Wolsey's spy.

Thomas sat on a stool, on the opposite side of the room, and rested his chin in his hands. He closed his eyes. Wisdom, dear Father. You promised to give wisdom to those who asked.

"I understand," Richard said, nodding in agreement. "But you should know that we share similar concerns, I believe. We are both entrusted with the spiritual care of the king's family."

Thomas nodded appreciatively but said nothing.

"I'm glad that you have finally met the princess. She is an intelligent girl," Richard said, changing the subject brightly, his light brown eyes twinkling. "The queen has insisted that her daughter's education be equal to that of the best-educated princes in Christendom."

Thomas smiled. That sounded like his Queen Katherine.

"The queen assumes that Mary may well be regent someday, though the English have never accepted a female heir to the throne," Richard added, eyeing the note from Wolsey that Thomas had left on the table. "I believe it would take some extenuating circumstances for that to occur."

Thomas stared at him, willing himself to ignore the comment. He wished he could speak freely, wished it was Father Martin, instead of this new priest. But he dared not speak his private thoughts.

Richard shrugged dismissively.

"Perhaps you heard? Juan Luis Vives, the *very* tutor who in- structed Erasmus in Greek, is coming to court. The queen wants him to tutor Mary in Greek," Richard said proudly.

"I had not heard that," Thomas said, grateful for the safer topic of conversation. "Impressive indeed! I want to meet him. He was at Oxford when I was there, but we never spoke."

"I am eager to meet him myself, "Richard said, smiling. "I will introduce you when he arrives. Hopefully, we will stay here for a few months. I think it benefits the princess to be with her mother. She is young, despite her age."

Thomas nodded again. The conversation was stiff, but at least they were talking. He could appreciate that Richard was trying to be friendly. That was a rare thing in the royal court—no one wanted to befriend a priest.

"It is certainly good for Katherine," Thomas said. And for him. Mary's presence would only improve the queen's temperament and make serving her easier. Perhaps now she would at least con- sider the king's request.

18

A Delicate Conversation

December 1528

"I have a very delicate question for you," Wolsey said sharply as Thomas's relief to find Wolsey alone—without Cromwell—dissipated. Would they ever have a casual conversation?

"Has our dear Katherine talked to you about her wedding night?"

Thomas frowned. What new scheme was the cardinal brewing?

Wolsey pursed his lips and raised an eyebrow.

"Perhaps the queen has had a bit of contrition about her wedding night. Perhaps she has confided in her *confessor*," Wolsey fished.

Thomas's eyes narrowed. He saw where this conversation was going.

"Which wedding night?" he asked, and Wolsey laughed lewdly.

"Either," he said through coughs. Then, composing himself, he cleared his throat. "Either would interest me."

Thomas was quiet. The queen had officially maintained that she had been a virgin when she married King Henry, an improbable proposition given her five-month marriage to his brother Arthur. But the queen fiercely held to this story, and Thomas had conceded that it was possibly true.

Everyone knew that Prince Arthur had been a sickly boy. Courtiers had told Thomas that he was tiny and frail for his age, half a head shorter than Katherine on their wedding day, even though she was a petite girl at sixteen. Indeed, Thomas had been told that some members of the Tudor household had begun preparing Prince Henry for kingly duties long before Arthur succumbed to the sweating sickness, just in case. Everyone knew that the prince could die young. Katherine had even told Thomas that her Henry—her Henry—had once confessed that his father always feared Arthur might not reach adulthood. He remembered his father hoisting him in the air and saying, "There, there, my little spare prince. You may be king, after all." And that was before Henry was tall enough to hold a sword above his head.

It was entirely possible that the weak, young Prince Arthur never consummated his marriage. Perhaps anything was possible behind closed doors.

"Queen Katherine has maintained that she was a maid when she and Henry married. This fact is very important to her." There was nothing more to say about it.

"Yes, yes! I am aware that this is her *public* confession," Wolsey said, eyes flickering with irritation. "She has expressed this much to me in private, although it has been some time since she confided in me. I had hoped that by now you had established a better rapport with her."

Wolsey cocked his head curiously. "I had thought such an obvious lie might weigh heavily on her soul. Perhaps she would divulge her sins to her priest."

"No, Cardinal Wolsey," Thomas answered truthfully. "But maybe she still does not trust me."

"Perhaps," Wolsey conceded. "And how did she respond to Mary's arrival? Will she give up her fight with the king?"

Thomas shook his head. "She has not changed her opinion."

Wolsey tapped the tips of his fingers together and held them to his lips.

"Why is she being so obstinate?"

Thomas was silent.

Wolsey narrowed his eyes.

"Have you spoken to her about the king's Great Matter since Mary arrived?"

"No, Cardinal Wolsey."

"And why is that?" Wolsey demanded.

"I did not think it wise," Thomas said carefully. "The queen is happy with Mary. Let her have that. She will need to make some difficult decisions soon. She is a practical woman, but she is stubborn. If you push her, she will never comply."

Wolsey flushed, sweat gathering around his tight white collar.

"Oh! I see you understand the queen better than I do!"

Thomas looked away. Perhaps he had said too much.

Wolsey nodded impatiently, swearing under his breath.

"But Thomas, you must understand that time is of the essence. Cardinal Campeggio will be arriving soon. The king needs this matter resolved as quickly as possible."

Of course the king wanted this matter resolved quickly. That was clear.

"The king wishes to remarry as soon as the Pope offers him the annulment. It would be *very* convenient if the queen would support him in this venture. As we have already discussed, it would be in the best interest of everyone in England. We need a male heir, and she cannot provide one!"

Wolsey pounded his fist into his hand and closed his eyes, and Thomas pressed his lips together. The less he said, the better.

"Do you know what will happen if the king does not get a prince?"

The cardinal rose from his chair.

"You have until Christmas to convince her to join the nunnery," he said. "If nothing changes, then we will have to take stronger action."

Suddenly, Thomas could see how desperate Cardinal Wolsey had become. If Queen Katherine refused to go quietly, if the Pope made it difficult for the king to get an annulment, if Wolsey failed to make the king's problem go away, King Henry might blame him. After all, Wolsey was the king's lord chancellor, the Archbishop of York, the man who had always made Heaven and Earth bend to Henry's whims—and now, he might fail. Cardinal Wolsey was afraid.

"Please, Thomas," Wolsey whispered hoarsely. "The king is very insistent on this matter. It would be very good for us, good for Katherine, and good for me, if it were resolved amicably. Try to convince the queen."

Thomas did not argue. For once, he knew that Wolsey was right.

19

YULETIDE

Christmas 1528

"Merry Christmas!" Henry roared as courtiers and honored guests matched his toast, raising goblets of sloshing mulled wine.

"Huzzah!"

Thomas watched the spectacle from the back of the Great Hall, laughter and cheers reverberating off the tapestry-lined walls. War, disease, and political hostilities were forgotten for the evening in the holiday revelry. The moment was now, and the king was in as generous a mood as Thomas had ever seen. For an evening, the king's Great Matter was tabled, and King Henry VIII was once again the charming prince his subjects remembered.

Or so Thomas hoped.

King Henry's tables overflowed with his wealth—steaming silver platters of his finest meats, succulent goose, wild turkey, a giant roasted boar, and the king's roasted venison, trophies of his most recent hunt. There were elaborately decorated minced meat pies, salted fish cakes, sweet bread, and more wine. And dispersed throughout the spread, like an afterthought, were plates of imported delicacies—figs, almonds, and oranges, many of them brought from Katherine's country, where the trees burst with winter fruit while England's trees stood bare.

Green garlands and boughs of holly hung from the ceiling and walls while hundreds of candles flickered from dozens of candelabras scattered about the room. The flickering reflected off golden plates, bathing the king's subjects in a warm, rosy glow. It was by far the most splendid royal banquet Thomas had ever witnessed, and he looked over at Katherine to see if even a bit of the holiday cheer had warmed her heart.

It had.

"The king is in fine fashion," Richard Featherstone whispered to Thomas as the two stood waiting their turn at the table. They would be invited to dine after the courtiers finished their meal and began dancing at the far end of the Great Hall. The king's musicians were already playing, and a troupe of masked courtiers was preparing additional entertainments.

Thomas had heard that holiday dinners were often that way in the royal household, crowded affairs of the king's entire household. The first group to be served was the company of the royal family and the king's closest intimates. The second course, of equal opulence, was served to the gentry and courtiers who did not fit into the first round. Of course, it was an honor to be at the first seating, but it was no slight for Thomas and Richard to be seated at the second.

Thomas watched the queen raise her glass. She smiled as she toasted the king. But her motions seemed rehearsed. She knew how to perform in court, but Thomas had spent enough time with her to tell from her hollow smile that she was humiliated, positioned several seats away from the king, near Princess Mary. The spot closest to the king was occupied by his mistress, Anne Boleyn.

"The queen is holding her own, I'd say," Richard whispered, following Thomas's gaze.

Thomas looked away, annoyed by Richard's ability to read his thoughts so easily. The priest had even asked that he call him Richard. It made him uneasy.

Cardinal Wolsey stood up.

"I would like to congratulate the king on his victories abroad and his faithful service to our great nation," the cardinal said, ringed hand over his heart. "This has been another prosperous year. Long live King Henry."

"Long live King Henry!" the crowd cheered in unison, pounding on the table to amplify the cheer.

King Henry's friend, the philosopher Thomas More, raised his glass. "And long live our Queen Katherine," he said.

"Long live Queen Katherine," the crowd agreed, although Thomas Abell noticed that the king seemed less enthusiastic about that sentiment, and he detected a slight amusement on the corner of More's lips.

Katherine nodded and smiled graciously.

"Merry Christmas to all of you," she said while the crowd continued their conversations and revelries.

The king took a long drag on his wine glass, and Thomas noticed that he reached for Anne, touching her gloved hand delicately. Katherine stiffened and turned away to face the lady who sat on her other side. With her back to the king, she began conversing with the lady beside her, though Thomas could not hear the words.

Surely, this was not the first time the queen had seen her husband prefer the company of her ladies-in-waiting. It was no mystery who fathered Bessie Blount's son. How humiliating it must have been for Katherine to see the king flirt with the women who combed her hair and laced her stays. Katherine had never mentioned it, perhaps out of loyalty to Henry, but now that they were all seated at the same table, Thomas saw the pained way Katherine watched Anne. No wonder they rarely came to court.

The king's fool, Will Sommers, a half-sized man in a multicolored silk jacket and floppy hat, romped into the center of the room, turned a somersault, and knelt before the king. Henry dropped the half-eaten turkey leg he had been enjoying and grinned at the fool.

"Your Majesty! Your Excellent and Great Highness! It is Christmas!" the fool declared.

"Yessss," roared Henry, raising his glass. "Indeed, it is!"

The courtiers raised their glasses and responded with a hearty chorus of "here, here" and "Merry Christmas!" until Charles Brandon, the Duke of Suffolk, pounded the table.

"Lords and ladies," he shouted. "Let the king speak!"

The crowd quieted, all eyes turning to the king.

"And what news have you?" the king asked Will, who had resumed turning cartwheels for the crowd. To the crowd's delight, he plopped on his bottom and faced the king.

"The bandits have arrived," Will announced as if he had just remembered his errand.

"Really?" the king roared jovially, tearing off a giant bite of turkey meat with his teeth.

Just then, the Great Hall doors flew open with a gust of cold air, and five young gentlemen burst into the room like a troupe of troubadours taking the stage. Their fine velvet jackets and silk stockings immediately revealed them to be members of Henry's court, but black masks covered their faces, obscuring their identities.

The crowd loved it.

"What is this?" Henry asked with pleasure.

One of the masked men dramatically slapped a note on the table in front of the king.

The king took another long swig of wine and tore the sealed message open.

"Ah-ha, I see. The women of my court owe a great debt! If it is unpaid, they are to be taken away and sold to Suleiman the Magnificent for his harem in Constantinople," he read. The ladies squealed and giggled as the masked men made great play of tying their wrists in a thick velvet rope.

"But wait," Henry said. "I will pay their debts with a wager if you like," he announced magnanimously, winking at Katherine's new lady, who immediately blushed.

"What wager does the king offer?" the head masked man said stiffly, his lines clearly memorized beforehand.

"A sword fight! To the death!" Henry announced, jumping to his feet. The room gasped.

The masked man nodded, and the fool, who had disappeared for just a minute, burst through the doors, rushing in with two comically small wooden swords, children's toys.

The crowd laughed appropriately.

"To the death!" the fool shouted. "Long live our one true king!"

"Long live King Henry VIII!" the crowd responded.

The king and the masked man took their stances and began fighting, slapping swords as the crowd cheered with each of the king's advances. Princess Mary watched every move her father's wooden sword made, wincing each time the masked man whacked at him. Queen Katherine held Mary's hand and watched her husband too, the corners of her eyes betraying a smile, though her hands covered her mouth in mock anxiety.

When the masked man jabbed at the king, Mary's hands flew to her mouth.

"Father!" she gasped.

The crowd laughed.

The king and the masked man performed their swordplay around the center of the Great Hall, in the best view of those sitting at the table, and the crowd began to pound the table and chant, "King Henry! King Henry!"

King Henry was in his best form, flushed and laughing, enjoying every moment of the masquerade, when his foot slipped on the green and white tiled floor, distracting him just long enough for the masked man to strike him across the chest.

King Henry flushed red and jumped to his feet, slapping the masked gentleman across the neck, drawing blood despite the blunt wooden sword. The crowd gasped and turned silent as the drama halted for a moment.

Then, as if on cue, the man fell dead in what looked to be a bit more realistic than the drama required.

Charles Brandon began drumming his hands on the table until the crowd of seated courtiers joined him, chanting "Huzzah! Huzzah!" while the king held the truncated wooden sword over the masked man's head.

"Our great king has vanquished his enemy!" the fool announced. "May it be so for ALL his enemies."

"Here, here!" Charles Brandon cheered. "Long live King Henry!"

"Long live the king," the crowd returned.

The king extended his right hand to the slain courtier. "Well done, John," he said, laughing as the other four bandits removed their masks.

But the courtier remained on the floor, eyes closed, pale, blood dripping from a gash on his neck.

One of the king's rescued ladies rushed to the young man's side. "John?"

She shook his shoulders.

"Call the physician!" she demanded, and two servants rushed from the room to get a doctor.

Henry returned to his place at the table, shrugged his thick shoulders, and took a long drink while courtiers gathered around the unconscious young man.

"Play!" King Henry barked at the trio of court musicians who held their instruments slack at their sides. He turned to Anne and flashed a quick, reassuring smile. She put her hand on his hand, and he looked at her face, his gaze lingering on her lips.

Within a few minutes, the king's physician arrived and rushed to where the young man lay unconscious. He tore off the boy's mask and slapped his cheek. John opened his eyes and groaned.

The crowd cheered.

The king nodded slowly as if the cheering was for him.

"The king is triumphant!" Will shouted, shaking his feathered scepter over John's face.

The king's physician swatted at the court jester. "Get that fool out of here," the doctor said as he positioned his shoulder under John's arm, hoisted him up, and led him out of the Great Hall. The young man would live another day, but his night was over.

Anne turned to the king and whispered something in his ear. He caught her eye and smiled.

Then he kissed her on her lips.

The crowd grew silent, stunned by the king's open carousing, making public what they had all whispered about in private.

Queen Katherine rose from her seat and followed the physician and the wounded boy out the door. Her night was over too.

"I suppose it is time for us to leave as well," Thomas said, turning to Richard, but the young priest had already found a place at the table and was enjoying his first bite of the king's feast.

Thomas quietly pivoted on his heels and left the Great Hall, turning his back on his place at the table.

20

HALL OF WITNESSES

December 1528

Thomas felt the stare of a dozen dead kings and queens as he kept in step with Cardinal Wolsey. Sheets of rain pelted the castle. Winter wind rattled the windows. A sudden crack of lightning illuminated the long, dimly lit corridor on the castle's north side, and Thomas was sure he saw ghosts behind the portraits. The cardinal and he were not alone as they discussed the queen's private matters. Thomas shuddered. He much preferred to walk in the garden, rain or not.

"Why did you leave the king's Christmas dinner?" the cardinal demanded. "You did not acknowledge your Sovereign Lord or bid him good night."

Thomas swallowed hard. Had his disgust toward the king been obvious?

"You left before you ate," Wolsey accused. "Was the king's generosity not enough for you?"

"No—yes," Thomas stammered, his stomach rumbling at the memory of going to bed hungry on Christmas Day. He had comforted himself with the thought that at least it was only the first night of Christmas. There would be more feasts before the season ended with the Twelfth Night. "I did not mean to be rude. I would have stayed ..."

"Then why did you, a loyal member of the king's household, leave without so much as a polite 'good evening'?" The cardinal stopped short, making Thomas almost trip over his vestments. "Thomas, it simply reflects poorly on me, *your mentor*."

Thomas shook his head. The cardinal's reputation had never occurred to him that night. His only thought had been to comfort the queen, though he hardly knew why. She seemed increasingly guarded.

"Cardinal Wolsey, it was not my intention to reflect poorly on you," he began. "When the queen left, I thought perhaps she needed a priest." As he spoke, a tinge of resentment sparked in his heart, heating his face. He had done nothing wrong to leave the yuletide festivities. The cardinal had no idea how much he would have rather eaten minced pies and candied oranges. "Queen Katherine seemed distraught. I thought I should follow her."

"Yes," the cardinal said. "I observed that." He eyed Thomas. "And did she confide in you why she was upset?"

"No," Thomas said truthfully as another flash of lightning lit up the face of Margaret Beauford, the king's grandmother, who had died shortly before Henry chose Katherine for himself. "She retired immediately to her chamber, and her ladies informed me that she would permit no visitors." It had been a wasted effort.

"What did she say to you in the morning?" the cardinal probed.

"We did not speak of it," Thomas said, remembering the queen's vacant stare as he offered her Mass the following morning. "She was very quiet."

Wolsey raised an eyebrow.

"She was quiet?"

"Yes," Thomas repeated. "She has scarcely spoken to me in the past few days. Her ladies tell me that she is distraught." *Distraught. That word again. Always distraught.*

"I see," said Wolsey, pursing his lips.

The two continued walking.

"Has she confessed to you that she was not a maid when she went to Henry's bed?" he asked.

"No, Cardinal," Thomas answered. Would the cardinal ask him every time they met? "She has not said anything more of it to me."

"Does she confess anything at all to you?"

Thomas stopped walking, weighing the consequences of speaking plainly to the cardinal. "Perhaps you are aware that our queen is quite scrupulous in confessing sins," he finally said. "She often worries that even the tiniest thought or action is sinful. I spend quite a bit of time hearing these sins, offering her penance, a sharp word spoken a year ago, an inhospitable thought she had about some visiting baroness five years ago, the time she slapped her nurse when she was a child. It is not unusual for her to sit in the chapel for hours, confessing and praying ... but you already know this about our queen."

The cardinal nodded thoughtfully. "I remember."

Thomas continued, "But she has never confessed to lying, not for something small or something more substantial."

As delicately as he said it, Thomas hated talking about the queen's most private matters with the cardinal. But at least Thomas could speak the truth. The queen had confessed nothing that he had to hide from the cardinal. If anything, Thomas had begun to trust her version of the wedding night story because she was so contrite in everything else.

"It seems that she would have confessed the sin of lying if she had been untruthful about consummating her marriage with Arthur," Thomas finally said. "She may be stubborn, but she is not a liar. I don't think she could lie and live with herself."

Wolsey shook his head violently.

"No, no, you give her too much credit, Thomas. Perhaps you have spent too much time with her, and now you are blind to her manipulations. ... Or perhaps it is just that she does not *trust* you, not fully, Thomas."

"Perhaps ...," Thomas said, and the two men continued walking along in silence. "But Cardinal, there is something I do not understand."

Wolsey raised an eyebrow, and Thomas continued.

"Why is the king so eager to prove that Katherine consummated her marriage with Arthur? It would seem ..."

Wolsey scoffed. "Thomas! Surely you understand that the queen wishes to diminish her relationship with Arthur, so she can argue that she was never really married to him, not in body at least." He shook his head. "It's preposterous. Katherine was a beautiful woman. You should have seen her. Auburn hair, golden smile ... To believe she spent five months with that boy, skinny as he was ... without ... How is anyone to believe that?"

"Yes," Thomas said quickly. "It just seems irrelevant when Pope Julius issued that brief approving of the king's marriage, *even if* Katherine and Prince Arthur had consummated their marriage."

The cardinal stopped short under a portrait of Henry VII. The king's long, narrow face looked down in sallow judgment. Wolsey grabbed Thomas's arm.

"What?" he demanded.

"The brief that Pope Julius sent Queen Isabella before she died, the one that granted Katherine and Henry permission to marry *even if* the marriage to Arthur had been consummated."

Wolsey looked at Thomas with wild eyes.

"Even if," the cardinal repeated. "Even if?!"

"Yes," Thomas said, searching for careful words. "I had thought you were aware of this." *It being so important to the king's argument!* "The queen has a copy of it, but the original is in Spain."

"You have actually seen this brief from Pope Julius?"

"Well, no. The queen has a copy, but the original is in ..."

"Spain! I heard you the first time." Wolsey's wild eyes searched the space above Thomas's head as if dead kings could give him counsel.

"We, of course, have the original dispensation here that permitted Henry and Katherine to wed in 1509. The copy is safe in *our* royal archives. It was necessary to get such a dispensation from the Pope, of course, to bless their marriage, especially since Katherine had been married to Prince Arthur; God bless his soul. But it says nothing about whether or not the marriage had been consummated."

Wolsey wrung his hands as he appeared to riffle through his memory frantically.

"I know, of course, that Ferdinand and Isabella had their concerns, and Isabella had written to me that she planned to write to the Pope herself." Wolsey covered his mouth. "Ah! Isabella wrote to me that she would request that the Pope put her concerns in writing. Yes! Oh, he must have ... but I had not realized," he said. "Perhaps the Pope sent such a letter directly to Queen Isabella in Spain! Oh my, Thomas! This information changes things considerably."

"Surely King Henry was aware of such a brief? Isn't Queen Katherine's copy in the royal archives?"

Cardinal Wolsey quickened his pace.

"No!"

Wolsey was almost trotting by the time they reached the end of the hall. He turned abruptly in the direction of his own chamber. "Thank you, Father Thomas," he said, a little breathless. "Your information has been very helpful!... The king will be most interested to know about this brief."

Wolsey dismissed Thomas with a wave and hurried down the hall, muttering, "As if! As if!"

Alone in the gallery, Thomas looked up at a new, towering portrait of King Henry VIII. The young king stood confidently, his lips pressed together. He neither smiled nor frowned, keeping his thoughts silent, his next move a mystery. Thomas swallowed hard and crossed himself. *Dear God, what have I said?*

21

THE QUEEN'S LETTER

Thomas felt the queen's hot stare as he advanced reverently into her chamber, conscious of both her presence and that of the Holy Host he presented on the silver tray. He sensed tension. Something was off. This would not be another silent morning!

The queen's favorite messenger, the young Francisco Felipez, and her last Spanish lady-in-waiting, Maria de Salinas, sat at her side. Francisco stared daggers at Thomas while Maria crossed her arms and scowled. Even Crimson, sitting erect at Katherine's feet, looked like he might lunge at Thomas.

The queen stood, her delicate hands clenched in tight fists.

"You!" she began. Crimson barked.

"You told Cardinal Wolsey that my mother asked the Pope for a second dispensation! One granting permission for my marriage even if, *even if!*" her voice broke. "And now that scheming Wolsey, proud as a peacock, has told Henry he believes that I am a liar. He wags his tongue, saying even my *own mother* knew I was a liar. He says, 'Even Isabella knew her daughter was used goods. Used goods!'"

Thomas quietly sat down on a stool and placed the tray of sacred bread and wine next to him.

"My Queen," he said quietly. "It was not my intention to harm you."

She cut him with accusing eyes.

"But you have, Father Abell, you have given my husband reason to malign me."

Thomas's stomach churned. How could he explain?

"I was surprised that the king and cardinal were unaware of the papal brief, the Pope's letter to your mother. I thought that such an important document was already part of the king's official archives."

He looked at Katherine, and she would not meet his eyes. Perhaps she had thought so too.

"I did not know that you spoke of something confidential," he said quietly. "I assumed, wrongly … I see now … that it was not common knowledge."

The queen's chin trembled, and angry tears welled in her eyes.

"*¡Me da rabia!*" She raised her hands over her head. "*¡Me hierve la sangre!*"

Maria de Salinas clucked her tongue and glared at Thomas. Crimson gave his tail a tentative wag and licked Katherine's hand.

"The queen say she is angry," she translated. "Very angry," she added, as she handed Katherine a tissue with the initials K & H embroidered in black thread. "Her blood boils like hot water."

Thomas nodded. He had needed no translation.

"It defames me," Katherine said, wiping hot tears. "It implies what is not true."

Thomas nodded thoughtfully, watching Katherine's face.

"And he will use this letter and say I am a liar. He will say *mi mamá* doubted me."

Katherine's eyes blazed until she dropped her head in her hands and sobbed.

Maria rubbed the queen's quaking shoulders.

"You have been a good wife and a good queen," she gently argued.

"If I might," Thomas began, carefully picking his words. "I do not believe the king's knowledge of the existence of this brief could harm you, Queen Katherine. Your mother wisely had Pope Julius put these words in writing so no one would ever be able to separate you and King Henry." He cleared his throat. "This papal brief is important evidence that the Pope allowed for your marriage to King Henry ... *even if.*"

Katherine looked up at Thomas through red-rimmed eyes.

"But at what cost, if people think I lied about Prince Arthur!"

Katherine crossed her heart when she said Arthur's name, and Thomas realized it was the first time he had heard the queen speak her dead husband's name.

Thomas took in a deep breath.

"Queen Katherine, it seems to me that this papal brief would only help your case, as now the king will have to claim that Pope Julius erred when he granted permission for you to marry him."

"Then why does Henry demand that I write to my nephew, the Holy Roman Emperor, Charles V, and ask him to send the brief here to England?!" she exploded. "Why does *Henry* want it? He plans to humiliate me!"

Thomas was quiet. As far as he could tell, the Pope's brief could only serve as evidence that King Henry's marriage to Katherine was legitimate and noble from the beginning. Having the brief physically present in England could only help her cause.

"Wolsey was just here," she said. "He demands that I write a letter, now, today, requesting Charles help me by sending the *original papal brief*. He stressed the *original!*"

She pulled out a parchment and began writing.

"Wolsey said that if I cannot help the king in this matter, then it will be time to send Mary back to Wales," she said. "He knows how to hurt me. Doesn't he? Was that also your idea, Father Abell?"

Thomas shook his head.

"No indeed," he said quietly. "I would never want them to take Mary from you."

"The king is sending his groomsmen to personally deliver this message," she said. "And I, yes, I will send my Francisco Felipez. He will tell my nephew Charles my mind."

She motioned to the young man, and he leaned in while she whispered in his ear. Thomas watched but said nothing. The queen suddenly looked up at him.

"Take away the Host, Father," she said. "I will receive Mass from a Dominican monk of my choosing. I have always found them to be worthy servants of the Gospel and not spies for Cardinal Wolsey!"

"As you wish." Thomas bowed and quickly retreated from the queen's chamber. As he walked down the hall, his pace quickened. Oh, that he could keep walking and never come back! How could he have been so careless in his conversations with Wolsey?

22

THE KING'S REQUEST

January 1529

"Your Majesty, you would have me sail to Spain tomorrow?" Thomas asked, although the king's request needed no clarification.

Henry smiled, the same smile Thomas had seen so many times before when the king wished to use his charm to get what he wanted. It was usually effective, although completely unnecessary. A cold command would have produced the same result. He was the sovereign.

"Thomas, as you know, this matter has lingered long enough. Our dear Katherine needs closure, and I need closure." Henry placed one of his large hands on his chest as if to cover his heart and, perhaps, his conscience.

Thomas nodded.

"Wolsey and I have come to the conclusion that it would settle matters greatly if you were to represent *me* to the Emperor Charles and personally request the original copy of this brief."

"Your Majesty," Thomas said carefully, clasping his sweating hands together. "It is my understanding that Queen Katherine has already written to her nephew and requested the original brief. I was in her presence three weeks ago when she dispatched her messenger. And I believe she did so at your request."

Thomas knew exactly when the queen had written the letter because it had been the last time she had allowed him in her presence.

"Ah, Father Abell, perhaps you do not know? The queen's young messenger boy fell and broke his arm in France," he said, smiling in a way that made Thomas uncomfortable. "So now I need a new detachment of messengers, trustworthy men that Wolsey and I know to be honest men."

Was young Francisco Felipez not honest?

"Wolsey has told me that you have been of great service to us," he continued. "You do speak Spanish, right?"

Thomas nodded, gravely watching the king's face. "I do," he answered slowly. "But perhaps, if I may, Your Majesty ... may I ask a question?"

The king nodded, though curtly.

Thomas swallowed hard. He had put this quest in motion. Perhaps he could bring it to an end before anyone else suffered a broken arm—or worse.

"Are you convinced that such a papal brief exists in Spain?" Thomas asked.

The king smirked.

"I see," he said with a knowing smile. "You do not believe all of her stories either."

Thomas was careful not to nod or acquiesce in any way. Like a mouse trapped in a corner, he felt the cat's stare, saw the flick of his tail.

"I do not wish to cast doubt on our good queen," Thomas said carefully. "But many years have passed. Queen Isabella and her husband, King Ferdinand, have passed. The queen's nephew is on the throne in Aragon, though he moves his residence about the country. I question only if such a physical document has survived in the Spanish archives."

The king narrowed his eyes.

"Did *she* not want me to send an envoy to Spain?"

Thomas took a step back and cleared his throat.

"I don't know," he said, trying to calculate the king's motives. It was so difficult to stay ahead in this game. "She seemed embarrassed by the brief, but I do not understand why. It seems to me that if such a dispensation exists, it would help her cause."

The king's face flushed a bit.

"Her cause is selfish and based on lies!"

Thomas bit his lip, trying his best not to flinch as the king shortened the distance between them considerably. His hands trembled.

"I mean to say, Your Grace, that I cannot see why the queen would object to having the Pope's dispensation here in England, where the court can consider it in their evidence."

The king smirked again.

"Well, you know, Katherine was quite *unhappy* when her mother first requested it." He chuckled. "I had forgotten about it, but when Wolsey told me you mentioned it to him, of course, I remembered the letter from her mother and how upset she was."

The king smiled.

"It was not the Pope's brief that irked her. Yes, of course, she wanted that. It was that the Pope granted us permission to marry *even if* Katherine and my dear, dead brother Arthur consummated their marriage. And that was *her mother's* insistence. Ha! Katherine swore to me that she was as holy as the Virgin Mary. Swore! But not even her mother believed her."

Henry's icy blue eyes narrowed as he moved closer to Thomas's face. "But I remember my brother Arthur boasting like a knight returning from battle. 'I was in *Spain* last night,' he said."

"SPAIN!"

The king's chest heaved like a horse brought to a sudden halt. His face was close enough for Thomas to almost feel the bristle of his red beard, his hot breath curling around his neck. "Spain," he repeated absently, then turned and spat on the ground.

Thomas stood in place, knees locked, heart beating like a pursued rabbit's. His legs trembled under his vestment. But he willed himself to stand still, eyes open, watching Henry. The king was so red he was almost purple.

"Tell me, priest, has she ever confessed that sin to you? The lying whore."

To Thomas's relief, King Henry turned and walked toward the diamond-cut window.

Members of the king's court had already retreated to the other end of the Great Hall, watching like deer in the woods, ready to run if necessary. But they would not. Thomas felt that they were somehow enjoying the spectacle of the king's temper. As long as his rage was not directed at them, they would relish repeating the story to a dozen gossiping tongues. The king called pious Katherine a "whore." That would make idle tongues rejoice.

The king's anger was not directed at him—not yet, at least. And he only hoped it stayed that way. He looked down at his trembling hands, but out of the corner of his eye, he caught Cardinal Wolsey studying his face.

"Your Grace," the cardinal said, emerging from the shadows, "may I offer some clarification here?"

Henry waved his hand.

"Thomas, as you know, Rome is preparing to send a legatine court here to try the merits of the king's request."

Thomas nodded, and the cardinal continued.

"The king wishes to have all evidence on hand so the court might make a wise and fair decision. Of course, he desires to be fair and even-handed with everyone involved."

Wolsey looked carefully at the king.

"Should such a dispensation exist—and I share your concerns, Thomas, that it is quite possible that it does not or perhaps never did exist ..." The king gave Wolsey a sharp look, but he continued. "We do not have the certified original document here, do we, Your Majesty? And that seems mighty unfortunate for our dear Katherine. Wouldn't you agree?"

Yes, it would be, but Thomas was careful not to nod while Wolsey's true motives were hidden from him.

"So, as our Sovereign King Henry has requested, we will send a reliable man of God, like yourself, Thomas, to get this important document, and then we will have all the necessary information for the legate court to consider in the spring," Wolsey said as if the whole matter was settled.

Cardinal Wolsey placed his hand on Thomas's back, pushing gently between his shoulder blades, walking him toward the doorway. With his back to Henry and the rest of the court, the cardinal whispered in Thomas's ear, "And when you get that papal brief, you will bring it back to me directly. No one else must see it!"

He placed his hands on Thomas's wide shoulders, turning him to meet his insistent gaze.

"Do you understand? The fewer people who know of its existence, the better."

"You want me to bring *you* the papal dispensation?"

"Yes!" Wolsey said. "And if anyone asks, you will say it was lost … a fire, a shipwreck, bad housekeeping. Be creative."

"But Emperor Charles will know. And then the queen will know."

The cardinal looked at his manicured fingernails.

"Thomas, I know that this is a difficult thing I am asking of you."

Wolsey paused and looked down.

"We must do what we need to do to help the king solve this matter. It would be better for everybody if no record of this *extra* dispensation existed. It embarrasses Katherine, as you know, and more importantly, it unravels the king's argument. He was prepared to argue that Pope Julius was unaware that Katherine and Arthur had consummated their marriage; when he granted permission for their marriage, he simply did not have all the information, information that would have prevented him from agreeing to such a damnable arrangement!"

Wolsey took in a deep breath.

"Now, you see, Thomas, if the brief is admitted as evidence in the case, then Pope Clement will have to contradict the opinion of his predecessor, and he may not be willing to do that."

The cardinal pursed his lips. "Thomas, Queen Isabella's brief just makes this whole thing... complicated. You must understand. I am sure you do."

Thomas said nothing, encouraged nothing. Bile burned up his throat. What trap was he being squeezed into?

"Thomas, if you care at all for the queen, for justice of any kind, the best thing you could do for our dear Katherine is to convince her to retire to a nunnery, like I have been telling you all along. The king will have his way, and the fewer people broken in the process, the better."

Wolsey sighed deeply.

"Just go to Spain. If you want a traveling companion, take Princess Mary's tutor, the priest Richard Featherstone. That expensive Greek tutor will keep the princess busy for the next few weeks, anyhow. Then the queen will have a witness to the fact that you asked Emperor Charles for the brief." Wolsey weaved the plan together with a rush of ideas. Then he grabbed Thomas's shoulders again and looked him in the eyes. "But Thomas, don't bring the original back to Katherine or let her send it to the archives. Bring it to me directly. Do you understand? I want it here so I can take care of it before anyone else sees it... Katherine will not mind. She doesn't want it here anyway."

To Serve the Queen

Tall Tree Press

23

OUT TO SEA

January 1529

Thomas leaned over the rail and vomited his breakfast into the swirling, gray sea.

The smell of decaying fish, the constant tossing of the water, the rising and falling of the deck were too much. He wiped his mouth with the back of his hand and closed his eyes.

The cold ocean breeze felt good on his face. He sighed. This simple channel crossing would be a long voyage if he could not tame his stomach.

"Not much of a sailor?"

The voice was unfamiliar, and Thomas glanced over his shoulder to see who had witnessed his indignities.

A Spanish gentleman with a black beard and wind-tossed, curly black hair smiled sympathetically at him, the corners of his dark eyes crinkling with amusement.

Thomas shook his head grimly.

"First time at sea," he said, turning back to look on the horizon. Ominous, gray clouds hung in the distance. Dark rain curtains closed over the channel. A storm was coming.

"It's a short distance to France, but I am afraid the weather will get worse," the man said, pointing at the clouds. "See, storm clouds are moving in now. Aye, winter storms can make a crossing take days, sometimes more than a week."

Thomas grimaced. More than a week?

"I am Juan de Montoya," the Spaniard said, tucking his wind-blown hair back before offering his hand. "I believe you must be Thomas Abell, the queen's priest. You and your companion Richard Featherstone are on the king's business, heading to Spain?"

The ship lurched, and Thomas grabbed the rail to steady himself instead of taking the man's hand. He looked over at Richard, standing on the far end of the deck. Had the Spaniard talked to him?

"You have been informed well," he said.

The statement served as a question, and Montoya smiled knowingly.

"*Sí, Padre*, the captain told me ... but I already knew," he admitted.

Thomas watched the man reach into a leather pouch and pull out a root. Had they met before?

"Try this," he said, handing Thomas a small root that had been cleaned and wrapped in a piece of parchment. "Ginger. Helps with seasickness."

Montoya pulled back his tongue to reveal a piece of the amber root.

"Learned about ginger years ago. My first sea voyage." He smiled in recollection. "Spent forty-five days headed to Hispaniola. Beautiful place. Paradise!"

Thomas took the package and carefully pulled a small nub off the root.

"Don't swallow it!" Montoya warned.

Thomas's eyes burned at the spice.

"*Sí, Padre*, chew on it a bit. Takes some time, but it will help."

Thomas nodded.

"Thank you," he said, pushing the ginger root under his tongue.

"When the rain comes," he said, nodding to the dark horizon, "stop by my quarters. We will share a drink. No?"

Thomas nodded, his stomach still lurching. He closed his eyes and felt the deck rising, falling, and rising until the breeze turned cold and rain began pelting his face.

"*Padres*, I am sure you will be glad when this storm has passed," Montoya began as Thomas and Richard found a place to crouch on a narrow bench in the Spaniard's tiny private cabin.

The ship lunged forward, and Thomas nearly fell off the bench. He hooked one of his feet under the bench leg and gripped the edge of a wooden table to steady himself. Surely, the channel crossing would not take a week!

Montoya placed a wooden plate of hard cheese and brown bread before Thomas and steadied it with his hand to keep it from sliding off the table.

"This is not my first sea storm." He laughed. "No, I have seen much worse. I believe this storm will be over ..." He rocked his head back and forth. "... before dawn. ... I think you will be fine, no?"

Thomas nodded and watched Montoya cut a piece of the hard cheese and tear off a handful of brown bread.

"You should eat," Montoya said with an easy smile.

Thomas was not quite sure he was ready to eat. The cabin was shifting, the hanging lantern swaying with every wave.

"It will help your stomach to put something in it," Montoya explained.

The bread was still fresh, something they might not get for days if the crossing continued for long. Thomas took a piece and handed it to Richard. This is the bread of Christ, broken for you.

Thomas took a bite of the bread and chewed it slowly. Richard did the same.

"How do you know our names?" Richard asked, looking around at Montoya's comfortable cabin. In addition to the narrow bench and table, the cabin was furnished with a cot, colorful pillows, and a desk with an ink flask and a stack of parchments.

"I am the servant of Eustace Chapuys, the new Imperial ambassador," he said. "Until last year, I served as a clerk in the queen's administration." He shook his head. "But, *Padres*, you must know that all of the Spanish are gone. *Sí*, I am sure you know this."

Thomas nodded knowingly. If the Spanish priests had remained in the queen's employment, he would still be in Oxford.

"Señor Montoya, I have not met Ambassador Chapuys," Thomas said slowly, forcing his thoughts away from his discomfort. "The queen is selective of her company these days, and I am not always present when she receives guests."

Montoya nodded. "But Padre, we know it is not only the queen who is selective of her company," he said with a raised brow. "It is the king, maybe Cardinal Wolsey, who decides, no?"

Thomas looked at him quizzically. "Is that so?"

"*Sí, sí.*" Montoya nodded emphatically. "And I know what is happening behind those closed doors! They say the king will marry his mistress, that whore, Anne Boleyn."

"I do my best to ignore court gossip," Thomas said, looking away.

"But you have heard?" Montoya pressed.

"Of course, we have heard," Richard said impatiently. Thomas shook his head, rubbed his temples, and said nothing.

"Hmm," the Spaniard said after a moment. "You are not one with loose lips."

Montoya clasped his hands.

"That is good," he said, "because there is more I should tell you."

24

THE SPANIARD

"You are carrying a message from the queen to her nephew, Emperor Charles V, no?" Montoya asked as he handed Thomas a goblet sloshing with French wine.

Thomas looked at Richard. Had he told anyone the nature of their business?

"How do you know this?" Richard demanded.

"The king has spies, *sí*? And Wolsey, no?" he began. "The queen has her people, too."

He waited for the priests' reaction, but Thomas only pressed his fingertips together and stared back. After an uncomfortable moment, Richard cleared his throat.

"We do not know your agenda, sir," Richard said, glancing from Montoya to Thomas.

Montoya nodded solemnly. "*Sí*, that is true."

Thomas nodded. "Señor Montoya, you have told us our business—but not yours."

"Ah." Montoya smiled broadly. "But your business is mine."

"How so?" Richard demanded.

"Chapuys sent me to intercept you," he said as Richard's eyes widened. "*Sí*, now you are listening to me. It is not the queen's desire for you to ask her nephew, Emperor Charles V, for the only copy of the Pope's brief. Please do not bring it back to England, *Padres*!"

"And that is worth a trip to Spain?" Richard asked, steadying himself as another wave rolled under the ship.

"*Sí!*" Montoya emphasized. "It is vital to the queen. She does not want the original brief in England!"

Thomas narrowed his eyes. "But *she* did not tell us this."

"No?" Montoya quizzed. "I am not surprised."

"If she did not want us to bring back the papal brief, then why did she not ask us herself?" Thomas asked. He watched Montoya's face, the shape of his mouth, the corner of his eyes.

"Ah." Montoya held his gaze. "Perhaps she does not trust her priests."

Thomas scowled and stood up. "Señor Montoya, I believe you know that the pope's brief is strong evidence for Queen Katherine's case. Why would she want it to stay in Spain?"

Montoya narrowed his eyes and looked directly at Thomas. "I think, perhaps, Father Abell, you know."

"We don't know what you are talking about," Richard said indignantly. "Other than it would be an embarrassment to the queen. We know that she was upset ..."

Thomas felt the blood rushing into his head. Richard was too talkative. The conversation had gone on long enough.

"King Henry sent me to Spain to get this document," Thomas interrupted Richard. "I am loyal to my king and my God, and the queen has not commissioned me otherwise. Who am I to subvert the will of both the king and queen? Especially on the word of a foreigner."

Richard smiled with relief. "Yes! As Thomas said!"

"Very well," Montoya said with a slight bow. "I respect your duty to the king."

Thomas smiled politely and turned to go, but he could not shake the feeling that he was being backed into a dark alley with nowhere to run.

Richard did not know about his conversation with Wolsey, and he was not planning to tell him either. Their conspiracy, if indeed that was what it was, did not need Richard's participation. He had no intention of adding Richard's involvement to his conscience.

And was he wrong for complying with Wolsey? What choice did he have?

It was true that Queen Katherine had never wanted him to get the papal brief, so how would she be any worse off if it landed in Wolsey's hands? Perhaps she would even thank him for keeping it out of English gossip. But what if Katherine changed her mind about using the brief in her defense? There was no guarantee Wolsey would protect him if the queen later demanded he be punished for failing to deliver the original copy of the Pope's letter, the one she had formally requested in writing.

And yet, handing the brief over to Wolsey was not right either. The thought made his skin crawl. When he agreed to serve the queen, he never intended to serve Wolsey as a spy—not really. He had always sought ways to tell the cardinal as little as possible and hold the queen's best interests at heart. But now—now, he was prepared to destroy evidence. How had it come to this?

If he subverted Wolsey's wishes, what would the cardinal do? Wolsey could dismiss him, disgrace him, or worse.

Thomas rubbed his throbbing head. *Oh, Lord, wisdom!*

The twilight sky bathed the horizon in golden light. It was a palpable peace after the storm, the last triumph of the day before the sun gave way to the night, but Thomas was anything but peaceful as he paced the damp ship deck.

He ran his fingers through his hair and mouthed the Latin prayer that had so often served to soothe his tormented soul.

"*Pater Noster...*" he began.

"Are you well?" Richard asked as he caught up to Thomas.

"Praying," Thomas said, continuing.

Richard fell in step with Thomas, continuing the prayer, nodding as he said the words aloud. When they finished, Thomas stopped, closed his eyes, and took a deep breath. When he opened his eyes, Richard was staring at him.

"The Spaniard?"

Thomas looked over Richard's shoulder. No other passengers were within earshot on the ship's deck, just a few hands tending to ropes at the starboard.

"No ... well, yes," he confessed. "He troubles me."

"I see that," Richard said.

The two continued walking. It felt good to move his legs.

"But what you said is true," Richard said, taking a half step to keep up with Thomas's long stride. "The king sent you on a specific mission, and the queen has not instructed you to do otherwise. All you have is her letter, which we know she wrote."

Thomas nodded, but his pace quickened as his steps fell heavier.

"But ... it's true. I do not think the queen trusts me," he said.

Richard looked surprised.

"Why do you say that?" he asked. "She speaks highly of you."

"Yes," Thomas said, and then paused. He was not sure if he should confide in Richard, but they were on this mission together, for better or worse. He deserved to know at least a little bit of what Thomas was thinking.

"The queen never wanted me in her household," Thomas said after a long moment. "Wolsey chose me. And I meet with him regularly. The queen knows this. Perhaps she thinks I am one of his spies."

Richard stopped walking.

"Are you?"

Thomas kept walking and said nothing for a moment before turning around and answering truthfully. "I hope not."

Thomas and Richard stood on the ship's damp deck, enveloped in a thick coastal fog, and watched as French deckhands scrambled aboard, offloading bundles and barrels from the ship's hold. When they disappeared back into the coastal fog, only the sounds of their boots and foreign chatter drifted back to the priests.

Thomas took in a long, deep breath. The air smelled of fish and tasted of salt. The aroma of fresh bread wafted up from the port-side village. They had reached the shores of France. His stomach growled, and he smiled. France! This was France. *"Ce pays est d'une beauté exceptionnelle."*

Richard laughed. *"Exceptionally* beautiful? Really, Thomas? It's gray and drab, like London in a winter fog. You can't even see the village from here." He pursed his lips thoughtfully. "Thomas, I think you just like hearing someone other than Anne Boleyn speak French!"

The corner of Thomas's mouth lifted. Perhaps. For a moment, the weight of England and Wolsey, King Henry, and Queen Katherine lifted off his chest. It was good to be on solid ground again! Good to be so far from court. He closed his eyes and let himself savor the moment.

When he opened his eyes, Richard was smiling at him. "I'll get our things," he said. "You enjoy your beautiful France."

Thomas looked out at the distant village emerging behind shifting fog. *Jesus Christ, Son of God, have mercy ...*

He felt a hand slap his back.

"Hola, Padre."

Thomas jumped, and Montoya laughed heartily. "I didn't mean to startle you." His brown eyes narrowed into his laugh lines, and he wiped tears away while Thomas smoothed his cassock and tried not to be offended by Montoya's sense of humor.

"You are returning to England?" he asked.

"Sí, tomorrow," Montoya said with a shrug. "But ... perhaps a good French meal first."

"You traveled a long way for a short conversation," Thomas said. "I hope Chapuys does not feel he wasted his money."

"Ah." Montoya shrugged as if their conversation was completely inconsequential. "Diplomacy is always a risk."

"Diplomacy?" The shifting fog was receding further ashore, and he could see the stone-cut cottages and the thatched roofs.

"*Sí*, of course, *Padre*. Chapuys worries that if the king is successful in divorcing his wife, then Charles V may have reason to defend her honor. He fears it will lead to war between the Empire and England."

"Indeed!" Thomas said, eyeing Montoya doubtfully. "Chapuys has told you this?" Montoya nodded gravely.

"*Sí*. And my master worries King Henry wants the original brief for himself, not for the queen," Montoya said. "He wants to have it in his possession so he can conceal it, no? He broke the young Francisco's arm! *Sí*, we know about that too. And we know that Wolsey sent you, his most trusted priest, to deliver the queen's message and get Queen Isabella's papal brief."

"Ambassador Chapuys thinks I am Wolsey's man?" Thomas asked, glancing over to see if Richard was still in earshot. He was not above deck, so Thomas turned his eyes back to Montoya, who continued without answering the question.

"We think—that is, the ambassador and I think—that Wolsey intends to destroy the evidence, the *only evidence* that this brief ever existed."

Thomas started to object, and Montoya held up his hands, "*Sí, sí*, the queen has a copy, we know. But it is only *a copy*. It is not *certified*. The original in Spain is the only document that will hold up in the Pope's court. We know this. The king knows this. And Wolsey knows this too! If that original comes to England..." Montoya made a guttural sound like a butcher clamping his cleaver on a chicken's neck. "If that brief comes to England, to Wolsey's England, it will disappear. Poof! No?"

Were Wolsey's motives that obvious?

"However," Montoya said, dipping his head and lowering his voice. "Padre, I made this journey because I believe you will *honor* the queen's true wishes. Margaret tells me that she believes you are a righteous man." Montoya's brown eyes held Thomas's, search-ing. "That is why I am here. Padre Abell, I am asking you to leave the brief in Spain, where Charles V will keep it safe. Perhaps ask the emperor to send an authenticated copy to the legatine court. Then the queen will have her evidence, and Charles V will keep the original safely away from Wolsey's hands."

"This is the message you wished to convey?"

"*Sí*," Montoya said with a slight bow. "And now I have delivered it."

25

THE FRENCH TAVERN

France

Thomas wrapped his cold, red hands around the steaming bowl of cabbage soup and smiled. It was good to be inside the old French tavern. Its low ceilings and half-timbered walls provided a cozy retreat from the relentless winter rain and biting wind. Even with the relative luxury of a covered carriage, Thomas and Richard were thoroughly soaked after a long day. And now, Thomas's whole body ached from the constant shivering. January was a bitter time to make a journey across France. No wonder wars were fought in spring.

"It is not bad," Richard said cheerfully, biting off a piece of brown bread. "Better than last night. Wouldn't you say so, Thomas?"

Richard was always drawing him away from his thoughts, into conversation.

"Yes," Thomas said with a polite smile.

The warm tavern *was* an improvement over yesterday. Last night, they had dined on stale bread alongside the road and slept in their coats, on mats, under the caravan. A constant drip from the canvas kept Thomas awake. And now he was more than tired. He was exhausted.

The courier, an old Frenchman named François, had assured Thomas they would make better time today. He promised, repeatedly, that they would arrive at a village with accommodations. Thus, they pressed through the rain and discovered François had not been wrong.

And delightfully, they were not alone in enjoying the cozy tavern quarters either.

All around them, travelers enjoyed wine, morsels of bread, and the ubiquitous steaming cabbage soup. Thomas listened with pleasure as a blend of French and English washed over him. He heard a phrase in Latin and then an answer in French. He understood both and covered his mouth to hide a smile at the French response. Languages were so delightful!

He closed his eyes and silently thanked the Lord for convincing his father that he needed a French tutor, though the old man said none of the boys in Colchester needed French for sheep farming. Who could have seen this day coming?

Father never said what had changed his mind, but one spring day, a tall, thin Frenchman with a leather satchel and a worn stack of French and Latin books arrived on the steps of the Abell estate.

Oh, how he missed Father! If only he could write him a letter and thank him. He would describe their journey across France. Father would have been amused and proud.

Unexpected tears sprang to Thomas's eyes. Though his father had been gone for more than a decade, it was moments like this that caught him off guard. Joy had a way of opening the heart to grief.

"Do you hear the king's tongue?" Richard asked, interrupting Thomas's thoughts again.

"No," Thomas said, hoping Richard had not observed his eyes watering.

He looked around and saw a low table with two men. They seemed to notice Thomas and Richard at the same time.

"Hello!" the Englishman shouted over the din. "Are you the priests the queen has sent to Spain?"

Thomas looked warily at Richard. Were they about to meet the men who broke Francisco's arm? The two were dressed as gentlemen. They hardly seemed the violent type, but Thomas had been surprised before.

Thomas nodded slowly without smiling. "Indeed. And who are you?"

The large Englishman hopped to his feet. He extended a thick hand, along with a hearty smile. "Edward Lee, ambassador of his Majesty, on an official mission to speak with the Emperor, Charles V. This is my companion Girolamo Ghinucci, Bishop of Worcester."

A Venetian who had bought a bishopric in England? Thomas had heard of such political arrangements before, and it always irked him. When Church positions were sold, corruption soon followed. He nodded coolly while Richard eagerly pulled two chairs to their table. Perhaps Richard would appreciate new companions.

"We are also on the king's business," he said enthusiastically. "Join us, please!"

Edward seemed happy to join Thomas and Richard, but the Venetian followed warily, stroking his thin mustache, his dark eyes darting between Thomas and Richard.

"It's been a terrible ride so far," Edward acknowledged. "Rain, rain, and more rain. About ruined my best breeches." He laughed heartily.

It seemed to put Richard at ease, but Thomas continued eating. He didn't laugh, not that he was trying to be antisocial. He just was not sure if the engagement warranted laughing at bad jokes.

"What business has our king with Charles V?" he asked pointedly.

Edward raised a bushy brow. "Thought you would know," he said. "Same as your business, I suppose."

He looked over at Girolamo and smiled. "We serve the king, same as you. We bring Charles V news of the king's intent to divorce his wife, Katherine. Could be a delicate subject, as you know, the emperor being related to the queen."

Thomas watched Girolamo's face. Was he scowling, or was that just how his face looked when he was thinking? Perhaps the Venetian bishop was just as tired of the king's Great Matter as he was.

"Yes, you could say it is a delicate subject," Richard said, raising a brow and looking over to Thomas.

Edward laughed. "Well, I can see we agree on that." He slapped his empty glass down and nodded to a buxom French woman meandering around the crowded room with a carafe of wine.

"I love the wine here," he announced. "And the women are not too bad either."

He winked as the woman filled his glass.

Thomas looked away.

"Sorry, Fathers." Edward laughed as he took a long drag on the wine. "A man is just a man."

Unless you take vows.

Richard looked away from the woman and took another bite of bread.

"If you like," Edward proposed, "we can travel along together, probably safer for all of us."

Thomas saw Richard look at him, but he did not say anything, could not say anything. Instead, he pressed his fingers together and listened to the man who wa*s just* a man, and thought that no amount of winter rain and wind could compare to the displeasure it would be to spend the remainder of their journey in Edward Lee's company.

"You two are delivering a message—that's what we were told—to the emperor, asking for a document that the king would find helpful." Edward looked between Thomas and Richard. "The king just sent us to make sure Emperor Charles gives it to you. Make sure we bring it back home to England. Same as you, you see."

"Two priests with an official letter from the queen are not enough?" Richard asked, sounding just a bit defensive.

The Venetian sniffed.

"Now, of course, it would be more than enough," Girolamo said in his trained, crisp articulation. "Except that the king wishes to send *me*, as well. I am an expert in canon law. I can explain to Emperor Charles exactly why our King Henry is entitled to an annulment. This is very important to our king. The emperor must be made to understand, clearly."

Girolamo ran his thumb over his fingertips and said no more.

"I see," said Richard slowly. "We should present the queen's request, and you will offer the legal arguments for the king?"

"Yes, you understand," said Edward as he pushed away from the table. "It's been a long day, gentlemen. The king has arranged fresh horses for you and a new groomsman to lead the way across France. So, we will meet in the morning, then?"

"No," Thomas said quickly. "No, I do not think we should arrive together."

"And why is that?" Girolamo demanded, a sudden, small fire burning in his beady, black eyes.

"It is very important to the king to retrieve the original papal brief," Thomas explained, eyes narrowing. "We should present the queen's request to Emperor Charles first. I believe that he will be moved by her wishes and comply. But if you arrive first, and he is not convinced of the king's case, he may be suspicious of the king's motives, and then he may not give us the brief."

"Suspicious?" Girolamo questioned. "Charles will have no reason to be suspicious. The king is in his full rights, and I will present it as such!"

"Yes, but perhaps he does not find your argument convincing? Then we will have lost the opportunity to get the brief," Thomas said.

Girolamo scowled.

"Now, now," Edward began, "we should travel together because it would be safer as we ride through this foreign land. And when we arrive together, we will decide who will speak first." He smiled. "No need for conflict among the king's men. We are of one mind and one mission. We will get a good night's sleep, rest from this cold day of riding, and be off tomorrow morn."

Edward left the group, walking in the direction of the French woman with a jug of wine. He touched her lightly on her elbow and smiled suggestively.

"Our livery will be ready at noon tomorrow," Girolamo said, watching his companion flirt with the local woman. "We need to make purchases here, so it will be impossible to make an early start, anyhow. But we should continue together. As the king has requested."

Thomas nodded. "We will consider it," he said and took another spoonful of his cabbage soup that was no longer steaming.

Distant, frosty stars provided the only light as Thomas and Richard crept around the livery stable, quietly retrieving their horses and waking their French courier.

François looked at Thomas with sleepy gray eyes and, despite quiet grumbles and incoherent French phrases, gave Thomas a reluctant nod. He ran his weathered hands over his face, rubbed his white chin stubble, and gathered his belongings in his leather satchel. He was ready to leave by the time Thomas opened the livery door and led the horses out into the narrow village street.

The moon had already set, but Thomas knew the night was only half over. As they walked the horses quietly through the village street, he heard the faint sound of Benedictine monks singing their Latin matins, sanctifying the night with their chant. It would be hours before the first rooster crowed and the vinedressers and clothmakers returned to their trades. And it would be even longer before Lee finished his breakfast and began looking around for the queen's two priests. But Thomas had no intention of waiting.

"You are certain?" Richard finally asked as they left the quiet village behind.

"Yes," Thomas said without hesitation. "When we get to the highway, go as fast as you can. We will pass our next stop. I mean to get to Loufur tonight."

Richard raised an eyebrow but said nothing.

Once the darkness gave way to twilight and the meager warmth of a rare, partly sunny day, Richard fell into a trot next to Thomas. "What are you thinking?" he asked.

"I am not sure yet," Thomas said hesitatingly. "I just knew that we could not travel with those Englishmen."

Richard laughed. "They were a pair."

Thomas did not laugh but flexed his jaw and looked straight ahead.

"No," he finally said, looking over to see if François was close enough to hear. "I don't trust them."

"Are you thinking of what the Spaniard said?"

"No," Thomas said quickly, and then, thinking that what he had said was not truthful, lowered his eyes. "Perhaps."

"We cannot trust his word against the queen's written word, Thomas," Richard said. "The king would have our heads!"

"Maybe," Thomas said, staring down the road.

Richard did not say anything, and the two passed a frozen meadow and dormant vineyard before Thomas returned to the subject.

"I do not know what to think," he said. "But I knew that I would not be able to think in Lee's company. We need to push hard and get to Saragossa first. That is all I know."

26

PILGRIMAGE IN SPAIN

March 1529

"This is as far as I go, friends," François said, handing the reins to Thomas. "My mother's village is a day's walk to the east, and you will continue this road south through the pass. In a few more days, the mountains will open, and you will be in Spain. *Voilà!*"

Thomas climbed down from his mount and handed the old Frenchman a pouch of gold coins, the king's payment for guiding his priests through France.

"*Merci beaucoup,*" Thomas said, lightly touching François's shoulders. "God bless you on the rest of your journey."

Thomas watched François walk, stick in hand, down the narrow eastward footpath.

"He looks like a pilgrim," Richard said with a smile as he and Thomas continued down the road into Spain. "I have always wanted to be a pilgrim. Travel to Rome. Kiss the feet of saints. See relics with my own eyes."

Thomas raised an eyebrow but kept watching as François moved farther down the road.

"No? Thomas! Are you skeptical of relics too?"

Thomas tilted his head and pursed his lips.

"I am not skeptical, not like Martin Luther," he said. "I think they can be helpful in pointing to the Cross. Erasmus said, and I think I agree, that relics can be unnecessary obstacles for people if they put their faith in the relics instead of God. It is better to focus on Jesus Christ."

"Are you sure that was Erasmus and not Luther? Sounds like Luther."

"I am sure," Thomas said emphatically. "It was Thomas More's friend, Erasmus of Rotterdam. In fact, he writes that he agrees with St. Augustine and Thomas Aquinas on this matter. He says that relics can be helpful, but they can also be like idols if people put their hope in them instead of seeking God for themselves. It's in his book, *Handbook of the Militant Christian*."

"I see," Richard said, raising his own eyebrow. "You have spent time considering this."

Thomas shrugged. "I consider everything."

Richard laughed. "I've noticed. More than you like to talk, it seems."

"Maybe."

Richard nodded and pursed his smiling lips. "Yes, it's true, Thomas. You can go an entire morning without uttering so much as a single word to me. Not so much as 'Why, look at the beautiful mountains!'"

Richard motioned at the distant Pyrenees, and Thomas glanced at him thoughtfully. "I don't mean to be rude."

"It is not rude." Richard shrugged. "It is just ... different."

Both men were quiet for a long minute until Thomas spoke up.

"I am sorry, Richard. Sometimes, I am deep in my thoughts."

Richard nodded and kept looking down the road.

"Do you know what you will do when we get to Saragossa? Will you tell the emperor what Montoya said? That the queen does not *actually* want us to bring back the Pope's letter?"

Thomas looked at the snowcapped mountains, marking the border of Spain, and shook his head. "I have to say something. I cannot simply deliver the queen's letter when I know it is false."

"False?"

"Yes."

"You know?"

"Yes," Thomas said, not turning to look at Richard. "The Spaniard told us the truth." From his peripheral vision, he could see Richard's raised brow.

"Are you sure?"

Thomas nodded and continued. "Yes, I am quite sure. The queen was angry with me." Thomas paused and looked over at Richard. "For telling Cardinal Wolsey about the Pope's letter."

"Oh." Richard stared at Thomas. "I did not know. ... You told Cardinal Wolsey? ... I didn't realize."

"Yes," Thomas said, quietly. Whatever judgment Richard felt was warranted. Thomas had told Wolsey. He had betrayed the queen's trust, and then he had led Richard to believe that he did not know what Montoya was talking about. He had withheld from Richard for lack of trust, and now Richard had reason not to trust him.

"I am sorry, Richard," he said quietly. "I was hoping my conscience would allow me to obey the king." Thomas shook his head. "I have been wrestling with my heart, unsure of what to do. But Montoya is right. The queen does not want this papal brief to return to England."

"Oh," Richard said with a hint of disappointment. "Why didn't you say earlier?"

Thomas kept his eyes on the road as a wave of shame crashed over him. "I did not know whom to trust. I am sorry ..."

Richard was quiet for a moment. "Don't apologize. These are difficult times. You know that I also care deeply for Queen Katherine and her daughter." He smiled and shook his head. "Those two are more alike than not ... stubborn." His face became serious. "But I fear that this matter with King Henry will not end well for them, or any of us."

Thomas shook his head. "No."

Richard stopped his horse and turned to Thomas, looking him squarely in the eye. "You can trust me, my friend."

Thomas felt a weight lift off his chest, and tears sprang to his eyes. He was suddenly grateful for the Lord allowing Richard to travel with him. *Friend?* It had been so long since he had had a real friend. He knew he should say something, but the words caught in his throat. He stared at the road ahead and nodded. When he finally glanced over at Richard, he saw he was studying his face.

"What will you tell Emperor Charles?" Richard asked.

"I am not sure," Thomas said, honestly. "We have to be careful." Whatever he said would have implications for Richard too. "It is no small thing to disobey your king."

27

The Aljafería Palace

April 1529   Spain

"Beautiful," Thomas said as he caught a white blossom gliding to the ground. "Oranges?"

"*Sí, Señor* Abell," the Spanish courtier responded. He smiled broadly, his olive skin crinkling around his brown eyes. "Sweet oranges. Do you like them?"

"*Sí.*"

Thomas closed his eyes and took in a long, deep breath. They had traveled such a long way, over many weeks, but finally they had arrived. The sun, the smell, the sound of the courtyard songbirds were balm for his soul. He opened his eyes as a gentle breeze blew, tossing a cascade of blossoms, like snow, to the marble pathway.

The courtier kicked the flowers that had begun to pile up on the walkway and apologized for their droppings. "The trees have been blooming for weeks now—two, maybe three weeks. In a few days they will be gone." He nodded to himself. "*Sí, quizás, tal vez.* They will be gone by the end of the week."

He made a clicking sound and motioned for Thomas and Richard to follow him, crushing the fragrant petals underfoot as they crossed the courtyard.

The three men walked toward an open room surrounded by arched columns, unlike anything Thomas had ever seen. Each archway was decorated with intricately sculptured geometric patterns, circle patterns, like lacework in stone. A series of high arches intertwined, holding up the edge of the ceiling like tall trees holding up a forest canopy, bidding the traveler to enter a private world of serenity.

"The Moors," the Spanish courtier said, noting Thomas's gaze. "The Moors built this palace five hundred years ago, *más o menos*. The Aragon kings added to it. Ferdinand and Isabella built the throne room." He grinned, eyes twinkling with pride. "The throne room is ... well, you will see."

They passed under the Moorish arches, past walls decorated with golden gilded floral designs and the calligraphy of Arabic messages long forgotten. They turned a corner and walked up a grand staircase to Ferdinand and Isabella's throne room, the only addition. They went through another elaborately detailed archway and into a long, empty room with a marble floor and high ceiling.

They had come to Katherine's world.

"Are those pinecones?" Richard asked, pointing to the golden sculptures descending from octagonal shapes.

"Yes," Thomas said, staring up at the golden pinecones repeating in a pattern across the entire blue and gold ceiling. "Fertility symbol, an old pagan custom."

The golden beams and supporting crossbeams created a lacework pattern, forming eight-pointed stars at each intersection with octagonal shapes inside each square. At the center of each square were curly golden flowers, culminating in the pinecones.

"Gentlemen, Fathers," the Spanish courtier interrupted Thomas and his gawking companion, "His Majesty, Charles V, Emperor of the Holy Roman Empire, King of Spain, Archduke of Austria!"

The courtier bowed low as Charles V and an entourage of his advisors and courtiers entered. Thomas swallowed the lump in his throat. The moment had arrived.

"I understand you are here on behalf of your queen, my dear aunt, Queen Katherine of Aragon," the young emperor said in crisp, well-trained English. "I imagine it has been a long journey for two priests."

Thomas stepped forward. "I have a letter for you from Her Majesty," he said, offering the sealed letter to the Spanish courtier, who reverently handed it to his sovereign.

Emperor Charles took the letter, broke the seal, and read it silently in their presence.

"She wishes me to send a brief with you, the original one, back to England," the emperor said, a look of concern on his face. "This is perhaps because of the matter between her and King Henry. I have been hearing reports of this from my ambassador in London."

Thomas nodded without saying anything. He could feel Richard fidgeting anxiously.

The emperor looked at them and then at the letter.

"I am familiar with that brief," Charles said. "It is among my grandmother's archives, Catalina's mother," he added with a smile. "I believe my grandmother queen requested it be kept here as evidence of the Pope's dispensation for Henry and Katherine's marriage."

"Perhaps she foresaw a circumstance in which such evidence would be helpful?" Thomas queried. How long had people worried about the legitimacy of Henry and Katherine's marriage?

Charles shook his head.

"I do not know. I do not have much memory of my grandmother," he said thoughtfully. "I was, of course, a young child in the Low Countries then, with my Habsburg family, when she passed. May she rest in peace, but I understand that she was a formidable woman." He laughed and spread his hands. "She was the visionary behind all of this—the unification of Spain, the marriage alliances of all her children, even funding Columbus. Never underestimate a Castilian woman!"

He shook his head and smiled proudly. "I am sure that you are aware of her reputation." He frowned. "But no, I do not think she anticipated Henry and Katherine would seek a divorce. She believed that her daughter was quite fond of her husband, at least in the early days."

"She is fond of him still," Thomas said, the blood rushing into his head. "Despite his ill treatment."

The emperor raised an eyebrow.

"Ill treatment?"

Thomas was quiet for a moment, feeling the eyes of Charles, the Spanish counselors, and Richard, who offered a subtle nod.

Thomas knew that his next move, his next words, could ruin his life. But to deny the truth, and his heart, seemed impossible. He could only press forward. And so, he opened his mouth and uttered treason.

"The queen does not wish you to send the original brief," he said suddenly, with more confidence than he felt. "Despite what that letter says. Queen Katherine composed it under duress. The king, whom she has been faithful to for nearly twenty years, compelled her to do so. I assure you, it was against her will."

Charles looked incredulously at Thomas and lifted his oversized chin in disgust. He shook his head.

"Father Abell, you mean to tell me that my dear aunt, the regent Queen of England, daughter of Ferdinand and Isabella, was forced to write this letter against her will!" His voice rose with each word, the clarity of the offense becoming greater with every passing second.

He shook the letter Thomas and Richard had carefully carried across England, France, and Spain. "This letter?!"

"Yes, Your Majesty," Thomas said solemnly.

Charles sat down on his throne and looked at Thomas with his intense, bright blue eyes.

"Then please tell me why you are here."

Thomas took a deep breath and glanced at Richard before continuing.

"Your Majesty, I do not believe that King Henry wishes to obtain this brief in good faith. He uses you and the diplomacy of your relationship." The words tumbled out more freely than Thomas had feared.

"I do not believe my king wishes to use this brief in the legal proceedings, despite how it looks. In fact, it is my belief that he has required Queen Katherine to request the original copy of this brief so that, upon obtaining it, he might destroy it."

The Spanish courtier who had guided them into the throne room gasped. Richard stared at Thomas. The truth was out. Not only did the queen not want the original brief to return to England, but Wolsey wanted it there only to destroy it. Thomas had known both of these facts the whole journey, and he had only let Richard know part of it. Richard's brow twisted, and Thomas could not decide if he was worried or angry.

The courtiers murmured among themselves until Charles flicked his hand in irritation. "Quiet," he admonished. "I want to hear the English priest. Father, please tell me why my uncle, the King of England, would seek to destroy this papal brief?"

"It is my understanding that papal briefs such as these are not registered in Rome."

Charles nodded. Thomas continued.

"The original that you possess is unique. And it is the only evidence that Pope Julius intended to bless this marriage, even in the event that the marriage between your aunt and her first husband, Prince Arthur, had, in fact, been consummated."

Charles stroked his chin. "Indeed. The only one? It is quite valuable, no?"

Thomas locked eyes with the emperor. "Yes, Your Majesty. Much is at stake."

Thomas was quiet for a moment, letting his words settle. He could feel the eyes of the court on him, and he glanced at Richard again.

"As you have undoubtedly heard from your faithful ambassador," Thomas continued, "our majesty, King Henry VIII, wishes to replace Queen Katherine with another woman, one capable of giving him a son." Thomas swallowed hard and continued. "The queen has passed her childbearing years and has only one living daughter, and that in spite of her six pregnancies, as you know."

Charles dipped his chin sadly, his eyes half closed. "Yes, it has been her lifelong sorrow."

"The king has come to believe that their marriage is cursed, that it should never have been made," Thomas explained, then paused.

The king and the handful of Spanish courtiers in the Throne Room watched him intently. It felt as if the whole world had been distilled to that place in time, that moment. He was on a stage he had never imagined, performing a play he had never wanted to perform, and his very words meant life to the queen and, perhaps, death for him. But he could not stop speaking. He glanced over at Richard, whose eyes had narrowed.

"The king has been saying, publicly, that Queen Katherine lied about her marriage to his brother. He has spread the insult that she consummated the marriage with Prince Arthur and then misled him to believe that she came to his bed a virgin. And for this offense, he says, God has cursed their marriage, for no man should marry his brother's wife and expect to produce sons."

Charles crossed his arms, his brow furrowed.

"He implies," Thomas continued, "that if she had not consummated the marriage to Arthur, there would have been no real marriage, no real reason for concern. But if she, indeed, consummated that marriage, then, the king insists, he and Katherine have been violating the law of God." Thomas paused, and Charles raised an eyebrow in anticipation. "The king now claims that they have been living in incest."

Charles made a sour face.

"The king has found a verse in Leviticus to confirm his fears," Thomas said. "It says in Leviticus that if a man lies with his brother's wife, then the union shall be unclean. And consequently, they shall be childless."

The emperor's dark eyes stormed. "That is troubling."

"But it is not the whole picture," Thomas said quickly. "In Deuteronomy, the law given to the Jews of old, God commanded that men marry their brothers' widows and produce heirs for their deceased brothers. It was commanded to provide for the support of widows."

"For the Jews, perhaps," Charles said skeptically, and Thomas felt the bitter irony. Katherine's parents had established the unification of Spain at the expense of the Jews, expelling them from Spain the same year Columbus left on his first voyage to the New World. And yet, here he was, an English priest using Jewish law to clarify Scripture and provide a defense for the Spanish princess.

"Yes," Thomas said quickly. "It is an old law, one that does not apply to Christian men under the New Covenant. But it is my conviction, and the conviction of others in England, that it does not conflict with the Scripture in Leviticus that the king wishes to use. In fact, the verses in Leviticus should be read with the Deuteronomy passage in mind, and this, of course, clarifies the situation."

"How so?" Charles asked. "Explain your logic and theology to me."

"If God commanded the Jews to marry their brothers' wives, in the case that the man dies and leaves no heir, then it cannot be an unclean or evil thing to do so," he said, watching Charles contemplate what he spoke. "God would not command his people to do an evil thing, not in the Law that he commanded Jews to obey for all generations."

Charles nodded. "That is logical," he conceded. "But what about the text in Leviticus, the one that torments Henry's soul?"

"I believe that Henry gives permission to his own soul to be tormented," Thomas said boldly. "He has chosen to be blinded by his own lusts and desires."

Thomas felt the heat rising in his cheeks as he spoke the indictment against his sovereign. Never had he spoken his thoughts so boldly.

"Your Majesty, forgive my insolence," he said. "I should say I believe that King Henry is troubled by Leviticus, not because of careful study of the Scriptures or inquiry into the Church's traditional interpretation of these. I believe that he is enticed by his mistress Anne Boleyn and wishes to find support in the Holy Scriptures."

"You find this distasteful?" Charles said, although the question hardly needed to be answered.

"I do not like to see Holy Scripture twisted for personal gain," Thomas said. "And yes, my sympathies are with your aunt. She has been a good wife and rightful queen. It would be an injustice for her to be displaced."

Charles was quiet. Thomas glanced at Richard, who nodded. Thomas continued.

"Your Majesty, it has become clear to me, upon inquiry of Church traditions and Scripture, that the Leviticus passage must refer to a man abusing the wife of his living brother, as in the case of adultery. I do not believe that it applies to the king and queen's holy matrimony."

Charles nodded. "I see."

"Yes," Thomas said. "It is my conviction that it is a simple case. Perhaps Pope Julius also saw it this way when he issued the brief consenting to their marriage, *even if* it had been consummated."

Charles stood up. "But you are telling me that my aunt, Queen Katherine, does not wish me to send this important brief to England? It seems to me, from what you have said, that it would only protect her from Henry's arguments."

Thomas nodded. "Indeed, I believe that it would. But, Your Majesty, the queen does not trust the king to safeguard the original document." He swallowed hard and glanced at Richard, who was watching him intently. Whatever consequences followed would affect Richard too.

"And Queen Katherine is not wrong. I know for certain that Cardinal Thomas Wolsey plans to destroy the brief." He was quiet for a minute, letting the accusation against King Henry's celebrated right-hand man, the highest and holiest member of the English church, stand. "He has confided this to me himself."

"*Cardinal Wolsey* has told you such?"

Thomas dipped his head. He had said it. He could not take it back.

"Then I will not send it!" Charles exclaimed with astonishment. "But Father Abell, what do you suggest I do?"

Thomas opened a leather satchel and pulled out a lengthy document written in Spanish. Richard gawked. Thomas had written the document during the long nights while Richard slept. Now he wished he had discussed it with Richard. He could have told him beforehand. Thomas pushed down a stab of guilt.

"Your Majesty," Thomas began, clutching the parchment. "I must also tell you that we broke company with an envoy from the king. Those men will arrive in the next few days, and when they do, I want you to be prepared." He stopped, aware of his presumption. "If you so wish."

"Of course!"

Thomas handed the emperor the parchment. "I cannot profess to understand all the diplomatic concerns you have to balance, but please, allow me to offer these as humble suggestions."

"Please."

"I have written a list of three possible actions that I think you could take without endangering your position with King Henry," he said. Then, more quietly, "and, if possible, without endangering my life." Thomas bowed slightly.

He looked gravely at the emperor. Having spoken his conscience, he was at the mercy of Charles V. Just one word of what he had said could send him to the Tower. He would never be a free man again. But what was said was said. There was no turning back.

Thomas held his breath as Charles began reading the document. He glanced over at Richard, who gave him a reassuring nod. Thomas exhaled. Good. Richard was still with him.

After what seemed like an impossibly long moment, Charles lifted his eyes and sighed heavily.

"You wish me to write to my ambassadors in Rome?" he questioned.

"Yes, Your Majesty. I do not believe the justice of the queen's cause will be honored in London. You could request your ambassadors use every effort to prevent the annulment proceedings from taking place in London. It must stay in Rome."

Charles looked to one of his counselors standing to his right. The man acknowledged the emperor with a nod. They could use their ambassadors in Rome to lean on the Pope.

"And so it shall be done," Charles said. He glanced again at the document. "What of this matter of sending an ambassador to London, an expert in canon law? Why not another priest like yourself?"

"It must be an official ambassador," Thomas replied. "If the legatine court assembles in London, the king will not refuse to hear an ambassador. It must be someone of that rank. Not another man of the Church."

Charles nodded. "And finally," Charles said, reading from the document, "you ask that my best legal experts write to the queen with any information that might help her case?"

"Yes," Thomas replied, his resolve weakening as he considered, again, the implications of what he had written. He suddenly wished to be out of the Throne Room, far from the opulence of Charles's court.

With that, he bowed slightly and asked his leave. He had done what he had come to Spain to do. He had honored the queen and his conscience. The matter was in God's hands.

28

CHARLES V AND THE KING'S MEN

A week later, Thomas and Richard were seated with the emperor's advisors when Edward Lee and Girolamo Ghinucci were ushered into Charles V's Throne Room. Thomas smiled to himself to see the awe on Edward's round face as he took in the grandeur. Girolamo seemed less affected. Perhaps his years in Rome had made him less impressed by royal extravagances.

"This is quite amazing, simply splendid," Edward gushed to the same Spanish courtier who had first directed Thomas and Richard through the Aljafería.

The courtier nodded and pointed toward Thomas and Richard. "*Sí, Señor*, a true work of art. Ah, and perhaps these are the Englishmen you seek."

Edward laughed heartily. "Indeed!" he said, but Girolamo looked suspiciously at Thomas.

Thomas heard footsteps approaching, and the Spanish courtier straightened to attention.

"His Majesty, Charles V, Emperor of the Holy Roman Empire, King of Spain, Archduke of Austria!"

"Welcome, Englishmen," Emperor Charles said, acknowledging Edward and Girolamo, who knelt before him, the Venetian kissing the emperor's hand.

"Thank you for welcoming us!" Edward said as he arose. "Being here in your most beautiful palace is an honor." He gazed up at the ceiling and the gilded inscription around the room. "It is exquisite."

Charles smiled good-naturedly, but even Thomas could see that he was impatient.

"I am eager to hear your business," the emperor said.

"Our king, Henry VIII of England, requests an audience with you," Girolamo said evenly. "We beseech you on behalf of him."

Charles nodded. "Yes," he said quickly, and Thomas caught Girolamo's eyes narrow. Did the Italian suspect that he had prejudiced the king against him? He felt a knot grow in his stomach. Would the emperor expose him for what he had done? How long until King Henry learned of his treason?

"We are here to discuss something of great importance to the king," Edward said, placing his hand dramatically over his heart.

"Yes," Charles V said slowly, in a way that put Thomas even more on edge.

"Well, of course, the king cannot be here in his own person..." Edward stumbled. "And so, we humbly ask that you would receive us and hear his explanation of this, his Great Matter."

The emperor cleared his throat and stretched a bit taller.

"Master Lee, Bishop Ghinucci," he said. "Perhaps I ought to save you a bit of trouble and tell you that I am aware that King Henry wishes to divorce my aunt, Katherine of Aragon, the reigning Queen of England, and to replace her with one of her ladies, solely for the purpose of producing a male heir. Yes, I have been informed!"

The emperor paused, and Edward waited, his mouth parted in anticipation of the emperor's forthcoming words. "And I am not sympathetic to your king's cause."

Edward immediately looked stricken. His face paled, but Girolamo nodded as if he had expected such a greeting from the queen's favored nephew.

"Perhaps you will give us the liberty to present the king's conscience," Girolamo said with the eloquence of an international diplomat. "We are not unaware of the offense it would seem to you and your family. The king wishes to make amends."

A courtier who had accompanied them stepped forward and laid a large, heavy wooden chest at the emperor's feet. The courtier opened it, and a murmur rippled through the Spanish company of counselors and courtiers. The trunk was full of gold coins. A bribe? *King Henry must think his wife's honor is for sale!* Thomas felt his cheeks flush.

The emperor did not seem amused either.

"Thank you for your gift," he said, narrowing his eyes. "But it is unnecessary."

Edward cleared his throat. "Your Majesty, you yourself are a married man," he began. "You understand the great gift of God that marriage is. Indeed, marriage is a holy sacrament." Edward nodded. "Our king has been grateful to Katherine for the many wonderful years they have shared together. But it has come to his attention, in his study of the Scriptures, that he, indeed, he and Katherine, have been living in a sinful marriage."

Charles cocked his head and crossed his arms.

Edward stopped short, and Thomas glanced over at Richard, who looked as nervous as he felt. The emperor waved his hand. "No, please continue, Master Lee. You said my aunt, Queen Katherine, has been living in sin?"

"Well, no, not simply your aunt, but also King Henry..."

Thomas watched the emperor's face grow cooler as Edward droned on about Leviticus, the Pope's authority, and the king's desire to amend the situation. Charles tapped his foot impatiently and seemed poised to end the conversation altogether, when Girolamo interrupted his colleague.

"Please, Your Majesty, allow me to explain," said Girolamo in a tone that Thomas thought was more sinister than sincere.

The emperor raised his bushy eyebrows and waved his hand but said nothing.

"You see, Emperor," Girolamo began, "the king deeply respects the Scriptures and all things holy."

No one in the room nodded in agreement, but the bishop continued, laying out Wolsey's argument. It made Thomas's skin crawl to hear Girolamo quote Scripture, but he fixed his eyes on the emperor. If Edward or Girolamo looked in his direction, he wanted them to feel that he supported the king's men, supported their cause. If they suspected Thomas and Richard had prejudiced the emperor, they would undoubtedly make trouble for them when they returned to England.

"King Henry has lost five children prematurely to death," Girolamo asserted, "and he has come to the unfortunate conclusion that this is not a mere coincidence. He and Katherine are under God's judgment because they acted outside of his goodwill. God, Himself, has punished them with the death of their children."

The room was quiet.

"That is unfortunate," Charles finally said. "What does King Henry propose to do about my aunt's honor?"

"Yes," Edward jumped in eagerly. "Our king is most concerned about his lady's honor. That is why he wishes to repent of this *unintended* sin." He paused. "Perhaps you have already heard that he has asked the Pope to annul his marriage…"

"But her honor," Charles interrupted Edward's rambling. "What will King Henry do to protect the honor of his queen, the mother of his very *living* daughter, Mary, Princess of Wales?"

"The queen could retire in comfort to a nunnery in England," Edward said cheerfully.

"God willing?" Charles asked. "Perhaps you mean if she is willing to go to a convent."

"She would be most comfortable there, Your Majesty," Edward argued.

"Would she?" Charles asked.

"Why, yes, Your Majesty, she would, of course, be provided for in absolute comfort, but she would also be given the leisure to pursue her own delights, music, and her intellectual pursuits. She is quite educated, is she not, Father Abell?" Edward suddenly looked at Thomas.

"Yes," Thomas said quickly. "She is most studious and pious. She has often expressed a desire to devote more time to studying the Bible and prayer." He glanced at Edward, who, thankfully, seemed oblivious to Thomas's true thoughts. "Perhaps living in a convent would not be disagreeable to her. Perhaps it would allow Queen Katherine more time to improve her mind."

Charles coughed to cover a slight smile and turned to Edward. "But is it her desire to be divorced from her husband, the good King of England?"

Edward faltered, "Well, as a matter of fact ..."

"No," Girolamo interrupted with a low growl. "We will not hide from you, Emperor, the fact that Katherine is not of the same mind as King Henry. She is not yet cooperating with the king."

"She wishes to oppose the king in this divorce?" Charles asked.

"Well, ahh ...," Edward began.

"Yes," Girolamo said clearly. "It is most unfortunate for her soul."

"How so?" Charles demanded.

"We do not wish for her to continue in this incestuous marriage," Girolamo said without apology. "We wish to help her do what is right for herself, her husband, and her country."

"Indeed!" Charles said. "Then can you explain to me why your king wishes me to send a copy of Pope Julius's communication with the late Queen Isabella, the one in which he gave a special dispensation for Henry and Katherine to marry, even if the marriage of Katherine and Prince Arthur was consummated?"

Girolamo shot a look at Thomas.

Charles followed him. "Your kinsmen, Father Abell and Father Featherstone, have presented the letter from Katherine in which she beseeches me to send this brief to England."

Thomas watched quietly as Girolamo looked from him to the emperor. Richard was looking pale, and Thomas silently prayed Richard would be wise enough to keep quiet.

"Yes," Edward ventured. "Our king requests the original."

"The original?" Charles asked, raising his voice slightly. "Why not a copy?"

"Your Majesty," Girolamo began in his even tone. "Perhaps you are also aware that the Pope's courts will decide this matter soon. Cardinal Campeggio has arrived in England, and even now, a legatine court is preparing to meet in London. Naturally, we are gathering all the relevant evidence."

"But I believe that the queen already possesses a copy of this brief," the emperor challenged.

"Yes, yes, indeed, she does," Edward stumbled. "But ... it has come to the king's attention that a mere copy could be challenged as a counterfeit ... a fake."

"A fake?" The emperor was clearly not amused.

"There are persons," Girolamo responded with his chin pointed high, "who would wish to impede this process. ..."

Emperor Charles did not let him finish. "Who?"

The room was uncomfortably quiet for a moment, and Thomas saw Edward look up at the gilded ceiling with its protruding golden pinecones.

"Queen Katherine," Edward said, and Thomas heard Girolamo whisper a Venetian curse. "Queen Katherine opposes the annulment."

"And why is that?" Charles demanded.

"Your Majesty, we have not come prepared to represent Katherine's concerns," Edward stammered.

"I see," Charles said vaguely. "And you wish to convince me to side with King Henry over his wife, my own mother's dear sister?"

Neither Edward nor Girolamo answered, and the emperor stood up. "Return this time tomorrow, and I will give you my response."

29

THE KING'S MEN ARE DISAPPOINTED

Thomas was silent, as he, Girolamo, Edward, and Richard walked solemnly through Isabella's famous arched courtyard, which had seemed so magical just a week ago. The white blossoms had disappeared, leaving behind tiny green bulbs emerging from the carcasses of petal-less flowers. The marble walkway had been swept clean of fallen blossoms, the sweet fragrance gone. There remained only the promise of oranges to come.

Despite his silence, Thomas could not help but feel a rush of euphoria. He knew he should be afraid that Girolamo would uncover his disloyalty to the king, but in the moment, he was so happy that he almost did not care. Richard had kept quiet, and Charles had played his part perfectly and sent them away without the brief.

"How is it that the emperor is so opposed to our king's position?" Edward asked incredulously once the group had left the Spanish castle, crossed the moat, and headed into the busy streets of Saragossa. Girolamo looked to Thomas but said nothing.

"Perhaps it is simply because of the family relationship," Richard offered practically. "Perhaps it was optimistic to consider Emperor Charles would think otherwise."

"But what shall we tell King Henry?" Edward asked, anxiously biting his lip.

"We shall tell him the truth," Thomas said, walking quickly. "We shall tell him you presented your case well, and the emperor was unmoved by your good arguments."

"He will not be pleased," Girolamo said gravely.

"Nor will Cardinal Wolsey," Thomas reminded them.

Girolamo pointed to an alleyway off the main cobblestone street. "I know a tavern there," he said, pushing past other patrons gathering in front of the door. He moved the English group into a low room with long tables and pewter mugs.

"Good," Edward said. "I was getting hungry. We can discuss this over food."

Thomas did not think he could stomach even the king's table, but considering it better not to let the king's men reflect on the reason for his anxieties, he agreed. "Food always makes bad news easier," he said offhandedly while Girolamo eyed him.

"Tell me, Father Abell, how did Charles receive you when you arrived?" the Venetian asked. "We were quite disappointed when you left us so abruptly."

Richard looked anxiously at Thomas, but Thomas smiled slowly.

"I apologize, Bishop Girolamo, that we did not leave you with a better notice. I had hoped that by arriving early, we would have an opportunity to present the request for the brief first," he said honestly. "As it was, the emperor seemed happy to receive us. He has quite a high opinion of his aunt, Queen Katherine."

"Yes, we see that," Girolamo said without humor. "And the letter? How did he receive that?"

"Ahh." Thomas shook his head. "He was a bit confused. And then suspicious."

"Suspicious!" Edward said.

"Yes," Thomas said, trying not to look at Richard squirming. "He wanted to know why King Henry required the original, and the original only."

"He made that quite clear today," Edward quipped. "Bringing in the original brief for our eyes to see and then snatching it back."

Edward covered his face with his hands. "What shall we tell the king?"

"Exactly what happened," Thomas said evenly. "He must know what Charles has done, and quickly, before we arrive home."

Girolamo slowly nodded.

"Thomas is right," he said. "I will write to the king tonight and report exactly what happened. Charles showed us the brief, made us swear it was genuine, and then had his scribe copy it in our presence. Three bishops swore to the accuracy of the copy and then sealed it."

"Yes," Edward interjected. "Three, not one or two, but *three* bishops, no less!"

"But it could have been a fake copy," Thomas said quietly.

Girolamo looked at him sharply.

"We are to suggest to the king that the copy Charles is sending him is a forgery?"

"No, no," Thomas clarified. "The copy that Charles is sending to him is a genuine copy, for sure. We cannot argue against that. We were present while it was produced! What I am suggesting is that we have no way of knowing for sure that the papal brief he showed us was legitimate at all. Who is to say the emperor did not instruct his scribes to compose that last night?"

Richard looked at Thomas in confusion.

"It is *possible* that the emperor has just authorized, in our presence and with three bishops present, an official copy of a forged brief," Thomas said.

Edward shook his head. "But the seal," he said. "We saw the papal seal."

"When was the last time you saw Pope Julius's seal? It has been fifteen years since any new documents have borne that seal. Each pope has a different one. I do not know about you, but I did not get a long look at that seal," Thomas argued. "Could it not be that Charles had one made to look like his? Maybe he never had the brief at all."

"But what of the three bishops who swore to its authenticity?" Edward asked.

"Perhaps they are indebted to Charles V."

"That is quite a conspiracy theory, Father," Girolamo said. "And not a very good one."

Thomas shrugged and averted Girolamo's gaze. He was right. He was a terrible liar, but perhaps it did not matter. If the proposed conspiracy confused Girolamo's suspicions, even for a moment, he and Edward might repeat it to Wolsey. And maybe that would be enough.

Besides, Wolsey would probably like the idea of a conspiracy. The king would shed no tears over the idea that the papal brief was possibly a forgery. Its existence only complicated the divorce proceedings. Nothing could make the king happier than believing that the papal brief, the special permission for his marriage, even if Arthur and Katherine had consummated their marriage, might have never truly existed and would definitely not appear in the courtroom.

"Well, at least he could have let us bring back the copy of the papal brief," Edward lamented. "At least we would not return to England empty-handed."

Girolamo raised his mug. "We are not coming back empty-handed," he said simply. "We faithfully delivered our message. The emperor, who is a close relation to the queen, quite naturally does not support King Henry in his wish to be divorced. That is beyond our control. Charles has said he will send a copy of the brief to the court, and now, it is simply time for us to return to England. We have acted judiciously. All will be well. Our king is gracious and just."

An uneasy silence between the four left Thomas wondering if even Girolamo believed his own words. They all stared at the table. Richard glanced nervously at Thomas, and for a moment, Thomas worried he had misjudged his traveling companion—that Richard was not his friend, but another of Wolsey's men, who would betray him to Edward and Girolamo. But Richard was silent.

Edward lifted his mug and proclaimed, "Indeed." Red wine sloshed onto the table. "Long live King Henry VIII!"

"Long live the king!" Richard quickly agreed.

Thomas said a silent prayer of thanks. Richard was an ally.

Catching Girolamo's gaze, he lifted his mug. "Long live King Henry VIII, the Sovereign King of our dear England!" *And long live Queen Katherine, Rightful Queen of England!*

Thomas tossed and turned, writhing like a fish caught in a net, until Richard touched his sweat-drenched forehead. Thomas woke with a start and sat up in the cold inn room, gasping, his breath hanging in the air like haunting specters.

"Nightmare?"

"Yes," Thomas muttered, still pulling himself from the morbid images that taunted his thoughts, foreboding images of death and torture, false smiles and hidden agendas, darkness, coldness, loneliness.

Richard made the sign of the cross over Thomas. "You did the right thing, Thomas," he said sleepily and turned over.

With a racing heart, Thomas stared wide-eyed at the ceiling, pulled the bedsheets closer to his face, and murmured, "Lord Jesus Christ, Son of God, have mercy." He closed his eyes and repeated it again, this time quietly beating his chest. He said the ancient prayer again and again until, at last, his eyes closed of their own will, and he drifted back into fitful sleep.

Moments later, the first rooster crowed, and the inn began buzzing in the predawn hour with the sounds of travelers rousing themselves for another early morning on the road. The journey back to England was long, the future uncertain, but it was a new day. Thomas rose, stretched his hands to the sky, and prayed the Lord's Prayer.

30

RETURN TO THE QUEEN

May 1529   Ampthill Castle

"Father Abell," Katherine began, her chin trembling as she met Thomas's eyes.

Thomas bowed slightly, his heart pounding.

"Thank you."

Her voice broke, and she looked away for a moment.

"Montoya told me what happened in Spain. And Ambassador Chapuys told me of your communication with Emperor Charles, how you presented our case, *my* case." Her light blue eyes held his. "I did not know you cared so deeply for my cause."

He could not break away from her gaze, so he held it.

"It was just, my Queen ..."

"I owe you an apology," she began, but he stepped toward her. He longed to grab her delicate hand and tell her he would defend her righteous honor as long as he lived. But he did not. He would not. It was not his place. He would let his actions speak. Her eyes watered. She knew.

"No, my Queen, I kept my intentions from you—indeed, from everyone. I needed time to decide how to act."

"You acted courageously," she said.

The room was quiet. The queen had dismissed her ladies in waiting, and now Thomas sat alone with Katherine, the rightful queen of England. They had spent many hours together, in her confessions and his sharing Mass, but there had always been a distance. Perhaps she had learned, long ago, not to trust men.

But he was not every man. He was Thomas Abell, a priest and a scholar. His body and soul belonged to God, his mind to knowledge, and his service to the Church and the Throne of England. He knew he held the queen's confidence, and now that they shared the intimate bond of vulnerability, he would not violate it.

Margaret bounced into the room, flushed as if she had just run down the hall. She smoothed renegade strands of hair, tucking them under her headdress as she spoke.

"The cardinals wish to see you, Your Majesty," she said breathlessly. "They are here."

Thomas could hear the sound of slow, heavy footsteps, and he watched as Katherine straightened her gray velvet dress. She took a deep breath and gathered her hands before her, clutching her rosary. She twisted the beads as her lips began to move silently. Moments later, Cardinal Wolsey and the elderly Cardinal Campeggio from Rome entered the queen's private chamber without invitation or apology.

Wolsey nodded to Thomas and spoke to Katherine as he held out an official Church document.

"Your Majesty, we are here to personally inform Your Highness that you have been summoned to appear before the legatine court to be held at Blackfriars on June 18th."

"It has been scheduled?" the queen questioned, receiving the parchment from Wolsey's hand.

"Yes," he said uncomfortably. "The king has consented to the Pope's court here in London. He will comply with our findings, and he expects your full cooperation."

The queen nodded. Thomas knew that she had been expecting the announcement, although he had hoped that Charles V's communication with his agents in Rome had been sufficient to move the proceedings to a more neutral ground. There seemed little chance the cardinals would rule against the king in his own castle. They would stand trial. The queen had only a few weeks to prepare. There would not be enough time for Charles V to send his legal experts. Perhaps other members of the queen's household would stand by her. He had heard that Bishop John Fisher was willing to speak out in her defense. But would it be enough?

31

THE TRIAL AT BLACKFRIARS COURT

June 21, 1529   London

Queen Katherine, the mighty Spanish Infanta, the reigning Queen of England, swept into the packed assembly room at Blackfriars exactly two decades after her spectacular coronation procession through London. That day, she had been dressed in virginal white, a triumphant young bride with auburn hair cascading down her sunlit back. With her coronation at Westminster, she had claimed her rightful place in the heart of her people. Today, dressed in black velvet and Spanish lace, she would defend it.

Thomas watched Katherine with a mixture of pride and anxiety. The queen's legal counsel had been able to postpone the trial over the weekend, but it was Monday morning, and the day had arrived.

Thomas had seen Queen Katherine privately humiliated in grief, her own sadness eroding her confidence. And it was good, so good, to see her walking tall, publicly standing for her rights, and in some ways, the rights of every Englishwoman. She would be queen, and it seemed that all of London had turned out to see her glory.

Thomas heard the women pressed along the cobblestone path shouting, "Queen Katherine!" and "Fear not!" He had even heard, "May God grant you victory over your enemies!"—a bold prayer repeated again and again.

Even King Henry seemed to be aware of the raucous adoration and ordered a courtier to beat the commoners away from Blackfriars' entrance. But even from behind the closed friary doors, the women's voices continued as a muffled din, a background noise that not even closed doors and bolted windows could fully shut out. It made Thomas smile.

When Katherine entered the friary, she acknowledged the protesters, pressing her hands together in a pious pose, nodding. "Thank you," she mouthed, though her voice was not heard above the noise. "Pray!"

As she moved into the assembly hall, surrounded by lords and ladies, courtiers and clerics, the cardinals and her king, she lifted her gaze to the ceiling as if fixing her eyes on an unseen realm. Her chest slowly heaved under a heavy cross pendant, and her lips moved in silent petition. Her fingers worked the rosary beads in her hands, and she walked deliberately, making her way through the crowded assembly room to the temporary throne Wolsey's men had constructed for her.

King Henry, having taken the easier route to Blackfriars by water, gliding down the Thames River to the tune of his own trumpets and regalia, was already seated on his temporary throne under a canopy of shimmering gold cloth. His dais, built slightly higher than Katherine's pedestal and positioned on the opposite side of the court from Katherine's, provided him with the perfect vantage to observe her entrance and the overwhelming support she garnered from their adoring people. He scowled.

The day that Thomas had asked Charles V to prevent was here. The Pope's legatine court would hear the king's annulment request in London. Together, Cardinals Campeggio and Wolsey would decide the fate of the royal marriage, but Thomas already knew how Wolsey felt about the matter. It hardly seemed like a fair trial.

Perhaps the letter Charles V sent to the Pope requesting the court be moved to Rome had not arrived in time to delay the London court. Perhaps the Pope could not be bothered by the quarreling of two English regents.

Thomas clutched his own rosary and willed his spirit to calm as his fingers remembered the prayers of his heart. He prayed for himself and for Katherine.

"Silence!" the court official cried. "The King of England comes into the court."

The crowd's murmuring ceased. The absurdity of it all, the King of England summoned to his own trial! In Henry's impatience, he had submitted himself to the power of the legatine court and agreed to a public display of his most intimate affairs. Now, all of London watched.

King Henry VIII rose from his throne, stood under his golden canopy, and addressed the two cardinals seated in makeshift, gold-covered judgment seats.

"Cardinals, representatives of his most Holy Pope Clement and the Church in Rome, I ask you to make a swift decision to determine whether my marriage is holy before God. As I have confided in you and in the Pope in Rome, I have been plagued with scruples, perpetually, since the beginning of my marriage with Katherine, and I ask you to deliver me from my concerns. I submit to your ruling, should you decide that my marriage is valid or not."

Cardinal Wolsey, dressed in his most ornate scarlet vestment and square cap, stood up. It was his turn to recite his lines, and Thomas could not help but feel that it was the worst play he had ever seen performed on any stage.

"Most gracious king and queen, I humbly acknowledge that I have received infinite benefits from Your Highness, both material and immaterial. Nonetheless, I *assure you* that Cardinal Campeggio and I intend before God Almighty to judge this ever-important case only according to the facts and our consciences."

Then the elderly Italian cardinal painstakingly stood, grunting as he put his full weight on his swollen, gout-stricken feet.

"Your Majesty Queen Katherine," he said, slowly addressing the queen. "We have considered your request to move this court to Rome." He paused, catching his breath, "And we have decided, for the sake of expediency, we will continue here in London."

A murmur erupted through the hand-picked crowd. From his place behind the barrister, Thomas could not tell if the people were more outraged that the queen's request was denied or relieved that the most sensational spectacle in recent history would remain in London. But in truth, it did not matter. The show would continue.

"Silence!" the crier interrupted.

"I assure you that as representatives of the Pope, and God Himself, we will judge impartially," Campeggio continued.

The cardinal sat down, and the crier shouted, "The court now calls Queen Katherine of England. Come into the court!"

As Katherine rose, Thomas felt the weight of every eye focused on his queen, his sole spiritual charge, and he remembered his promise to pray for her. He rotated the rosary in his hands. *Father in Heaven...*

"Cardinal Thomas Wolsey, Cardinal Campeggio," she addressed the judges. "I repeat my request that this court be adjourned and moved to Rome, where it can be heard in front of an impartial audience. As the servant of our king, Cardinal Wolsey, I do not believe that you possess the impartiality to hear this case according to the facts and your conscience, as you say."

Wolsey did not nod, but he let her speak.

She turned her attention to King Henry.

"My dear husband, our Majesty King Henry VIII, I have but one thing to say to you. You have told the court of your scruples concerning our marriage, but we have been married for twenty years. Now ..." She blinked, her chin trembling. "Now is not the time to speak of your scruples ... having been silent for so long!"

Again the crowd erupted in murmurs. This time, Thomas was certain Katherine held their approval as he heard "Aye, aye" and "Amen" echoing throughout the hall.

"Silence!"

The king looked stricken.

"My dear Katherine," King Henry began, "I remained silent only because of the great love I have for you." He placed his hand over his heart. "I had sincerely hoped that our marriage would be declared valid in the eyes of God."

He paused for a moment and then shook his head.

"But Katherine..." His voice took on a darker tone. "Do not believe for a moment that by moving this court to Rome, we will have a more impartial setting."

He paused, the heat rising in his cheeks. The room fell silent.

"Are you *not* the Queen of England?" he spat. "Do you not trust your own courts to judge you fairly?"

Katherine silently faced him, chin slightly elevated, eyes fixed on his throne, while he continued to lecture her on her English duty.

Then suddenly, while Henry was still talking, Katherine stepped down from her dais and began picking her way through the crowd. His voice fell silent as the crowd murmured and dispersed around her.

When Katherine arrived at Henry's feet, she dropped to her knees, her thick velvet robes spilling around her.

"My King, my dear husband," she began with outstretched hands.

Henry reached down to pull her up, but as soon as he let go of her shoulder, she knelt again.

"Consider my honor, your honor, your daughter's honor," she pleaded. "You should not be displeased by me defending our honor."

Thomas could hear the crowd murmuring. Katherine was giving the performance of her life, and she only had eyes for the king.

"You must consider not only our marriage and your own concerns, dear husband, but also the reputation of my country, and my relatives who have invested so much in the Spanish-English alliance."

With this, Henry tried to interrupt her, pull her to her feet, but she continued pleading. She reached out and grabbed the king's red silk slippers, holding both feet in her hands like she might kiss them or wash them, whatever he chose.

"When I appealed to Rome, it seemed reasonable for the matter to be settled there. This present court has already become the subject of suspicion, Your Majesty. And furthermore, as you know, the case was already begun in Rome," she said.

She rose slightly and clasped her hands as she so often had in the royal chapel.

"Surely, my Lord, as it is your desire to have the Holy Church determine the validity of our marriage, *surely* that would be best done in Rome with the Pope himself presiding over such an important affair."

Henry's face flushed, and his hands trembled. Did his conscience truly trouble him, or was he just embarrassed by Katherine's public display of affection?

Henry waved his hand as if to dismiss Katherine. He rubbed his hands and cleared his throat. "Please, dear Katherine, of course, of course, I have our honor in mind," he said. "Whatever you think is best."

The moment he uttered the words, the crowd began murmuring.

Cardinal Campeggio looked at Cardinal Wolsey and nodded gravely.

The queen rose laboriously, smoothing her crushed dress, and curtseyed low, never taking her eyes off Henry. She straightened her back and held her head high, as if absorbing all the crowd's approval as they muttered, "Well said," and "Long live the queen." The crowd parted as she began walking back to her side of the courtroom, but instead of returning to her throne, she kept walking.

"Call her back," Henry demanded. "The court is in session. Call her back!"

The crier shouted above the din of the crowd.

"The queen is called back to court!"

But Katherine was already out the door.

"They are calling for you, Your Majesty. Will you not return?" Thomas asked breathlessly as he caught up with the queen. She was stepping up into her carriage, her attendants already gathering up her dress as she mounted the coach.

"No!" she said, her cheeks flushed with passion, her eyes brimming with tears. "This court is fixed. Will Cardinal Wolsey rule against his sovereign?" She shook her head, her golden earrings bouncing in agreement. No, he would not. No one knew this better than Thomas.

Thomas climbed into the coach beside the queen. If she was leaving, he would follow.

They left in silence, the noise of the crowd fading with every hoofbeat. He took Katherine's hand as the hot tears rolled down her cheeks.

32

WHEN CARDINALS FAIL

The cardinal sat at his desk with an open bottle of wine, papers strewn across the table. The trial was well underway, and things were not going as smoothly for the king. Crumpled parchment and bits of spent candles littered the floor. Clearly, it had been a long night.

Wolsey glowered at his attendant, and the young man departed a bit too eagerly, Thomas thought.

"What happened in Saragossa?" Wolsey demanded when the two were alone.

The old cardinal looked like he had not slept in days. His hands trembled, and he squinted as if tormented by a headache.

"Are you well, Cardinal?" Thomas deflected.

"No," the cardinal moaned. "Not at all."

He looked at Thomas warily. "I have slept very little these past few weeks, the king's Great Matter, and all... It weighs heavily on me, very heavily."

Thomas frowned, a pang of sympathy invading his heart. Was it the cardinal's fault that he had been tasked with the impossible job of making the king happy?

"That Fisher," Wolsey began, "that Bishop John Fisher is making this so much worse, charging up the court in Katherine's favor, complicating the truth of this matter." Wolsey shook his head and closed his eyes. "He is an evil man, simply evil."

"Evil?" Thomas asked, raising an eyebrow.

Wolsey eyed Thomas. Perhaps he should just let the old cardinal rant.

"He makes this process more difficult, confusing the public, confusing Cardinal Campeggio... Confusing me," he confessed, closing his eyes again. He pressed his hands to his head. "It is the definition of evil."

Evil because his convictions are inconvenient to the king? Thomas looked out the window into the bright summer light, thinking about Fisher's speech, his defense for the sanctity of marriage and the Pope's authority to grant it. There was a conviction behind his words, a courage that Thomas admired.

"Bishop Fisher said it was a cause he was willing to die for."

There was a hint of admiration in Thomas's voice, and Wolsey looked up at him wearily. "Yes, I know, Thomas!" He closed his eyes and cradled his head in his hands. "The king, my king, my dearest friend, asks this of me, this simple task of the highest churchman in England, and I cannot give it to him. Oh, Holy Mother of God, this will be the ruin of me."

Thomas shifted uncomfortably but said nothing. Wolsey shook his head, and then suddenly his brow furrowed, and he turned his full attention to Thomas.

"So, Thomas, what really happened in Saragossa?"

Thomas took in a deep breath. "My cardinal," he said deliberately. "We have spoken of this at length. The emperor would not suffer the original document to leave Spain." He sighed. "I presented you with the certified copy."

Wolsey shook his head and narrowed his eyes. "Yes, but *why?*"

Thomas's stomach churned. He remembered Father Martin's words about keeping his thoughts to himself, and he simply held Wolsey's gaze until the cardinal dropped it. Finally Wolsey turned his attention to a parchment on his desk.

"Well, Thomas, I still have to report to the Pope and the king. Pray that God gives me wisdom."

Thomas smiled. That was a prayer he could pray.

July 1529   Greenwich Palace

Thomas walked slowly, keeping pace with the queen as they rounded the royal rose garden at Greenwich Palace. Red, pink, white roses, each one open and fragrant in the prime of its summer glory. But the queen seemed oblivious, anxiously turning her rosary as she walked. Every few steps, she stopped to pray and then continued walking. Thomas moved in rhythm with her and listened.

"Bishop Fisher is representing you well," Thomas finally said when Katherine had made her way through her rosary beads and seemed exhausted with the practice. The sky darkened as the afternoon sun slid behind gray clouds. "He raised several good points with the cardinals. They seem hesitant to rush to a judgment."

Katherine stopped walking.

"But will they move the court to Rome?" she asked. "It needs to be in Rome."

"That would be ideal," he agreed. Katherine asked for what only Heaven could give, and was satisfied with nothing less. How could he, her counselor and friend, prepare her for the very real possibility that the king would find a way to get what he wanted—even if Wolsey failed to convince the Pope—even if Rome never consented to an annulment?

"The king has asked me again to consider a nunnery," Katherine said, looking at the ground. "He is living openly with his mistress, and he wishes me to be out of the way."

Thomas held his breath.

"But to give in to his demands, to be stripped of my crown, for my Mary to be bastardized ..." A crackle of thunder boomed across the summer afternoon sky. "I think it's going to rain," she said as the drops began falling in rapid succession.

"My Lady!" Margaret yelled, dashing to catch up to the queen with her own scarf unfurled and ready to place over the queen's head. "Let's get you into the palace." Despite her urgency, the young woman was giggling, and the queen caught her mood, laughing heartily as they hurried clumsily into the castle.

The rain came in a torrent, and the two laughed as the king's gardener ran across the yard, wheelbarrow in tow, soaked to the skin.

"Well," Katherine said. "That was something."

Something was something. Better than the waiting. And Thomas smiled, grateful for the distraction.

"Your Highness." A young household servant bowed low as he spoke. "An urgent message for you."

The queen took the parchment from the boy, opened it, and closed her eyes.

"Sweet Mother of God, Jesus, thank you, thank you."

Thomas and the ladies in waiting gathered in close.

"The Cardinal Campeggio has adjourned the court," she said, wiping away tears. "He says it's a harvest holiday in Rome." She covered her mouth, concealing her smile, but the corners of her eyes creased in delight.

Margaret stared. "In Rome?"

"Yes," Katherine said, rereading the note, "in Rome."

Thomas laughed out loud. So that was how the old cardinal would solve the crisis. Delay. Delay. Delay. And if all else fails, adjourn. They were back in limbo—a purgatory of indecision. At least it gave them more time. But time to do what?

To serve the queen. What had Father Martin said? Others would take up Katherine's cause—already Bishop Fisher was doing that. Thomas should listen to Katherine's confession and offer Mass. He took a deep breath. He could do that.

33

WOLSEY FALLS

October 1529

"You wished to see me?" Thomas asked as he entered Wolsey's darkened privy chamber. The cardinal was alone, shades drawn at midday, looking very much like a child who had been scolded by his tutor, wild with anxiety for the punishment awaiting and quieted with the knowledge that what would be would be.

"Yes," said the cardinal softly. "I've given my wealth and possessions to the king—York place, Hampton Court, the Manor of More, the horses, the furnishings, my collection of Flemish tapestries, my gold and silver plate, all of it," he said with a deep sigh. "It seems that it would be best for me to serve our dear King Henry in Yorkshire. And thus... I am leaving tomorrow... by the first light of dawn."

"I have heard," said Thomas. "I am sorry."

The announcement was not news to Thomas. The whole court and everyone in London knew of the king's vengeance on Cardinal Thomas Wolsey. The king was charging him in his own royal court for *premunire*, an ancient convention designed to prevent Church officials from overstepping their bounds. In Wolsey's failure, he had become an obstacle in the king's path. Wolsey, it seemed, had forced the will of the Pope into an area of the king's authority. He had crossed the king and done it for the Church. Never mind that Wolsey had worked tirelessly for the king to prevail.

Thomas shuddered. Oh, how the mighty have fallen!

Even Katherine had warned that if Wolsey failed to give Henry what he wanted, the old cardinal would face his wrath. And now that the Blackfriars legatine court had been indefinitely adjourned, without a victory for the king and his increasingly demanding mistress, King Henry turned his frustration on Wolsey.

"Anne Boleyn never liked me," Wolsey complained. "Not since I got in the way of that affair with Percy... No, no, she never trusted me to do for the king what was right for the king, and, alas, now it is too late. She holds the power, and I, the king's faithful servant, have been discarded, as it were."

Thomas listened quietly. Katherine herself had never trusted Wolsey. She resented his influence over her husband, and she was free in telling Thomas so, but neither of them could have predicted the downfall of such a great man, the Alter Rex, the one who commanded both Heaven and Earth, both church and secular affairs.

"What really happened in Saragossa?" the cardinal asked abruptly, sounding very much like a jealous lover. "I could really have used the original papal brief, undermining the queen's claim to her precious virginity. The least that I could have done was destroy it and prevent the queen from ever using it.... Lee told me that while Charles berated him about the *validity* of the king's marriage and the *dishonor* of his divorce, you were silent—silent, Thomas. You said nothing."

Thomas pursed his lips. They had already talked about this.

"Lee told me you helped Ghinucci write his opinion that, perhaps, the papal brief was a fake, a possible counterfeit," he chuckled. "That was a good one, Father Abell. After all, you knew it was not."

He looked critically at Thomas.

"It got me thinking," Wolsey said, large green eyes narrowing. "If you are such a good actor, what are you playing at? What is your game?"

Thomas smiled. At one time, Wolsey's threat would have left him shaking in his shoes, but not anymore. Too much had happened—too many miles on the road to Spain and back. And Wolsey was not, well, Wolsey anymore.

"I do not play games, Cardinal," he said. "I am an honest man."

"But?"

"I was hoping to help Lee by suggesting ways the document *could have been* falsified, but I never said that I thought it was. It was obvious to all of us that we had seen the real thing. I merely pointed out the conditions under which the brief could have been considered to be a copy, hypothetically."

Wolsey rubbed his hands together.

"Why did Charles insist on keeping it in Spain?"

"I think you know," Thomas said.

The cardinal smiled. "So, you told him to keep it there."

Thomas held the cardinal's piercing gaze steadily.

"Charles understood the value of the brief. You underestimated him, Cardinal, if you thought he would send it to England and risk all evidence that the Pope had made allowances for the king and queen's marriage... even if it had been consummated."

"Even if!" Wolsey shook his head. "*Even if* I live to be a hundred years, I hope I never have to hear those words again." The cardinal turned wistfully to Thomas. "But the queen still holds to her claim that the marriage was never consummated with Prince Arthur? She was *virgo intacta*?"

"The queen has not changed her story."

"And she will not," Wolsey said. "She is the most stubborn princess ever born to kings."

Thomas smiled.

"But Thomas, is it true that you are faithful to the Crown?" Wolsey asked with more anxiety than threat.

"Yes," Thomas said. *To the queen's crown.*

"That's good," Wolsey said, still watching Thomas's face. "We have to support our king... to the end."

34

REFLECTION IN THE GARDEN

December 1529   Greenwich Palace

The crisp morning chill permeated Thomas's winter vestments, piercing through his clothing despite the extra woolen layer he wore between his ecclesiastical robe and his linen tunic. He shivered and wrapped his arms around his chest, stamped his leather boots, and rubbed his red hands together. How long would it take the queen to arrive for her mid-morning walk? Was it his imagination, or was she slowing down, taking longer to wind through her daily routine?

He looked across the royal garden.

The final leaves had fallen from the trees. Two weeks ago, he had noticed the first frost, and now it greeted him every morning as he walked silently through the palace garden in his daily predawn ritual of private prayer and contemplation. Wolsey was gone, and the winter was coming fast. Soon, the days would be colder, shorter, darker.

The rosebushes had gone dormant, and the gardeners had swept away nearly every fallen leaf. They had even brushed and groomed the sand walkway, preparing it for the coming layer of snow that would surely fall any day. Brown winter sparrows hopped along the path, pecking for the bits of stale bread the gardener tossed.

Walking toward the king's fountain, Thomas reached into the pool to retrieve a single brown leaf that had fallen in. As he reached, he caught a glimpse of his reflection, his quiet, stern face now framed with gray hair. When had that happened? How long had he been in the queen's household, two years? It felt like more. Soon, his last batch of Oxford students would be graduated and moved into new roles—hopefully serving at country parishes all over England, far from the politics of London.

What would become of him?

Would he serve the queen until she grew old and died?

Would the king force Katherine into a nunnery and disperse her household? Would Thomas go back to Oxford? Perhaps he could return to Essex and be near his family? The queen had given him a benefice, a prize for his loyalty and service, a parish in Bradwell in Sussex. He could retire there, serve as a parish priest, and live off the proceeds of the land. Though he had never seen the little village of Bradwell or the surrounding landscape, he smiled to think of its woolly sheep, the rolling fields of green, the wandering chickens, and the children singing as they walked along the village path. It could be like Heaven on Earth.

But would King Henry allow any of it?

Cardinal Thomas Wolsey had lost everything. He was nearly under house arrest in the far northern country of York, and there were rumors that the king still was not satisfied. Perhaps Wolsey had been wrong. Maybe the king would hang the clergy.

Thomas looked back at his reflection. Would the king turn against the clergy loyal to Katherine?

Thomas heard the crunch of gravel behind him and looked up to see the queen and her ladies turning into the garden. The winter sparrows flittered away. What good was it to worry? The birds neither sowed nor reaped. The heavenly Father fed them. Was Thomas not more valuable than these? Worrying would not add a single hour to his life.

Thomas rose and greeted the queen. One day at a time. That was the only way to serve the Lord.

35

A GATHERING OF PRIESTS

August 1531   London

A year had passed since the Pope announced a Roman harvest holiday, and still, the king had not gotten the annulment he so desperately wanted. Court gossip whispered that Henry followed Anne Boleyn around like he was bewitched, a fool. The king never called for Katherine, and she rarely attended his state dinners and lavish feasts. When the occasion required her presence, she wore black like a widow and treated the king with all the pained civility of a jilted lover. The next morning, she would spend hours in confession, exorcising the evil thoughts that had come to her, unwanted, as she saw the king dote on his mistress.

Thomas had come to dread these public appearances with the queen and found himself agreeing with her every time she justified her excuse for not attending such affairs. It was safer for the queen's household to stay as far away from the king's household as any royal palace would allow two parties to be.

Thomas had just heard that the queen's household would soon all be leaving together. Within a fortnight, the queen and all her servants would be moving to their own residence, entirely away from Henry. So Thomas was more than a little surprised when one of the king's pages dropped him a note, summoning him to the king's private quarters.

When he arrived, he recognized everyone around the table: his friend Richard Featherstone, John Fisher, John Forrest, Thomas Cranmer, Arnold Baker, Thomas More, and a dozen more. The shoulder-to-shoulder assembly of black-robed clergy gathering in King Henry's privy chamber was a short list of the royal household's elite chaplains, confessors, and secular priests like Thomas Wolsey, who served as royal administrators. They were all men Thomas Abell had come to know over the past four years in the royal household.

These were the men who offered the daily elements, prepared sermons, listened to the confessions of the royal family, and humbly offered spiritual advice when queried. They served independently of each other, rarely consulting even among themselves. They had certainly never been gathered in assembly. Why had they been summoned?

As Thomas looked around at the collection of men, tall and short, young and old, one thing seemed similar for all: each man crowding around the king's privy table had a reputation for piety, a trait that had once made them attractive for the king and queen's household. But as Father Martin had said, the world was changing quickly. It was possible that the king no longer favored any of them. He certainly held John Fisher at least partly responsible for his failure at Blackfriars.

Thomas caught Richard's glance and nodded. Whatever was about to happen, they were together, like they had been in Spain. The old bishop, John Forrest, also gave Thomas a slight smile. Thomas knew that he was a loyal man of strong conviction. He would stand with him too. *Be strong and courageous. The Lord is with us.* Thomas felt his rosary under his cloak. *The Lord is with us.*

When the heavy wooden door opened, it was not King Henry who emerged but Thomas Wolsey's administrative clerk. The stoic Thomas Cromwell, with a heavy ledger and ink-stained fingers, stood before them, scowling as if he had already delivered his bad news.

"Fathers, priests of the royal household." He addressed them solemnly. "It has been two years since Thomas Wolsey departed for Yorkshire... and then passed on." He paused. "Of course, Sir Thomas More has served the king as the Lord Chancellor." Cromwell nodded to More, who sat at the end of the table, arms crossed, face drawn.

Cromwell continued, "I have called you here this morning to renew your affection and loyalties to the Crown," he said as if he were not threatening them but inviting them to a tea party in the rose garden. "And I want to warn you, King Henry has grown weary of clergy who are more loyal to Rome than his court. Yes, you are priests, but you are Englishmen as well. The king demands to know if you intend to support him and his God-given right to rule these people with fairness and justice or if you will support the foreign princes who manipulate the Pope."

"We support our king! Long live King Henry!" said a young priest with a thick head of curly blond hair and fat cheeks. Thomas recognized him as Arnold Baker, a Cambridge graduate.

"Long live King Henry," the priests parroted without making eye contact with each other.

"May God bless our king forever," said Thomas Cranmer, the king's new private chaplain. He pressed his hands together in a dramatic act of piety. "We support the king."

Cromwell nodded with satisfaction and motioned to Cranmer. Cranmer stood up.

"The king has requested the universities of England, the educated theologians of his realm, to prepare opinions of his case, to give biblical responses to his concerns about his marriage." Cranmer spoke with gravity. "The Pope's legatine court has been in recess for more than a year! And our good king needs a definitive answer as to whether his connection to Queen Katherine is legitimate or not. He cannot wait forever."

Thomas listened.

"He may ask any one of you to also help draft an opinion," Cromwell added, opening the leather-bound ledger and taking out a stack of printed parchment that he had squeezed between the folds of the book.

A young clerk standing beside Cromwell took his cue and began distributing the pieces of printed parchment, an official notice detailing the king's request for academic opinions.

"I am posting these official requests today. They will be sent to Oxford and Cambridge as well as Paris and even Bologna and Padua," Thomas Cromwell announced. "King Henry is hopeful to garner not only support for his position but honest opinions concerning Pope Julius's decision to overrule the Levitical code as he did when allowing Henry's marriage in 1509. The king is increasingly concerned that Pope Julius erred in his dispensation, and if this is the case, we seek the learned opinions of European scholars. Should they agree with the king, it may help Pope Clement to view the king's position with favor."

Cromwell smiled for a brief second.

"We think that perhaps Pope Clement is already of the same opinion as King Henry, but he may be reluctant to publicly profess that his predecessor had made an error, which is quite understandable. However, if the universities consider this difficulty and conclude that Pope Julius erred, then it will clear the way for Pope Clement to undo the damage that has been done."

Thomas looked at the parchment in his hand, requesting, in Latin, the opinions of scholars worldwide. Cromwell made it sound so simple and logical, like trading cattle or bartering for wool. Undo? How could a pope undo twenty years of marriage? Could Princess Mary's life be undone?

"I am notifying all of you, because the king may ask a few of you to contribute to these academic responses. I am sure that you all remember how our esteemed Thomas More and others have helped draft theological statements for the king in the past. This is no different."

Thomas looked at More, but the great philosopher was staring at the parchment. He looked a little pale, and he did not lift his head at the mention of his name. A chill ran up Thomas's spine. Perhaps this time *was* different. *Lord, Jesus, Son of God, have mercy on us...*

36

SMITHFIELD

"Do you think More will help the king?" Richard said in a low voice as he and Thomas left the king's privy chamber and headed into the crowded courtyard. "He looked like he was going to be ill."

"I thought *I* would be ill," Thomas said. "I have opinions about our king's interpretation of Leviticus, but I would rather not share any of it with him." He shook his head. "I don't know why Cromwell is singling us out. Surely there are plenty of clergy who agree with the king's actions."

Richard looked gravely at Thomas. "The king seems to be moving in that direction. I think he is planning to expose those who disagree with him."

Thomas looked down at the cobblestone under his long strides. "I hope you are wrong."

"Perhaps ..." Richard stopped abruptly. "Thomas! Speaking of those who disagree with the king, have you heard about the nun from Kent?"

"Elizabeth Barton? The one who sees visions? Her work is ... interesting. My sister Agnes wrote to me about this. She said there had been miracles, one boy from their village and another woman from Colchester. Agnes was excited."

"Yes!" said Richard, cautiously glancing around as they continued walking. "But she has become quite political."

Thomas raised an eyebrow. "How so?"

"She says the king has no right to divorce his wife. Says God will punish him for his wickedness. Punish England too."

"She says this publicly?"

"Yes!" Richard nodded emphatically. "She tried to meet with the king, but he would not see her. But she stayed in London anyway. She is out preaching in the marketplace, Smithfield."

Thomas stopped.

"Smithfield? She is not afraid?"

"I suppose not."

"St. Bartholomew's Prior?"

"Yes, the same place."

"Oh," Richard said with a sudden spring in his step, caution forgotten. "And it's Bartholomew's Feast Day this week! Gingerbread, jugglers, acrobats! Feel like stretching your legs a bit, Thomas?"

Thomas laughed. Why not? A little merriment could go a long way to lift his spirits. And who could ever turn down a chance for gingerbread?

The two priests walked in silence, leaving the castle courtyard and wandering through the narrow cobblestone street. They passed the imposing white Tower of London and headed up the hill toward the outskirts of the city, where a large marshy field had given way to a monastery and marketplace.

Smithfield was a hub of activity, a place Thomas remembered fondly from childhood trips with his father. Farmers drove their cattle and sheep to the open field, while local merchants set up tables around the friary to sell their soap and leather goods. Now, at the end of the summer, there would be fresh vegetables and farmers' wives with honeycomb and baskets of eggs. And on Bartholomew's feast day, there would be gingerbread too.

Thomas smiled at the memory. How he missed Father! He could almost hear his voice in his head, warning him that where money changed hands freely, there would be pickpockets, cutpurses, beggars, and street performers, all types of sinners and sorry fellows vying for the loose change that would so inevitably fall from the hands of hardworking men into the muddy palms of vagrants.

To sober those who would take advantage of the carnival at-
mosphere, there was always at least one unfortunate youth shack-
led, wrists and ankles, in the sheriff's stocks. Women would drag
their dawdling boys along, lecturing them about the hazards of
immoral living. The boys would scowl and peek at the young men
in stocks, heads hanging, hands dangling, mud on their faces.
Thomas remembered it all so well.

But the real deterrent to crime was not the soiled stocks and
young men cringing in shame. The harrowing row of old elm trees
lording over the boundaries of the ancient open space was the real
terror. For children old enough to understand, those high trees
testified to the full extent of the law.

In addition to the wool trade and fresh gingerbread treats,
Smithfield was also a place of regular public hangings, executions, heretic burnings, and worse, the old elm trees often serving as the scaffolding from which these poor souls hung. The no-
torious William Wallace had met his end here—hanged, drawn,
and quartered—and Thomas knew that he would not be the last.
The grotesque, bloody stakes along the Thames River stood ready,
waiting for the next unfortunate head.

The nun from Kent was either brave or foolhardy.

"Queen Katherine is setting out for Wolsey's old estate, The
Manor on the More," Thomas said as they walked toward Smithfield. "The king has ordered her to go."

Richard nodded. "It has come to that," he said with resignation,
"a separation."

"It seems. The king left without saying 'goodbye.' Queen
Katherine was beside herself. But I am sure you heard about that."
Thomas shook his head. "I suppose you will return with Mary's
household to Ludlow?"

"For now," Richard murmured. "Until I am replaced."

"Replaced?"

"Thomas, surely you must realize that the king is putting pres-
sure on not only Katherine but also Mary. He demands the child
denounce her mother. His spies are throughout the household,

reporting back to him. I've seen the way the new clerics look at me. It is only a matter of time before Cromwell ferrets out all who hold allegiance to the queen."

Richard wiped a bead of sweat from his forehead.

"And then?"

Richard stopped short. The two had come to the outskirts of Smithfield, and they could see a crowd gathering around a young woman in a nun's habit. She was standing on an overturned apple crate, dramatically waving her arms and shouting, her shrill voice echoing off the distant stone walls of Bartholomew's monastery.

"I think that must be her," Richard said. "The nun from Kent."

"God will not approve of this deceit," Elizabeth Barton screeched in a voice not quite used to shouting in public. "He has shown me that if the King of England proceeds with this folly, it will have dire consequences for England, for this country, and for you!"

Thomas and Richard eased into the crowd, keeping close to the back of what seemed to be a hundred onlookers. Why didn't the friary guards shut the spectacle down? Were the king's spies watching the crowd even now, noting dissenters?

"You speak against God's anointed king?!" a fat merchant in leather breeches shouted.

The crowd murmured, and Thomas heard a volley of slurs and insults, both against the king and his mistress, as well as the nun and her overturned apple crate.

The nun from Kent began shaking. "It is God who is against the king. I have seen it. Aye! Yes, I have seen the king's future in a dream."

The crowd hushed.

She closed her eyes, stretched her arms above her head, and moaned.

Thomas crossed his arms. What was this performance?

"God almighty has shown me that if this king continues in his sin and folly, if he discards the wife of his youth, his queen ..." The crowd began making booing sounds.

One man growled, "The king's sin will be the downfall of us all!"

"If the king leaves his wife and marries the harlot, Anne," Elizabeth Barton said, raising her voice to a fevered pitch, "King Henry will not live a year, not seven months more, before he will die."

Someone gasped. The nun from Kent really was prophesying the king's death. How long until this would be recognized as a threat, a treasonous outburst?

"Yes," the woman said, wagging her outstretched finger. Her whole body shook like an invisible fist was wrestling her tiny frame, and then she stepped down from the apple crate and collapsed into the arms of two other nuns who stood at her feet. "The king will die," she gasped as if she herself physically felt the pain of whatever ailment would cause his demise.

"We should leave," Thomas said. "Thomas Cromwell's spies are surely taking note of the crowd."

With the abrupt conclusion of the nun's ecstatic performance, the crowd murmured. Arguments broke out. A young man threw a spoiled squash at the nun, followed by other people throwing rotten fruit at him.

Thomas heard a man shout, "Treason! She speaks treason against the king!" But another voice said, "The king dishonors God!" Another squash flew into the air, landing beside Thomas's feet. Frothing brown squash flesh exploded over his black vestments. Other rotten vegetables flew, and then the shouting turned to shoving.

"Let's go," Thomas said, grabbing Richard's elbow and pulling him away from the fray. "I've seen enough."

37

A Separation

August 1531

Thomas gripped the carriage bench, bracing himself against the violent jostling of the royal coach as it lumbered through the English countryside, away from London and King Henry, away from his court and his Great Matter. The queen looked distressed, closing her eyes and clutching her rosary in one hand, the velvet-upholstered side of the coach with the other. How much farther to the queen's new residence? How many more potholes would they endure on the road to exile?

"Are you well, my Queen?" Thomas asked, although he had asked the same question a half hour ago.

Katherine nodded, not opening her eyes. She was likely about as well as he was.

When King Henry moved into Cardinal Wolsey's expansive Hampton Court, he informed Katherine that she would have to find other accommodations. There was simply not enough room in Wolsey's mansion for Katherine and the woman he so desperately desired.

The king suggested another of Wolsey's estates, The Manor of the More, a large, remote house about twenty miles northeast of Hampton. And like most things in life, Katherine complied. She would do the king's bidding, so long as she kept her title as queen.

Although the journey was a dawn-to-dusk horseback ride, the queen's entourage moved at a turtle's pace, stretching the trip into a multi-day affair. The queen's intimates traveled with her, her ladies-in-waiting, her priests and counselors, as well as a physician, horsemen, cooks, and a small host of soldiers.

The soldiers seemed a bit excessive, Thomas thought, as the entire countryside seemed to be brimming with the queen's devotees yelling, "God save the queen!"

At each encounter with peasants, Katherine leaned out of the coach window, demurely nodding and pressing her fingertips together, intimating that she was praying for them. The women often cried as Katherine's carriage passed. Were the tears for his lady or their own woes? Surely, the women of England had their own heartaches and betrayals, sicknesses, disappointments, and depravities. But perhaps that was why they loved Katherine. Though nobly born and well-fed, she suffered no less than they.

A violent jolt threw the carriage forward with a loud crack, and Thomas felt his body lurch forward, his shoulder slamming into the queen and her lady Margaret.

"By God's heart ..." Margaret exclaimed as Thomas pulled himself off, examining first the blood on his hands and then the queen's terrified face.

"Are you harmed, my Queen?"

But before she could offer a weak affirmation, the master of the queen's guard thrust open the carriage door.

"Queen Katherine? Are you well?"

Confused and bleeding, Thomas pulled himself up and offered the queen a hand. She placed her ringed hand in his, and he settled her back on the carriage bench.

"Yes," the queen said slowly to the soldier as if trying to convince herself. "I am fine."

"We hit a hole in the road, a large one!" the guard explained.

Another soldier ran up to the carriage's open door. "Your Majesty, one of our horses has gone lame, and the carriage wheel will need to be repaired," he said. "The nearest town would take a few hours to walk to. With a horse, our men can reach it in an hour and, perhaps, send back help."

The company of soldiers gathered around the carriage, facing out against the twilight-bathed forest, preparing for whatever attack could be imminent. Sometimes, potholes in the road were built as traps to catch wealthy caravans. The queen's soldiers would take no chances.

Katherine suddenly laughed.

"I remember a time Henry did this as a game," she said, covering her mouth with the memory of her surprise. "His men, dressed as bandits, rushed into my room and would have me believe that the castle itself was under attack ... until Henry rushed in to save the day." She smiled. "Henry was always the hero."

Margaret took Katherine's trembling hand and caressed it.

"This is not the king's doing, my Lady. We cannot stay here along the road in the darkness," she said, looking to Thomas for guidance.

Thomas wiped the blood from his mouth. He must have caught his lip on something sharp.

"You are bleeding, Father," Margaret said.

"I am fine," he said. "Attend to the queen."

"Send three or four men ahead into the nearest town," Thomas said to the captain of the guard. "Bring back the best carriage they have for the queen. I will stay here with whatever men you have left."

The soldier nodded. "We will send three, and three will stay here. That is all we have," he said. And Thomas suddenly realized that the queen's detachment of soldiers was scarcely sufficient.

"Leave me with a crossbow," he said. "I'll stay close to the queen and her ladies."

The soldier handed Thomas a crossbow, and Thomas uttered a prayer of thanks for the times his father had taken him hunting.

Dusk turned to darkness while Thomas and the women stayed in the carriage, listening to the wild sounds of night. Thomas held the crossbow awkwardly while the queen pulled the wool blanket close around her and shivered despite the warmth of the late summer evening. An owl hooted. Then fell quiet.

"I knew Arthur would not live," Katherine confessed into the darkness. "When I saw the line of sweat on his brow and the servants told me I had to leave the chamber, I knew. Yes, I knew that he would die, and I would be a widow."

Her voice broke at the thought, and tears welled in her eyes.

"I don't know if I loved him," she said. "I told myself that I did. It was my duty to him. But I am not sure that I *knew* what love was meant to be until Henry took me in his arms and told me I was the queen he wanted."

A single tear trickled down her face. "Wanted," she whispered again.

Thomas could barely see the queen's face in the darkness. But he knew he needed to say something.

"I am sorry, Your Majesty," he finally said. He wanted to say, "My Dearest Queen Katherine, you have always deserved the love of your king," but he could not. The guards around his own heart stood at duty, and he would not push past. It was better to be silent about what could have been for the queen, for himself, for anyone. Better to live the life God granted.

The queen wiped away the tears.

"Arthur loved me. He was shy and awkward around me, but I do believe that in his heart he loved me," she finished with a half smile. "I think."

Her face softened in the warmth of the distant memory.

"You know, I was very young when my mother told me that I would be marrying the King of England. She instructed my household not only to call me *Infanta* but also the Princess of Wales. She wanted me to know that I was destined to be the Queen of England. That is how she raised me."

Thomas heard the slight sound of twigs cracking and distant footsteps approaching. He gave Margaret a quick warning, nodded to the queen, tightened his grip on his crossbow, and then stepped out of the coach into the frosty night air.

"Who goes there?" he demanded.

38

THE MAID OF KENT

"An audience with the queen," a shrill female voice demanded.

The woman and her companions approached in the darkness, without a lamp to guide them, and Thomas could not make out their faces under their thick hoods.

"Who are you?" he demanded, sounding more like the captain of the guard than the queen's favored priest.

"I am a fellow follower of Christ, a maidservant of the queen and His Majesty, a daughter of the Church," she said as she walked closer. The heavy cloak covered part of her face, and even in the moonlight, Thomas could not see anything more than her chin.

"Do not come closer," he demanded, even as the gravel crunched under her small boots. "Tell me who you are."

"I am Elizabeth Barton, a nun from Kent."

Margaret let out a quiet gasp, and Thomas could hear the queen whispering to her from inside the royal coach. He stepped forward.

"Why do you come to us at night?"

"I think you know," she said, and Thomas felt his skin crawl. He swallowed hard. He never trusted those who claimed to know his thoughts, especially young women who might.

"The queen will not meet with you," he said defiantly. "I do not wish to upset her with your ill-conceived delusions."

"They are not delusions, Father," she said evenly.

"I have heard your message in London," he said. "The queen will not entertain it. Please leave."

The young woman was quiet, but she was now close enough for Thomas to make out the contours of her face, the same he had seen at Smithfield. She was young—likely no more than twenty years old. She had large eyes and a short, freckled nose. What was this woman doing traveling the highways at night, approaching royal carriages, preaching the king's death? She would not end up well. He wanted no part of it.

"I speak for the Lord," she said in the same determined, even tone. "He bids me come and speak to you this evening."

Thomas shifted his weight. He should not be listening to this.

"How did you find us? Have you set up an ambush?"

Thomas felt the three soldiers training their weapons on the woman and her two companions, whom he could now make out to be other young women and not armed bandits.

"No, Father," she said, taking another small step toward him. "I was asleep in my bed when I heard the Lord say, 'Go, speak to my queen. You will find her on the road to The More.'"

"Someone informed you."

"Nay, sir. No one but our Lord."

"And so you have come," Thomas said. "But the queen will not speak to you."

Elizabeth's young lips parted into a charming smile. "But she can hear me, can she not?"

Thomas said nothing for a moment, then said, "Leave, sister. This is not a safe place for you or your companions."

"I am not afraid of you or any other man," she said, smiling. "I listen to God and what he tells me."

"I wish her to leave at once," came the queen's sharp voice from the coach. "She is not welcome. I love and serve my husband, the king! We do not wish his death now or ever."

Thomas took a step toward the nun, pointing the crossbow in her direction.

"Leave!"

"King Henry will die if he marries that whore, Anne Boleyn," Elizabeth shouted as Thomas took steps toward her, and she took steps backward. "I have seen it in a dream. God has revealed it—warn him!"

With that, Elizabeth Barton and her companions turned and disappeared into the darkness.

Thomas stood in the middle of the empty path, heart pounding. Would he have sent an arrow into the young woman's heart if she had threatened his queen? He wished he had not let her speak at all. The queen did not need to hear those disturbing prophecies. How was it that Elizabeth Barton was so sure? Was she another Frideswide? Or was she possessed?

"Leave!" he whispered, though Elizabeth Barton was long gone. "Leave!"

39

RATTLED

"She rattled you," Margaret said, watching the way Thomas's hand shook as he held a spoonful of porridge up to his lips.

He set the spoon in the bowl and tucked his hands under his habit. He really was not hungry anyhow.

"No," he lied. "I am fine." But he could not lie, not even to Margaret. She could see plainly that the nun of Kent had gotten to him, and even several hours later, in the safety of the village inn, he was shaken.

"Yes," he confessed. "The nun's message makes me anxious."

"Why?" Margaret asked.

"I don't know," Thomas said. How should he explain what he did not understand?

Margaret nodded and took a spoonful of porridge.

"Perhaps the nun is right? Perhaps God will judge Henry for abandoning Katherine?"

Thomas looked around the room.

"You should be careful what you say, even here, so far from the court," he whispered.

"I know," she said quietly, her eyes on the porridge. "But perhaps the nun from Kent is not crazy? I think she is brave."

Thomas shook his head.

"It's not what she says that concerns me. It's something else."

Margaret cocked her head as if curiously waiting.

"It feels... evil," he finally said.

Margaret looked confused. Then dismissive.

"It was a long night," she said. "I suppose you did not sleep?"

"No. It was so late when we arrived that I could not still my mind," he said.

"Hmm," Margaret said. "You should get some rest now. Let us sit with the queen."

Thomas smiled. After all these long months of serving the queen, he was beginning to feel a bit of familiarity with her household. And with Richard Featherstone back in Ludlow, young Margaret was the closest thing he had for a friend. And that was at least a small comfort.

"Thank you," he said. "Perhaps you are right."

But alone in the stuffy inn room, with daylight streaming through the spaces between the curtains and the wall, he could not sleep. His mind would not allow rest, though his body demanded it. When his heavy eyelids finally closed, his mind ravaged him with fearful images: the queen alone on the highway; the king dying in bed and wailing for solace; the nun, wicked and sexual, flaunting her young body, her exposed arms and neck reflecting the moonlight.

He woke up with a gasp.

He could not allow the nun to meet with the queen. There was something deeply disturbing about her, and it was not just the words she said. Elizabeth Barton was right and wrong at the same time.

God might very well judge King Henry for his betrayal. He could end his life in an instant, or God could grant the king a long life. He would do as he willed. He would, indeed, judge Henry for his sin, as he would judge every man who lived and died. One day, he would judge Thomas. He thought of this every day he knelt before the cross.

Thomas stood up and made the sign of the cross over his heart.

"Pater noster, qui es in caelis." He would do the only thing he knew to do. He would bring his troubled heart, his mind, his soul to the Good Shepherd.

"Have mercy on me," he whispered in English, "a sinner."

It was not up to him to judge the king. That was for God alone. He would serve God and serve the queen. He would not entertain those who enjoyed whispering about God's judgment falling on his king.

A knock on his door startled him.

"Father Abell," he heard Margaret whisper. "She is here."

40

ELIZABETH'S WARNING

"I thought I made myself completely clear last night," Thomas said with as much authority as he could muster. "The queen will not entertain your company. If you persist in trying to meet with her, I will have the queen's guards throw you into the street."

Elizabeth Barton smiled, her blue eyes dancing with amusement.

"I am not here for Queen Katherine," she said with more charm than Thomas was used to hearing in a nun's voice. "I wanted to speak with you."

She reached out and touched his wrist with her delicate fingertips.

Thomas felt the warm shock of her touch and pulled back sharply.

Elizabeth laughed, her eyes closing pleasantly for a moment. She looked so relaxed. He felt so tense.

She slowly parted her lips.

"I wanted to apologize for ambushing your company last night," she said. She seemed to be studying him, looking for clues.

Thomas hardened his face. The nun from Kent was not trustworthy.

"I wanted to speak to the queen, of course," she began in a demure voice that sounded more like the women of the court, the women of the queen's household who occasionally came to him to confess their sins of ill thoughts against their lady and minor acts of avarice against each other.

"I wanted to be obedient to God, but also I wanted to speak to you," she said, lowering her eyes.

Thomas said nothing.

"You are not what you seem," she said with amusement. "You seem so offended by me, but you yourself have distanced yourself from King Henry. And I believe that on at least one occasion ..." She paused, her blue eyes lighting up with anticipation, "I believe that you, Father, have acted quite treasonously."

Something of terror arose in Thomas as he felt the nun reading his most private journal. Who had this young woman spoken to?

"I see from your face that I am correct," she said boldly. "I believe you have been disloyal to King Henry. And I believe this happened on a long trip he sent you on. Am I right?"

Thomas looked around. No one was in earshot as they were the only two people lingering in the inn's empty dining room at midmorning. All other patrons had headed on to their journey or out into the village to make their daily allowance and provide for their families. The queen and her attendants had found places to rest in the unoccupied, moderately furnished village inn. Thomas was alone with the young woman.

"I do not wish to speak to you," he said quickly, although he desperately wanted to know how she knew him and what she planned to say next. Part of him even wished she would touch his wrist again.

"Then do not speak," she said, placing a single forefinger over her lips. "Listen!"

Thomas nodded slowly, his mind racing, his stomach turning. His soul reached out silently for help. *Pater noster, qui es in caelis.*

"You will not remain at court," she said.

But Thomas already knew this was true. The king had already threatened to banish the queen permanently from court, and he would, no doubt, follow her. Why should he remain in the company of the royal household anyhow? He would continue his post, serving as the queen's chaplain as long as he was needed. If he were to be released from that duty, he would return to Oxford, continue teaching, or perhaps take up work in the parish again. He had no desire to remain in court.

And perhaps that was an easy prognostication for the false prophetess of Kent. It must have been obvious that he would not remain at court. He felt himself exhale a breath he had been holding in.

"I do not think you have anything to say that I do not already know," he said. "And I think it is time that you leave."

"You will have to choose," she said quickly.

Thomas looked around again. They were still alone in the empty room. Only wooden chairs and tables could bear witness against him if they were called to give an account as to why the queen's chaplain entertained the king's enemies.

"I serve both the king and the queen," he said. "By serving the queen, I serve my king."

"You know that is not what I speak of," she countered boldly. "You will be forced to choose between serving *God* or the king. It is coming. I have warned you. You will not be able to remain hidden for long."

She stood up.

He remained sitting.

"Be bold, Father Abell."

"Please leave," he finally said, but without any of the confidence he had mustered earlier. What she said may very well be true, but her style, her voice, her very body unnerved him.

"As you wish," she said as her long skirts brushed past Thomas and the empty wooden tables as she left the dining room. Thomas looked down and took a deep breath. When he looked up Elizabeth Barton was gone, but he was not alone. The innkeeper and his wife were standing in the doorway, watching, listening.

—◦❖◦—

"What did she say?" Margaret whispered hoarsely as they jostled along in the royal coach.

Thomas looked over at the queen, who had fallen asleep, her head resting precariously against the side of the coach, relaxed in long-overdue sleep.

"She said nothing," Thomas said uncomfortably, adjusting himself in the seat opposite Margaret. He was accustomed to close proximity with the queen's women, but now Margaret suddenly felt too close. She sat across from him, her very knees nearly touching his. He wished the coach would stop and give them all a moment to stretch out, walk around, relieve themselves.

"She said nothing at all?" Margaret questioned.

"No," Thomas said slowly. He looked at Margaret carefully. She was not the nun from Kent. She was the young woman who had served the queen faithfully for the four years he had been in her service. She was not a woman of loose lips or compromised character. He could trust her.

"She apologized for startling us on the road last night," he said truthfully.

Margaret nodded. "Was that all?"

"And she said that she wanted to speak to me directly."

Margaret raised an eyebrow.

"And?"

"I did not want to let her speak ..."

"But you did?"

How much should he tell Margaret?

"She wanted to prophesy that I would not remain in court long."

"Oh." Margaret looked confused. "That is all?"

"Well, no," Thomas said. "Of course, that is no real prophecy. Anyone listening to the gossip would make that prediction. ... The king is not likely to bring the queen back any time soon, and I have no plans to return to court without her."

Margaret nodded impatiently. "Of course, yes. Did you tell her so?"

"Perhaps, somewhat."

Margaret nodded. She seemed satisfied, but only for a moment. "But was that all?" she asked, still the curious child.

"No," Thomas said slowly. This was a long journey to be making with the queen and her ladies. How many days more until they arrived at their destination? He looked over at the queen, who still seemed quite unconscious. "She warned me that I would have to choose between serving God and serving the king."

"Oh," Margaret said, still looking a bit confused. She let out a sigh of relief. "I should think that is becoming abundantly clear," she said quietly. She raised the same eyebrow again. "And not only for you, Father Abell."

Thomas closed his eyes and leaned his head back on the coach. He knew he could trust Margaret. She was one of the good ones.

41

Universities Weigh In

February 1532

Thomas walked through the Great Hall at the Manor of the More. It was smaller than the great halls in King Henry's other palaces, but it was the queen's residence, free of the demands of the court and the prying eyes of Cromwell and the king's operatives. After six months of living east of London, the estate had begun to feel like home, at least temporarily.

But peace can only last for so long.

"Father Abell," Margaret sang as she caught Thomas gazing up at a stern old baron in the Great Hall. "A messenger from the king is here to see you."

Such messengers were regular occurrences. Over the past few months, Thomas had assumed the role of informing Cromwell of the queen's health, her wishes, and, above all else, her desire to spend time with her precious Mary, a longing that had turned into a dull ache. How could a father be so cruel as to use his own daughter as a pawn to get what he wanted from her mother? There were things about kingship that Thomas could never understand.

The messenger bowed and handed Thomas the parchment.

"The king wishes your services in London..."

He stopped reading.

"What is the message?" Margaret asked, her curious smile fading.

"The king is calling me back to London."

"Oh?"

She placed her hand on Thomas's vestment sleeve.

"Why?"

"The king is drafting a response to the universities' theological conclusions." He looked at her curious brown eyes. "Thomas Cromwell requests I come to London... to help with the effort."

Thomas could tell by Margaret's puzzled look that she was as surprised as he. Didn't Cromwell suspect his loyalties were with the queen? Was it a test?

"Perhaps it is because you are an Oxford tutor?" Margaret suggested.

"Possibly," Thomas said. He sat down heavily on a padded stool set against the wall and closed his eyes.

Even a few weeks earlier, he would have welcomed the opportunity—any opportunity—to leave The More, to expand his intellectual capacities beyond the service of the queen. But the weeks of serving had begun to settle his soul. He had taken Father Martin's advice to heart. He had listened to Katherine, prayed with her, sat with her. And now she and her ladies felt as much a part of his family as Father Martin had. The thought of leaving now, even for a short time, filled Thomas with grief.

And there was the matter of conscience. What would the king do if he refused to write a treatise approving the marriage? Perhaps the nun from Kent was right. He would have to choose. Did he have the courage it would take to stand up to the king? Henry could throw him into the Tower of London. He could confiscate all his worldly possessions. He could chop off his head. Thomas felt a wave of nausea. *Jesus Christ, Son of God, have mercy.*

❖

March 1532   London

Thomas scanned through the first stack of parchment pages. Most of the sixteen universities focused on the Levitical code, which prohibited a man from marrying his brother's wife. He frowned. No doubt, the king had offered a handsome prize for their opinions.

He stretched and yawned. Going through the material would take more than a few days.

"Father Abell." Thomas Cromwell stood unannounced in the doorway. It was always so unnerving when he did that. How long had he been standing there, watching him in silence?

Thomas raised an eyebrow and said nothing.

"The king is eager to hear a summary of the opinions. Can you prepare that by next Friday?"

Next Friday?

It would take him from dawn to dusk, without much time for eating or sleeping, just to read through the opinions, let alone draft a summary by the end of next week.

"Of course," Thomas said dryly. "It will be difficult, but I'll manage."

"I thought you might say that." Cromwell smiled with a sniff. Perhaps he enjoyed the thought of Thomas crouched at a wooden table by candlelight, doing the bidding of the king against his will.

"Would you prefer to have an assistant?" Cromwell asked.

Thomas eyed him evenly. *An assistant or a spy?* "If you think it would be helpful."

"I do."

Cromwell stepped aside, and the young, round-faced, blond cleric who had been so eager to endorse the king at Cromwell's assembly last fall stepped into the cavernous room.

"I'm Arnold Baker," the priest said in a high but confident voice. "We met last summer at Hampton Court."

"I remember," Thomas said with a nod. He looked at the parchment in his hand. "You are proficient in Latin? Of course, you are. I suppose we had better get to work."

"As far as I can tell," Arnold Baker began speaking, though Thomas continued reading. The sun was setting, and he wanted to get through one more draft by candlelight. "It seems that the French are generally in favor of the king's point of view, and the Spanish are not. Well, I suppose that is no surprise."

Thomas looked up, straightened his back, and looked at Arnold through blurry eyes. It had been a long week, and it was only Wednesday.

"It seems to me that we can report back to the king and the Privy Chamber that the French are in favor of his annulment," Arnold continued. "Generally speaking, they are."

Was the young man testing him?

"I don't think that is quite true," Thomas said, examining Arnold's earnest face. "By my count, there are at least four universities that wrote that Pope Julius had the authority to dispense in the area of Henry and Katherine's marriage and that he made *the right* decision. So no, I would not agree that the French are *generally* in favor of the king's position."

"Well, generally," Arnold repeated weakly. "Generally."

Was this why Cromwell had planted the young man in his research committee of two?

"With respect, Arnold, we were asked to make a serious review of this material. Why should we say the French are *generally* in support of King Henry's position when we can say with certainty ..." He picked up a parchment. "... that at least four of sixteen, or one-fourth of them, disagree?"

Arnold cleared his throat and looked over his shoulder to be sure the two men were alone.

"You may write that in your report," he said in a low voice, "but it is not what the king wants to hear. It would be far safer and more expedient to finesse the facts just a bit. We are not saying that the French are *all* in agreement with the king, just generally speaking so, and three-fourths is quite a majority. Wouldn't you say so?"

"If the king asks, I will give him the exact numbers," Thomas said, turning his attention back to the stack. He had spoken with cardinals and kings, and he had no intention of compromising the truth now to please Henry, not over numbers and percentages. It was not his opinions that he was offering. They were only tasked to report on the opinions of others. How could the king hold them accountable for the message they relayed?

Arnold was not wrong to be worried about the report. But worried or not, they had a job to do, and they would report as truthfully as they possibly could. The world might be turned upside down, but they still had the truth, and they would speak it whenever they were asked. At least Thomas would. He had to.

Thomas picked up the Oxford and Cambridge opinions. He had saved the English ones for last, both looking forward to and dreading reading the opinions of his former colleagues. He longed to know how Father Martin would respond. Had he been among the Oxford scholars? Thomas scanned through the papers, reading the academic Latin as easily as he would read English. No, it did not appear that Martin's name had been included.

Thomas sighed. They were almost done with the task. They would be ready to deliver the report to Henry on time if Arnold did not cause too much trouble.

Out of the corner of his eye, Thomas saw Arnold scribble "French support the king" on his parchment. The young man glanced up at Thomas, then wrote "generally."

So, that is the way this will go.

"Father Abell," a young page in the doorway said quietly as if to soften the abruptness of his interruption. "There is an urgent message for you."

42

FATHER MARTIN'S GIFT

Oxford

A lump formed in Thomas's throat as he stood over his old mentor's bed. The man lay unconscious, breathing laboriously through dry lips and flushed cheeks. Two nuns and a young priest, one Thomas had never met, sat on stools by the bedside, rotating worn rosaries through sweaty palms.

"Father Martin," Thomas whispered.

The old man did not respond, but Thomas could hear a familiar catch in his tortured breathing. Priests who attended the dying knew it well, the death rattle.

"I came as soon as I could," Thomas said, the lump in his throat dissolving into tears. He had ridden hard through the night to get to Oxford as soon as he heard the news. He had finished the report for Cromwell as the moon set and gotten on his horse within the same hour. Now, he wished he had just let Arnold write the report.

Thomas touched Father Martin's hand. It was flushed with the fever of a soul on fire, a tired old man warming himself at Heaven's holy hearth. Thomas wiped away a tear.

"I am so thankful for you," he whispered. "You have been a true father to me. Thank you for your counsel, your teaching."

Thomas closed his eyes. *And your love.*

"How long has he been like this?" he asked the young priest.

"Since yesterday afternoon," he said quietly. "I think his soul is ready to go. Father Atwater administered last rites this evening. Students and priests have been coming to say goodbye. He is just hanging on. Maybe he was waiting for you."

Thomas nodded. Why had it been so long? When was his last letter to Father Martin?

"Father Martin, you blessed me so many times. And you blessed others, so many others." He cleared his throat. "So, Father, my Father, I bless you in the name of Jesus. Go to Him, your True Shepherd."

Even as he said it, Thomas felt the weight in the room lift. He took a deep, easy breath and gently kissed the old man's brow.

Father Martin coughed, opened his eyes, and looked past Thomas and the young priest, as if he were seeing something just beyond the smoke-stained rafters and thatched roof. Then he smiled faintly. Father Martin always talked about the joy of seeing his Savior's face. Was he seeing Heaven?

His smile faded, and his face slowly grew gray. His thin lips turned a pale shade of purple. How many times had Father Martin said, "Be faithful to the end, Thomas!"? And here he was, at his end, the appointed day that would come for them all.

Thomas sat down heavily and suddenly felt very tired. He leaned his head against the cold stone wall and closed his eyes.

"Father Thomas Abell?"

Thomas focused blurrily on the young priest standing before him.

"Yes?" Thomas answered groggily, blinking. How long had he drifted off?

Late afternoon sun washed through the incense-filled room. A trio of servants surrounded Martin's feather bed, cleaning his body. A couple of nuns knelt beside an altar, praying the rosary and weeping.

"Father Martin wanted you to have these," the young priest said, handing Thomas a thick packet bound in twine. It was a stack of loose papers in Father Martin's own handwriting. And even a quick glance revealed that the unpolished notes were about the king's Great Matter.

"Thank you," Thomas murmured.

He thumbed through the papers. Father Martin had entrusted his thoughts to him. It was a tremendous gift. Trembling, and nearly breathless, he began to read.

"It is now the duty of English priests and theologians to suffer their opinions be heard ..." Thomas smiled at Father Martin's eloquent introduction. The old priest's name had not been included with the scholars on the Oxford paper, and now he knew why. He would not compromise his duty to God to please the king.

Thomas scanned his mentor's notes. The Leviticus and Deuteronomy verses were not in conflict. Just as he and Father Martin had discussed a year ago, the passages addressed two different situations. They, in fact, worked in harmony, clarifying each other. Leviticus called a man taking his brother's wife unclean, but that applied to a living brother. The rule was to protect women against abuse and incest. It described a specific form of adultery and guaranteed that God would not bless the children of such unions. Father Martin made it sound so simple.

The Deuteronomy passage required a man to marry his dead brother's wife if his brother had died without leaving an heir. The son of the second marriage would be considered the older brother's heir, and the Jews were commanded to do this with consequences befalling them if they did not. They were *required* to marry their dead brother's wife. *Required.*

Thomas paused.

"But why should we, who live under the Law of Christ, care about these laws that do not apply to us?" he read. The universities had argued that Henry and Katherine's marriage was against the laws of nature, the laws of God, and that the Pope had no right to go against God's nature and law.

"The Deuteronomy requirement demonstrates that such marriages are not against the law of God or the law of nature," Thomas read, his heart quickening.

He scanned the paper. St. Jerome. St. John Chrysostom. Theophylact of Ohrid. Thomas laughed; of course, Martin had included Theophylact! The eleventh-century orthodox archbishop's commentary on the Bible had just been translated into Latin. Martin had been so excited to read it and share it with his students.

Martin referenced Thomas Aquinas, his teacher Albert the Great, and Saint Gregory. Father Martin had searched the canon, just as they had talked about. But what was this? Tertullian's name was written in the notes and circled. The third-century theologian was not without fault, and priests who read and taught his work knew how to quote the good without stepping into his heresy. Martin had not spelled out his thoughts on Tertullian, but even as Thomas stared at the name, he knew.

Several of the university opinions had quoted Tertullian's writing on marriage, but they failed to note they were quoting the books the Church had already declared heretical. Was it an intentional misrepresentation of Church doctrine? Thomas's face flushed. Nothing frustrated him more than misinformation.

"Will you be joining us for the Friday morning Mass?" the young priest asked as he passed through the room. "A Mass for Father Martin's soul will be later, of course. This is the regular Mass at our parish."

He continued talking while Thomas willed himself to pay attention and turn away from the king's Great Matter, the university's misleading interpretations of Church canon, and their perversions of Scripture. Perversion! That was exactly what it was. And a great sin too! How could men of the cloth willfully twist what God had said was good for the Jews and make it a despicable thing?

"I'm sorry," he stammered, only then realizing the priest was still looking at him. "What were you saying?"

"It's getting late," he said. "And I believe that you missed sleep last night—perhaps you will stay tonight. Our morning Mass will be the regular Friday morning Mass, but in two days, we will have the wake and the Mass for Father Martin's soul."

"Father Martin's soul," Thomas repeated almost deliriously. "Friday morning?"

"Yes," the young priest repeated. A look of concern crossed his face.

"Tomorrow morning is Friday morning?"

"Yes," the young priest said. "Of course."

Thomas jumped up.

"I need to get back to London!"

Thomas raked his fingers through his disheveled hair.

"I have to go. I am sorry. Please understand. I think Father Martin would want me to go."

Thomas hastily packed Father Martin's notes into his leather satchel and ran out the door. If he hurried, he could get to the privy chamber before Arnold Baker presented their findings to the king and his counsel. He had one more opportunity to set the record straight. He would speak up, for Katherine, for Father Martin, for God.

43

Night Ride

Thomas held the reins tightly, the leather bands cutting into his hands, drawing blood. It was painful. But the pain was good. It kept him awake. So did the cold wind, biting through his tunic. In his haste to leave Oxford, he had forgotten to retrieve his woolen cape from the chambermaid who had taken it to the wardrobe when he arrived to see Father Martin.

Father Martin. His heart ached with the weight of unshed tears. The grief would come later. It had to. He needed to focus on the road with its potholes and uneven terrain. One false move and his horse could stumble into a ditch.

His body ached with cold, but none of it mattered—the pain, the cold, the grief. Nothing mattered except getting to the king's privy chamber before Arnold presented their summary. He would not let his name be associated with a lie. He would not let the young priest misrepresent him.

It was *not* the unanimous counsel of university academics that the Bible forbade a man to marry his brother's widow. Faithful theologians all over England and the continent disagreed with the king's interpretation of Scripture. He had to give voice to Martin's thoughts. He had to speak up for those who could not speak up for themselves. This was why God had placed him in the king's house. He knew it.

Pope Julius had *not* been gravely wrong. His permission for Henry and Katherine to marry had been in agreement with Holy Scripture and Church tradition. To assert otherwise would not only dishonor his queen, but it would break open the floodgate against Church authority and the sanctity of marriage. The very soul of England lay in the balance. Nothing could be more important than him getting to London before dawn.

Thomas gripped the horse with his cold knees and leaned forward in the saddle. He would ride all night if needed. He had ridden last night, and he could do it again. The road before him seemed hazy, like murky water. Was he falling asleep? He would not. He could not. He would think about the theologians who offered their opinions that Katherine and Henry's marriage was against God's law. That stirred his blood enough to keep him upright in the saddle.

Thomas was aware of the stars, the gently rolling Thames River, the quiet houses and villages as he rushed past. He knew that most men would not dare to ride the highway alone, especially not the main road between Oxford and London. There were too many vagrants, too many desperate, hungry men waiting for a wealthy cleric or drunk nobleman to stumble past in the night. But Thomas was neither wealthy nor drunk, and somehow, he did not care if there were highwaymen lurking.

His purse carried only a few coins, nothing more than would pay for a meal or two and a night at an inn along the way. He had no jewelry. The only thing of importance on his body were the notes from Martin, and he had already read them. He had an uncanny ability to remember almost perfectly what he had read, and Martin's ideas were not just on the parchment. They were forever etched into his consciousness.

He leaned in, focused his weary eyes on the road, and kept his horse running at a pace that would have alarmed any farmer who happened to be awake and walking about on his property, half past midnight.

"Hey!" he heard a shadowed voice cry.

Then Thomas's horse stumbled on an obstacle neither of them had seen. Thomas flew forward over the horse's head, and the world went black.

"I've sent my lads to fetch the doctor," the milkmaid said when Thomas's vision came into focus. The sun was up, but it was early morning, and the dew hung heavily in the air.

"You took quite a beating, Father," she said reverently, pressing her handkerchief to Thomas's bleeding cheek. His head throbbed, and his whole body ached. He moved his legs. Yes, they were fine. So were his hands, though raw and bloody from clinging to the leather reins. Leather reins. Horse.

Thomas tried to sit up but lay back down, groaning. "Where is my horse?"

The woman shook her head.

"My son and me just found ye along the road just now. We were bringing me pitcher of milk to the ladies in town. They buy it straight from me every morning. First thing. Never fail. Me boy walks with me, but when we seen you, we know you need the doctor."

"Thank you," Thomas croaked.

The woman looked at the metal pitcher of milk, hesitating as if debating what she should do. She sighed.

"Take the milk, Father. I think you need it more than the ladies this morning."

She dipped a ladle into the metal pitcher and lifted it to Thomas's parched lips.

"God bless you," he said, drinking. He was suddenly aware that he was both hungry and thirsty.

"What are you doing in these parts before dawn?" the woman asked with a hint of suspicion. "It's not a normal thing for priests to be a travelin' by their lonesome."

Thomas groaned. Of course not. And for good reason.

"I need to get to Hampton Court this morning," he said, though he was sure the words sounded ridiculous coming out of his bloodied face. "There is a... meeting that is important."

"The king's house?" the woman said.

She dipped the ladle back into the pitcher and offered Thomas another drink.

"You must be an important priest," she said, eyeing his wounded face.

"I am not important," Thomas groaned. "Not at all."

"What is your name?" the woman demanded.

Thomas closed his eyes. His head throbbed. How far was he from London?

"Eh?"

"Thomas. I am Thomas Abell, chaplain to Queen Katherine of Aragon."

"Oh, sweet mother of God," the woman exclaimed. "And here I am in my regular clothes."

She crossed herself and dipped her ladle in the milk pitcher again. Thomas hated that her generosity grew at hearing his royal connection, but he was thirsty and hungry. He drank heartily.

"Thank you, madam." He closed his eyes. The light was so bright. "How far are we from London?"

"Oh, a good spell if you plan to walk." She looked him over. "You are not planning to walk the whole long way, are you?"

"If I must," he said, struggling to sit up. "I must."

"It's a bit faster by boat," she offered brightly. "There is a lad from the village who will take you for a price. I don't suppose the thieves left you with any gold?"

Thomas patted his belt. No. The little purse was gone.

"I did not have much with me," he said and lay down again to close his eyes and think.

—◦✦◦—

"I found him just like this," he heard the woman say, and when his eyes focused, there was a kind, older man with a short gray beard and spectacles and a wide-eyed boy standing over his shoulder.

"Can you move?" the doctor asked.

"I think so," Thomas muttered, sitting up. "I need to get to London this morning. It's of utmost importance to the Queen of England."

"He is the queen's priest," the dairy maid said with a beaming smile. "Our Katherine. Are you still thirsty?" She offered Thomas another ladle while her son watched. She swatted him away. "We will eat later," she whispered harshly.

"I'm okay, madam," Thomas said, feeling a bit of his strength returning. "Give it to the boy. He did a good thing by fetching the doctor."

"Yes, Father," she said humbly.

The doctor felt Thomas's arms and legs and examined his head wound.

"You are still bleeding, Father," he said, pressing his hand against the wound. "We need to stop that before you go anywhere." He ripped a long strip of linen and wrapped it tightly around Thomas's head.

"Why are you headed to London in such a hurry?"

"I am expected at the King's Council today," he said, looking around to see if there was a cart or horse in sight.

"Today!" the doctor said, then chuckled. "Well, that is a bit unfortunate, I would say."

"Indeed!" Thomas said, peering down the road. Maybe a hired coach would give him a ride. Money would be no issue when he arrived in London.

"I would say you are a good day's walk, maybe four, five hours by coach to London," the doctor said. "I do not think you will make it."

He looked critically at Thomas.

"Will the king have your head for missing his meeting?"

"No... he is not expecting me."

The doctor looked at the dairy maid, who nodded knowingly. "He is the queen's chaplain. Queen Katherine," she repeated proudly.

"I'll fetch the river guide," the doctor said. "That is the fastest way."

44

Not Unanimous

Not Unanimous

"Your Majesty, noblemen and priests, I believe that there is nothing more to discuss," Thomas heard Thomas Howard, the Duke of Norfolk, conclude in his heavy northern accent. The chambermen pushed the heavy wooden doors open and forced their way into the crowded Privy Council.

The duke scowled at the interruption, but the usher threw up both hands.

"Your Majesty, gentlemen, I beg you to forgive me, forgive me."

The packed chamber of lords and noblemen looked past the high-pitched servant to Thomas and began murmuring to each other. Thomas felt the bandage around his head and smoothed his dusty priestly garment. A sight he must be! The winter sun was fading to twilight, but he had arrived in time, if barely. The council was seated. The meeting had not concluded. There was still a chance. It was now or never.

"Gentlemen! Father Thomas Abell, Chaplain to the Queen," the usher said, stepping back to give Thomas space, though Thomas needed no real introduction. Most of the noblemen had seen him by the queen's side at court appearances and state dinners.

"Father." The king nodded with a slightly amused smile. "You arrive quite late."

Thomas cleared his throat. *Jesus, have mercy on me, a sinner. Give me courage.*

"Your Majesty," he said, looking steadily at the king's blue eyes. "I apologize. I met with some ... resistance along the way to London last night."

Murmurs rippled through the crowded room.

The king nodded. "Resistance? It appears someone intended to take off your head!" The men laughed at the king's joke until Thomas Howard clapped his hands. "Gentlemen!"

"You do not appear to be well," Henry said with what almost seemed like genuine concern. "You need not have come. Your associate, Arnold Baker, has already presented your findings. Well done! Your summary is quite relevant, very important to our situation."

The king smiled. Thomas did not. Instead, he froze.

It was the moment. He had the words to say, the arguments, the thoughts of a week of unslept nights. He had rehearsed all the reasons why the king's marriage was valid and why the universities were wrong. But now, standing in the presence of the king and his men, he was as silent as a guilty child. But he was no guilty child. *When you stand before kings, the Holy Spirit will give you words to speak.* He swallowed hard. *Jesus, help me speak.*

"It is quite remarkable that the French are so supportive of His Majesty," Thomas Cromwell said pointedly. "And unanimous at that!"

The king looked quizzically at Thomas.

"It was not, Your Majesty," Thomas said as the room fell silent.

"Not what?" the king asked.

Thomas held the king's gaze while his own cheeks flushed with unspoken words.

"Father?"

"Your Majesty, the French universities were not unanimous in their findings. It is true that many of them supported your request for an annulment, but a few theologians found that Pope Julius was correct in validating your marriage to Katherine. It was not, as your good counselor said, unanimous."

A chill fell across the room until the king shrugged.

"Do you mean to say your associate misled me?"

There was no backing down. Thomas spotted Arnold Baker cowering at the far end of the room, his blue eyes suddenly round in his pale face.

"No," Thomas said quickly. It was one thing to put his own life in danger, quite another to implicate the young Arnold Baker. "Perhaps it was a miscommunication. I believe Father Baker meant to report that many, even most, of the French universities were supportive of the king's cause to seek an annulment. But perhaps it is more accurate to say that not all are supportive."

"Oh," the king said, looking Thomas over from bandaged head to dusty robe. "Are you certain?"

Out of the corner of his eye, Thomas could see Arnold shaking his head slightly as if begging him to reconsider.

"I am certain," Thomas said. "I read them all myself."

The Privy Council murmured.

"Perhaps Katherine's priest would like to inform us of the French conclusions," Thomas More said, leaning forward, watching him intently. "I would like to hear the reasons given for their dissent."

The nobles began talking and murmuring until the king pounded the armrest of his chair, silencing the men.

"No, no," the king said with noticeable agitation. "We have had enough of this conversation for today. This meeting has already gone past the afternoon meal, and I have grown tired of the conversation," he said. "We have a good cockfight prepared before sunset, and I am eager to see if my lady's bet will be the winning bird."

The king flashed another smile to his nobles and then looked coldly at Thomas. "We will finish this conversation tomorrow morning," he said fiercely without a hint of amusement. "I need to hear what these so-called French experts have to say about my marriage."

The meeting was over, but the conversation had just begun.

45

WAITING

The next morning came and went, but no messenger arrived. Instead, Thomas felt the royal household around him buzz with its regular activity, cleaning and stoking of fires, making breads and beds, and carrying on, sunrise, sunset. No one requested his presence.

By evening Thomas heard through the servants' gossip that the king's party had ridden out for a hunt. They would be gone the rest of the week.

What should he do? He sent a message to Cromwell. He had concluded the task. They had written a report, and Baker had presented it before the king's privy council. Did he have leave to return to the queen's household?

Thomas waited. A day passed. The silence was deafening.

"Pater Noster, qui es in caelis," he prayed as he paced around the king's austere guest room. Nothing made him more restless than uncertainty. But Henry's silence, at least, made space for Thomas's body to heal as he waited, languishing in the king's guest room, but he could not shake the feeling of uselessness. Surely there was something more useful he could do than wait and pace the room like a man rotting in the Tower.

Write it down.

The thought stopped him short. If he wrote down his objections to the university's findings, other Englishmen could read it.

Priests. Noblemen. Lawyers. Merchants. Any man or woman with the ability to read could consider the logical arguments Martin had outlined.

If Thomas wrote it, perhaps, maybe, he could get it to a printer in France or the Low Countries to publish. William Tyndale had found a way to publish Scripture and bring it back to England. Perhaps he could do the same.

The thought made him tremble. Tyndale was a fugitive, a condemned man. What would happen if Thomas Cromwell stormed into his chamber, unannounced, and found him composing such a treatise? Would he have time to toss it into the fire before Cromwell crossed the room? And how would the king respond if he finished the book and printed it? Thomas had spoken the truth in Saragossa, and miraculously, it had gone unnoticed by the Crown. Would Thomas be so fortunate the second time around?

But fortune had little to do with his escape from Wolsey's prying questions. Thomas was sure that God had protected him as the cardinal fell out of the king's favor. He had been quietly tucked away, serving the queen, as Wolsey lost his titles and wealth. And now, the great Wolsey was gone, dead, having fallen ill on his return to London. The threat of King Henry finding out about Thomas's disloyalty in Saragossa was all but over. God had protected him then, and now, if God was pressing him to write out a response to the king's theologians, he must write.

Thomas stepped out of the room he had been waiting in for three days and found the usher who had pushed his way into the privy chamber.

"Can you fetch me parchment?" he asked. "I'll need a stack of sheets."

By candlelight, Thomas began carefully writing his thoughts on the parchment. With the king's own paper and ink, he would construct his argument against Henry's annulment. When the king called him for an audience, he would be ready to make his case.

Thomas picked up the quill and wrote his response in his native tongue, crossing out words, forming his thoughts carefully in English. By the end of the week, he had a well-crafted response, nearly a hundred pages long. The sun rose and set, but the king never called him.

Thomas paced the room, staring at the stone floor, and thought about the queen, Father Martin, and his own father. What would he have told him to do? Should he send word to the king? No. He should wait. He could wait. He would wait.

The next morning, Cromwell returned Thomas's correspondence. The king was moving on to more pressing matters; after all, he governed the entire great kingdom of England. He was a very busy royal monarch. He would not be available to meet with Thomas for quite some time. Thus, Thomas was free to return to the queen, where she would undoubtedly appreciate his spiritual counsel and services in a location far, far from the royal court.

Thomas folded the letter carefully.

Free to go.

He paced the room and picked up the stack of parchment papers. Cromwell had said the king would publish the universities' response to the king's Great Matter. He himself had helped compile that information. His compilation of the university's findings would be printed and distributed. It would be read by people all over the continent, although only those who read Latin would be able to read it.

Latin.

Thomas looked at his stack of papers. He had written his response in English, the language of the king's own government, the language of parliament and the people.

He began pacing the room again. He knew what he must do. He would leave Hampton Court, but he would not return to the queen, not yet.

46

THE PRINTER

March 1532   Antwerp

Thomas was grateful for the pounding rain, as he ran along the Antwerp streets, watching for puddles, pulling his borrowed leather-hooded cloak around him. The rain provided an excuse for the hood. The hood provided a place to hide. And he had every intention of hiding as he made his way down the street in the middle of a busy day.

Entering the low doorway, he removed his hood and smiled to see another familiar face illuminated by a single candle in the corner of the dimly lit room.

"William!" he said before looking to see who else occupied the printer's musty shop.

William Tyndale embraced his old friend, slapping him affectionately on the back, causing raindrops to scatter onto the printer's ink-drenched floor.

"I don't go around using my name here," William said. "I am sure you know, the king has me for a criminal these days." He winked as if enjoying the notoriety.

Thomas looked at his friend. He seemed to have the same boundless energy, the same mischievous look, that he had always had at Oxford. But there was a seriousness weighing him down all the same. Thomas saw it in his eyes.

"I may well be on the king's outlaw list myself soon," Thomas confessed.

Tyndale raised an eyebrow. "Are you joining the Lutherans?"

Thomas Abell laughed. "Still trying, friend?"

"Of course," Tyndale smiled broadly. "Always."

"What do you have here?" he asked, looking at Thomas's bulging leather satchel.

"A book," Thomas said sheepishly. "Some things I needed to write."

"And you are here because you could not print it in England?"

"Maybe I thought a trip to Antwerp would be a nice thing to do in March," he said, still smiling because he was with William, and it had been so long since he had seen the face of a friend he could trust. They both laughed.

"I hate to break up this reunion of old friends," said a balding round man with a leather apron and ink-stained hands. "But if we are going to get this book published, we need to begin as soon as possible. We never know when our operations will be interrupted."

Tyndale nodded gravely. "Indeed."

The printer reached out to shake Thomas's hand. "Merten de Keyser, publisher. I believe we have been corresponding about your response to the universities."

"Yes," Thomas said, observing Tyndale's curious glances. "I'm Thomas Abell, priest, chaplain to Katherine of Aragon, although, as we discussed, I do not want my name associated with the book, not for now."

"Indeed!" William Tyndale said, rubbing his hands in glee. "Now I am intrigued."

Merten de Keyser proceeded to explain the printing process to Thomas, complete with the time associated and the costs. At the mention of money, Thomas produced a piece of paper.

"It is a deed to my benefice in Bradwell in Sussex, and I am prepared to forfeit that in the event that the book does not make its profit."

Merten considered the deed for a moment.

"This is not our typical arrangement," he said, shaking his head and handing the deed back to Thomas. "I take half the cost upfront in cash. Your king's coin or imperial gold."

Thomas looked doubtful.

"How much are we talking about?" he asked.

"It will cost £20, perhaps £25, for a print run large enough to distribute it on the Continent," the publisher said.

Thomas was quiet. "Perhaps I have £10, but I don't have the rest. It might take a few weeks to arrange my affairs and get it to you."

Merten pursed his lips. "Father Abell, I am sure you realize that this is risky business, not just for you, but for me and my wife. The authorities have shut us down at least once, and we have to be prepared to move to another town and start over at any moment."

William nodded. "Aye, this is true, Thomas. I was with Martin Luther in Worms until last year."

"And why are you here, William?"

Tyndale smiled. "Surely you know, friend. We are continuing our work on the Old Testament."

Thomas nodded, of course. And here he was, aiding and abetting an enemy of the Church. William must have noticed his discomfort.

"Of course, you know, Thomas, I have also written my opinion on the king's request for a divorce," he said. "We are of the same mind."

Thomas sighed. At least they agreed on that.

"Merten, I believe that I have 10 pounds credit with you from our last book," he said suddenly.

Merten acknowledged this with a skeptical nod.

"I would like you to advance that to my dear friend Thomas Abell. When his book sells, he will be good for it." William winked at Thomas. "Or perhaps Her Majesty will be able to cover the loan before we are even finished printing it?"

Thomas was too surprised to process an objection. What could he say? What would the queen say to know that William Tyndale, an enemy of the Pope and Crown, had financed his book, a defense of the Pope's legal right to affirm their marriage? These days made for strange alliances.

"But William, you have not even read the book," Thomas said after a moment of consideration. "What if you find something you object to in it?"

William crossed his arms and pursed his lips.

"Well," he said after a moment's pause. "I think that I know you pretty well, Thomas. I'll read it ahead of time if you want my feedback, but I trust that what you have written will be carefully considered and respectful."

Thomas opened his satchel.

"You should read it first," he said, "before I accept your generous proposal."

He handed the bundle of pages to his friend, and Merten retreated to his cabinet to begin preparing the tools he would need.

"*Invicta Veritas*," William read aloud. "*The Unconquerable Truth!* Latin?"

He laughed, and Thomas was taken back to Oxford and all of their late-night conversations about Latin and the need for translating the Bible into English.

"No," Thomas said. "Just the title. They were the only words that fit, but the book is in English."

William smiled. "Um-hmm."

Thomas nodded knowingly. "I want every literate Englishman to read this."

William smiled again. "And so do I."

47

INVICTA VERITAS

May 1532

"Have you read the book they are all talking about?" Richard Featherstone whispered as he and Thomas walked through the large open gate, into the garden at Bishop's Hatfield in Hertfordshire.

This house was only a day's journey from London, but it felt like a world away, and a welcome relief for Thomas. Surrounded by rolling green hills dotted with sheep and country cottages, Thomas felt his spirit relax. Like the spring butterflies dancing among the meadow flowers, he felt lighter. As far as he was concerned, the further Katherine moved from London and the king's court, the better for both of them. Each mile down the country road meant more freedom to live outside the king's growing scrutiny.

But King Henry's was not the only watchful eye that Thomas hoped to avoid. Ever since his encounter at the Privy Council, Thomas was becoming increasingly aware that Cromwell was the new power to contend with. He was confident, calculating, cold. Thomas had no idea how far the king's new advisor would go.

Cromwell had King Henry's ear, and he undoubtedly stoked the king's disapproval of all things related to Katherine. Unlike Wolsey, Cromwell had no longstanding relationship with the queen, no personal reason to show forbearance. She was not *Our Dear Kather-*

ine to him. She was an obstacle to the king's happiness and prosperity.

Thomas looked around.

Two of the queen's maidservants, local ladies chosen by Cromwell's contacts, walked along the other side of the garden. They seemed absorbed in their own happy world, distracted by their girlish conversations as they ambled along, shoulder to shoulder, giggling and whispering, hands pressed to ears. Whatever was amusing them was lost to Thomas, muted below the sound of spring birds chirping and new leaves rustling in the trees. Perhaps he could speak openly to Richard without fear of them reporting back to Cromwell.

Of course, he had read the book. He had held the first copy, smelled the drying ink, and stroked the simple bookbinding.

"*Invicta Veritas?*" Thomas asked coolly, concealing a slight smile.

"Yes! That is the one," Richard said. "Quite a bold name. *The Unconquerable Truth?* Everyone at court is talking about it."

Thomas nodded and feigned interest in a butterfly landing on a rosebud.

"Interesting," he said dispassionately, too dispassionately. Was he fooling his friend? "Has the king read it?"

"Oh yes!" Richard laughed. "You should hear him railing, 'Rubbish! It's all rubbish!'"

"He is angry, of course," Thomas said thoughtfully. "It was quite scathing."

Richard looked curiously at his old friend. "Yes, yes, it is, Thomas!"

The two men stood silent for a minute, as Richard searched Thomas's face.

"Thomas, you know that when the king finds out who wrote it, he will not be kind. His full wrath will fall on whoever wrote it," Richard finally said. "But I think you know that, friend."

Thomas looked away. There was no need for pretense. Richard already knew his biggest secrets. He had been with him in Saragossa. If he wanted to betray him, he would have done it long ago.

"When did you write it, Thomas?" Richard asked. "It *had* to have been you. The book had all the same arguments we talked about on the way home from Spain, and so much more!"

Thomas shook his head. He could not tell Richard. The less he knew, the less he could be tortured into confessing. It was better that Thomas pay for his own convictions and not anyone else. Already, Arnold Baker had been sent to a monastery, far from court, where he would be less likely to exaggerate reports of the French support. King Henry had punished Arnold Baker and, seemingly, forgotten Thomas. That made little sense, but so much of King Henry's decisions seemed impulsive and unpredictable. The best thing to do was to serve God and stay away from Henry. If that was even possible.

Publishing *Invicta Veritas* was hardly progress in Thomas's attempt to stay away from Henry. But somehow, he never really felt like he had a choice. To be silent was to shut up fire in his bones. He could only be silent for so long while the spiritual leaders of England called good evil and evil good. There was a time to speak, and that time was now.

Richard kicked a rock that had fallen across the walkway.

"Some people think Thomas More wrote the book or someone associated with him."

"No," Thomas said quickly. "It could not have been More's work."

"No?" Richard raised a brow. "Well, no, of course not. I think that the idea of More writing it under Henry's very nose at court is ridiculous, of course... But it's more than that. The writing is nothing like More's *Utopia*. It's not nearly as polished or..."

"Or what?" Thomas asked. It was a new experience to hear a critique of his work.

Richard frowned. "Well, it's not the same style. The vocabulary and cadence are... "

Thomas looked intently at Richard while he continued.

"Well, different ... just not the same caliber as Thomas More's writing. ... I think that ...

"Enough," Thomas said, coughing to conceal a smile that was quickly spreading into a self-conscious grin. "I wrote it in a hurry. It's not supposed to be *Utopia*. It's just a response to the European universities."

Richard stopped short and looked around to be sure there was no one else in the garden.

"So it was you!"

"Well, I thought you suspected."

"Yes, yes, I did. It is just that ... well, I need to know all about it."

Richard slapped Thomas affectionately on the back. "Well, done! I can't believe you did it." Then he stopped for a minute. "Of course, I did not mean to compare it to *Utopia*..."

"It's fine," Thomas said, laughing. "I am no Thomas More. Honestly, it would be a relief to talk about it."

Richard gaped at his friend, and his tone became serious. "Thomas, the king will kill you if he finds out."

"I know."

The two men said nothing for a moment.

"I gave my life to God a long time ago. If I die, my conscience will comfort me." He took a deep breath, the words now spoken aloud sounding both brave and hollow at the same time. Could he live what he said? Somehow, saying it out loud to Richard helped him believe it. "The truth is I thought I would pay with my life when we returned from Spain. God has given me three more years."

Richard grunted.

"Perhaps it was God's mercy that the king sent you and the queen's court away, out of sight, easier to forget you. But really, Thomas, *The Unconquerable Truth*? It is going to be more difficult to ignore that. You are a quiet one, but when you have something to say, you don't mince words."

Thomas shrugged. "The truth will set you free."

Richard gave him an amused look. "I hope you are still saying that from the Tower."

"So do I."

The two men walked in silence.

"Father Martin left me his notes," Thomas finally said. "I wanted to make sure that his arguments were heard."

"But the ideas were yours too," Richard said. "You have held these convictions for a long time—why come out now?"

Thomas walked along thoughtfully. He had been asking himself the same thing. The truth was, he felt that he had been late in giving his support to the queen. He had hoped that it would be enough for him to do as Father Martin had counseled him: listen to the queen, say Mass, serve her needs.

But then, when the scholars began saying that Henry and Katherine's marriage was a violation of God's law and the laws of nature, he simply could not be quiet anymore. To call a good thing bad or to say something God said was good was now bad ... it was all too much. And then, God said, *Write it down*. What else could he do?

"Cromwell suspects you," Richard finally said. "The court is abuzz with people reading *Invicta* and discussing who would be so bold. Cromwell asked me privately where you have been the last year. He wondered if you had made a trip to Antwerp."

Thomas raised an eyebrow. Not even the queen had known about his secret trip to the lowlands. She'd assumed he had been in London all that time.

"Of course, I told him that, to my knowledge, you were with the queen. Your service to her is very important to both of you," he said.

"I was in Antwerp," Thomas confessed. "Just for a fortnight, long enough to see the first copy pressed. Others brought the book into London last month."

Richard smiled. "You are brave, my friend, a true son of the Church. I want to hear all about it."

"Well, wait until you hear who paid for it," Thomas said with a smirk.

48

The Queen Learns About Invicta Veritas

Thomas stood in the doorway and watched Katherine pace the room. With trembling fingers, she twisted her rosary. She prayed aloud only part of the petitions, her quiet voice fading as if her anxious thoughts were winning the battle in her mind.

She looked up.

"Thomas!"

Katherine ran to her priest, heels clicking the cold stone floor, hands outstretched like a child.

Thomas grabbed her hands and searched her troubled gray eyes.

When had she begun calling him Thomas? Was it when he confronted the nun of Kent on the road to The More? Or was it earlier? When he returned from Spain, she had called him Father Abell. It must have been somewhere along the road between here and London.

The last few months in exile had been different from the previous years, and Thomas had grown to treasure Katherine's hard-earned trust. Ever since Saragossa, he knew *that she knew* he could be trusted. But he doubted she knew the depth of his affection for her. It was somewhere between the feelings he had for his sister Agnes and his own long-gone mother.

If he had married, could he have felt this way about a wife? Probably, he did not allow himself to think about it too often. But this familiarity, *this love* he had for his queen, felt like a holy affection—one that even Father Martin would have understood, though the intensity bothered him. It exposed his heart, even if only to himself. He swallowed hard. But still, she called him *Thomas*.

"My Queen."

Katherine's eyes swam in unshed tears, and now, as he held her hands with the affection of a son comforting his mother, she let them fall, sliding quickly down her weary face. How often had she wept in the privacy of his presence? The sight of her weeping never failed to reach deep into his soul and tug on his carefully guarded heart. He had become her safe place, and in doing so, she had exposed his heart to a new danger: Love.

"Margaret tells me Thomas Cromwell has sent a dispatch for you," she said, voice trembling. "He believes you wrote the book that troubles the king."

Thomas dropped the queen's hands and sat heavily on a stool next to her.

"My Queen, perhaps you are speaking of the response to the universities?"

"The universities?"

"Yes, the universities that have offered their opinion that our Lord, the king, has a right to annul your marriage." He said it delicately and respectfully. Even after all these years, he hated to bring up the divorce. But there was no avoiding it—it was an affront to her dignity every time it was mentioned.

"Oh," she said simply, twisting her fingers around the lace of an unfinished embroidered handkerchief. The stately black "H + K" mocked her.

Katherine was no child, no fool. Though far removed from court, she was well informed through less discreet sources. The Spanish ambassador, Eustace Chapuys, updated her in all his letters, as did her former ladies-in-waiting. Thomas knew that *she knew* about the king's request to the universities, and that many of them had come out in support of Henry's desire for a divorce.

"Chapuys wrote to me about the book, *Invicta Veritas*," she said, looking curiously at Thomas. "He did not know who could have written it."

Thomas took a deep breath. The book was still anonymous, and he would rather keep it that way. Telling Katherine would only increase her anxiety.

"How could Cromwell blame *you*?" she said. "When have you had time to write a book?"

A look of horror crossed her face.

"London? Did you write it when you were in London?"

Thomas was quiet, not acknowledging Katherine's question. But his silence was enough.

"Oh, Thomas!" She grabbed his hands again and searched his face frantically. "Cromwell will arrest you! The king will show no mercy!"

"King Henry will do nothing except what God allows," Thomas said with more hope than real faith. "May God save the king," he added, crossing his heart.

Hadn't the Apostle Paul commanded Timothy to pray for kings? He would pray for Henry's soul, though the words sometimes dripped with unrepentant bitterness for the man who made Katherine's life so miserable.

"Yes, God save the king," Katherine responded. She walked quickly to the cold hearth and poked at the ashes.

"Thomas, if Cromwell is coming here to arrest you, then you must leave! Immediately! You must find another place to live, at least until the king forgets about all of this."

"He won't forget, Katherine," Thomas quietly acknowledged.

"But you will not stay here and wait for him to arrest you," Katherine said, straightening her back. She spoke as a queen giving a command, something Thomas had not heard in a while. In a strange way, it gave him hope.

"Where should I go?" he asked, never dropping her steely gaze. "Bradwell? My sister's house? Cromwell knows where all of my family lives."

Katherine shook her head. "No, of course, not. You cannot go home, and I don't think you should go to Bradwell either." She began to pace, once again twisting her rosary and muttering prayers in half whispers.

Thomas nodded politely, unwilling to interrupt her prayers.

"I have a friend in ..."

"No!" Katherine said. "I don't want to know. I want to tell Cromwell's men that I have no idea where you are!" She sat down heavily and picked up the unfinished embroidery. Did she think Henry would ever wipe his eyes on it? She poked the dark thread through the fabric and pulled it up.

"Yes, then. You are right. I will leave today."

Katherine nodded, still looking down at the embroidery.

Thomas felt a deep ache in his chest. The king had abandoned Katherine, and now, here he was, leaving too. The thought pierced his heart. He had never wanted to hurt her. Why had he not foreseen that writing *Invicta* would lead to this?

49

A FRIEND IN LONDON

London

"You are the king's priest?" the balding man asked as he slowly cut a generous slab of hard, white Cheshire cheese and passed it to Thomas on a pewter tray.

Peter Danielson's townhome was less elegant than the royal palaces Thomas had lived in, but it was certainly far better apportioned than the homes of most inhabitants of the English capital city. The man and his fine home represented a growing class of merchants and artisans, people without blood connections to the nobility. They were men educated in working Latin and higher mathematics. They ran complicated, international businesses and paid their taxes on time. New money flowed through their coffers with enough left over to finance new industries and, apparently, to buy contraband books.

Men like Peter Danielson were rapidly rebuilding London in their own way, with their own ideas, ideas that often ran contrary to traditional religion. It made Thomas uneasy. England was changing, and in more than one way, and he longed for the safety of tradition. If only the Pope had answered his repeated request for asylum. He could be safely in Rome. But it seemed the Pope wanted no more trouble from England. Thomas would have to turn elsewhere for protection.

"My post is with Queen Katherine," he said carefully. Though William Tyndale had told him Danielson could be trusted, he wanted to gauge the man for himself.

Danielson ran his hand over the wooden table. It was an exquisite piece of Dutch workmanship. He had just told Thomas that his company's ship had arrived with it last week, along with a very heavy wooden clock concealing a crate of Tyndale's latest New Testaments.

Thomas nodded, trying to mask his conflicting thoughts about Tyndale's unauthorized edition of God's Holy Word circulating among Londoners.

"William writes that you could use a safe place to harbor for a bit," Danielson said critically, eyeing Thomas from his collar to his flowing black robes. "He failed to mention that you were a priest, let alone one who worked for the royal household. Will this put my family in danger?"

Thomas held his gaze steadily.

"I do not know," he said honestly. "I am a fugitive of the king, but I do not think my presence here could be traced. Our only common acquaintance is William, and the king's men would not know of my association with him. I have barely seen him since our Oxford days."

The man nodded.

"But you are a priest? Do you agree with Thomas More that William Tyndale is a heretic?"

The question, though expected, made Thomas uncomfortable. It was a conversation he had quietly bowed out of since he began focusing on the king's Great Matter and the university's blasphemous twisting of Scripture. In his concern for the queen's plight, there had been little room for him to consider Tyndale's English translation of Scripture. Perhaps he had intentionally not thought about it for fear he was changing his mind in a way the queen would not understand.

The truth was that he wanted William Tyndale and his friends to be treated honorably; their ideas debated civilly, like they had done all those late nights at the Old Bear. But that was something Thomas More seemed unwilling to do. It seemed More feared hell itself would devour England if he allowed the Protestants any bit of civility.

"I am a priest, and I am loyal to our Church traditions and the Holy Pope in Rome," he said without flinching. "I agree with Augustine on this matter. There may be corruption in God's Church, but the Church is my mother, and I love her as I love my queen."

Danielson crossed his arms and glowered at Thomas.

"Thomas More tortures men for reading Christ's words!"

Thomas shook his head and met Danielson's stormy gaze. "I do not condone that."

Danielson exhaled, but he kept his arms crossed, watching Thomas.

Thomas studied Danielson's face. What could he say that was true, loyal to the queen, and diplomatic? *Jesus, help me.*

"William Tyndale and I were good friends at Oxford," Thomas finally said, smiling slightly at the recollection. "We talked about ideas. We agreed on more than we disagreed ... at that time." He sighed. He knew from recent conversations with Tyndale that there were now more than a few things they would disagree on, as William's study of Luther had brought him to embrace more than one unorthodox view of the sacraments. But he wished his friend no ill; God could clarify what was amiss. He was confident that God would complete the good work he had begun in his friend and bring him to full truth. But just as importantly, there was still one thing that he and Tyndale agreed on, at least in principle.

"I agree with William that there ought to be an English translation of the Bible available for all men to read," Thomas said, raising his chin, hoping for a bit of common ground with his host. He left unsaid his conviction that it be an official Roman Catholic version.

Danielson raised an eyebrow. "And how would your queen feel about this?"

"We have not discussed it," Thomas confessed. Their relationship was not like his friendship with William or even his fellow priest, Richard Featherstone. He and Katherine never discussed new ideas. With her fierce loyalty to tradition in general and the Holy Roman Catholic Church in particular, Thomas doubted the conversation would ever go far. Her own parents had done far worse to heretics than Thomas More could have imagined. And she had been raised to believe that punishing apostates was the sacred duty of good Christian rulers. Ferret out the heretics before their unbelief spreads like a cancerous sore! Better for a few to burn than a nation be damned.

Thomas could not reconcile this way of thinking; it felt so foreign to Jesus's teachings, but he also knew good men who would disagree with him. It was best to keep his thoughts to himself and care for the queen's other matters. She was in no position to be burning heretics any time soon.

Danielson nodded.

"But you are loyal to Katherine, and you have written the book everyone is talking about?"

He said it both as a question and a statement. *Everyone?*

"I have written a work, published anonymously in Antwerp, challenging the king's interpretation of Scriptures. I believe he has twisted them for his own purposes," he said.

"Indeed!" Danielson said. "I have read *Invicta*, and I believe that many among Tyndale's friends agree with you."

Thomas pursed his lips thoughtfully. Danielson had read his most private thoughts on the king's Great Matter. He knew him better than most, although they had just met.

"My thoughts on an English translation of the Bible have changed over the years," he said carefully. "After spending time with William, I am beginning to think that if more Englishmen read Scripture for themselves, corrupt theologians who have taken bribes from a crooked and lustful king would not be able to pull the wool so easily over Englishmen's eyes."

As Thomas criticized King Henry, he felt his cheeks burn. He was not accustomed to speaking his criticisms of Henry out loud, and he certainly had not spoken so freely on his growing conviction that the Bible should be made available in English. Although he still hoped, against hope, that it would come through legitimate Church channels. A Roman Catholic-approved English translation would be a windfall for everyone.

Danielson nodded slowly, a toothy smile emerging from behind his thick beard.

"I see why you need hiding, Priest."

Thomas winced. Would his presence put Danielson and his family in jeopardy?

"Perhaps I can help the household in some way," he said quietly. "I am hoping Cromwell's warrant will expire in a few months, and the king will go back to other, more important matters."

Danielson raised an eyebrow. "Months?"

"I can look for other..."

"No, Thomas. You are a friend of William Tyndale. You are an odd Catholic priest, perhaps, but you are a friend, and you are welcome in my home."

Tears of relief stung Thomas's eyes. True Christian hospitality was a gift. He would not take it lightly.

"Perhaps you will not mind," Danielson continued, "but you should know that a collection of London's best *heretics* gathers here on occasion to do, as you say, debate the great issues." He smiled broadly. "They would enjoy including you in the conversation—if you wish."

Perhaps no generosity was without obligation.

"I would be grateful for your hospitality."

Danielson tore off a piece of hard bread and chewed it slowly, watching Thomas with amusement. He handed a piece to Thomas.

"Hopefully, you are still saying that in a month's time."

50

Tyndale People

In a month's time, Thomas was still enjoying his stay with Danielson's family. Like the family he grew up in, Danielson, his wife and their five children rose before dawn, even before distant cocks crowed the new day to life. Thomas could hear the children in the room below him praying their morning matins, welcoming the day. As far as he could tell, for being heretics, they still prayed the same prayers he did. It filled him with a warmth he had not felt in years.

Everyone in the Danielson home had their chores, including Thomas. Having lived with servants most of his life, Thomas enjoyed the manual labor, and there was still plenty of time left for him to study and write. He worked on his biblical Greek studies and reviewed what he was learning with Danielson's bright young sons, who were learning to read the Bible in the original Greek, just like he and Tyndale had encouraged the young scholars at Oxford to do. And every night, the family read from Tyndale's Bible.

The first night Thomas joined Danielson's family, he edged to the back of the sitting room as the family gathered around the hearth. Danielson's wife, Susanna, reached behind the egg basket, pulled away the string of drying onions, and found the rag bundle that concealed the Tyndale New Testament. She gingerly handed it to her husband.

The humbly bound book was so different from the chained vellum versions of the Vulgate Thomas cherished. This one, though larger than a prayer book, could be held in one hand. The leather binding, though new, was already worn.

Thomas could imagine a day when every English household had a Bible like the one in his hand. The thought filled him with joy, and yet, he still had lingering concerns about the translation process and how people would treat the Bible once it became commonplace.

For Thomas, going to the library to read the Word of God in Latin had been a holy treat—an activity saved for special days, a reward for years of Latin study. It was a privilege afforded to those who had earned the right to read Scripture and pass it down to others.

Danielson carefully opened the book to the page he had read the night before and began reading from Matthew, the teachings of Jesus, the story of the Sower. It was both foreign and familiar to hear the parable in English. Thomas leaned in. What English words had William chosen for the passage he knew in Latin?

The youngest of Danielson's children fidgeted, wiggling in his mother's lap, but the other four children sat quietly, eyes focused on their father. One of the girls, seated at her mother's feet, twisted the blond hair that fell disheveled outside her sleeping cap. Her younger brother sat rigidly on a three-legged stool. He sucked his fingers while he listened. *A farmer went out to sow a crop.*

Thomas, of course, knew the story and had read it to his Oxford parish in Latin, but to see the children's faces, hearing the story for the first time, somehow dramatized it in a way he had never heard it before. A farmer went out to sow a crop. These children, this next generation of Englishmen, were soil right before him. This was Tyndale's dream: children hearing God's word in their native language. Tears sprang to his eyes. *William, I wish you could hear this.*

If only the Bible could be legally printed in England like it was in France and other Catholic countries, which allowed the vernacular Scripture. There had been no official papal edicts forbidding the Bible in English. That prohibition had been the work of Parliament after the Lollard uprising. There was no reason that there could not be an official translation sanctioned by both the king and the Pope. Surely, it would benefit all.

Thomas closed his eyes and prayed it would be so.

When Thomas opened his eyes, he saw Danielson watching him. The children turned their gaze to Thomas. He smiled. "Do you want to read the Scripture?"

It did not sound like a challenge, but Thomas hesitated. The Bible was still contraband, officially illegal. Possessing a copy of the book was enough to warrant arrest. And yet, he had written a book like that too.

He opened his palms.

"Thank you," he said, cradling the leather-bound book in his hands. This was the project William had worked so hard on. He gently turned the delicate pages to the first chapter of John. He knew that part by heart in the Vulgate. Like an Italian tune or an English melody, the Vulgate's Latin version of John 1 resonated as it flowed out of his mouth.

"In principio erat Verbum et Verbum erat apud Deum et Deus erat Verbum," he breathed out with a sad smile. He had not been much older than Danielson's boys when he'd learned those beautiful lines. He smiled at the children's faces and then looked at the page in his hand. "In the beginning was the Word and the Word was with God: and the Word was God." He smiled. *Well done, William.* It was a perfect translation.

Danielson smiled too.

"Please continue," Danielson's middle son, the one with curly brown hair and freckles, said. "I like hearing them both."

Danielson's sons had gone to grammar school, so like many other young men in the new middle class, they had a working knowledge of Latin. Unlike most people in England, they could understand both Latin and Tyndale's new translation.

Thomas sat with the family for at least an hour, reciting what he remembered of the Vulgate and comparing it to Tyndale's translation. Most of it matched well.

"Thank you, Father Thomas," Susanna said, absently kissing her toddler's sleeping head. "But I do think it's time the children get to bed." She smiled, and Thomas handed her the New Testament, ready to be hidden away among the family's provisions. *Real food*, Thomas thought, *daily bread*.

Although Thomas enjoyed the family Scripture readings in English, he missed the daily Mass—receiving the Body and Blood of Christ and remembering His sacrifice. He felt so close to God in those moments of worship. To miss them made him feel cut off from Christ's Church. Danielson's family attended the local parish together on Sunday mornings, but Thomas had not gone for fear that he would be recognized.

"Just wear regular clothing," Danielson's middle son suggested. "Maybe people will not recognize you in breeches and a cap."

The thought made Thomas smile. He had worn nothing but his priest's habit since his ordination nearly twenty years earlier. He wondered what regular breeches and a common shirt would look like on him.

Danielson must have wondered too, because the next Sunday morning, as the family rose with the dawn, the man climbed up into the attic where Thomas had made his temporary home. He handed him a bundle.

"I hear you miss attending Mass," he said with an amused look. "Try these on. I think you would be surprised how different you look."

51

MASS IN LONDON

Thomas fidgeted uncomfortably in Peter Danielson's leather jerkin and breeches. The merchant was several inches shorter and quite a bit wider, making the outer garment both too big and too small. Thomas tugged on his inner linen shirt, pulling down on the doublet that was slightly too short and cinching the baggy breeches. Thankfully, his own gray woolen stockings covered the difference in the length of their legs. Was it obvious he was wearing another man's clothes?

"You look fine," Susanna Danielson whispered as they ducked into the little chapel. He cleared his throat and looked ahead.

Londoners from the local neighborhood quietly filled the pews, taking their worn places while priests in floor-length black robes arranged the elements on pewter trays. An older priest swung a bronze incense pot side to side down the parish aisle, creating a trail of fragrant smoke. Thomas closed his eyes and inhaled deeply. It was good to be home, even in a place he had never been.

Thomas did not recognize any familiar faces, not among the parishioners or the priests, and why should he? His entire time living in London had been in the royal court. His only chapel had been the queen's chapel or whatever cathedral he had accompanied her to. Occasionally, he excused himself from the royal company and strolled to the village parish nearest Greenwich Palace. Still, those experiences had been few and far between. Now, sitting with English people, experiencing worship in the borrowed clothes of a London merchant with Lutheran leanings, he felt a wave of relief, like a foreigner coming home. These were his people. This was his church.

It reminded him of his childhood parish at St. James Church in Nayland. His father, a wealthy wool trader, insisted the family was in church every week. Most villagers were sure to make it to church on Easter, attending confession at least once during Lent. But Thomas's parents were pious people, observing every religious day and participating in every sacred feast. His earliest memories were candlelit halls and processions at Corpus Christi. He remembered his tall father, removing his shoes and creeping barefoot to the altar on Good Friday. "Never take Christ's sacrifice lightly," he would say.

"The king quotes Holy Scripture when he says he ought to divorce the queen," he heard the priest say to a large man in front of him.

"But I have read *Invicta*," the man whispered. "Everyone in Parliament is talking about it. My cousin let me borrow his copy. It's quite... convincing."

Thomas felt his heart beat faster. He wanted to slip away and hide in Danielson's attic, but he also desperately wanted to hear the conversation.

"Hmm," the priest said. "I heard that the king ordered that book burned in Oxford. It's rubbish, apparently."

"But have you read it?" the man asked.

"Well, no," the priest said, straightening his long black robe. "You cannot be expected to read everything printed these days."

"I can tell you that the writer is quite upset with the king for twisting Scripture. He says God commanded the Jews to marry their dead brother's widow if she does not have any children to take care of her, and it is no bad thing to do it neither. Matter of fact, they were commanded to marry 'em. God said they had to do it. So, it wasn't evil." The big man stood a little taller. He must have enjoyed explaining the argument to his priest. "So now, we don't hold to the Old Covenant, of course, but saying God told the Jews to do something against the law of nature," the man shuddered, "is just plain wrong. It's like saying God is evil. And that book says that is blasphemy."

Thomas felt his heart leap. *The man understood!*

The priest crossed his arms. "Well, Big John, that sounds interesting, but we know nothing about the writer. He could be a clever heretic for all we know."

Thomas felt his cheeks burning.

"He is not a heretic," Danielson interjected. "I've met him, a likable fellow—a trained priest, actually."

"Really?" The priest raised one eyebrow. "You've met him?"

Thomas turned to leave. He did not trust himself to stay.

"Good sir." The big man grabbed Thomas's elbow as he turned to exit. "I don't believe we have met. You are a friend of the Danielsons?"

"Yes." Thomas breathed heavily, straightening his doublet. "The Danielsons have offered me hospitality during my stay in London," he said simply. He could feel the priest staring at him.

"I am John Bowler; my friends call me Big John," the man said, patting his robust girth. He nudged the priest. "My brother, our priest, says it's one of the seven deadly sins—gluttony. He's probably right."

Thomas forced a smile. He knew it was appropriate to give his name and say something light and charming. But he could not. He had spent so much of his life defending the truth in all forms that he could not think of a false name to give for himself. George. William. John. He just could not make the words pass through his lips. So, he stood uncomfortably in Danielson's breeches and hoped God would intervene. He did.

Just as Thomas thought he could no longer continue the pretense, someone rang a light bell, and the priest began the Mass.

Thomas knelt with the Danielsons in prayer.

"Thank you, Holy Father," he whispered. The palms he held together were sweaty, though the chapel was cold. "Keep me in your peace."

When the Mass concluded, Thomas remained at the altar, kneeling before the Host.

"Jesus, Savior of my soul, guide me," he whispered. The world was confusing; right was wrong, and wrong was right, and all he wanted to do was be faithful to the end, to hear those precious words: *Well done, good and faithful servant.* At least, that was what his soul wanted. His flesh, he knew only too well, wanted many things.

"Jesus Christ, have mercy on me, a sinner," he whispered, pressing his fist against his chest.

The priest who had listened to Big John put his hand on Thomas's quaking shoulder.

"Do you want to make a confession?" he asked discreetly.

What could he say? To whom could he confess his sins? And what was sin, and how was God redirecting him? Thomas looked up at the priest and wondered if the young man could see the torment in his eyes. Of course, he could. He might deceive kings and cardinals, but in the presence of the Lord, he felt his soul stripped bare. He was undone, and he knew the priest could tell. He had been on the other side of that exchange too many times not to know what it was like.

"I am not sure where the Good Shepherd is leading," Thomas said simply.

"Do you need to confess?" the priest asked again.

"No," Thomas said. "I think I just need guidance."

"Do you want to talk?"

Thomas hesitated. Of course, he wanted to talk. But he wanted to talk with Father Martin or maybe even his friend Richard Featherstone. How could this priest he barely knew give him any advice, any assurance that he was on the right path?

Thomas shook his head.

"Perhaps later," he said thoughtfully.

"Then please, come by the church tomorrow morning. Maybe then you will be ready," he said with a measure of youthful confidence Thomas found annoying. Had he been like that? Probably. It didn't matter. There was nothing the young man could say that would help his restless heart.

52

A CONFESSION

Despite what Thomas had told himself and the young priest at Danielson's church, he found himself standing on the threshold of the rectory on Monday morning, knuckles pounding on the heavy wooden door. He was still wearing Danielson's breeches, though he kept his priestly collar concealed under his shirt this time. He would keep his identity hidden from others, but for himself, he needed to remember who he was. He was Thomas Abell, a Roman Catholic priest, a servant of God, and chaplain to the Queen of England.

"You returned!" the young priest said with a look of astonishment when he opened the door. It was clear that he had been eating his morning meal. Bits of bread clung to the corners of his lips, under his uncombed beard.

"Have I come at a bad time?" Thomas asked.

"No, no! Not at all," the priest said in a voice too high to be convincing. He looked down the alley to see if anyone else was with Thomas, a peculiar custom that Thomas had begun to observe everywhere. *Was everyone in London checking alleys? When did we all start living in fear?*

"I was reading the book Big John gave me," he said. "Perhaps you heard us talking about it yesterday."

Thomas nodded, trying not to register anything that would give himself away.

The priest clasped his hands.

"But I am sorry, that is not why you came here," he said apologetically.

If only he knew, Thomas thought, but he was quiet, letting the sound of distant children distract him from his fears. The priest must wonder what sin he had come to confess. The realization filled Thomas with shame and then a bit of irritation for feeling shame. He had done nothing wrong. He just needed direction.

"I wanted to take you up on your offer for spiritual counsel," he said. "There are so few I can speak with."

The priest looked concerned, and Thomas remembered again how very young he looked.

"I am sorry," the young man said. "My name is Andrew Wilmouth, but I did not get your name, and Danielson did not tell me."

"My name is Thomas," he said quietly. He looked past the priest into the open rectory behind him. "Perhaps we could go inside?"

"And that is why I am here in London, and I don't know what to do next ..."

Andrew sat wide-eyed on the end of the pew, with one hand covering his mouth.

"You wrote Invicta Veritas?" he finally asked.

Thomas nodded.

"Oh," the young priest said. "And now there is a warrant for your arrest? Cromwell is looking for you? But nobody knows that you wrote this?" He picked up a copy of the book, and Thomas stared. It was the first time he had seen it outside of the printer's shop, and it looked so harmless in the young priest's hands.

Andrew folded his hands and wrinkled his brow. "Well, you don't seem to have committed any of the seven deadly sins, and

I don't see any carnal sins. Have you neglected to do an act of mercy?"

Thomas was quiet and then shook his head. "No, my conscience is clear about that."

"Well," said Andrew. "What did you want from me?"

Thomas stood up. *What was he thinking?*

"I am sorry. I think I just needed to talk to someone."

He started to go, and Andrew grabbed his arm. "Please, Father, I don't know how to advise you, but at least let us pray together. I can do that."

The two priests walked into the empty church, and Andrew lit a candle and knelt.

"We can ask for wisdom. St. James says God will give wisdom to anyone who asks," Andrew said in a way that made Thomas smile. He remembered being a young priest. It always felt awkward to give spiritual counsel to older men.

"Yes," Thomas said, nodding. "That is true." He had just heard Danielson's wife read that passage from the Tyndale Bible. Perhaps he had read it once before in the Vulgate, but it had been a long time ago. Maybe he had forgotten it.

The two men knelt, and Thomas whispered, "Holy Father, give me wisdom to know what to do."

The men were quiet for a long time, and finally Thomas said, "Andrew, I believe it is time for me to speak up. Will you let me use your pulpit?"

Andrew smiled. "Indeed!"

To Serve God

Tall Tree Press

53

A PUBLIC PROFESSION OF FAITH

August 1532   London

Thomas peered over the high lectern at the sea of unknown faces swirling below him. Men, women, children. He scanned them until he found Danielson's upturned face and steady gaze. Danielson nodded. The corner of Thomas's mouth lifted into a slight smile, and he closed his eyes. *Thank you, friend.*

Thomas touched his silver cross necklace and smoothed his long vestments. He had chosen his best chasuble, the one Katherine had commissioned for him when he returned from Spain. It was white with gold banding and a subtle floral damask design that matched the red damask that Katherine's ladies wore at court. It was good to be wearing his own clothes again. It was good to represent his Queen. He was doing the right thing. It was time to speak.

Father Andrew stood at the front of the congregation, shifting his weight and clasping his hands awkwardly. *Was he worried too? He should be.* Father Andrew straightened his back and announced there would be a special address from a friend of the parish.

English faces turned and looked up at Thomas, suspended in the pulpit above them. He inhaled deeply and let go of the edge of the gilded lectern he had been squeezing. *Jesus Christ, have mercy.* The people before him did not know who he was or where he had been. He could speak with anonymity. But he chose not to.

"My name is Thomas Abell," he said, clearing his throat. "I am the chaplain to our Majesty, the Queen Katherine of Aragon, the rightful queen of England."

Thomas heard a few soft gasps and then the silence of a fully attentive body.

He swallowed hard and straightened his back to its full height. *Look them in the eyes*, he reminded himself. *Make them see.*

"There has been confusion about Katherine's position as our queen, particularly what the Scripture says about marriage, ah ... the king and queen's marriage," he began. "And, as far as God has permitted, I would like to tell you what I believe to be true."

Thomas explained the reasons for marriage and why the Church included it as a holy sacrament. Then, he talked about the argument Henry VIII made that his marriage was invalid. Speaking evenly, looking from face to face, he was aware that every word he spoke would raise the ire of their all-powerful monarch, yet he continued. Thomas carefully explained why it was offensive for King Henry to use Leviticus to dishonorably dispose of his wife. It was an offense against their queen, but also against women everywhere, and ultimately, God Almighty, whose words the king twisted to get his own way.

When he was finished, there was an uncomfortable silence until an old woman in beggar's clothing called out, "And what would ye have us do?"

The church fell to murmuring, and Thomas held up his hands for silence.

"Please, please, I ask you to pray for the queen. Pray for the king, as Scripture demands, and pray for England."

Andrew motioned for everyone to rise.

"Let us do that now," he said, and one by one, the crowd fell to kneeling, silently pleading to God for the royal family. Some prayed liturgical prayers, holding their rosaries as they prayed. Others whispered spontaneous prayers. *Lord, have mercy. Christ, have mercy. Lord, hear our prayers.*

Thomas's eyes filled with tears. It was more than he had hoped for. *Thank you, God. Bless Katherine and Henry. Your will be done on Earth as it is in Heaven. Amen.*

54

ON THE ROAD

The next morning, Thomas gently placed his hands on Danielson's children and blessed them: *Father God, protect them and hold them in your loving hands.* Would he ever see them again? Lord willing, but perhaps not.

He embraced Danielson, now a brother and a friend, and touched Susanna's shoulder affectionately.

"Thank you," he said, tears welling as he held Susanna's gaze. "You opened your home to me, at your own risk and expense. May God bless you ten times over." He made the sign of the cross over the family and their humble home.

Then he quietly walked down their cobblestone alley onto the main street and into the London crowd rushing from one place to another. The city was always moving, and it was time for him to move too. It was time to speak up, time to listen for God's direction, and time to say whatever He instructed him to say. But where?

As Thomas walked along, he saw a detachment of the king's soldiers pass by, headed for the king's palace. Their armor glistened in the bright morning light. What would life in the royal house have been like if circumstances had been different? Would he have ever learned to enjoy court life? Would he have always felt like a stranger, a professor without a classroom?

It was late summer now, and the word on the street was that the king had made up his mind to divorce Katherine and marry

Anne. He would not wait for the Pope's consent. He would grant himself permission. He was, after all, the supreme King of England, the representative of God on Earth. Why should he not also be the head of the church in England?

Thomas shook his head. What arrogance! He grimaced and kicked a loose cobblestone.

Pray for those in authority.

Thomas nodded in agreement with the Spirit's conviction. *Yes, Lord, bless King Henry in your mighty name. Give him the grace to repent of his sins. Help him lead our country well.*

As Thomas passed through a market square, a shrill voice stopped him short. He knew that tone, that voice, that message. It made his skin crawl.

"Harken my words," the young woman cried. "If the king divorces his wife and marries the Whore, he will die in seven months' time. Mark my words!"

Elizabeth Barton! The nun from Kent! She was back in London, standing high above the crowd on the top of an ox cart.

A small group of strongmen stood around Elizabeth like the king's own guard, protecting her from the insults of the crowd as she made her shocking proclamation. Curious Londoners: men, women, and children, lingered along the road, listening. The king would die in seven months! England would be forced into turmoil as men rallied for power. Poverty! Peril! A famine! Chaos would ensue, not unlike the chaos that surrounded this Elizabeth Barton from Kent.

Thomas saw Elizabeth's bare, outstretched arm and looked away. Were the people simply drawn to the unusual sight of a young woman speaking publicly, her creamy white arms reflecting the summer sun, her blonde hair dangling suggestively outside of her black veil? She seemed to have abandoned her black habit for an ill-fitting peasant dress that revealed more of her arms and chest than any respectable sister of the Church would allow. It felt wrong.

Thomas hugged his satchel closer and kept his eyes low as he edged through the crowd.

Why should he react so strongly to her? Their messages were different. She prophesied the king's demise and death; he simply disagreed with Henry's theological arguments for the divorce. He prayed for the king's welfare, and Thomas knew his Queen Katherine did the same.

"You," Elizabeth shouted, stopping in the middle of her sentence. "Have you harkened to God's call?"

Thomas looked up and, as if against his will, locked eyes with the nun. She was pointing directly at him, and he felt the heat rise in his cheeks as the crowd stared. He said nothing. Lowering his gaze, he hurried past, through the crowd. He would not engage with Elizabeth Barton.

"You must choose!" he heard her shout as he turned down the nearest street.

The cool morning turned into the hot afternoon, and the thickly packed neighborhoods gave way to the countryside. Thomas walked with his back to the sun, instinctively walking East, toward Essex and his family's ancestral lands. Was he longing for the embrace of home, the familiar, a place where he could take refuge from this political jockeying and constant fear? Maybe. But home, *that* home, was a distant memory. Only his sister Agnes and her family lived in the house. He could not endanger their lives by going there. Already, he had written to Agnes and told her that he was well, but he would not put her family in danger.

This road was his and his alone. He had written *Invicta Veritas*. No one else should pay for his decisions. "Holy Father, guide me," he whispered as he walked. He felt for the rosary at his belt and rotated it between his finger and thumb, remembering the prayers of his youth. He said them in both Latin and English and, just for fun, he tried to remember them in Spanish.

When he was tired, he rested under a tree. He had not packed any food, and he was getting hungry. The thought of the queen's table made his stomach growl. How he would love a bit of fresh bread, roasted pheasant ... Even a stew of turnips and parsnips would do.

Would he spend the rest of his life in exile? What if the nun from Kent was right? What if the king perished? Would Katherine and her daughter return to court? Would they rule England? He would not allow himself to hope that was possible. *God bless King Henry.* He would pray for his sovereign. Scripture and Church tradition commanded him to do so. He could do no less, even if it killed him.

55

CARTHUSIANS

"Are you well?" a cautious young male voice inquired.

Thomas opened his bleary eyes and saw a group of monks surrounding him, their heads silhouetted in the bright morning light. From their simple white vestments, Thomas recognized they were Carthusian monks, holy men given to silent prayer and meditation, men of God rarely seen outside their cloister walls.

Each monk carried a basket overflowing with apples, and Thomas's stomach growled.

"Ye hungry, Father?" an older monk said quietly, as if not quite used to hearing his own voice. He handed Thomas a piece of ripe, red fruit.

"Yes," Thomas said. "Thank you!"

He closed his eyes and offered a silent prayer and, with a crunch, bit into the late summer apple, so much better than the king's best cake or his grandmother's gingerbread. He wiped the juice from his cheek as he uttered another thank you to the watching monks.

Thomas stood up and stretched.

Sleeping under a tree in summer was a fine holiday for young people, but his bones were used to royal beds, or at least the comfortable straw mattress in Danielson's attic. Every muscle ached. But he was grateful for the breakfast.

"Are you Carthusians? From the London Charterhouse?" Thomas asked. Though they had spoken to him, they stood quietly among themselves. Not simply men of few words, the Carthusians were a silent order, spending their lives in prayer and meditation. The lay brothers of their order were permitted one day a week to speak as they went about business that took them beyond the friary walls.

"Yes," the oldest one said simply. "We are the brothers."

Thomas searched the Carthusians' quiet faces. What would it be like to live in silence, contemplating God? It was a life Thomas deeply admired.

When he was a young student, Thomas had walked past the high monastery walls in Oxford. He had thought that it would be nice to retreat fully from the world. He tried days of fasting, both food and silence, to see if he could be a monk. But he could never last more than a day or two. Maybe God made some priests for silence and some for words.

But now, more than ever, the silent life of Carthusians allured him. Could he retreat into the confines of the monastery and leave the world behind? Did the silent Carthusian monks even know about King Henry VIII and his plans to divorce Katherine? Would they care? He would not disturb their peace—or his own—by talking about it.

But as it turned out, the lay brothers were happy to make use of their free talking day. They had learned much about the outside world and were eager to get back to London to tell their brothers before a new week of silence began. They invited Thomas to join them for the walk.

Thomas did not have the heart to tell them he had just come from the city, and something in his spirit told him it was good to return with them. Perhaps a few hours with the brothers would clarify his journey. So, he picked up his bundle and began walking with them.

When they asked about his business on the road, he explained everything without holding back.

"Ye be speaking of the king's divorce?" one of the Carthusians asked after Thomas explained his predicament. Thomas nodded. There was no point hiding. The monks might have been sworn to silence, but the Lord had released him to speak freely in defense of Katherine's marriage. He would do so.

The men walked along, listening to Thomas, until one stopped and set his basket down.

The other men gathered around him, set theirs down, and proceeded to kneel and pray. Thomas joined them. In the quiet prayer, he recognized that his heart was disturbed. *Oh, my soul, why so downcast? Put your hope in God.* It was good to remember God in the moment.

When they silently stood and began walking, one of the younger monks spoke up. "We have just heard that the king's man, Thomas Cromwell, intends to shut down the monasteries."

Thomas raised an eyebrow.

"How would he do that—and why?"

"Perhaps ye know that Cardinal Wolsey, God bless his soul, was planning to consolidate some of the friaries," the young man began explaining.

Thomas thought about Frideswide's Abbey and the construction that he and Father Martin had walked through just a few years earlier. He had heard that after Wolsey's death, the king was continuing the work. He planned to build a college.

"Yes," Thomas said. "I have heard about Wolsey's work in Oxford, but what of Cromwell's closing monasteries?"

The monk quickened his pace, and Thomas matched his stride. "Yes. And the king may sever ties with Rome altogether."

Thomas stopped short. Was Henry's passion for Anne so consuming he had forgotten his own soul?

The monk looked gravely at Thomas.

"It is true, Father Abell. The process is beginning now."

Thomas continued walking. *How? Why?* What would it mean for the monks throughout England—the last hope for the sick and poor? Who would care for the farmers in years of drought and plague? Disbanding the monasteries would devastate the most vulnerable people in England.

"He plans to take the land for himself, pay off his debtors, and fill the royal coffers again."

Thomas felt the heat rise in his cheeks and the burn of acid in his stomach. Blasphemy and pure evil! Would God allow it? Henry was a gluttonous king who squandered his country's wealth in vanity wars. He depleted the royal treasury to satisfy the lusts of his flesh. How much had he spent on the Field of Cloth of Gold in France and on the lavish banquets he threw every time an influential statesman arrived at his doorstep? He had bankrupted England to serve his own ends. Would he now rob the Church, the very instrument left to serve the poor? It could not be so. *God Almighty, have mercy!*

If Katherine were at court, she would not have allowed it. She had always been a good influence on her husband, gently pointing him in the right direction. Although Thomas himself had not been in the royal household to see it, older servants had told him that in the early days, Henry and Katherine had always attended Mass together. One parish priest told him that on every Good Friday, the majestic King of England removed his shoes and crept barefoot to the foot of the cross. The Pope had given him the title "Defender of the Faith!" How could a man who had dined his whole life on Holy Eucharist spit on his Mother and forsake his Father's faith?

"We will not allow it, of course," the Carthusian monk said with a sad smile. "We may be silent, but we will not be put away, as some of the monks are prepared to do. We cannot be bought off with a few pounds and a cottage in the country. We serve God and whatever he says. If this costs us our lives, well, then our lives we will part with."

It was more than the old monk had said all morning, and Thomas could see that he meant every word.

The other monks nodded solemnly, and one of them crossed himself.

"We are all in agreement at the Carthusian House. We will not surrender to the king," he said.

So, this was what the world was coming to. The king was setting himself up against not only the Pope in Rome but Christ's church in

England. The nun from Kent had been right. Thomas would have to choose, and not just between Katherine and Henry, the monarchy or the Church. It might come to a choice between obedience and life itself.

But it was not a difficult choice. He had made it long ago when he knelt and made his priestly vows. As for him, he would serve the Lord. St. Paul had said that to live was for Christ, and to die was gain. He had just read that in Tyndale's New Testament.

Thomas looked down the dusty road ahead. Like Father Martin had said, the world was shifting. Who knew what tomorrow would bring? If he went with the monks, perhaps he could stay with them—if not for the rest of his life, then perhaps for a season.

"Then I will go with you," he said.

Thomas and the Carthusian monks walked westward all afternoon and arrived at the London Charterhouse just before Vespers. The monks nodded silently to Thomas and went inside the great church, but Thomas did not follow them. Instead, he reverently stood in the garden outside the main church, listening to the monks sing the Gregorian chant. The Latin words washed over him, nourishing his soul. He had heard the choral music many times before in Oxford and in the king's court, but this afternoon, in the midst of his own inner turmoil, he found the song hauntingly beautiful, like salve on the bitterness of his soul. He could stay within the walls of the monastery forever.

But I don't want you to.

Thomas closed his eyes, pressed his hands together, and tried to free his mind of every other thought. *Lord, where do you want me to go? My life is yours. If it is your desire for me to spend my life in solitary contemplation, then I will. I will learn how to be present with you in the stillness.*

Thomas took in a deep breath and knew that someday he would do that very thing. But not here. Not with these brothers.

One day they will take you by the hand, and lead you where you don't want to go.

Thomas felt a lump in his throat, the longing. What was it about this journey that exposed the crevasses of his soul? The more he opened his heart, the more he felt the pain of his longing, the need for the fullness of God, the knowledge of the Almighty, both heart and head. Oh, that he would drink deep from the Fountain of Life! But it was not to be here.

Thomas opened his eyes. A bird was perched on the monastery wall. It was free to fly anywhere, so untethered to this world. And perhaps, so was he.

Unlike the monks he met on the way, Thomas was free to go. His vows had not tethered him to a place—only to a person: the Lord Jesus Christ and His Church on Earth. *Where should I fly, Lord?*

To the king.

Thomas jumped as if someone had slapped him. Could that have been the Spirit, or was he going crazy? He had seen priests lose their wits due to sickness or extreme pressures. Was he leaving all sanity behind? No. It was the same quiet voice he had heard a moment before.

Yes, Lord. I'm listening.

Thomas could still hear the Gregorian chanting. It filled the hall and bounced off the stone wall around the courtyard. He was sure that people passing by could hear it too. Male voices rising together like a rolling river, a community of sound.

"I'm listening, Lord," Thomas whispered.

Talk to him about the book. He will listen.

Thomas sighed. It was more than he could do on his own strength. He knelt in the garden. With all the monks inside offering evening prayers, he was alone. He trembled as he spoke.

"Yes, Lord Jesus, if it is the last thing I do, I will obey."

He made the sign of the cross and rose. By the time the monks filed silently out of the church, Thomas was already walking through the streets of London, heading for York Hall, his heart in his hands.

56

A VISIT WITH THE KING

"Your Majesty, the priest Thomas Abell," the crier called out as Thomas entered the Great Hall. He strode with holy confidence despite the weakness in the pit of his stomach.

Like the first time he entered that familiar hall, the room was full of courtiers and administrators. He recognized a few of them, and from the look on Anne Boleyn's face, more than a few recognized him as well.

"Well, would you believe it? It's my poor Katherine's good priest, Thomas Abell," King Henry said, magnanimously extending a hand. Perhaps he had arrived on one of the king's rare "good" days.

"How is my dear sister, our faithful queen dowager?"

Thomas smiled sadly. "Our dear Katherine is well in body, though distressed in spirit."

Henry frowned. "I see."

It was the kind of polite exchange everyone expected, but Henry looked curiously at Thomas as if not completely surprised by his unannounced entrance.

Courtiers who had been engaged in other conversations sidled closer to the king. They moved close enough to enjoy the inevitable spectacle of Henry's wrath. They looked positively gleeful in anticipation.

Thomas pushed down a stab of irritation. Just a few years ago, they spoke well of him; some of them regularly came to confession when he held Mass. But that was back then, before the trial at Blackfriars, before the queen was banished from court, before the king's Great Matter became the black shadow that eclipsed the sun.

Thomas Cromwell, who had been leaning ever closer to the king, whispered something that Thomas could not hear. The king's face darkened, and whatever confidence Thomas had enjoyed a moment earlier vanished. A stab of panic punched him in the gut. What was he doing here? *Steady me, Lord!*

"Cromwell informs me ... that his sources tell him ... that you, Thomas Abell, wrote that wretched piece of rubbish against my divorce!" His ruddy cheeks took on an even darker hue as his temper appeared to rise with every word he uttered. "You said that England's best theologians are blasphemers. Isn't that a bit much, Father Abell? Blasphemers?"

King Henry took a step toward Thomas, and Thomas told his knees to be still.

"I came to the church in humility, *repenting* of my incestuous relationship with Katherine. I *relinquished* my right to be married to her, and I respectfully *requested* the Pope annul our marriage, and you, YOU, construe my motives and suggest my scruples are merely my lust!" The king's voice grew louder with each accusation. "You ally yourself with enemies of the Crown to oppose me! It is treason!"

The entire room was quiet, except for the snickering of the king's colorful fool who squatted in the corner, his fat hands stuffed into his mouth.

"What have you to say for yourself, man of God!" the king demanded.

Thomas swallowed hard. The king's words reverberated through the Great Hall.

"Thank you for giving me audience, Your Majesty," Thomas finally said when he found his voice. *You will speak before kings... Jesus, help me.*

"How brazen it is for you to come here today," Henry shouted. "Guards!"

Thomas held up his hands, a form of surrender, not so much to King Henry, but to the God who had sent him into the fray.

"I wish to speak to you about *Invicta Veritas*. As you have said, I am the author."

A murmur rushed through the room as Thomas Cromwell broke into an uncharacteristically wide smile. "As I thought," he said.

"She said you would come!" the fool exploded, jumping up and hopping from one foot to another. "The lady, the witch from Kent, she said, she said, she said you would come."

"Get him out of here!" Henry bellowed, but when the guards moved toward Thomas, he interrupted, "Not the priest! The fool!"

The room fell to murmurs, and Thomas felt the watchful eyes of every courtier. Anne Boleyn's stare pierced his resolve like daggers. *Steady me, Lord.*

The guards grabbed the cackling jester as Henry turned to Thomas.

"Did the nun from Kent send you?" the king asked.

"No," Thomas said, confused. Why was the nun involved? He shook his head. "No!"

"Is she an acquaintance of yours?"

"No," Thomas replied hoarsely. "I know who she is, but she is no friend or ally."

King Henry looked at Thomas curiously. The storm seemed to have blown over a bit. How could the man change moods faster than his servants could change his waistcoat?

"You look better than the last time I saw you," Henry finally said.

Thomas touched his face.

"Yes," Henry said with a smirk. "You were a bit black and blue. Protesting that your companion had so inaccurately reported the results of the French universities. I believe you objected to the word *unanimous* when it was more like three out of four, six out of eight, whatever it was ..."

Henry glanced at Thomas Cromwell, his personal accountant and mathematician.

"Five out of seven," Cromwell stated with a respectful nod.

"You do have a penchant for accuracy, Father Abell," the king said, his eyes narrowing. "But we never discussed it, did we? ... Let's take a turn."

The king placed his heavy hand on Thomas's shoulder and turned him toward the high-arched door leading out of the Great Hall. Thomas willed his heart to slow down, his knees to stop shaking, and his mind to think clearly. *Jesus Christ, Son of God, have mercy.*

Thomas Cromwell and the king's bodyguards stepped in line, several yards behind them, as they walked out of the Great Hall and down the stairs toward the garden.

"I do my thinking in the garden," the king said simply, as if his angry outburst had never happened.

Thomas nodded. It was a good place to think, and also a good place to meet with God. *God, meet with us!*

"Explain your argument," Henry said quietly as they entered the palace garden. Cromwell and the other men were just out of earshot. "I have read it ..." He stopped and looked at Thomas. "It is rubbish, of course, but since you are here, and if my dear Anne has her way I will never see you again, I would like to know ..."

The king started walking again. Then in an almost humbled tone, far away from the ears and eyes of Anne Boleyn and his courtiers, he whispered thickly, "I need to know."

Thomas looked at Henry out of the corner of his eye. Was the king truly tormented by his conscience? Perhaps he was not too far gone. *Lord Jesus, is this why I am here?*

"Your Majesty," Thomas began, "I wrote the response out of my love for Christ and the Truth ..."

"Please! Priest, save me your pleasantries." Henry waved his hand dismissively. "We all love Christ and the truth. Explain to me your argument before I send you to the Tower."

The Tower. Thomas shivered at the thought of the cold fortress looming over the Thames. He forced the image away and took a deep breath.

"Your Majesty," he began and proceeded to outline the logic of his response, along with supporting Scriptures and Church history.

Henry seemed to listen.

"You do not believe, then, that the Leviticus passage applies to me and Katherine?" he asked with what seemed like genuine interest.

"No," Thomas said.

"And you do not support the annulment?"

"No," Thomas said.

"You are a brazen one, Father Abell," he said with what sounded like resignation. "Even More would not give me his honest opinion when he resigned."

Thomas thought of the last time he had seen Thomas More, sitting quietly in the king's Privy Council. More had looked tortured even then. Somehow Thomas doubted More would stay silent for long.

The king interrupted Thomas's thoughts with a guttural growl.

"Fools and traitors! You holy men talk like you know how to run a country. I was right to get rid of Wolsey. You and he are cut of the same cloth!"

Thomas disagreed on both points, but to dissent would ruin the progress he had just made.

"And please tell me, Priest, how is it that this witch from Kent showed up this morning and said you would be coming to see me? And just as she said, five hours later, you came?" the king asked with his brow raised.

Thomas stared at the king in disbelief.

Elizabeth Barton could not have known six hours ago that he would be barging into the king's Great Hall with an urgent need to talk to him. He himself had not known until an hour ago, when he stood in the Carthusians' court. "Your Majesty, that is a complete mystery to me," he said.

"You have not seen her? You are not allied with her?" the king asked with what seemed to be either confusion or irritation, most likely both.

"No," Thomas said, shaking his head. "I do not like her ... style."

"Style?"

"I do not find her respectful, Your Majesty," Thomas said tactfully, but as soon as the words left his mouth, he felt a pang of regret. Passing judgment on Elizabeth Barton to save his own reputation felt less than holy. But still, he spoke the truth.

"I see," the king said, watching Thomas's face carefully. "You know she predicts my death? Seven months from when I marry my Anne."

The king's tone had changed, and Thomas wondered if, in some way, he was reaching out for comfort, assurance that the wrath of God would not fall on him, assurance Thomas could never give.

"I have heard this, yes," Thomas said.

"And do you believe God will strike me dead if I divorce Katherine and marry Anne?"

It was a bold question, one made to Thomas alone, with no audience, and Thomas could not help but hear the vulnerability behind the question. This King Henry was once the king who had crept barefoot to the cross on Good Friday. This King Henry had believed in the power of God. He had tasted the Eucharist. He knew the truth, and at least a part of him still feared God. Perhaps.

"My King," Thomas said carefully. "God has not revealed that to me, and I cannot say if He has revealed it to the nun either. We must each seek God for ourselves, humble our hearts to his Word, and confess our sins before him. We each stand before God alone, servants and kings, saints and sinners."

The king smirked.

"I hear what you are not saying!" he said. "You question my scruples."

The king's mouth twitched.

"You celibate priests know nothing of the burden of securing a successor. You can afford to have high ideals because you do not have millions depending on you for their daily bread."

But we do, Thomas thought. Every priest is concerned about raising up the next generation of faithful, and every priest is responsible for providing Bread and Wine. *It is exactly what we do.*

But Thomas said nothing.

"You should leave before Thomas Cromwell reminds me to make an example of you," the king said with a flick of his hand. Then, just as suddenly as he was irritated, he sighed. "Father Abell, I am so weary of all of this."

Thomas saw the king's shoulders stoop, and he knew the man had told the truth. Despite his revulsion, Thomas felt a bit of compassion for the king, so tormented by his own sin.

"If you see Katherine, give her my regards," he said quietly.

Thomas searched Henry's eyes. Perhaps there was a good Christian somewhere inside the king!

"I regret that this situation has caused her pain," he continued quietly. "In the beginning, we had so much hope together." Henry looked wistfully into the distance, where Anne Boleyn and her flock of ladies had emerged into the garden and were walking toward them. And as quickly as it had begun, the moment, the glimpse into what could be, was over.

"You should leave before I regret this conversation, Father Abell," the king said and then added in a cracked voice, "but please, bless me first."

And so, Thomas did.

57

EXILED

Thomas was not a mile away from the palace when he heard the thunder of horses rushing up behind him. When he turned to see the king's guard, the captain called out to him, "Halt, ye there, Father! The king demands we apprehend ye!"

Thomas stopped in his tracks. Had Henry already changed his mind? Of course he had. How long could the king's good mood extend while Anne lived under the same roof? Thomas lowered his head and waited for the guards to approach.

Jesus, Savior of my soul, have mercy on me.

When the lead horseman drew near, he stopped his horse and thrust a sealed parchment at Thomas.

"I have been ordered to see that you receive this correspondence from King Henry," he shouted as if Thomas were not standing three feet away from him. The wiry young commander watched Thomas open the red seal, but before Thomas's eyes could cover the text, the man had turned the guards around and was rushing back to the palace.

Thomas stood alone in the street and read the king's hastily scrawled words.

"You are dismissed from the court, the king's household, and Katherine's services. Leave London and do not return on the pain of death."

And that was it.

He was exiled.

Thomas laughed out loud. That was it.

He raised his shaking hands. *Thank you, Lord Jesus. Thank you.* He kicked a rock into the open sewer paralleling the street. Who needed London? He was a free man again. He could live!

Thomas grinned. He had faced off with the lion, and he had walked away. But just as quickly as he celebrated, he began to quake, shaking from head to toe. He found an overturned crate, sat down, and put his head in his hands. He had nearly faced the gallows. His head had nearly been on a spike over the Thames River. He had almost died. *Thank you,* he whispered out loud as he covered his face with his hands. Long-suppressed tears pushed through his shattered defenses and rolled down his face.

He was dismissed from royal service and banned from London. Released and banned. That was it. But what now?

October 1532   Oxford

Crisp autumn air filled Thomas's lungs as he walked briskly, turning down the country lane, heading back into the collegiate city. Warm afternoon light illuminated the trees—oak and maple, beech and chestnut. Their changing leaves rustled in the breeze, bright yellows giving way to orange and red. He exhaled. It was so good to be back in Oxford.

As he walked through the old city gates, he patted the sack of goods he had just purchased from the farmer's wife—a small loaf of brown bread, a handful of fresh eggs, a slab of hard cheese, a few turnips, and an onion. It was not provisions for a king's table, but it was his own. He could make a few meals for himself and indulge in a few at the tavern with old friends. It would be enough.

Enough.

How many times had he longed for this very thing? Back in Oxford, back to learning and teaching and writing. Back to life as it had been.

But it was not—and would never again be—as it had been. And a nagging tug in his heart warned him that it would not last forever either. Was he Peter returning to fish? *My life is yours, Jesus.*

As Thomas neared the church on Bear Street, he noticed a crowd gathering around a small fire. Who made a rubbish fire in front of a church?

As he drew closer to the smoke, the hair on the back of his neck stood up. This was no routine rubbish fire; on the contrary, the fuel for the fire was the most expensive type: books!

A crowd of young men, mostly seminary students, were singing a hymn, and when they finished the stanza, Thomas heard a young man shouting about honor and righteousness amid cries of "God save our king" and "Long Live Henry VIII!"

"What are they burning?" Thomas asked a freckled young student as he neared the edge of the ruckus.

"I'm not sure," the boy said, bouncing on his tiptoes to see over the tightly packed crowd. "I just got here, but I reckon they are burning Tyndale. It's usually Tyndale."

The student chuckled. "You know, good old King Henry financed Tyndale's latest New Testament. He and Wolsey, God rest his soul, bought so many copies of his first book to burn that ol' Tyndale had enough coin to bankroll a new run. Now he's got near the whole of the New Testament in English."

Thomas smiled to himself. William. He always managed to come out alright.

The young man hopped up and down, looking over the crowd to see the book stack next to the fire. Thomas strained to see too.

"Oh ... no," he announced, shrugging his shoulders. "I was wrong. It is not Tyndale at all. They are burning that new book, *Invicta Veritas*, the one that says the king's theologians are blasphemous ..."

Thomas didn't wait for him to finish. He pushed his way through the crowd until he was standing directly in front of the fire. And indeed, the boy was right. There, in front of the fire, was a stack of *Invicta Veritas, The Unconquerable Truth*, about to go up in flames.

Thomas stretched out his long arm as if by reaching out, he could stop the burning, but his arm went limp. What could he do? He was close enough to feel the flames and smell the pages burning, and yet he stood there, too shocked to feel anything. *Invicta Veritas* was hardly six months old, and it was already feeding the fire like any rebel heretic at Smithfield.

And yet—it was just the book.

Thomas watched the mesmerizing orange glow devour his work and felt a sad consolation. This was hardly the end of *Invicta Veritas*, this book, or any of them. It was and would always be *The Unconquerable Truth*. No fire could quench the Truth.

Like a martyr freed from his body, the life, the real life, of the book would go on in conversations and debates. Already men were publicly discussing his arguments at Parliament. The king himself had given him an audience, in one divinely apportioned moment, to consider the arguments of the book. Thomas had done what the Spirit had prompted him to do. He had written *Invicta*. And now ... it was out of his hands. There was nothing he could do to stop men from burning it on the streets of Oxford. But there was nothing *they* could do to stop the message from lingering in the thoughts of Englishmen.

The student who had been praising the king picked up another copy of *Invicta* and ceremoniously threw it into the fire. Thomas was close enough to see the book crinkle as the fire consumed it, first in a burst of flame and then slowly peeling it down, the pages of the open book gently flipping on the current of the fire's core. In a moment, the book was consumed.

Tomorrow it will be forgotten, black char. Cold ashes. Soot. In a week, dust on the houses. Ashes to ashes. Dust to dust. Thence I came. Thence I shall return. God, teach me to number my days that I may gain a heart of wisdom.

The raging fire was mesmerizing. Thomas could hardly look away.

But when he looked up, he saw two old colleagues. Had they spotted him? The two were deep in discussion. One looked in Thomas's direction, and when their eyes met, the professor looked away. Was it disgust? Shame? Thomas had called out the Oxford establishment for caving into the king's whims, and now here he was, a free man, walking about Oxford, tutoring again, for Christ's sake, even while the king demanded his book burned. How long would his liberty last?

Thomas saw one of his colleagues notice something behind him. When he turned, he saw them too, a detachment of armed men forcing their way through the crowd, making their way toward him.

"You," a beefy one said, roughly grabbing Thomas's left arm. "You had better come with us!"

The other guard snatched Thomas's knapsack with the food provisions and hooked his right arm. There was no escape. He was coming with them.

The three soldiers rustled Thomas out of the book-burning crowd and walked him to a pub where a cloaked man sat in the back corner. The men pushed Thomas into a seat at the table and set the bag in front of the man whose face was concealed in the shadows.

"What is this?" the cloaked man asked. "Banned books?"

He opened Thomas's bag and swore.

"I was hoping for another copy of Tyndale or at least Luther," he said in a tone that Thomas could not decipher. Thomas narrowed his eyes. *Was the man earnest or mocking?*

"I'm not a Lutheran," Thomas said, although, as soon as he said it, he realized that it was a fact that no more helped than hurt him.

"I didn't think so," the man said, removing his cloak and moving closer to the candlelight. "You are that brazen Papist, Thomas Abell, the writer of *Invicta Veritas*."

Thomas Cromwell!

58

ARREST

"Am I under arrest?" Thomas asked, rubbing the red mark on his forearm where the soldier had grabbed him.

"No," Cromwell said dryly. "Not at the moment. I suppose it depends on whether you cooperate."

Thomas listened. He hardly felt cooperative.

"The king let you go," Cromwell said, "though I told him it was a bad idea. Gave you liberty to leave London, but it so happens that we have reconsidered. We think it best we keep you *safe* for a while." He smiled ironically. "Why, I believe if my men had not intercepted you when they did just now, you would have been burned along with your little book of lies."

"The king bade me stay away from London, on pain of death," Thomas said evenly. "I have complied. I have ... "

"Priest," Cromwell interrupted, "you are an irritation, a pebble in the king's shoe. And that, dear man of God, is not a good place for anyone. The king might forget you, but as long as your book is being discussed in Parliament and in churches, it is causing a row."

Cromwell clenched his fists.

"As you saw for yourself, Father Abell, your words incite violence." His eyes widened. "The king does not take kindly to riots in his streets, either in London or Oxford. Would God approve of all this disorder?"

Thomas was silent. He had spent hours with Cromwell in Wolsey's presence. He would not cower to him now. He had done nothing wrong. He had obeyed the king's orders.

"We've decided to detain you for a few weeks until the king decides what is best for you," Cromwell said, looking down at the little bag of provisions. "Do you have any other worldly goods you wish to bring with you? We've prepared a nice room for you at the Tower. I believe it has a splendid view of the Tower Green. Tall ceilings, large hearth ... quite lovely actually."

Cromwell gave a brief, humorless smile.

Did Cromwell hope to frighten him? He was being sent to the Tower of London! The futility of it all! It had simply been a matter of time before the king sent someone after him. But framing the arrest as a benevolent attempt to protect him from angry mobs in the street was more than Thomas could handle. Something seemed false, and nothing irritated Thomas more than dishonesty.

59

THE TOWER OF LONDON

November 1532   Tower of London

Thomas ran the palm of his hand over the soft sandstone walls, the confines of his cavernous tower cell. How long would these walls hold him?

How long, Lord?

He looked out the tall glass window onto the courtyard of half-timbered houses, the expansive lawn, and just beyond, where White Tower, a prominent Norman castle built five hundred years earlier by William the Conqueror, dominated the center of the walled fortress. Thomas's own forefathers had been with the Norman conquerors, invading the English Isles. And now, here he was, an Englishman, a priest, a confidant to the queen—watching as a prisoner from the Tower cell.

How long, O Lord? How long?

The fortified complex of towers and castles was far more than a giant prison. The castle walls held chapels and guestrooms for visiting dignitaries. Thomas himself had been there many times, saying Mass in the royal chapel and attending to the queen during her stay in the White Tower.

He was also well acquainted with the posh prison cells scattered throughout buildings in the tower complex, some with exquisite carpets and furniture, some as bare as a hermit's hovel. More than once, he had been in the luxury prison cells, accompanying the queen as she visited the nobility who found themselves, at least temporarily, on the other side of Henry's affections.

Often those gentry came and went in quick succession, as Henry used their short stints of captivity to encourage their loyalty. A month or two in the Tower had a sobering effect on men of prestige. Freedom was a powerful motivator.

But Thomas never thought he would find himself a prisoner in the Tower of London. He imagined worse, of course. When he had picked up his quill and began writing *Invicta*, he knew it would likely be the death of him, though he imagined death might come in the form of hanging or being unceremoniously cut down by a soldier's sword or perhaps being thrown into one of London's numerous dungeons or prison halls around the city. He never thought he would end up in the most prestigious fortress in the heart of London. Somehow, he always thought those places were reserved for men closer to the throne.

He ran his thumbnail across the soft stone surface, leaving the slightest trace. How many men before him had done just that—run their hands across the wall and watched as their nails dug a soft trench?

The weather had turned from the crisp October sunshine to a bitter, damp November. A frigid draft blew under the door and through the empty fireplace.

Though the prison cell was large for one lone man, it was not comfortable. It lacked furniture or floor covering. Except for the one straw mat and blanket he used to sleep on, the room was bare. And the enormous hearth was empty.

Thomas stared ruefully at the dressed stones adorning the fireplace. It was large enough to turn a roasting Christmas goose or maybe even venison. With enough coal, the room could be as warm as a midsummer's day. But on this bitter day in November, the hearth was barren, cold, useless. No one had brought him firewood, though his financial holdings would have easily bought a roomful of winter wood.

Even the birds had given up on the chimney ever being used. A loud raven nested at the top, and sometimes Thomas could hear her scratching and moving around. She must be able to see all of London from there, like the top of a cathedral tower.

But Thomas was in no cathedral, neither in body nor soul. He was cold and hungry and tired of the inactivity. He had been alone for nearly six weeks with no end in sight. And he had not been questioned, not charged, not even formally arrested. He had simply been brought to the Tower and forgotten.

Forgotten.

The loneliness curled around his heart and whispered lies: *You are alone. You wasted your life for this, and it has come to nothing. You will never be remembered.*

Thomas sank to the cold stone floor, void of carpet or rushes, and covered his face with his raw, red hands.

Lord Jesus, have mercy on me, a sinner.

He said it again and again until hot tears sprang from his eyes. If it was all he could do, it was what he would do. It was his only defense against the tormentors of his soul.

Have mercy on me, Oh God. Hide me in the shadow of your hand. I am yours. I have always been yours. Do not forget me here. Don't let me go down to the pit.

Lord Jesus, have mercy on me, a sinner.

Lord Jesus, have mercy on me, a sinner.

He beat his breast methodically with the breath prayer, drumming his knuckles on his chest like he was keeping time to an invisible instrument that only he could hear. He gave no thought to the number of times he uttered the prayer or the time of day. When he was completely exhausted, he lay down on the cold floor, his cheek in the dust of men long gone, and fell asleep.

Moments later, he heard the warden turning the key to his cell. Food?

They had forgotten yesterday. Would there be anything more than stale bread today? He longed for even the smallest bit of meat, perhaps cabbage stew or mashed turnips. But even a bite of bread would be heavenly.

He froze.

The warden was not alone. He heard a second voice, a female voice.

The heavy door screeched open, and Thomas saw the grumpy old guard and another face he recognized, one he would never have expected.

"Susanna Danielson!" he croaked.

His own voice felt rough and unfamiliar to him. He stood weakly to his feet, swaying as his vision blurred and threatened to send him back to the floor.

"Are you well, Thomas?" she asked, grabbing his elbow and supporting his thin back.

He nodded, but it must have been obvious to Susanna that he was not strong, because she rushed to her basket and pulled out a loaf of warm bread. "Please, Thomas—Danielson asked me to bring these gifts from the fellowship."

The fellowship. The gathering of Tyndale readers and Lutheran sympathizers.

He bit into the soft bread, his stomach growling loudly as he closed his eyes and chewed slowly. *Thank you, God. Thank you.* This was the rescue he needed.

Susanna handed him a flask, and he gratefully sipped it, allowing the refreshing ale to wash down his dry throat.

Susanna grabbed his hand.

"We are praying for you, Thomas." Tears filled her eyes. "The children pray for you every night—especially Lilly."

Thomas's eyes filled with tears as he remembered Danielson's children, the youngest girl, the one with curls, who sat on her mother's lap during the evening Bible readings. "Lilly," he said with a smile, the very name of the child brightening the interior of his prison cell. "Your sweet Lilly."

"You are weak," Susanna said with concern. "Have they been feeding you?"

"Sometimes," Thomas confessed, and Susanna threw the guard an accusing glance.

"Have you written to the queen? She would like to know where you are and how you are being treated."

"No," Thomas confessed again. "I have no paper or ink, and I did not want to trouble Her Majesty anymore."

"I think she would like to know," Susanna said thoughtfully. "I'll bring you paper and ink. You can write to her tomorrow."

She looked at the guard, who shrugged. It would be allowed.

"You have not been charged?"

"No," Thomas said.

The injustice of the situation hung in the air.

"There are some in Thomas Cromwell's household who attend the fellowship," she whispered. "That is how we knew you were here."

Thomas nodded.

"Thank you for coming," he said.

The Protestants had come to his aid, and he could do nothing but accept. He closed his eyes and pressed his dirty palms together. "Thank you."

60

THE QUEEN FINDS OUT

Thomas stared at the blank page. He turned the quill in his left hand, uncertain what to say. He must not alarm the queen.

Another cold gust blew under the cell door, setting off a shiver—and then a hacking cough. Thomas had not been well for weeks. It was time to let Queen Katherine know his needs. She would want to help. But how?

Thomas was cold, sick, and hungry, yes, but more than that, he worried that he had been forgotten. Why had Cromwell not formally arrested him? Why had he not been charged? Wasn't it against the law to hold an Englishman, a member of the gentry at that, without charging him? Was King Henry holding out for a moment to formally charge him with treason?

Treason was the catch-all charge that encompassed so many different offenses against the king. To fall out of favor, to give comfort to the king's detractors, to defy his authority in battle or in print, would send anyone to jail for treason.

But the swift punishment for treason was more than imprisonment. It was death, the most painful kind, the so-called French prescription. The accused was to be hanged by his neck, pulled down from the gallows while he was still alive, cut open, his vital organs removed, and burnt before his terrified eyes. When death eventually overtook the poor man, his body was quartered.

The thought made Thomas shudder. Thankfully, he had never witnessed the horrible spectacle, but he had seen the telltale signs—bloody courtyards and dead men's heads skewered on pikes across the Thames River.

He had walked beneath the stare of hollowed eyes more than once. He knew the price for challenging the king's authority. But he had not been formally charged—not yet. The uncertainty of it tormented him. Had the king simply forgotten about the pebble in his shoe?

Thomas sighed and began writing. He would simply tell Katherine his situation and wait to see what happened. It made no sense to protect her from the truth. If the king wished to make a public spectacle of him, the queen would learn of it anyway.

My Queen, I have learned to be content in whatever circumstance I am in, he wrote. He paused and nodded. It was true—at least he hoped it was becoming more true as God refined him. His life was in the Lord's hands, but Susanna had been right. It was time to tell Katherine.

"Is there anything more you wish for?" the lieutenant guard asked gruffly as he handed Thomas a large bundle with fresh blankets and an extra serving of food.

When Thomas's letter reached the queen, the response was immediate: firewood, fresh clothing, extra food, and ample paper and ink to write and make his case known.

"Yes," Thomas answered with a new sense of confidence. "I want to say Mass in the Tower chapel."

The guard simply nodded. The queen was still the queen in England.

61

CHRISTMAS IN THE TOWER

Thomas held the Eucharist high above his head and closed his eyes.

"*Per ipsum, et cum ipso, et in ipso, est tibi Deo Patri omnipotenti, in unitate Spiritus Sancti, omnis honor et gloria, per omnia saecula saeculorum. Amen.*" Through him, with him, in him, in the unity of the Holy Spirit, all glory and honor is yours, almighty Father, forever and ever. Amen.

The deep tones of the Latin Eucharistic prayer echoed off the stone walls of the chapel nave. His heart soared, and tears stung his eyes. It was more beautiful than he had remembered.

He looked down at the faces gathered around him. Young and old, men and women, family members and servants of prisoners in the Tower. Like the prisoners locked alone in separate cells, they too were suffering. But at least they were here together in the Tower chapel. And now they would partake of the Holy Bread. It was the very essence of Christian community.

"Corpus Christi," Thomas said. *The Body of Christ.*

The Lord's body was broken for them long before any of theirs would be broken. Jesus died for him, Thomas Abell. In the moment, that was all that mattered, and it overshadowed anything he had written in *Invicta*. The Lord's body was broken for him, Thomas, a sinner. He was redeemed by the cross.

After Thomas offered the Eucharist to the others, he bit into the Host. *Taste and see that the Lord is good.* His heart lifted. Every burden—caring for Queen Katherine, defending her marriage, all considerations of the future, every anxiety and fear—fled. He was not alone. He had never been alone. The Lord Jesus was with him, indeed, inside him, the greatest mystery of all time, the Incarnation, Emmanuel: God with us.

Thomas opened his eyes, an unconscious smile lingering on his lips. *Oh, how good and pleasant it is when men dwell together in unity.* The Body of Christ brought them together, even in their bondage. *Thank you, Lord.*

"I hear that you were permitted to say Mass," Thomas Cromwell said as he sauntered into Thomas's cell, which now boasted a covering on the wall, as well as a heavy quilt on top of the straw mattress and a wooden table with an inkwell. A small fire crackled in the hearth. On the table lay a loaf of brown bread and an orange. The orange was a special gift from Eustace Chapuys, the Spanish ambassador.

Thomas slowly set down the lute he had been playing and nodded. "Yes."

"How did that happen?" Cromwell demanded, picking up the orange and tossing it absently. "Who granted a prisoner of the Crown to say Mass?"

By what authority ... Thomas watched Cromwell's face carefully.

I'll tell you if you tell me by what authority John the Baptist preached. What could he say? What should he say? There was no need to involve anyone else in his trouble. He had learned that lesson the hard way.

"I do not know," Thomas said truthfully. "I simply asked and it was granted."

Cromwell pursed his lips, examining Thomas's face. Was he looking for the truth? Was he stalling?

"No matter," Cromwell said dismissively, setting the orange on the table.

Thomas let out a breath he did not know he had been holding. Clearly, Cromwell had not come to punish him for saying Mass.

"As you know," Cromwell began, "the queen has been quite ... active in her support of you. She is insisting you be released."

Thomas nodded, a feeling of hope rising in his chest. Though his heart told him to be careful. Men like Cromwell rarely gave favors without strings attached.

"I have not been charged," Thomas reminded Cromwell evenly. "How long is it lawful for the king to hold me without charge?"

Cromwell grunted.

"Even a Papist like you should know there is a wide moat between official, legal requirements and what the king has the liberty to do."

Thomas was quiet, not dropping Cromwell's challenging gaze.

Cromwell drummed his fingers impatiently on the leather packet in his hands.

"Even so, Father Abell, I did not come here to discuss your charges," he said with a pause. "It is not particularly advantageous for us to retain you here, as it is just causing more difficulties with the queen. And other members of the public." Cromwell looked around Thomas's well-furnished cell.

"You have a few friends."

Thomas nodded humbly. How he did, he did not know. Whatever he had was a gift from Him, the true king of the world. And if he only had Him, it was enough, but he could not deny that it warmed his heart to hear those words, "You have friends."

"Christmas is coming soon," Cromwell said. "The king has more pressing matters to deal with than placating Katherine. There is only one matter the king wishes to discuss with his brother's widow, as I am sure you are aware."

He sighed heavily, and Thomas looked at him curiously. Was Thomas Cromwell also growing weary of the king's endless pursuit of Anne Boleyn?

"We have decided that we would like to return you to Katherine's household," Cromwell said after a pause.

Thomas smiled broadly. Words never sounded sweeter.

"But we cannot permit you to continue speaking against the king's divorce," Cromwell added quickly. "You have said your piece, and the king does not require you to recant or take it back. Simply do not continue to speak your opinion ... at least until Easter."

"Easter?" Thomas asked. "Why Easter?"

Thomas Cromwell shook his head. He would give no more information than was necessary. "That is what the king has decided. Take care of Katherine and keep her out of the king's sight."

Thomas nodded. He would not question the gift. If the Lord allowed, he could be silent for a few months. He bowed his head. "Yes, I can do that."

62

THE PRINCESS DOWAGER

December 1533   Buckden Castle

Thomas walked silently with Katherine, their feet crunching fallen leaves as they ambled down the garden path. Winter had gone and come again. The neglected red and white rosebushes had bloomed and faded, leaving only a hint of stray petals crushed along the walkway.

The world had changed.

In the twelve months since Cromwell released Thomas from the Tower, King Henry had secretly married Anne Boleyn, the object of his seven-year pursuit, and then publicly crowned her queen in June. By September, Anne bore the king another child, but it was not the prince Henry had longed for.

The king continually moved Katherine farther and farther from London, demanding her ladies and servants refer to her as "Princess Dowager." And with each move, Katherine's position worsened. Buckden Castle, with its foul medieval moat and drafty rooms, had been their home for the last few months, and while it was far from the palace Thomas thought his queen deserved, he hoped they could remain there indefinitely. The life of exile had taken its toll on her body. The golden-red hair framing her face had all turned a dusty gray, and her face, once plump, now seemed worn and tired.

Queen Katherine paused to rest and drew a breath.

In the silence between them, Thomas could hear the village children playing in the distance. Their voices caught on the wind and settled into Buckden's courtyard. How sweet and mocking their voices seemed. Thomas looked compassionately at Katherine as she gathered her fur shawl tightly around her neck and placed her hand on Thomas's forearm. Did the queen still grieve her dead children?

Katherine's steps had been especially slow this afternoon. Was she sick or simply sad? When Thomas first returned from Charles V's court in Spain, the queen often outpaced him as she confided in him all of her fury and frustrations. But now, Thomas found himself slowing his stride to walk by her side. Whether or not her health was deteriorating, one thing seemed obvious: her fight was gone.

While Thomas was in the Tower, Katherine had passed her forty-seventh birthday, and she no longer claimed she could bear a child. Her maids whispered to Thomas of the change, but no one dared to talk directly to her about it. There had been no monthly bleeding since last spring, and no one held out hope for an heir coming from Katherine's womb. She was officially too old to bear a son. If Henry relented and returned to her, she would have nothing left to give him but her love and devotion.

But the queen's household also knew it was far too late for even that consolation.

Katherine had long stopped pleading with Henry to preserve their marriage. She would never acknowledge his marriage to Anne Boleyn or consent to an official annulment. And she would never retire to a nunnery. Her marriage vows were for life, and she would be the Queen of England until her last breathing day, but she knew that she had lost. She had lost her Henry, both his love and respect, and her heart would never fully recover.

She plodded along in silence. But in her quiet, Thomas recognized a new peace. Katherine had stopped wringing her hands.

Though Henry had spoken publicly about his scruples, there was no doubt Katherine had suffered more from them. For years,

Thomas had continually reminded Katherine of God's love, His forgiveness for past sins, and His acceptance of her continual repentance. And yet, she agonized, torturing her body with fasting, kneeling for hours on the cold stone floor, wearing garments of horsehair.

But something had changed. Now, as the queen walked beside him, she no longer asked Thomas to plead with God to forgive her of some unintended sin. Had she come to accept her barrenness as God's will? Or had she simply given up on trying to please Him?

As they walked in silence, Thomas hoped, in some small way, that his writing *Invicta Veritas* had helped her to accept that the deaths of her children were not punishment for violating the Leviticus passage. She had done no wrong by marrying Henry. Her marriage was not cursed because she had been the wife of Henry's older brother. She was simply not meant to bear a prince for the king. That was the painful truth.

The faithful servants of God did not always get answers to their questions. Sometimes they had to be satisfied with the very Presence of God himself. Jesus had promised to be with his children. They were never alone.

Thomas offered this counsel a dozen times, first whispered through tears of his own, and finally simply stated, wearily, as a matter of fact. It is what it is. There was not much more to do than to trust. Perhaps Katherine had come to accept that truth, both bitter and sweet, as well.

They would learn to live with a compromised peace. The queen would not have her king or her princes, but she would have her household, her dignity, and her place away from court.

But Thomas knew that even that could be a short-lived peace.

The king was growing insistent that everyone, especially Katherine's household, address her as the Dowager Princess, Arthur's widow. She was not, and in his depraved mind, had never been, his lawful wife or the legitimately crowned Queen of England. To address her as such was a grave insolence that would not be tolerated.

But it wasn't true.

And truth mattered.

Katherine had been the Queen of England. She had been King Henry VIII's lawful wife. To call truth a lie and a lie truth was beyond Thomas's capacity. Black was black and white was white. He knew that many of the king's servants merely saw his lady's title as a technicality. Why not say what the king wants to hear? Hasn't it always been this way? The king makes the rules, and his subjects comply.

But to Thomas, this was no small matter: a queen was a queen, in life and death. Henry could strip her of that title, but he could not change the past and say she had never been his queen. No one could change the past, not even an all-powerful king. Altering the past was beyond the scope of human power. Henry could say what he wanted to, but it did not make it the truth.

And Thomas, God willing, would stay on the side of truth.

"Father Abell!"

Margaret ran to Thomas, her damask skirts flying around her, brown eyes wide in her pale face, like a frightened child.

Thomas held out his hands to her, and she grabbed them, stopping only to curtsy to the queen. "Your Highness," she acknowledged.

"Father, the house is surrounded. Please, help me take the queen inside!"

Thomas wrapped his arm around Katherine and began moving toward the Great House. Margaret followed on Katherine's other side, caressing her arm, coaxing her along. Queen Katherine moved more quickly, though she stumbled every few feet, whispering prayers through trembling lips.

Thomas nodded in agreement. *Lord, protect our queen.* He could hear the queen's men scrambling through the house, bringing out armaments, preparing for whatever battle was at hand.

Before they passed through the garden gate, Thomas heard men pounding at the great door. "Charles Brandon, Duke of Suffolk, here on the king's business. Open the door at once!"

The queen looked at Thomas.

"Tell them to open the door," Katherine said resolutely. "If my Henry commands, we must open the door."

Thomas nodded.

"Open the door! The queen commands!" Thomas shouted, though everything in his gut warned him to keep it closed.

As soon as the servants opened the door, Brandon rode his horse into the courtyard, turning over potted plants, wielding a thrashing whip. A dozen men on horseback followed, each armed with weapons, swords, and spears.

"What is the meaning of this intrusion?" Katherine demanded, standing tall despite her diminished stature. "Why do you barge into my home like a castle under siege? By what authority do you come here in this manner?"

"The king's, my Lady." Charles Brandon smirked and nodded in mock respect. "Princess Dowager."

The queen narrowed her eyes.

"Princess Dowager? How long have you known me, Charles? Have you forgotten your place?" The queen's cheeks burned hot as she voiced her unspoken grievances. "I was the one who begged Henry to forgive you when you married his sister Mary! I pleaded for you and Mary when he made plans to banish you from England. I have always been a friend to you and Mary, and now ... " The queen's voice trembled with bitterness. "Our friendship means nothing?"

Charles Brandon stared hollowly above the queen's gaze.

"I am a servant of His Majesty King Henry VIII and his rightful queen, Anne," he said with less bravado. "The king has been notified that you persist in calling yourself queen in defiance of his authority, and he has demanded that you be removed to Somersham."

The queen stood her ground. "No," she simply said, her lips tightening into a thin line.

Brandon did not look at her. He continued to stare above her head.

"Men!" Brandon shouted. "Release the staff of their positions. They are no longer needed."

Brandon's men unmounted and dispersed through the house, whips in hand, demanding Katherine's household leave immediately. Thomas watched, helpless to interfere, as Brandon's soldiers traipsed into every room of the house. One by one, the cooks and maids, horse handlers and gardeners, clerks and administrators left. One older gardener, who had been with Katherine longer than Thomas could remember, stood his ground in the courtyard, refusing to move while Brandon's men whipped him. When the old man fell to his knees, they kicked him. He covered his head, moaning.

The queen watched in horror.

"Please, let's go," Thomas suggested, more as a demand than a request. There was no reason for his lady to see her household staff abused.

By the time Thomas and Katherine had climbed the spiraling staircase to Katherine's upper tower room, the uproar had subsided. From the narrow chamber window, they could see the queen's servants, Margaret among them, streaming away from the house, running down the country road toward the village. Good, at least no one else would be in harm's way.

Katherine locked her door, and Thomas positioned himself in the hall, just outside the queen's door. He would not leave her, no matter how convincing the duke's whips and words would be, but he would give her space, dignity.

"Tell them I am not leaving," Katherine shouted from behind the door. "I will not allow Henry to remove me again and send me off to the marshes!"

Katherine had been forewarned of Henry's demands. A week earlier, there had been a letter from Thomas Cromwell informing Katherine that she would be removed to Somersham, a notoriously remote house in the western marshes, a drafty castle known for its foul air. More than one noble who lived in the remote house had succumbed to the plague, and people whispered that the place was cursed. Cromwell had specifically written that it was Queen Anne's wish that the Princess Dowager be removed to Somersham, and Katherine could not help but feel that the action was designed not only to get her out of the way but to hasten her demise.

She would not go.

"I am the queen," Thomas heard her say quietly on the other side of the door, and then, through sobs, "I am his wife. She has no right to send me away."

"I am here, my Lady," Thomas said to Katherine on the other side of the door. "I will not leave."

More sobs.

"Thank you, Father. Pray with me."

Thomas led her through the Lord's Prayer and a prayer of petition. They were not alone. The Lord was with them. He whispered these comforts to Katherine and felt his own spirit agree, though he wondered how long they could continue like that—Charles Brandon occupying the house, the staff gone, the queen self-imprisoned in her own room.

Charles Brandon waited until sundown, letting Katherine mourn in her own room alone. Thomas could hear the men helping themselves to whatever they wanted in the house. Like any raiding party, they made themselves at home, even in the queen's residence.

Thomas sank to the wooden floor. His stomach rumbled. In the fading light, he could see stars and the full moon shining through a tiny keyhole window.

Lord Jesus, have mercy on me, a sinner.

He closed his eyes, resting his head on the cold stone wall.

Lord Jesus, have mercy on me, a sinner.

Thomas could hear Brandon pacing and shouting. It seemed that a few of the household servants had stayed. Thomas could hear the duke addressing them.

"Who told you that you must address the Dowager Princess as Queen Katherine?" he demanded.

Silence.

"Speak when you are being spoken to!"

He heard a shuffle, a slap, more silence, and then a whimper, then heavy footsteps.

Brandon burst into the corridor, grabbing Thomas by his vestments and forcing him to stand.

"Father! Is it true that you instructed your lady's household to address her as Queen and only as Queen?"

Brandon's eyes were aflame with fury, a fire no doubt fueled by the queen's store of wine that he had been drinking all night. Thomas stared at him silently. He was not required to incriminate himself to the king's brother-in-law. The duke was not his judge.

Brandon slapped Thomas across the face.

"Speak, Priest!" he demanded.

Thomas felt the sting of the slap and slowly turned his face to expose the other cheek, never breaking the duke's demanding gaze.

Brandon chuckled, a guilty laugh. The gesture had not been wasted on him.

"I see," he said. He narrowed his cold eyes and slapped Thomas's other cheek, this time drawing blood from his nose.

"Stop!" the queen squealed from behind the door. "Stop, Brandon! You have no right to strike a man of God! Shame on you! For the love of Jesus and His Mother! Stop!"

Brandon groaned and glared at Thomas, his body swaying from drink.

"I'll deal with you in the morning," he finally said and walked away, stumbling down the dark corridor.

Thomas wiped the blood from his nose and smarting cheeks.

Lord Jesus, have mercy on me, a sinner.

63

Long Live the Queen

With the first hint of daylight, a shaft of pale pink light pierced through the keyhole window. Thomas rose to his knees and knelt below the small hole in the wall, placing his hands on both sides of the opening.

In the receding darkness, Thomas could just make out the path moving out of the shadows away from the Great House entrance. Even in the faint light, he could see a steady stream of villagers flowing toward the castle—men and women, horses and oxen, marching like an infantry at dawn. Farmers carried pitchforks and scythes. Women held torches and wielded heavy branches. One man drove a pair of oxen laden with a sturdy tree trunk. Did the rescue party intend to ram Buckden's sealed portcullis?

As he looked closer, Thomas saw Margaret walking with a group of village women. Her arms were linked with two young women Thomas did not recognize. Even in the dim light, he could see Margaret's set jaw and flushed cheeks. She was coming back for her queen!

Thomas grinned and clasped his hands. *At last! They were not forgotten.*

As the crowd grew closer, Thomas spotted Peter Smith, the queen's financial advisor, and Melvin Watson, her best legal counselor, and dear Leah and Lilly, two of the queen's youngest chambermaids, arms linked as they marched toward the house. He had once suspected them of being Cromwell plants, but no—they were faithful to the queen!

"Release our queen!" one man shouted.

"Long live Queen Katherine, true queen of England," a high-pitched young woman yelled. A chorus of voices agreed.

"Hear! Hear! Save the queen!"

"Long live Queen Katherine, the true queen of England!"

By the time the dawn gave way to a tepid winter morning, Thomas could see that the mob of townspeople surrounded the castle. He smiled, though his stiff cheeks ached with the movement. "Queen Katherine, Queen Katherine, the true Queen of England," echoed off Buckden's red brick walls.

"Do you hear them, my Lady?" Thomas spoke through the closed door.

"Yes!" Katherine exclaimed, and Thomas heard her shuffle toward the door to unlock it. Together, they walked to the window. Thomas pushed open the glass pane, and Katherine leaned out, waving like the Spanish Infanta on her coronation procession.

A young woman in the crowd yelled, "It's the queen!" And one by one, the crowd knelt, men removing their hats and laying down their rustic weapons.

"Thank you!" Katherine shouted with all the dignity she possessed in her finest moments. "Thank you for coming. My precious people! As you can see, I am here, and I am unharmed. Thank you for your kindness and gracious support."

She wiped a tear from her eye as the crowd took up the chant again.

"Long live Queen Katherine, the true queen of England!"

The crowd continued the chant, undeterred even when a steady rain began to fall on them, until finally, the castle door creaked open, and the duke, dressed in armor, stepped out.

"Be dispersed!" he shouted. "I am the Duke of Suffolk, here on the king's business! Be gone. Go back to your houses and fields."

The crowd fell silent, but no one moved.

"Long live Queen Katherine, true queen of England!" A child's voice came from the back of the crowd. And the mob picked up the refrain, punching pitchforks and sticks into the air. "Long live Queen Katherine, true queen of England!"

"Silence!" Brandon shouted. He put a hand to his head as if to protect himself from a physical assault. Clearly, his night's drinking had caught up to him. He swayed and turned back into the entryway, lowering the portcullis behind him. *Was he retching in the courtyard?* The man was in no state to negotiate with a mob.

Several hours later, with the mob still cheering and threatening to break down Buckden's door, Brandon knocked gently on the queen's chamber door.

64

TRUTH AND CONSEQUENCES

It was a sober Charles Brandon who knelt before Katherine later that afternoon. He was quiet, and outside, Thomas could still hear the queen's supporters, demanding her release. Brandon took the queen's hand and opened his mouth to speak.

"Perhaps we should start this conversation again," he said, looking into Katherine's stormy gray, distrustful eyes.

The queen was silent while the voices of the crowd gathered around Buckden reverberated through the castle. "Long live Queen Katherine! Long live the Queen of England."

Was Charles Brandon intimidated by the crowd? Thomas studied the duke's anxious face and wondered how King Henry would respond to reports that his trusted friend and brother-in-law, the Duke of Suffolk, had bungled the process of removing Katherine and incited a mob protest.

Throughout the day, many villagers had returned to the town, bringing back even more people to surround the castle. By Thomas's estimate, the crowd had doubled in size since dawn, and the people showed no signs of leaving. Young men made fires to keep warm, and grandmothers in woolen shawls walked through the crowd with bread baskets, distributing generous provisions. The loyal townsfolk looked prepared to keep the vigil going until they were satisfied that their queen was safe.

"I am willing to discuss the king's demands," Brandon began. "But tell the crowd to go home. There will be hell to pay if this mob burns down Buckden."

Thomas looked at Katherine, twisting her embroidered handkerchief in her lap. Surely Katherine knew the townspeople would never burn down the castle. Did she understand that the villagers were her last bargaining power? What would keep Charles Brandon from forcibly packing her up and carting her off to Somersham?

"No," she said slowly. "I cannot ask these people to leave. They are eager to see that I am protected, a job that you should be doing as well."

Brandon pursed his lips and narrowed his eyes.

"Katherine, you know that King Henry could easily muster an army. And if I send word, then he will. Our sovereign king will not be mocked."

Brandon was not wrong. He might have been in a tight spot for the moment, but it was only a matter of days before the king heard of the uprising and sent reinforcements. Although that could end badly for the duke as well. The mob reflected poorly on the king's popularity and authority, and anything that hurt Henry was bound to hurt the person who caused it. There was no telling what retribution could fall on Charles Brandon, the Duke of Suffolk, if he could not quell the situation quickly.

"I will not be removed to Somersham," Katherine repeated, clenching her teeth and glaring at the duke.

Brandon nodded slowly. "Very well, Katherine," he said without using any title, an omission that struck Thomas as an insult. "I will not remove you today. I will return to the king and tell him that you refused... but you must call off this mob immediately."

Katherine held her gaze steadily. "And my household? Return them immediately."

"Yes," Brandon replied eagerly, as if he were gaining the upper hand. "All of them."

She looked at him, studying his face, and Thomas could not dismiss the warning in his gut. Brandon had surrendered his goals too easily. It could be a trap.

"You will respect the queen's wishes to remain with her household here in Buckden?" Thomas interrupted, eager to clarify the duke's concessions.

The duke glared at Thomas.

"Yes," Brandon said. "I will return to King Henry and tell him that the Princess Dowager refused to be removed and that it is my recommendation she remain here at Buckden."

The queen looked at him suspiciously. Brandon had used her despised title.

"And you think he will agree to that?" she asked.

"He may," Brandon said.

Thomas looked at Katherine. Would she give in to Brandon? She stood up.

"Tell the people to leave," the duke said. "For their own sake," he added. "Their pitchforks will not fare well against the king's swords."

The queen looked toward the window.

It was one thing to protect her dignity and quite another to protect the people God had given her to govern. She was a queen to her last breath. Thomas had no doubt she would always put the health and safety of her people first.

Katherine walked gingerly toward the window but stopped midway.

"Call my household back first," she said suddenly. "I need to know that you will at least make good on that promise."

"As you wish."

Brandon whispered instructions in a young soldier's ear, and ten minutes later, the portcullis creaked open. A dozen members of the queen's household returned while Thomas and the queen watched through the window.

"Now tell the crowd to leave," Brandon demanded.

The queen looked to Thomas, and with the slightest motion, he shook his head.

Brandon glared at Thomas. For a moment, Thomas feared he would feel the backside of the duke's hand again. His cheeks throbbed.

"The queen must disperse this crowd!" Brandon said, raising his voice. "What other assurance do you want?"

The queen looked to her priest.

"Put it in writing," Thomas said. "In the presence of the queen's council."

"I have no authority to override the king's wishes!" Brandon argued. "I offer this compromise at my own peril. I only promise to return to the king empty-handed, saying the queen refused. I cannot ensure she will not be removed from this place in the future!"

"Even so, write it down."

The duke stalked out of the room and returned a few minutes later with the queen's lawyer and Margaret. When the queen saw Margaret, she gasped, and the young woman ran into her extended arms. "My Queen," she whispered.

The duke clapped his hands loudly.

"No, no, no! You must not address the Princess Dowager as queen!" he protested. "Anne Boleyn is the Queen of England."

Thomas looked past the queen to the open window. The voices were still reverberating up the walls. "Long live the queen!"

Margaret's cheeks burned. "She is my queen," she said, lifting her chin.

"My staff will address me as instructed since the beginning," Katherine said, straightening her back and staring defiantly at Brandon.

Careful, Katherine. Don't overplay your hand.

The duke ignored Katherine and grabbed Margaret's wrist.

"Let her go!" Katherine cried. "She only seeks to honor me."

Brandon twisted Margaret's delicate wrist while the queen shrieked.

"For the love of Jesus and His Mother!" she yelled.

"Who instructed you to ignore the king's orders?" Brandon demanded as he twisted Margaret's arm.

As Thomas jumped to his feet to defend Margaret, a soldier flanking Brandon unsheathed his sword. He shoved Thomas back into his seat.

The duke gave Margaret's wrist one more twist, and she cried out. "Please stop! I address my lady as queen because I made an oath!" Brandon dropped her arm, and she touched it gently. "We all swore to serve her as our queen."

"What do you mean?" He looked suspiciously past Margaret to Thomas.

"When we entered the queen's service, we made an oath to serve her as our queen, the crowned Queen of England," the maid-servant explained, giving Katherine a slight smile.

"So?" Brandon challenged. "Make an oath to serve her as Dowager Princess of Wales! You place your own life in peril by refusing the king's authority!"

The queen squared her chin, and Thomas placed a protective hand on Margaret.

"Please do not harm the lady," he said evenly. "She is an innocent woman trying to serve to the best of her ability. You have no cause to harm a good servant of the Crown."

Brandon turned his irritation on Thomas.

"The Crown? This woman denies His Majesty's authority and his lawful marriage to Queen Anne! Can you not see? This is treason." His words echoed through the chamber, but no one answered.

Brandon narrowed his eyes at Thomas. "You! Priest! You told them not to address Katherine as the Princess Dowager! Didn't you?"

Thomas did not answer the accusation. He would not lie to the duke, and he had no reason to tell him the truth. He simply stared at him defiantly, silent, challenging Brandon to strike again. But Brandon was not deterred.

"I know that you did, in fact, tell the queen's household that to make a new oath to the Princess Dowager, *as Princess Dowager*, was to agree to a lie. Other servants have told me this already!" He jabbed his finger accusingly at Thomas. "Father Abell, you told them that lying was a damnable offense against God. You *told them* that if they swore an oath to Katherine in any other title than they already had, they were lying before God. Did you not?"

Margaret looked at Thomas.

"Is this not true?" Brandon demanded.

What could Thomas say? Brandon's assessment of the situation was twisted, but Thomas *had* told the servants that making an oath to a lie was the same as agreeing with it. He held the duke's gaze; silence would speak the truth for him.

Brandon searched Thomas's face and swore.

"I will be true to my word, Katherine," Brandon said, turning to the queen. "I have returned your household staff. And I will return to the king and tell him that you will not be moved."

He looked down at Melvin, who was quickly writing his words on parchment.

"I will sign this document stating as much," he said. "And I will leave your premises tonight."

"Then I will disperse the crowd," the queen conceded.

"But only after you leave," Thomas added.

Brandon looked sharply at Thomas. "Yes, only after. But I think that perhaps you should accompany me to the gate so the people will not turn against me. In fact, perhaps you should accompany me all the way back to London."

Thomas shook his head. "No, I don't think it will be necessary for me to return with you to London."

Melvin finished writing, and Charles Brandon took the quill to sign it. He handed it to the queen.

"Yes, Father Abell," he said, his tone turning icy. "I believe that it is necessary."

Turning to Katherine, he continued. "Madam Princess Dowager, I must inform you that I will not be able to leave your priest here in Buckden. There is a warrant for his arrest, and I will be taking him with me."

All of the blood drained out of Thomas's face. He could not go back to the Tower, the cold, the hunger, the utter loneliness. The room suddenly felt inescapably small, and he had the urge to break free, run and run and run until the duke's archers shot him down. But how would his death serve the queen? He focused his attention on Brandon's cold glare.

"On what charge?" he finally managed to say.

"For being a royal irritation," Brandon said with a triumphant glare. "Perhaps you know there has been a warrant for your arrest since midsummer. Thomas Cromwell has looked high and low in London." He shook his head. "I have no idea why the secretary did not realize you would be right here by Katherine's side. I think he was under the false impression that you would be hiding among the Protestants."

The duke laughed at the joke, and Thomas swallowed hard. *The Protestants? Oh, dear Jesus!* Images of Danielson and his family flashed through his mind. He was glad Cromwell had not found him hiding in their attic. If he was going to return to the Tower, it was better that he not take anyone else with him.

"Cromwell sent me back to the queen a year ago," Thomas said carefully. "He sent me here himself. I have been careful to do exactly as I was instructed."

Brandon narrowed his eyes.

"Except you told the household of Madam Princess Dowager to address her as queen," he said. "That was a grave mistake, Thomas Abell."

A soldier stepped forward with chains to bind Thomas.

"Charles! Please! Father Thomas has become my family," the queen pleaded.

"Your king is your family! He is your dead husband's brother!" Brandon snapped. "How dare you utter such treason. Thomas Abell clearly turns your heart against the king's will that you accept your fate."

Thomas took a step toward the queen. The soldier standing beside Brandon unsheathed his sword again and stepped forward. There would be no running away. *Lord Jesus, Son of God, have mercy.*

Thomas placed a hand on Katherine's trembling shoulder. Had the duke planned to arrest him all along, or had he simply pushed him too far?

"If there is a warrant for my arrest, then it is only a matter of time," he said quietly. He had received numerous letters from Danielson and Richard Featherstone, urging him to be careful and stay away from London. The letters had not specifically mentioned a warrant, but Thomas was not surprised. He had half expected it. The king was becoming increasingly hostile to those who disagreed with him.

Thomas knelt and kissed the queen's hands. "Queen Katherine of Aragon, you are my queen and will always be." He turned to Brandon. "Do not remove the queen. I will return with you to face the king."

Brandon nodded. He did not correct Thomas's use of Katherine's title but sighed in relief. "We will leave before nightfall," he said.

Katherine squeezed Thomas's hand and wept.

65

THE ROAD BACK

He saw her face, inches from his, those green eyes, those supple lips, that suggestive smile.

"Run. Run while you can, Thomas. Run. Run. Run. Run!" Her voice turned into a drumbeat in his head, over and over, again and again, and echoed with his own desires. "Run. Run. Run while you can! Curse the king and save yourself."

But ... No. No. No! Bless and do not curse.

Thomas woke up with a start, gasping for breath like a fish out of water, the very words caught in his dry throat. *No. No. No.* How dare the nun from Kent haunt him in his sleep! How dare she appeal to his most carnal desires.

"Be gone!" he whispered out loud, and he was suddenly very wide awake.

He looked up at the frosty stars gliding across the dark sky. The fire was rapidly reducing to embers, and he estimated that there was only about an hour before dawn. The duke's soldier, who was assigned to guard the camp, had drifted off to sleep, propped up against an oak tree. They had only traveled a short distance from Buckden before making camp. He could find his way back to the village and beyond if he wanted. If ever there was a time to run, it would be now.

Thomas felt his wrists. He was not chained. He had never been formally arrested—he only knew of the warrant from Charles Brandon. Who knew if that could be believed? The last time he saw

Thomas Cromwell, the king's administrator had told him to stay out of Henry's way. And he had done just that, and more. He had not written about his opposition to the king's new marriage, and he had not spoken out either. In fact, he had done exactly what Cromwell had suggested. He had returned to serve Katherine and comfort her in her grief. Why would Cromwell arrest him now?

It did not make sense, but so much of court politics made no sense. It was as if the very ground were shifting under them all. What had been good was now bad. What was bad was now celebrated as good. Perhaps it was no longer possible to merely be quiet about what he disapproved of. From the letters he was getting from London, he knew that it was now required for the king's servants to publicly approve their sovereign's decisions.

Still, it did not have to involve him.

His dream, though troubling, was not wrong. He could slip away and let the king's problems be the king's problems. What good could ever come of him rotting away in the Tower?

If he left now, he could be a few miles away before sunrise. He could run, and who would blame him? But where? He could not return to the queen. He could not go back to London, certainly not to Danielson's house. Essex was out of the question, as was Oxford. He would have to go somewhere entirely new, and he would be a fugitive of the Crown, maybe for the rest of his life.

One day, they will take you by the hand and lead you where you don't want to go.

Running would serve no one but himself.

Lord Jesus Christ, Son of God, have mercy.

Thomas closed his eyes and opened his hands.

Lord Jesus Christ, Son of God, have mercy.

Tears slid down his cheeks. He could not go back to the Tower.

Lord Jesus Christ, Son of God, have mercy.

But what choice did he have? What choice had he ever had?

"My life is yours, Savior," he whispered out loud in the darkness. "Take me where you will."

The soldier resting against the tree stirred as if troubled by dreams of his own. He grunted and returned to sleep. Thomas rolled over on the hard ground, pulled the thin blanket around his shoulders, and stared into the darkness. In the morning, the caravan continued on to London.

66

WHAT CHARGES DO YOU BRING?

Thomas shivered in the cold, his breath visible in the cavernous Tower room. It was the same cell he'd left a year earlier. But this time there was no fire in the hearth, no blanket on the straw mat, no bread on the wooden table. Not even the memory of the Spanish ambassador's orange lingered.

Thomas crossed the empty room and touched the wall. His faint line was still there, just below eye level. He touched it, running his finger over the scar. It was barely the length of his hand. Prisoners make marks on walls, tallying the passage of time.

He rubbed his thumb into the line, and a thin layer of sandstone gathered under his nail. Prisoners mark time, waiting, waiting for release, for deliverance, or maybe ... for death.

Thomas pressed his forehead against the wall. Would there be any release for him?

The world was upside down and inside out. As long as Henry VIII sat on the throne, he made right wrong and wrong right. The very world he created imprisoned Thomas. There was no escaping his authority.

Thomas clenched his fists until the nails cut into his cold hands. Was it all in vain? Had it been out of his own pride and stubbornness that he wrote *Invicta Veritas*? Surely, his life could have been easier if he had been allowed to stay in Oxford, teach students there, and abide by the quiet, academic life he had wanted when he chose the priesthood.

But no. He had chosen to follow his Lord Jesus, and he alone had taken him to London, to the queen, and now, to the Tower. He touched the wall and began tracing his finger along the line.

"Lord Jesus Christ, Son of God, have mercy."

He traced the line again, this time harder, his voice louder.

"Lord Jesus Christ, Son of God, have mercy."

More sandstone gathered under his thumbnail.

"Lord Jesus Christ, Son of God, have mercy."

He repeated his prayer mantra over and over, each time tracing his finger deeper into the line. After an hour or more, the line was perceptibly deeper, but only barely. The quietness of the room enveloped him, threatening to crush his soul. How could he endure such loneliness? He walked over to the empty hearth.

"*In principio erat Verbum et Verbum erat apud Deum et Deus erat Verbum.*" He recited all that he remembered of the Latin Vulgate, beginning with the John 1 passage he had recited for Danielson's children before reading Tyndale's English version.

How was Danielson? And Tyndale?

Being deprived of food and warmth was one thing, but being left alone, isolated from human companionship and news from the outside world, was almost more than he could bear.

"Lord Jesus Christ, Son of God, have mercy."

He returned to the window, found his line in the wall, and pressed his thumb deeper into it. He could see the Tower lawn, now covered in winter snow. A black raven hopped across the yard, leaving a trail of triangular tracks behind it. Thomas smiled. *Hello, bird. I remember you. God sent ravens to feed Elijah. Maybe he sent ravens to the Tower too. A gift, perhaps?*

The sound of footsteps climbing the stone staircase startled Thomas. It was not dinnertime. He turned expectantly to the door and heard a voice he knew. "Thomas, are you well?"

—◦❖◦—

"They have not charged you?" Danielson asked incredulously.

"No." Thomas shook his head. It baffled him. How small of a pebble in the king's shoe was he to be thrown into the Tower but never charged? It had been a month—a long, dark, cold month.

"I will write some letters and see what is happening," Danielson said with concern.

"I don't want to bring trouble to you or your family," Thomas said with a cough.

Daniel handed him a bundle, which he had brought under his arm.

"This is for you," he said. "They would not let me bring you paper and ink. I asked. They said no, but the guard said you could use a covering for the cold nights. I think he heard you coughing."

Tears sprang to Thomas's eyes, and he clutched the bundle.

"Thank you, brother," he said huskily. "You have fulfilled the Lord's words of visiting the prisoner. May God return his blessing to you a hundred times over when he returns."

Thomas made the sign of the cross over Danielson, who bowed his head humbly.

"Ah, Thomas," he said in a whisper. "Unfold the blanket carefully."

Thomas held Danielson's eyes, but neither of them said anything. Instead, Thomas looked past his friend to the heavy prison door and understood that the guard who had let Danielson into the cell was standing outside, listening. He nodded.

"Time's up!" the guard announced impatiently through the door. Thomas might have had all the time in the world, but apparently, the guard did not.

Danielson grabbed Thomas's thin hands.

"We are praying for you... every day."

Thomas closed his eyes in gratitude. "Thank you. I pray for you too."

Later that night, after the stars emerged and the guards had retreated to the warm fire at their guard post, Thomas carefully unrolled Danielson's blanket. Neatly packed inside the folds of the heavy, gray woolen blanket was a potato sack concealing a hard object, slightly wider than Thomas's hand.

Thomas smiled and gently pulled the Tyndale New Testament out of the sack. He turned it over in his hands, eyes filling with tears. Such a precious gift must have cost Danielson a fortune. He held the Bible up to the moonlight pouring through the open window and found the first chapter of John.

"In the beginning was the Word, and the Word was God ..."

Those words, so precious to him in both Latin and English, were more than bread and gold to him. They were life. He was not alone. The Word of God, made flesh, was there. Immanuel. God with us. God with him in the Tower.

67

PRISONER THOMAS

1536

Days turned into weeks, and Thomas hung onto life, eating the stale bread his guards brought him, accompanied by the occasional bowl of gruel and watered-down mead. His soul feasted on the Tyndale New Testament, and when the darkness overcame the cell, he lay on the straw mat and recited everything he could remember. His cold breath hung above his lips like frosty phantoms in the empty cell.

How long, O Lord? How long?

I waited for Him, and He heard my cry. He lifted me out of the pit.

Psalms.

The memory of a lifetime of liturgy and prayers, both Latin and English, fed his soul while his body wasted away. By the time the winter snows melted and spring birds began chirping outside his window, he knew whole chapters of Tyndale's New Testament by heart. And he could wrap his bony hands around his thigh. How long could his body and soul endure deprivation and solitary confinement?

There was no word from Cromwell or the king, and he now felt sure that he had been forgotten. He heard whispers in the hall and conversations below as people passed through the Green, but no one brought him news of the outside world. Not even Danielson had returned. Perhaps he had not been permitted a second visit.

Did his first visit bring suffering to his dear Susanna and their children? The thought brought chills to his already cold body. *Jesus, protect those dear children.*

When the loneliness was overwhelming, Thomas walked to the window and placed his palms against the wall.

"Lord Jesus Christ, Son of God, have mercy."

He traced his thumb against the lines he had begun etching in the stone. He felt the first one, now the length of his thumb, and then the second, an intersecting one, like a cross. "Lord Jesus Christ, Son of God, have mercy."

Day in and day out, he went over the image, praying and scratching, bits of soft stone gathering under his long thumbnail.

He heard the call—"Prisoner Thomas Abell!"—as the heavy boots climbed up the stone staircase to his cell.

Thomas stood up and looked at the door. The guard never announced his food. He just delivered it—unceremoniously sliding it into the room on a tin plate—a modest offering. He left it without conversation, just enough to keep him alive in body, if not soul.

"Yes." Thomas's voice cracked, weak from lack of human conversation. "I am Thomas Abell."

Would this be the day of his death? His heart stopped. He feared the coming pain, and yet, the promise of Heaven and a release from the years of prison were on the other side of death. If today were his last, he would not complain.

The prison door opened. A beefy guard, one he had seen only once before on the day he was arrested in Oxford, and Thomas Cromwell stood at the top of the staircase.

Thomas Abell stood up straight, suddenly fully awake, shaking off the stupor after days of isolation and deprivation.

"Master Cromwell," he said to the man he knew must be responsible for his arrest and detainment.

"I've been asked to inform you that your name has been added to a list," Cromwell said without wasting time on pleasantries. It was as if the two men had never met, never shared a conversation in the king's chamber, never spoken in Oxford, never discussed his fate in this very cell. Cromwell's face was hard, cold, impassive.

But Thomas Abell remembered the man, Cromwell. He looked him in the eyes, daring him to acknowledge his suffering. *Why am I here? Have you forgotten the pebble in the king's shoe now that you have tossed it out?*

Cromwell looked beyond Thomas, examining his bare quarters, his empty hearth, the single straw mattress, and the gray woolen blanket. Finally, his eyes rested on Thomas's.

"Have I been charged?" Thomas asked, ignoring Cromwell's announcement that his name now appeared on a list. Thomas longed for the official charge, for closure, yes, but also for an opportunity to understand his offense and, perhaps, to formulate a reasonable defense.

But Cromwell would offer him no relief from his legal limbo.

"No," Cromwell drawled, pacing uncomfortably around Thomas's world. "Parliament has been quite busy with certain changes, new measures that you will undoubtedly be hearing about soon enough if you have not heard already. I suspect that when it is convenient, there will be an official charge to formalize your imprisonment."

Cromwell laughed. "But I am not sure why that matters, priest. The king does as he pleases."

Thomas looked down at the floor as Cromwell continued. "Surely, you are learning this lesson."

The world was indeed shifting rapidly.

So much had changed even since the last time Cromwell barged into Thomas's cell. This time, there was no mention of Thomas having powerful friends, no mention of the king tiring of hearing his wife's complaints, and no offers to release him if he kept away from the pulpit and printing press. No hope of release.

"I hear no news of the outside," Thomas said evenly, consciously trying to form his words without bitterness. "I do not know what is happening in Parliament. I have been permitted no visitors for the past four months, as I have kept count."

Thomas Cromwell rubbed his hands and sighed with a hint of exasperation.

"I have not come here to inform you of Parliament or the king's business," he said matter-of-factly. "We do not need anything from you. That is, unless you are prepared to repent of your obstinate disregard for the king's authority. Perhaps you wish to make a statement supporting his God-given authority and his *rightful* marriage?"

Thomas said nothing.

"As I thought," Thomas Cromwell dismissed. "Your friend Featherstone said the same."

Thomas raised a weak eyebrow. *No, not Richard Featherstone too! How many more, Lord?*

Thomas Cromwell waved his hand as if everything was trivial.

"Father Abell, as I was saying, I'm only here to inform you that your name has been added to a list of supporters and conspirators implicated in aiding Elizabeth Barton in her treasonous activities."

The blow hit Thomas in the gut, a one-two punch. He was maligned with the nun of Kent, and his dear friend Richard was also in jail, perhaps somewhere in the Tower complex. He sat down on the wooden table, placing his long, bony hands over the knobby knees protruding from his thin vestment.

"The nun of Kent?" he asked incredulously. "What have I to do with that blasphemous woman?"

Thomas Cromwell paced to Thomas and looked down at him, arching his eyebrow.

"I was hoping you would tell me," he said. "I was surprised to hear your name mentioned in that circle. I had not known you to be in conspiracy with her. Her style is a bit ... different from yours."

He smirked. "I doubt she read your *Invicta Veritas*. If the poor soul can even read two words together on a page." He laughed at his own joke. "Although she was a pleasant sight."

"Was?" Thomas winced.

"Yes," Thomas Cromwell said, his eyes narrowing. "You really are not hearing any outside news, are you?"

Thomas shook his head.

"King Henry finally tired of her mischief," he said. "When he and Anne Boleyn had been married for seven months, and Henry still lived, he knew the nun was a false prophet, a circus queen, an agitator. We arrested her."

Thomas Cromwell shook his head. "It didn't take her long at all," he said. "Started squealing left and right that she had been tricked; she had been used and abused. All manner of men had coerced her into making her ill predictions."

Thomas felt sick. What had the woman said?

"She named a dozen or so men in His Majesty's service, including you and the bastard Mary's tutor." Thomas flinched.

"I had nothing to do with Elizabeth Barton," Thomas said, eyes locked on Cromwell's. "You know I never lie," he said. "Knowingly," he added with a prick of conscience.

Cromwell studied Thomas's face.

"This is your reputation," he said. And Thomas wondered who had spoken of him. Were the rumors that Cromwell associated secretly with the Tyndale heretics true? Would that help him?

"Of course, I am aware of the nun," Thomas clarified. "I heard her speaking in the street, and she attempted to meet me, twice, to deliver a message to the queen."

Cromwell lifted an eyebrow.

"I wanted nothing to do with her," Thomas said. "I feared that her rebellious spirit would be ruinous to herself and all those associated with her. She cursed the king. I prayed for him, even though I believe he was wrong in his treatment of Katherine, his wife."

Thomas spoke the last two words slowly, recovering the smallest sense of boldness. If he was going to be executed for treason, he wanted it to be for honest reasons. He supported the queen and stood by her side, but he offered no curses against the king, and he had never supported the nun from Kent.

"I am sure that you remember the king has asked his subjects to refer to his brother's widow as the Princess Dowager," Cromwell chided without breaking Thomas's stare.

Thomas nodded. He remembered.

Cromwell placed his hands together, his fingertips touching his lips.

"Elizabeth Barton was hanged at Tyburn for her crimes against the king and his queen," he said. "Her head was on a spike, just out there," Cromwell said, waving in the direction of the Thames. "You should know that her conspirators will likely suffer the same fate."

Thomas felt weak. He grasped the side of the table.

"I am no conspirator. I never endorsed her in any way."

He looked up at Cromwell, whose face had softened.

"You have not been charged yet," Cromwell said.

Thomas watched as Cromwell looked over the wall at Thomas's "T." His eyes lingered there for a minute and then fell to his straw mat. Then, to Thomas's horror, Cromwell's gaze rested on the partially covered Tyndale New Testament.

"You might want to keep that book covered," Cromwell said in a low voice. "You may not have had anything to do with the nun from Kent, but that book is still illegal."

Thomas searched Cromwell's face. Was there a hint of humanity left?

"Why didn't you send a letter or a messenger with this news?" Thomas asked. What could make the king's chief minister interested in a forgotten priest who had been abandoned in the Tower months ago?

"I wanted to see you for myself," Cromwell answered. His voice dropped. "Things are changing rapidly, Thomas. I know that you had powerful friends helping you before, and they petition me regularly, still, but don't expect the same rescue this time. Watch yourself. You look like someone who needs a meal."

Thomas's stomach rumbled, and Cromwell pulled a loaf of bread out of his leather satchel. It was still warm.

"Bread," he said, "from Susanna." He rose without another word. And then, as quickly as he had come, the king's secretary was gone.

68

A Writing Tool

Thomas stared at the bent stylus in his hand. The small, tarnished tool was pewter, valuable, and unmarked. How had it come into his world? Had it been a strange dream? He rubbed his eyes and looked across the room at the broken window. Shards of glass sparkled on the floor; a draft poured through the window. No, it had not been a dream. A raven from the Tower had dropped it through the broken glass pane.

Thomas rolled the stylus over and over in his palms. If only it were a quill, a writing instrument with a neat little pot of ink. If only...

Thomas walked over to the wall, placed his hands on the "T," and smiled. He touched the stylus to the stone and began scraping. Yellow powder, the stone's residue, slowly appeared under the knife. He began sketching a new line and another. A few minutes later, he had the outline of an H, then an O, and an M. The light began fading, and he sat down on the straw mat.

If they would not give him paper and ink, he could still write.

In the weeks that followed, Thomas fell into a routine of sorts. Wake up with the dawn. Pray. Read. Walk around his cell a hundred times, praying. Read. Walk and pray again. He thought about the Carthusian monks and laughed, first with bitterness and then with gratitude, to realize his sweet Savior had given him the desire he had once wished for. He had solitude with his Lord.

Thomas ate when the jailors passed his food rations through the door. Occasionally, one of the guards, a younger man who lowered his eyes, passed Thomas a note. Usually, it was a thin parchment with bits of news written out—by Cromwell, Thomas suspected. It helped him make sense of the fragments of conversation he overheard drifting through the Tower lawn below him. This was how he found out about Katherine's death. The simple message read: "The Princess Dowager is dead." Thomas sat, head bent over the parchment, as the soldier watched. "Our queen is gone," Thomas said quietly. The soldier touched Thomas's shoulder lightly, made the sign of the cross, and left.

Thomas ate nothing that day. The shallow wooden bowl of thin broth and stale bread sat untouched while he stared out the window. Katherine was gone. Her fight was over. She had been faithful, so faithful. Tears spilled over his cheeks as he tasted their saltiness on his lips. *Lord, have mercy on Katherine's soul.* He wiped his eyes on his frayed vestment sleeve and sighed. She was free. He smiled. She was safe. No one would ever harm her again. She was with the true Lover of her soul. He exhaled. His job was done.

Every afternoon Thomas turned his attention to the etching on the wall. Those were the lonely, hungry hours when he remembered family dinners, state dinners, and even bread and ale shared in the kitchen with the queen's household servants. Any of it would have been a feast for body and soul. Sometimes, it was too much to think about. He turned his sorrow into art, beauty for ashes. He carved his name on the wall.

Thomas was not the first prisoner to decorate the Tower walls. Another prisoner, perhaps many years before him, had left his name there. It was a simple name with no date or embellishments.

Just a name. Peter. And when Thomas saw it, he prayed for Peter's soul, whoever he had been. Had his life ended in this room? Had he been released? Or had he been dragged out for a public execution? Released only in death?

Another man, or perhaps the same prisoner, had left the sign of the cross, the ageless sign of comfort for the suffering. How many times had the man's dirty fingers traced that simple cross, prayed the same prayers Thomas now prayed? *O Lord, do not forget me!*

Thomas prayed the Psalms, prayed the liturgy, prayed every prayer he could remember, and when Heaven felt too far away, he lay prostrate on his straw mat and let himself sob into the gray woolen blanket. That too was prayer. Man was not meant to live alone.

In the waning hours of the day, as Thomas thought of his family, those beautiful faces around the table, he remembered things long forgotten: the sound of his sisters' giggles, his father's stern but patient look, his mother's fresh bread, the way she looked at him when he brought her the fallen nest of sparrow eggs. He had lost her so early and had left home not much later. He had traveled far and wide and been a student, then a teacher and a priest, and finally the confidant of the queen. Now she, too, was gone. And here he was, in the Tower, listening to the sounds of life passing by, drifting up from the distant streets below.

All of the memories made him think about who he was, and slowly his family emblem began to emerge under the pewter stylus—the shape of a bell with a deep A carved in the middle. It was an old family tradition, a lighthearted pun his father enjoyed. They were the "A-bell family."

A bell, an instrument to call people to worship, to remind them to pray, to alert them to danger. Was he that bell? He carved his name, "Thomas," above it. Yes, he was Thomas Abell, and he would ring true. Every night, before the last light faded, he touched it—his family name in stone. And he remembered who he was.

The world may well have forgotten him—the scholar, the lawyer, the priest, the chaplain of Katherine the queen—but he would remember who he was. He thought about the many times he could have avoided his fate. He could have gone along with Henry's whims and recognized his authority as the head of the Church. He could have ignored his compulsion to write *Invicta Veritas*. He could have remained hidden, finding life somewhere on the continent or in Italy under the protection of the Holy Roman See. He could have run away that last night, and in his heart, sometimes he felt his soul run down that road, away from London and its dreadful tower. But in the moment when it mattered, he had not run. He had been faithful, and that gave him comfort.

As days turned into years, with only a trickle of news coming from occasional letters and visits, Thomas doubted that his life contributions had made any difference at all. He had been a little proud of himself when he defended Katherine to her nephew in Spain. Oh, shame—the very thought brought heat to his cheeks now. He had been nothing heroic, only obedient to the message God had placed on his heart. Writing *Invicta Veritas* had been the same. What else could he have done with the words God burned into his soul? To ignore Him would have been a more dreadful prison than any fortress of stone.

No, he had done nothing heroic—like the widow who gave her two mites, he had only given what he had.

69

Release

July 30, 1540

The summer morning was warm, two hours after sunrise, when Thomas heard the heavy footsteps marching up the stone tower, ascending the steps to the cell that had been his home for six and a half years.

Is it time, Father?

Thomas closed his eyes and whispered, "Lord Jesus Christ, Son of God, have mercy."

The steps grew louder. There must have been a half dozen of them.

The heavy prison door flung open, and Thomas knew the jailor was not bringing breakfast. There would be no dinner either. Two days earlier, he had heard the thunderous crowd gathered on Tower Hill, the executioner's cry, the cheering, the screaming, the public mocking. The king had executed his own best advisor, Thomas Cromwell, on a public block for all to see, all except those in the Tower.

The window in Thomas Abell's cell faced the courtyard green and the old Norman castle White Tower beyond, so Thomas had not seen Cromwell's head roll off the block. But he had seen the man's face just before his execution.

As the detachment of soldiers, guards, and priests marched Thomas Cromwell past Thomas's tower, Cromwell craned his neck to look up. His horror-stricken eyes met Thomas's. "Pray for me," his lips said, though his voice was lost to the wind and the din of the crowds.

And so, Thomas prayed for him, earnestly.

Cromwell was the reason Thomas was in the Tower. Cromwell had authorized his arrest and denied his petitions. He had largely ignored Thomas, left him alone, forgotten him for years, and never finalized an official charge against him. King Henry and Cromwell had deprived him of all dignity and the most basic human contact, but Cromwell had asked Thomas to pray for him. And so, Thomas did.

As the crowds roared and cheered, Thomas prayed. He prayed for mercy, prayed for comfort, prayed for Cromwell to repent of his sins and enter God's grace. And as he prayed, compassion flooded Thomas's soul. God had given him seven years to adjust to the horror of the Tower. He had made peace with the deprivation and looked upon his imprisonment as a precious gift, an opportunity to share in the sufferings of Christ as he waited for his redemption. Years earlier, he had begun to long for Heaven, to eagerly await the face of his Savior whom he had grown to love so much. Death would be his release. And so he prayed Cromwell would be ready too.

And now, two days later, the king's men were coming for him.

"Get up!" a young soldier Thomas had never seen demanded. "Today, you pay your debt to your sovereign."

Behind the soldier, a timid, balding priest trembled as he stepped forward.

"Arnold?" Thomas asked, recognizing the pale-faced priest who, nearly a decade earlier, had falsely reported to the king that the French unanimously supported his divorce.

The man, no longer young, cleared his voice and ignored Thomas's personal address.

"Father Thomas Abell, I am here to offer you one last opportunity to repent of your rebellious treason before you enter Eternity," he said gravely, though his voice cracked when he said *Eternity*. "You have been sentenced to death for your conspiracy with one

Elizabeth Barton, the so-called nun of Kent, and for treason, by means of your refusal to recognize your king as sovereign over the church in England, and for your continued support of the king's enemy, the See in Rome."

It was the first time Thomas had heard an official charge against him. He did not bother to request a trial. There would be no justice for him. The king had murdered Cromwell, Thomas More, Bishop John Fisher, the gentle Carthusian monks Thomas had met along the road, and even the object of his original desires, his wife Anne Boleyn. Thomas Abell held no hope that the king, or any of his appointed judges, would find mercy for him. It made no difference that Elizabeth Barton had been dead for years or that Thomas had not written about or spoken in support of the Pope since his arrest. His last communication with the Pope had been a plea for asylum the same year *Invicta Veritas* was published. The Church had seemed supportive at first, but later, in a political maneuver to diminish tensions with Henry, had denied the request. The Church in Rome had left Thomas in Henry's hands long ago. They could hardly be considered secret allies.

But it did not matter. Thomas had long realized that his life was in God's hands. The king had no power over him that God had not ordained. God was still sovereign, the true sovereign over England.

"I am ready to face my Lord," Thomas simply said, courage bubbling up as he spoke.

The oldest guard huffed.

"You may be ready, priest, but it won't be quick. King has ordered you killed by the French prescription. You are to be hanged, drawn, and quartered."

The words would not register in Thomas's weary mind. He simply nodded.

Lord Jesus Christ, Son of God, have mercy.

Two guards marched Thomas down the stairs he had walked up nearly seven years ago. He stumbled as if he had forgotten how to descend, and a younger guard grabbed his forearm, encircling it in his thick fist, and spoke in a cracked, husky voice. "Come along, priest. It won't be long."

Thomas glanced up. The soldier's face was drawn, white, his lips nearly colorless. Was he afraid?

"Jesus, Christ, Son of God, have mercy on us sinners," Thomas prayed aloud as he watched the young soldier's face. The man pursed his lips and nodded in agreement. Sinners. Sinners, both.

The older guard grunted and pushed open the heavy tower door. Warm light poured over Thomas, enveloping his whole body—sunshine. He stopped and smiled at the sun.

The guards nudged him forward, through an open gate and into the city streets below the Tower. They began walking and Thomas realized they were passing Tower Hill, where an angry crowd had gathered two days before. The metallic smell of stale blood hung in the air, and Thomas did not look over to see if Thomas Cromwell's blood still stained the pavement. The look on the young guard's face said enough. Thomas's weak knees trembled.

"Jesus, Christ, Son of God, have mercy," Thomas whispered.

Jesus walked to his own death. Jesus carried his own cross. *Jesus, be with me!*

Thomas stumbled, and the younger guard wrapped his strong arm under him, lifting him so much that his feet barely touched the cobblestone street. Thomas looked down at his boots, cracked from years of decay.

"Our Father, who art in Heaven ..."

Thomas looked up into the sky. *Our Father in Heaven!* He was almost there. A smile broke out over his lips, and a bubble of joy filtered upward through his hollow chest. Tears stung his eyes. Heaven. Joy! For the joy set before Him, he endured the cross, scorning its shame. *Oh, Jesus, give me joy!*

Through a tangle of overgrown hair, Thomas could see they were not alone. A crowd of people were gathering. Some hung along the street, and others solemnly fell in place behind him as if barring his way back to the Tower, should he have the energy to turn and run.

Thomas did not recognize anyone in the crowds, and why should he? Children had grown up. Men had grown old since he had been in the Tower.

Thomas stumbled, falling headlong onto the cobblestone street. A sharp pain seared through his bloodied palms and knees as his vestments, the same clothing he was wearing seven years earlier when he last knelt before Queen Katherine, ripped.

"Get up!" the older soldier demanded, grabbing Thomas by his shoulder, effortlessly tossing his emaciated frame back on his feet and exposing his bloodied knees. "Can't keep the executioner waiting."

The younger guard resumed his position, supporting Thomas under his ribcage. "Almost there," he said barely above a whisper. "Almost."

The soldiers rounded a corner and entered a square thick with people shouting and talking. On the square's far end, Thomas recognized Bartholomew's monastery and a row of elm trees. Smithfield! He could laugh and cry. It would be Smithfield.

The crowd parted as the soldiers made their way through the square to a huddle of five condemned men. Three were strapped to stakes, piles of straw tied to their feet, and a torch burning menacingly just a few feet away. The other two men were attached, arm-to-arm, with the men staked in the kindling.

The soldiers pushed Thomas toward a man lashed to a stake and began wrapping Thomas's right arm with the man's left arm. The man groaned as the rough rope bit into his arm, drawing blood.

"You'll feel the heat," the older soldier spat, giving Thomas one last shove, "but the king doesn't mean to let the fire kill you."

Thomas turned to look at the man he was lashed beside. It was a face Thomas had never seen before. He squeezed the man's arm, and the man returned the squeeze, wrapping his weak fingers around Thomas's forearm. Strangers, brothers, the same.

Thomas craned his neck to see the other condemned men. The angry crowd faded into the distance like the ringing in his ears as he searched the men's faces. Was there anyone he knew? None. He looked down at the dusty cobblestone street until a familiar voice startled him.

"Thomas! Thomas!"

Thomas raised his head. One of the other men lashed to a man at the stake was shouting at him. Thomas looked at the balding man with an emaciated face and long, scraggly gray beard and recognized his friend's gray eyes.

"Richard!" Waves of joy and sorrow collided. "Richard!"

How sweet! How sad to share death! Thomas held Richard's eyes until the soldiers turned his back and lashed his other arm with the prisoner's on the pyre.

"King Henry VIII has decreed that you face judgment with these here," roared a man Thomas could only see through his peripheral vision. The man was standing on a makeshift platform, waving at the three pairs of condemned men, now lashed back-to-back with each other.

The people cheered, pushing in closer until the guards barked at them to stay back.

The man attached to Thomas began to quake. "Please," he choked, "have mercy!"

Thomas stretched his fingers along the man's arm until he found his hand. He grasped it, holding it with all the strength he had left.

"Lord Jesus Christ, Son of God ..."

"You are hereby sentenced to die, the lot of you," the man on the platform shouted. "You three, Protestant heretics, are sentenced to death for your blasphemous denial of the Body of Christ. And you three ..." He pointed a finger at Thomas. "... are sentenced to death as traitors. You have continued in your obstinance, denying the Royal Supremacy."

The crowd cheered like a drunken mob, but when Thomas looked up, he saw a ring of women holding each other and praying, weeping like the women at the foot of the cross. Was Susanna Danielson there? Margaret? *Jesus Christ, have mercy on my sisters.* Surely, his friends were not seeing this sad spectacle.

"It's the king's wish that your sentences be carried out together!" the man continued. "You are all enemies of his Majesty."

The crowd roared. Thomas closed his eyes. He had seen enough.

"Jesus," he whispered. "Jesus."

Thomas heard the crackle of the fire behind him and smelled the smoke rising from the kindling. He let out a long sigh of relief as he felt a leather strap loop around his neck.

The sound of the crowd faded, and suddenly, Thomas was in his father's field. It was springtime. The birds were singing. The wildflowers swayed in the evening breeze.

Thomas began to run.

Fresh air filled his lungs. He stretched his legs toward the edge of the clearing, running, as joy pulsed through his veins. In the distance, he could almost see them: his father, his mother, Katherine, the saints who had gone before. He was almost there. He was almost home. He pressed on.

EPILOGUE

Thomas Abell died on July 30, 1540, alongside Richard Feather-stone, another Catholic priest named Edward Powell, and three Protestants, including Robert Barnes, the young student from the Oxford pub. King Henry went on to execute his fifth wife, as well as many other political opponents, former friends, and allies.

It was not until his third wife that Henry VIII finally got his prince, but the sickly young heir did not live long. As King Edward was approaching adulthood, he died, leaving the throne to Kather-ine of Aragon's only daughter, Mary.

But Mary was no kinder to her enemies than her father had been. She became known to history as *Bloody Mary* for the 365 Protestants she killed, most of them martyred at Smithfield, where Thomas had died just a few years earlier. Violence begetting vio-lence.

In 1886, Pope Leo XIII honored several English martyrs, includ-ing Thomas Abell, whom he declared "Blessed Thomas Abell."

William Tyndale worked on his translations of Scripture until he was arrested in Brussels. He never returned to his homeland, but he thought of England in his dying moments and prayed, "Lord, open the eyes of the king."

Three years after Tyndale's death, King Henry VIII authorized an English version of the Bible, based mainly on Tyndale's work. By the time King Henry died in 1547, there was an English Bible in every English parish.

Author's Note

I have endeavored to adhere as much to the known historical timeline and facts as possible. However, like any novelist, I have interpreted Thomas's motivations and relationships in a way that seems most probable. This is particularly true of Thomas's relationship with Queen Katherine.

Historians do not know when Thomas's loyalty to Katherine began, but they seem to agree that the queen likely did not trust Thomas when he arrived in her household. And it would make sense if she felt that Cardinal Wolsey had placed him there to keep an eye on her.

We know from the historical record that Queen Katherine sent Francisco Felipez to Spain with verbal instructions to subvert the king's mission to bring back the papal brief. It is true that Felipez suspiciously suffered a broken arm along the way, prompting the king to dispatch a second convoy, including Thomas Abell, whom Wolsey had every reason to believe would be loyal to the king's cause.

The queen's Spanish servant, Juan de Montoya, accompanied Thomas, and according to the historian Jon Lander, likely convinced Thomas to disregard the king's mission and convey the queen's true message to her nephew, Emperor Charles V.

We do not know whether Thomas had decided to support Queen Katherine before this moment, but we do know from the historical record that he made his allegiance fully known in April

1529 when he stood before Emperor Charles V. Everything else he did stemmed from that decision.

It is unlikely that Princess Mary's tutor, Richard Featherstone, accompanied Thomas on the journey to Spain, but I decided Thomas needed a Sam Gamgee, a faithful friend who would share his convictions, so I wrote him into that part of the story. Featherstone was executed alongside Thomas, so King Henry must have considered him equally a traitor.

Elizabeth Barton was also a real historical person. Much like I depicted her in the book, she was a complicated personality who eventually recanted everything she said and named all kinds of people in her downfall. At the height of her influence, she met with King Henry VIII. But after the king married Anne Boleyn without dying the horrible death she predicted, Henry began doubting her ecstatic prophesies. Elizabeth was arrested and executed in the first few months of Thomas's imprisonment, but six years later, his supposed association with her was mentioned in the Act of Attainder announcing his execution. Most historians think it is very unlikely that Thomas Abell supported her. It's more likely that Parliament piled on the accusation to justify the executions. Thomas was never given any kind of a trial.

Thomas Abell is honored as a martyr in the Roman Catholic Church. Although he lived through the early stages of the English Reformation, there is no indication that he questioned any particular Catholic doctrine. However, I have allowed him to wrestle with different debates that would have been part of the conversation in his day because I think he cared about ideas. He was an Oxford academic, a priest, and a scholar, and I wanted to give him a robust intellectual curiosity.

In particular, I placed Thomas in conversations about William Tyndale and his efforts to translate the Bible into English. This was mostly a creative decision with little historical evidence; however, I do think that it is historically possible for many reasons.

William Tyndale and Thomas Abell were contemporaries who attended Oxford around the same time. Thomas was also known for being a polyglot when that was uncommon, so if anyone would have opinions about the Bible being offered in a language other than Latin, I think it is likely that Thomas would have. But probably the most interesting historical coincidence that puts Thomas in connection with Tyndale is that they both wrote a book denouncing the king's divorce and used the same publisher in Antwerp. That publisher, Merten de Keyser, was known for publishing both Tyndale's Bible and a French Catholic version of the Bible.

In his arguments in *Invicta Veritas,* Thomas seems particularly offended that European academics had twisted Scripture to justify the king's desires. This high view of Scripture made me think he might be sympathetic to William Tyndale's efforts to put the Bible in the hands of common Englishmen.

It is also worth noting that the issue of translating the Bible into English was more of a problem with the English government than with the Roman Catholic Church at this time. French Catholics had a French translation that Rome tolerated, although French authorities eventually banned it.

English opposition to vernacular translations dates back to John Wycliffe in the 14th century and his unauthorized, handwritten translation from the Latin Vulgate. The Lollard movement, a pre-Reformation evangelical movement based on Wycliffe's translation, became so politically threatening to the establishment that Parliament passed laws making it a capital crime to possess a Wycliffe Bible. So, by the time Martin Luther translated the Bible into German, the English Bible had been outlawed for a hundred years. Thomas Abell's cautious attitude about Tyndale's translation reflected the greater Catholic position, which viewed unauthorized versions with suspicion but did not entirely outlaw them.

There is no historical record of Thomas owning a Tyndale Bible or reading it in the Tower of London. However, it is possible. Despite being banned, Tyndale copies were prevalent in London. Catholic historians have noted from Thomas's prison correspondence that he was deeply familiar with Scripture. However, he obtained it, it's clear that he loved and respected the Bible.

Many people have asked how the Abells in America today are related to Thomas Abell. That is a mystery I have not yet solved. Our ancestor, Robert Abell, arrived in New England in 1630, almost a century after Thomas Abell carved his name in the Tower. I have not made a direct connection to him; however, I know that the Abell family has always used Thomas's iconic London Tower symbol as a badge of honor. Before I knew anything about the historical Thomas Abell, I knew the bell symbol. Many people in our family used it in their personal signatures, and I have vague memories of my parents using it to mark household items they wanted returned, like borrowed books, toys, and casserole dishes.

My interpretation of Thomas Abell has inevitably been shaped by the men in my family who share similar characteristics, intellectual curiosity, artistic sensitivity, commitment to the truth, loyalty, and uncompromising integrity. My father, Robert Abell, to whom this book is dedicated, particularly embodies these noble attributes. And because he was not just a good man but a good dad, my world was shaped by these ideals long before I ever began researching Thomas Abell.

ACKNOWLEDGEMENTS

Thank you to all the friends and family who encouraged me on this long journey from good idea to finished book. I am especially grateful to the Northwest Christian Writers Association for encouraging and equipping me to begin writing fiction again.

I am thankful for the hard work of my editors, Julie Frederick, David Aretha, and Allison Ramirez. I learned so much from all of you. Also, thank you, Hannah Linder. You created a beautiful cover.

Thank you to my sister, Serenity McCaw, and her husband, Marc, who accompanied me on my research travels in England. Thank you to my friend Camilla and her husband, Richard, who hosted me in England and were among the first friends to celebrate my research journey. I will always remember Richard asking me, early on, "So who was this Thomas Abell?" It struck me as the primary question that guided all of my early research. Even as I gathered facts, I kept that question before me: "Who was this guy?"

I need to thank the extremely helpful librarian at the British Library, who not only arranged for me to read the electronic transcript of *Invicta Veritas* but also printed it out for me—my most valuable souvenir of that trip. I am sorry I cannot thank you by name, but thank you anyway. Your contribution to my research cannot be overstated.

And thank you to the West Bergholt History Group and Gill Poole, who mailed me copies of Jon Lander's book, *The Queen's*

Champion. Reading that book was a game changer for my research. Thank you, Jon Lander, for your original research!

I have to thank my family, my amazing kids, and especially my parents, who have always believed in me and encouraged me.

Thank you, Dad, for reading the first draft and telling me you could not put it down. I hope you find the final draft even better. But more than that, thank you for showing me what a man of truth looks like. Your lifelong example of fearless integrity served as my model for understanding why Thomas Abell made the choices he did. Thank you for your faithfulness to your family and, ultimately, to Jesus Christ. If every child had a dad like you, the world would be a happier place.

And Mom, thanks for being my unquestionable cheerleader. Your love and support have buoyed me through many moments of self-doubt, and I am so grateful. My writing is a product of a wonderful childhood, filled with rich conversations and a hunger for more of the things of God. You set the tone in our home for that. Thank you!

Thank you to my Uncle David Abell, whose interest in our family history first introduced me to Thomas Abell. Your encouragement and support throughout this process have kept me going!

To my husband Kip, my adventure partner, my soul mate, and my best friend for more than thirty years, thank you for seeing me through this project and supporting my dreams. I am so blessed to be your wife.

And Blessed Thomas Abell, as you join us from that Great Cloud of Witnesses, thank you for your example. I hope I have conveyed your story well. Forgive me for what I have gotten wrong, and perhaps you can fill me in on the details someday. I look forward to that meeting in Heaven.

Lastly, thank you, Jesus, for your sacrifice on the cross. May your Kingdom come and may your will be done, on Earth as it is in Heaven.

HISTORICAL TIMELINE

- 1485 – Henry Tudor defeats Richard III at the Battle of Bosworth and becomes King Henry VII, founding the Tudor dynasty.

- 1489 – Marriage treaty signed between England and Spain: Prince Arthur (Henry VII's eldest son) is betrothed to Princess Katherine of Aragon.

- 1497 – Thomas Abell is born.

- 1501 – Katherine of Aragon marries Prince Arthur at age 15. Arthur dies five months later.

- 1509 – King Henry VIII ascends the throne and marries Katherine, his brother's widow, with a dispensation from Pope Julius II.

- 1516 – Princess Mary is born, the only surviving child of Henry and Katherine.

- 1518 – Queen Katherine makes a pilgrimage to the shrine of St. Frideswide in Oxford to pray for a living son.*

- 1527 – Henry begins seeking an annulment of his marriage.

- 1529 – Thomas Abell travels to Spain to deliver both the Queen's written request and her true wishes to Emperor

Charles V.†

- 1529 – The Legatine Court convenes at Blackfriars to judge the marriage. Queen Katherine makes a dramatic public appeal and refuses to participate.

- 1532 – Thomas Abell writes and later publishes "Invicta Veritas," defending the queen's marriage. He is arrested in October and released before Christmas.

- 1533 – Henry secretly marries Anne Boleyn. Archbishop Thomas Cranmer declares Henry's marriage to Katherine invalid. Katherine is stripped of her title as queen and sent into exile. Princess Mary is declared illegitimate. By December Thomas Abell is arrested again and sent to the Tower.

- 1534 – Parliament passes the Act of Supremacy, declaring Henry the Supreme Head of the Church of England.

- 1536 – Queen Katherine dies at Kimbolton Castle (January 7). Anne Boleyn is executed later that year (May 19).

- 1540 – Thomas Cromwell is executed (July 28). On July 30, Thomas Abell is martyred at Smithfield.

Footnotes:

* Queen Katherine's pilgrimage to St. Frideswide's shrine in 1518 is documented in historical sources. However, her meeting with Thomas Abell at the shrine is fictional.

† Historical records confirm that Thomas Abell was acting as Queen Katherine's chaplain by 1528, though the exact date of his appointment is not known.

About the Author

Theresa Abell Haynes is a journalist and historical novelist dedicated to bringing hope through inspiring stories. Her debut novel, *The Queen's Priest: The Story of Blessed Thomas Abell,* recounts the true story of Katherine of Aragon's priest who defied King Henry VIII and spent the last seven years of his life in the Tower of London.

Theresa holds a master's degree in the Religious Roots of Europe from Lund University in Sweden and a bachelor's degree in journalism. She contributes to Christian news publications, blending her love of history with storytelling.

Theresa lives in the Pacific Northwest with her husband of 30 years, Kip. She enjoys reading good books, hiking, raising chickens, and, when it is raining too much, traveling to other places.

Join Theresa's free email newsletter to hear about her next book!